ONE LIVES, ONE DIES

One lives or one dies: that's the law of revolution. But sometimes when one dies, things aren't as final as they seem. Especially in Bolivia.

A new prison governor calls the old man in. 'Who are you? What is your name? Why are you here? Unless you can tell me what your crime was, you are going to have to be released.'

Ernesto wills himself to silence. Twenty years of torture and suffering make him suspect a trap. But when he is released, he puts into action his plan for a terrible and macabre revenge on the torturers and betrayers. When the world's press finds out what really happened to Che Guevara in 1967, Ernesto believes he will be a front page sensation.

Phil Tanner, a secret warrior from Britain's beleaguered Intelligence Service, picks up the trail. But he is only one of a clutch of agents from the CIA, Russia and Cuba who are desperate to grab Ernesto before the news breaks. One sad, shuffling old man, once the hero of a radical generation, is hunted down by the espionage machines of both sides of the political divide.

David Brierley's new novel is frightening, bizarre, gruesome and nerve-tingling by turn. Each chapter promises a fresh surprise – and for some of the characters the surprise is far from pleasant. From the jungle of Bolivia to Britain, America and South Africa, we watch the pack close in on the most famous guerrilla fighter ever.

by the same author

COLD WAR
BLOOD GROUP 'O'
BIG BEAR, LITTLE BEAR
SHOOTING STAR
CZECHMATE
SKORPION'S DEATH
SNOWLINE

ONE LIVES, ONE DIES

David Brierley

COLLINS
8 Grafton Street, London W1
1987

William Collins Sons & Co. Ltd
London · Glasgow · Sydney · Auckland
Toronto · Johannesburg

BRITISH LIBRARY CATALOGUING IN PUBLICATION DATA
Brierley, David
One lives, one dies
I. Title
823'.914[F] PR6052.R4432

ISBN 0-00-223037-2

First published 1987

Photoset in Meridien by
Rowland Phototypesetting Ltd,
Bury St Edmunds, Suffolk

Printed and Bound in Great Britain by
Robert Hartnoll (1985) Ltd., Bodmin, Cornwall

This one's for
Christel and Albert, bless them

Mistrust even your own shadow

CHE GUEVARA

PROLOGUE

These are the facts. This is how it was.

If it is possible to mark the beginning of the end, it was 11th March. Yes, that early. On that day two recruits deserted. There had been other defections among the Bolivians, but none as serious as these. The deserters gave information to the military about the strength of the guerrilla bands, their weapons and the site of the base camp.

Or was it the capture of the jeep which had deeper significance? Tania had driven down from the capital La Paz bringing the Frenchman Danton. He had recently flown in from Havana with a message that Castro maintained was 'too confidential to be written'. Tania disobeyed her orders, which were to return at once to La Paz. Instead she hung about the base camp, waiting for Ramón to return.

The army found her jeep because Tania had been careless in concealing it. They could scarcely believe their luck. Here were papers giving details of the underground organization in La Paz and the identity of Ivan, the Cuban officer assigned to it. Right from the start the wider support in the cities and the mines was compromised.

Yet Tania had an excellent reason for waiting in the camp: she had a passion for Ramón.

Tania, Ramón, Danton, Tuma, Pacho, Inti – these were not their own names. The mystique of being a guerrilla demanded that a fighter rechristen himself. It was the first small step on the long journey to heroism. Also, if he was captured his true identity would be hidden. Did they truly believe that? The false names would be a flimsy defence blown away in the first fury of interrogation. Ramón in particular would get no respect from the torturers, for he was the leader.

At last the Bolivian government knew for certain that guerrillas were preparing for revolution and the area in which they were training. And what the Bolivians knew, the Americans knew the day after. But what could the Bolivian army do? It was made up of pathetic, illiterate, abysmally trained, poorly armed Indian recruits. Even Ramón pitied the 'little soldiers'. 'This is what we do after an ambush,' he insisted. 'We strip them naked and take their guns and set them free. Let them go back to their camp and say how well the revolutionaries treated them. Then they will prefer to surrender to us rather than fight and be killed.'

In truth the army was the least of the guerrillas' problems. Disease, hunger and accidents sapped morale. Ramón led them on tremendous marches which left the men exhausted. There were quarrels, suspicions that the rations were being unfairly shared. In any group there is always one trouble-maker. Here it was Marcos. He behaved like a child, swearing at his comrades, alerting army patrols with wild shooting, disobeying orders. Marcos was a member of the central committee of the Cuban Communist Party but Ramón warned him he would be expelled from the guerrilla group.

Marcos pulled open his shirt and clapped his hand over his heart.

'Shoot me,' he demanded. 'I would prefer to die.'

This piece of opera did not impress Ramón.

Revolutionaries – even famous ones – have great faith in slogans. March, Ramón said, had been the Month of Purification. Now it was time to attack. They crossed the Nacahuasu river at night and lay low until dawn before continuing. Tension gripped everyone, for soldiers and peasants were everywhere in the area. On 10th April a skirmish near Iripiti left three soldiers dead, but also one guerrilla. In the late afternoon the army returned and seven more soldiers were killed. A fortnight later in another skirmish a guerrilla died. And not a single peasant had been recruited. They remained suspicious and untrustworthy, which was a puzzle to Ramón. Didn't they *want* the revolution? As often as not some surly herdsman had to be kept prisoner and only released on the promise of not running to tell tales to the army. But the army seemed always to be on their tracks.

During May, more ambushes, with the number of soldiers

killed mounting, but slowly: three dead and two wounded, another three dead and one wounded, two dead. Not much for one month when revolution in the whole continent was Ramón's grand design. The number of sullen and lying peasants who had been held prisoner for a day or so was higher. 'Tell your friends,' Ramón would say, 'tell your friends we have come to liberate them.' No response. Out of sight, did the peasant spit on the ground?

Food and water remained great problems. There were days of starvation, or sharing one small bird between half a dozen men; then days of feasting. This gluttony had its revenge next morning: belching, farting, vomiting and diarrhoea. 'A real organ concert,' Ramón called it.

Night and day the guerrillas kept on the move. There was no time to rest properly. They never slept in real beds. Ramón noted it was six months between baths. During this time more pigs, tapirs and parrots had been butchered than soldiers. In June the winter rains started, drenching tropical downpours, or a daylong drizzle with cold winds from the south. Every day they marched, hacked paths with their machetes, toiled up hills, forded rivers, scaled cliffs. On, on, on. If you kept moving you had the illusion of progress. But they achieved only one ambush in the month, killing four soldiers. And disaster for them, the guerrillas' deputy leader Tuma had his liver shattered by a bullet and died. It was a black day, Ramón lamented, for each guerrilla killed was a major defeat.

The next month was the same: hours of marching through wild country, repairing tracks before they could be walked along, sleeping in fields, fighting violent stomach upsets more than the army. One skirmish led to the capture of a small army post, and one dead soldier. Then for three and a half weeks they were continually on the move, up mountains, down canyons, enduring rain, fog, cold and heat. At the end of the month the guerrillas themselves were surprised in an ambush and lost two men. Their escape was wild and desperate, down the middle of a river. For Ramón it was bitter knowing they were reduced to twenty-two men, two of them wounded, himself plagued by chronic asthma. And something else he had to recognize: the army had learnt to use his own tactics of stealth and ambush against him.

By August they had had nine months of guerrilla life. Of the six original fighters, two were dead, one had disappeared, two were wounded and Ramón admitted he himself was a 'wreck'. Ammunition was low, they ate their own horses for food, medicines were finished. They had only one small mare to carry their stuff. Ramón, goaded into losing self-control, stabbed the animal in the neck to spur it on, opening an ugly wound.

The radio brought news of clashes between the army and the other guerrilla band, with reports of comrades killed or captured, the discovery of the caves with their reserves of weapons and medicines, and of the trial of Danton. Each day and sometimes by moonlight they marched until they dropped from exhaustion, shivering in the cold and eaten by mosquitoes. After one clash with the army, the guerrillas retreated until some were too weak even to climb out of a ravine, and they slept the night separated into three groups. They were racked by hunger and ate their last horse. But worse, there was no safe water. Some men fainted, others drank their own urine, which resulted in diarrhoea and further dehydration. One of the guerrillas quit; the others were demoralized.

September brought increasing pressure from the army: mounted patrols, dogs, spotter aircraft, foot patrols that fired machine gun bursts into the bush. 'Why?' Ramón puzzled. 'Why the new aggressive spirit?' He did not know American Green Berets had taken over the training.

On the radio they heard of the death of Tania, killed trying to cross a river. Ramón paid it little attention. To his comrades he dismissed the report as a piece of propaganda. To himself . . .? The next day the radio reported that the President had attended Tania's burial. Ramón received this stoically. His emotions were more roused by criticism from communist officials in Hungary who had denounced him as pathetic and irresponsible. 'I would love to get to power,' Ramón raged, 'just to strip the masks off these cowards and lackeys and rub their noses in their own dirty tricks.'

Troubles crowded in. It had been months since they had had contact with their comrades in the capital or the other guerrilla group. They had to rely on radio news, never certain where the border was between truth and propaganda. Quarrels among the group erupted daily. The local people fled in fear at their approach. At one village Inti gave a lecture in the schoolroom to fifteen peasants. The men sat silent and amazed. There were no converts.

Three weeks after their last combat, the guerrillas themselves fell into an ambush. Three of them were killed, two wounded, two ran away. In the following days the army was everywhere. They could hear warwhoops and bursts of gunfire; they saw sunlight flashing off equipment as close as the next hillside. What was happening? The radio was no help, being censored. Twiddling across the dial brought news from a Chilean radio station that the Bolivian army now had the *terroristas* cut off. All day they could see soldiers, dogs and mules passing along the trail above them, but there was no longer any thought of lying in ambush. Survival was the limit of ambition.

The end was drawing closer. In their heart of hearts did they accept that? The army had become a real fighting force; the peasants gave no aid to the guerrillas and indeed were informers. Yet Ramón insisted to himself that the spirits of the remaining guerrillas were high. He had doubts only about Willy, who he thought would take advantage of a scuffle to run away. Which, as it turned out, was the final irony.

Days passed when the guerrillas did little but shift camp and keep out of sight. It was safest to travel in the hours before dawn. They lay up in shelter during the day, merely sending out scouting parties to search for water. Army patrols were constantly on the move. From the Chilean radio station Ramón learnt that eighteen hundred soldiers were scouring the country for them. Break out into a new area, he decided, make a fresh start.

7th October marked eleven months exactly since the guerrilla group had been set up. They rested until the afternoon when an old woman herding goats entered the canyon. They took the woman prisoner, as they had done with countless other peasants. She led them to her house, where she had one dwarf and one crippled daughter. The woman was given fifty pesos to keep quiet and Ramón warned: 'Don't say anything about us. Do you understand?' She understood, though whether she would keep quiet Ramón doubted. Better to kill her? No, what would happen to the girls. The guerrillas packed their gear and trekked up the

Yuro canyon by moonlight. At 2 a.m. they halted near some potato fields. They were too tired to go further.

Fifty pesos didn't buy the woman's silence for long. That same night she reported the incident to the nearest army post. At 6 a.m. Lieutenant Prado and his Ranger unit were ordered in pursuit. In the past weeks there had been hundreds of such sorties to trap the guerrillas. This time it wasn't a false alarm.

Once the guerrillas had been identified the Rangers divided into two squads. The first squad took care of the sentries, the second squad tried to outflank the main group, which had scattered among boulders. The guerrillas began their last combat with four men already wounded, others sick with stomach cramps and swollen feet, and all of them exhausted. But they offered fierce resistance. As the firing continued, Willy went to help a wounded comrade who was pinned down in an exposed position. The wounded man was Ramón. Willy hoisted his leader over his shoulder and staggered further up the canyon where he tried to stem the blood from Ramón's neck and leg wounds. Four Rangers who had got close ordered him to surrender. Willy reached out to grab his rifle and was killed before he could fire a shot. Ramón could see more soldiers arriving and the remnants of his own little guerrilla band dispersing, some to escape, others to be gunned down.

'Stop!' Ramón shouted.

Below him an officer was directing the firefight. Half a dozen guerrillas were sheltering behind rocks and shooting as the soldiers crawled to new positions. It was a matter of minutes now, of seconds.

'Don't shoot,' Ramón called out to Lieutenant Prado. 'Don't kill me.' And then, because he could see it was hopeless: 'I am Che Guevara. I am more valuable to you alive than dead.'

CHAPTER 1

Try hard enough and you can put the blame for much of what happened on sex. It's always safe to blame sex.

For Philip Tanner, a secret warrior from Britain's beleaguered Intelligence Service, sex played a prominent part. It always had, which he'd done his best to conceal from his bosses. On this occasion he had been absent for the best part of two months in South America, polishing old friendships, reassuring contacts that Thatcherite Britain was still a power in the world. Tanner called South America 'my patch'. Some patch. His return to Britain was delayed by certain business in Rio. The *cariocas*, as anyone who has been there will agree, are a compelling reason for delaying one's return. Such eager breasts, such rolling hips, such direct looks. Just a weekend, Tanner promised himself, a lovely long weekend which somehow stretched out to include the next weekend.

He had stayed in the district called Flamengo at the Hotel Gloria. Dear old Gloria, he reminisced, still game for anything. The swimming in the bay was dangerous – dip a toe in, the story went, and it would shrivel and fall off before your eyes. Catch a man like Tanner risking water up to his waist. But Copacabana wasn't far away. Nobody swam there much either. The beach was more for getting yourself noticed. Copacabana girls were good at that. They had a simple secret: they took three bits of string and two tatters of cloth and called it a swimsuit. Day by day Copacabana beach was living proof to Tanner that man is a warm-blooded animal.

Tanner had a cold home-coming. His house in south London was deserted. His wife Denise had cleared out her clothes and some of the furniture and their joint bank account. Tanner rocked on his heels while he took stock in the living-room. The gaps were as if a looting mob had passed through. Or a thief had sneaked in and stolen his marriage. A space on the wall held the dust outline of the Braque etching. It had been a birthday present from Denise and now she had taken it back. The bookcase was like a mouth with teeth drawn. The TV set remained but there was a vacant space under it. She's taken the bloody video, he registered. He focused on that gap rather than on the bigger gap in his life. Shit, she's a right cow. She's walked out with the tape of *The French Connection*. That showed a mean spirit because she didn't even like the movie and he did.

The video player and that particular tape, perhaps others. His mind was full of that instead of the bigger disaster. Did it mean something? Was Denise dropping clues? Such as: I'm going somewhere which has a TV but not a video player. Such as: *The French Connection* is a man's movie so that's why I want to take it. Such as: I've snitched the Braque etching because it shows Eros chatting up Eurybia.

The marriage had lasted over a decade. It had run into quicksands from time to time but whose marriage didn't, Tanner wanted to know. 'Quicksands? Quicksands?' Denise had shrilled. 'Do your women know you think of them as quicksands?' When she was in one of her shrill moods there was no point in trying to reason. Anyhow, she'd known the kind of man he was before their wedding night. Damn right she had. And revelled in it. Had she imagined, like other hopeful brides, that she would bring about a miraculous change in her husband? Fond hope. You could have traced the fading of that hope by the fine lines that had accumulated round her eyes and the tautness of her mouth as she added up the number of nights that work prevented Tanner from coming home to bed.

'Denise?' he called out. 'Denise? I'm home from the wars.'

He was going to add something more – something about only the brave deserving the fair – but he lost heart. She was gone. He knew without being told. It wasn't cowardice that prevented her having a face-to-facer. She was perfectly capable of coming at him with claws out and spitting with rage. It was obvious that during the latest absence she had decided she had had enough. Or not enough, and had gone out in search of someone who could offer her more. Such as a man with a taste for mayhem in his movies and a touch of Eros when it mattered. She saw no point in listening any longer to Tanner's excuses and lies.

Finally, as he surveyed the rape of the living-room, he allowed his eyes to settle on the envelope. It was on the mantelpiece above the blocked-up fireplace, a white envelope addressed: Philip Tanner. It brought a chill sweat to his palms and his forehead. He picked up the envelope and held it a long time as if his fingers could extract the message without his having the pain of reading it. He recognized Denise's writing, of course. He wasn't sure he wanted to know what she had to say and he didn't like at all the fact that she had used his surname. The formality made him sick in his guts.

He wasn't certain what to expect in the letter. Accusations? Solicitor's name? Address of her new home? A final plea for his reform? Perhaps an emotional torrent plus an assertion of her undying love which would allow him to work his way back? Tanner had the idea this was the kind of thing a woman wrote in a leaving letter. He tore open the envelope with his thumb and unfolded the sheet of paper. It read in its entirety:

> I have decided the time has come to get out. I have no wish to catch AIDS from you and die.
>
> Denise

There had been a time when Denise used to dot the 'i' in her name with a little 'x', like the promise of a kiss to come. This time she'd punched the dot so hard it had gone through the paper.

Tanner reported for work at his head office the following morning. Hershey wanted to see him and since Hershey was his Controller there was no avoiding that. How did it go? Tanner shrugged. 'I feel I've visited the cats' home and had to stroke every bloody animal.' What about Buenos Aires? How about Astiz? 'He wants more money. I told him he should be proud to work for one of the world's staunchest democracies. Do you know what he said? He said, Had I any idea of the price of steak in Argentina these days?'

Tanner kept his private troubles to himself. He didn't know how to get in touch with his estranged wife and he could make no sense of the turmoil of his feelings. So, overlooking his ten days' sport in Rio, he claimed some of his accumulated leave and took himself off to Nerja on the Costa del Sol. He thought a spell on his own would help him see the future more clearly. Being early in the season the sea was cold but the sun hot. He didn't have much time for introspection after all, for the first wave of Swedish girls had already come on holiday.

So Tanner was away as the first events unfolded. He didn't return to the Bunker – that ugly building in Lambeth – until well into May. His private problems were still no nearer a solution and he welcomed the crisis as an excuse to lose himself in work.

CHAPTER 2

Later she screamed. No one came running. People did scream from time to time but that was your privilege at El Lucky Dip. You paid good money and you were entitled to scream, even to make other people scream. Mostly the screams weren't for real, not pain screams. They were screams for effect, even screams of pleasure.

After Eulalia screamed and no one came, she jumped off the bed and went into the corridor and screamed again. Jośe who was down at the end watching television told her to shut up, she was disturbing the other clients. Saturday night was more of a screaming night. This was Sunday.

Later she screamed but at first she didn't. It was the most frightening, the most sickening, the most awful thing to happen in all her eighteen years. She called out to the Virgin Mary and Santa Teresa for help and protection and forgiveness for her sins. Did they hear? Were they listening to the prayers of a little Brazilian ex-virgin who'd ended up in another country and wasn't able to make herself properly understood? If the Holy Mother didn't speak her language, she must nevertheless know the torment in her heart.

'I won't do it again. I will be good. Reform, you understand the word? Never again do the Canadian Nurse – oh forgive me, I shouldn't talk of such things. It's just they ask me. The men. They say they hear of the Canadian Nurse. What can I do? They beg me. They say they did not know such pleasure existed. One man even tells me he can die happy now . . . oh, oh . . .'

Eulalia sobbed at what she'd just said and then she'd looked at Camoeres and screamed.

When she had first seen Camoeres she could tell he was excited and knew what it was that excited him. Men! They got that shine to their foreheads and that glitter to their eyes and that idiot's half-grin to their mouths. That was eagerness, impatience. But Camoeres, he had been trembling. He'd asked for her, only her, waited for her, though it wasn't much fun for a night out sitting with José, watching television, and drinking La Paceña beer at twice the going rate. He'd waited half an hour. No wonder he was trembling, his imagination working enough for two poets.

She didn't know it but he'd been waiting not just half an hour but the best part of a month since the rumours about her began to circulate. But Camoeres had first of all had flu and then he'd had to go away with his wife on a visit to her aged mother. Eulalia was certain he was married. They all were. Men of Camoeres's age had been married for longer than she had lived and that was why they came to El Lucky Dip.

'There is Manuelita,' José had tried. 'Some people say she is pretty.'

'The Brazilian,' Camoeres had said. 'Or I might as well go home.'

That certainly was part of the attraction. She came from Brazil and had the hot blood of African slaves in her instead of the thin Quechua blood of the local girls and her body moved to the beat of tribal drums. It was true she did not come from Rio but from São Paulo. Never mind, that was exotic enough. God knows why she had come to Potosi, this frozen city in Bolivia – God and a certain priest whose idea of communion was less than holy. In São Paulo, in her slum, her family had lived in a shanty. In Potosi you were already rich if your family had a shanty. The poor made their homes in the street.

Camoeres was not wearing a uniform but she decided he was a military man, which was not too far from the facts. He wore a suit of a sober colour. It had – as she took the jacket from him – the smell of incense as if he'd worn it that morning to go to church. She let him take his own trousers off because sometimes if a man was very eager and aroused you could hurt him. Camoeres was already aroused. She unbuttoned his shirt and slipped her hands inside and felt the pouch of his stomach. It was not the stomach of a poor man. And then lower. And he had caught her head, his fingers in her hair, and twisted her face up so he could stare at her. In his eyes was a kind of pleading. Do your work, do it well, the Canadian Nurse.

She laid him down and crouched beside him, as if she was praying or begging or mad. In her slum it was known as the Canadian Nurse, though she did not know why. No Canadians lived there and the only nurses were at the clinic and their hands were more often filled with the bodies of undernourished kids. On Camocres the Canadian Nurse worked as it did with every man, only more so. He had the orgasm at the end of the world, his muscles straining, his spine arching, his skin blotchy like an over-ripe mango, his mouth gaping. 'Eu ... Eu ... Eu ...' Trying for her name, she thought, gasping it, exploding with it. Of a sudden he fell back as his frenzy collapsed. He didn't move.

Some men were like that.

She settled by his side. After ten minutes he still had not uttered a word, of gratitude or amazement. She was bored. Sunday nights were the same the world over. Why didn't he chat to her? She would not understand more than one word in twenty but when she had arrived two months before it had only been one word in thirty. She was learning. She was not stupid.

'What is your name?' she asked. She knew that in Spanish.

He didn't answer.

'What is your name?' she repeated in the São Paulo mush that passes for Portuguese.

Apparently he had no name. She sighed.

'What is your wife's name?' she asked with a sly look. That should rouse him.

Silence. Perhaps he was in mourning for his wife and too sad to talk about it.

No, that was not likely. She moved her hand, wondering if a second visit of the Canadian Nurse would arouse him. It would bring a man back from the dead, so they said.

It was then, when nothing stirred, that she learnt the truth. Oh horror of horrors, nightmare made real, punishment for a million sins, Camoeres was dead. He had died, in her bed, at her hands. She had killed him with pleasure.

*

'You know where you are?'

It was a tone of voice between a question and a statement.

'Bolivia,' the prisoner answered.

'Bolivia.' He thought about the answer. 'The Republic of Bolivia,' as if that was a different place altogether. He hesitated, which wasn't like him. But the situation was unusual. 'I didn't expect you to say Tibet. *Of course* Bolivia. But where?'

The prisoner frowned, staring at his sandals. 'Potosi.'

'Outside the city of Potosi. Agreed. But *where* are you? Be precise. Don't you know?' Silence. 'Look at me. Why don't you answer?'

Because sometimes a question held a hidden trap. A wrong answer and the world exploded round you, inside you too. The world exploded in your body, in your head, right inside your skull, deep inside your being.

'The . . .' The prisoner had to force a breath into his lungs, a breath that took a long time. 'The special place.'

'Yes.'

'And . . .'

'And what?'

He wore gloves, white gloves with a curly pattern on the back. Burglars wore gloves not to leave fingerprints. But he wasn't a burglar. Other people wore gloves so their hands didn't get soiled. The doctor had worn gloves.

'The special place, you said . . . What were you going to say?'

The left glove was off. Now he was peeling off the right glove. The doctor had done that except his had been long rubber gloves not white cotton. Smears on them, vomit, blood, his blood. The doctor had dropped them on the concrete floor and walked out. A doctor was meant to heal the suffering. A doctor was not meant to be a participant saying: *Put it here, try there, never mind the blood, then let me do it.*

'And . . .? And what?'

'And, *señor*.'

'Not that. What were you going to say?'

'I don't know anything.'

'Don't know anything? What do you mean by that? You've got to be more precise.'

This must be the hidden trap. The prisoner kept his eyes on

the other man's hands. He got out a packet of cigarettes and a box of matches. That was why he'd taken off the white gloves. He didn't smoke with gloves on in case the nicotine stained them. Now he was fitting a cigarette into a holder – surely that would keep the gloves from getting stained? Such fussiness. The man wore a uniform with ribbons sewn on the left side. Bolivia hadn't had a war for half a century so what gallant actions had won him the medals? All the army had done was shoot miners and beat peasants to the ground and bring him to . . . Stop, don't brood.

'At least do you know who I am?'

Think. Where's the trap? None.

'You're the new Governor.'

'Of course you've heard. In prisons there is always gossip. You are like grandmothers with nothing to do but gossip. That is how you pass your days.'

He stopped, watching the prisoner through a cloud of smoke. He waved the smoke aside and inspected him again. Smoke got in the way. Smoke made everything less *precise*. Wasn't that his word?

'So I suspect you know what happened to the previous Governor?'

Careful.

'I only heard gossip.'

'Ill-informed, no doubt,' the new Governor said. 'Señor Camoeres had an accident, a heart attack in tragic circumstances. He was investigating an illegal immigrant from Brazil at the time and in trying to arrest the person, the exertion brought on the coronary attack.'

Why are you telling me this? Why so many lies? Always there is the official story and there is the truth. How could they expect to keep the truth hidden when so many people had been at El Lucky Dip? The reality was so juicy, improving with each telling. The fiction was so clumsy – who ever heard of a prison Governor making investigations?

When the new Governor put out his cigarette he doubled it over in the ashtray, only half-smoked. It lay folded up, a neat corpse. No, most of the corpses he'd seen hadn't been neat. They had been twisted, mashed-up.

'As I say, a tragedy. For Señor Camoeres naturally, for his wife, for this prison.'

For this prison? How could that be? Camoeres had been harsh and selfish and greedy.

The new Governor looked down at his desk, shuffled some papers together and knocked them into line.

'Your name is Ernesto Carballo.'

'Yes,' the prisoner said. 'Yes, Señor Governor.'

The Governor nodded. The prisoner was responding to firm treatment, the new realities. If he was going to co-operate, matters would be easier.

'How long have you been a prisoner?'

'I came to the special prison in 1979.'

'That wasn't the question I asked. Be more precise. Before you were here, you were in a prison hospital.'

Carballo had begun to sweat. Nothing he could do about it. It came suddenly like a summer storm – no way you could stop that either.

'Yes.'

'Therefore you had to be in prison before you went to the hospital. That is logical. But not here – nobody remembers you.'

There was the trap. But he had seen it, not fallen into it. Camoeres had remembered him. Camoeres had been transferred here as Military Governor of the special prison and that had been one of the most sickening mornings, seeing Camoeres again, seeing Camoeres's eyes narrow and the look in them that said: Be careful, very careful, or a terrible accident will happen to you. But now the accident had happened to Camoeres.

'I don't know,' Carballo said. 'I had lost my memory.'

'Yes. Yes.'

That had been during the Amnesia Period of Bolivian history. The dictator Banzer had gone. There had been elections but the military didn't like the results. It seemed every week a new general decided to have his turn at being President, postponing the time when Siles would come to power. As democratic rule edged nearer there had been a great burning of papers, withdrawing from exposed positions, changes of name and occupation and responsibilities, switching of bank accounts. This particular sick man in the prison hospital – suddenly no one admitted knowing him. His papers – if he had ever had any – had vanished. Medical records – what were they? It was a conspiracy in which he joined – even his memory had drifted away. No one wanted to look too closely at his body or hazard a guess how the wounds had been caused. Temporary papers were issued in the name of Ernesto Carballo. As is the way, the temporary papers took root and became permanent. Carballo convalesced. He grew stronger. He was well enough to be discharged – but he couldn't be. To be admitted to a prison hospital you must have been transferred from prison. A prisoner has committed a crime and his punishment must continue, even if no one knows what it is for.

'You have been eight years here.'

When Carballo nodded, sweat dripped from his eyebrows. Suppose enquiries were going to be made. Suppose the truth became known. There were certain people who knew about him and they were still alive. Carballo knew they were alive. He had seen a photo of one in a newspaper. Another time he had been in the recreation room when the old television set had shown the news. The picture had wavered and objects grew strange ghosts round them. The mountains caused that. A certain uniformed official was shown and a shadow had grown above his head, like a halo. That had been only last month.

The Governor patted his hair. It looked perfect, like a wig, no strand breaking free. He said: 'There is no *record* of who you really are, no *record* of your crime, no *record* of how long you were sentenced to imprisonment.'

I never was. Carballo beat that thought down in case it slipped out.

'I have been reviewing certain cases in the period since I have taken up my duties. I find a number of irregularities. I am a military man and I dislike irregularities. They show a lack of discipline. This is a special prison. It is for holding special categories of prisoner: ones who are dangerous to the state, ones who have taken up arms, spies, traitors, certain categories of foreigner. It is not intended as a repository for the left-overs no one knows what to do with. Do you understand?'

Carballo nodded. He had been standing throughout the interview. He straightened up, getting more discipline into his backbone.

'What were you imprisoned for?'

Carballo stared at the parting in the Governor's hair and shook his head.

'How long ago were you put in prison? Think, man.'

Carballo frowned. Let him see me thinking. He pursed his lips, tighter, tighter. Let no word escape.

'Where was your original prison before you were admitted to the hospital? Come on, you've got to do better than this. Try to remember.'

Sweat trickled. Lines of it came down his cheeks. The sweat could have been tears, remembering the anguish. Eyes had watched, lips had twitched, hands had approached to . . . Blank out the memories, blank out the mind lest a word betray him.

'I . . .'

'Yes?' The Governor leant forward. 'Well?'

'I can't.'

The Governor collected papers and slid them in a folder and initialled a chit of paper pinned to the top.

'Unless you can tell me what your crime was,' the Governor said, 'you are going to have to be released.'

'You should shave. It is important to keep your self-respect. Do you understand – self-respect?'

This is great, Morton thought, this is fantastic, this is the pot of piss at the end of the rainbow, this is so unbelievable I've got to believe it, pure poetry.

'I understand self-respect. I don't understand how I buy razor-blades without money. Sir,' Morton added because there was a sharpening of the look the Governor was giving him. Insubordinate *gringo*, that is what the Governor was no doubt thinking. Put him in the cell with the cockroaches.

'Not having money is no excuse for the crime you committed.'

Is this the crime of not shaving, Morton wanted to ask. Definitely the cockroaches if he didn't watch it.

'Sir,' he said, 'sir, please understand. I *did* have money until a couple of months ago. It wasn't money like millionaires have money, but enough to pay for hotels and food and transport. But when I was arrested, they disappeared my money.'

'Explain what you mean: they "disappeared" your money.'

'Like what happened in Argentina under the dictatorship. They disappeared citizens they didn't approve of. Well, I had money, pesos and dollars, and they disappeared it all.'

'Why did you not lay a formal complaint against these people? If what you say is true, of course.'

'Of course.' Morton thought about that, about how the arrest had taken place, about the court hearing, about the judge and a certain gentleman vanishing together into a back room while the court took a recess, and how the judge came back and sentenced him to imprisonment for a term of fifteen years, 'or less if the President grants clemency'. *Fifteen years?* He had hardly been able to take it in. He was being led away when his brain unlocked enough for him to stop and turn round: 'How do I appeal to the President?' The judge had been a little taken aback. 'It must be done according to the usual custom, on the correct form.' 'Well, where do I get a form?' 'You must wait. The forms are being reprinted.'

'I asked why you did not lay a complaint against them.'

'I could not lay a complaint *because* they had taken my money. I could not afford a lawyer.'

'Your embassy would help one of its citizens. That is one of the functions of an embassy.'

'The British embassy . . .' Morton thought about them. 'Maybe they were celebrating the Queen's birthday. Maybe they were celebrating the Queen's corgi's birthday. They were busy. Then a very important office boy came to see me – one morning and back to La Paz in time for a vital cocktail party – and explained that the Foreign Office had a rule about not interfering in the process of a country's justice.'

'That is quite correct,' the Governor said. He was peeling off his gloves, selecting a cigarette and inserting it in a holder. Morton watched and then went on.

'What justice, I asked him. These *muchachos* have planted evidence, arrested me and stolen my money. I am told that because I am a foreigner and because of the seriousness of the crime and because others are undoubtedly involved and mustn't be warned, the judicial process will take place in a special court. This boy wonder said: "See how the trial goes, old chap, you might get off – though they can be hard on foreigners who muscle in on their drug trade." *Haven't you been listening? How can I have a fair trial when it's being done in secret and the evidence has been planted?* Do you know what he said? He said: "Don't shout, old boy, they might hear you and you don't want to upset them unnecessarily."'

The Governor turned his face aside to blow out smoke but kept his eyes on the prisoner. 'I find this story extraordinary.'

'I too find it extraordinary,' Morton said. He looked at the Governor. He also found the Governor extraordinary. Someone had told him the Governor was an admiral who had been transferred to lick the special prison into shape. But how can he be an admiral? How can Bolivia even have a navy when it has no coastline, no outlet to the sea? Ah, they patrol Lake Titicaca. But what does the navy actually *do*? They patrol, he had been told, up and down. And for this they need admirals? No, they have the admirals and because of that they need the patrolling.

The Governor folded his cigarette into the ashtray and gave his attention to a document from the file on his desk.

'You were convicted of dealing in dangerous drugs,' he read.

'Sir, sir, please explain to me. Bolivia is a beautiful and proud country but it is also very poor. The richest people are those who trade in cocaine. They are very, very rich. They are richer than the government itself. They even offered to pay off Bolivia's national debt provided they were left to do their business in peace. These very, very rich people are never arrested. I am a photo-journalist. I make my living taking photographs for magazines and picture libraries. I am not rich. If I smuggled cocaine I would be rich. But I do not, and I am not rich. Would I have been staying in the Hotel Turista if I was rich?'

'Three-quarters of a kilo of the purest cocaine was found in your camera case.'

'Sir, please, first how did those officers know to look in my camera case? Who would have told them? Second, how could I travel with cocaine in there? I'm not a tourist with a camera round my neck. The cocaine was in the space normally occupied by my camera when I travel. Third, after Potosi I had a reservation to go to Santa Cruz. Why should I take cocaine to Santa Cruz? Santa Cruz is where the cocaine comes from. That is crazy.'

But Morton had had time to realize the truth: Bolivia *was* crazy. The whole country. *Loco.* Reality slipped away and craziness settled in its place.

'You speak our language well,' the Governor said, as if that was another charge.

'I have had time to practise in the special prison. Also I have travelled to other countries in Latin America.'

The Governor picked up his passport and inspected the pages one by one. Morton wanted to say to him: See, I have been travelling in South America, not smuggling cocaine to the United States. But he kept quiet. It was better.

'Peru,' the Governor said with some distaste. 'Did you like Peru?'

'I was robbed in Peru.'

'Did you report this to the authorities? Did they do anything?'

It seemed an obsession with the man. Morton shook his head. 'It was my fault. I was careless. It was a girl who stole my money. I was sleeping.'

Thinking of the girl at El Lucky Dip, the Governor said: 'You should take care with girls of that kind.'

Morton shrugged. 'She was English. Somehow with an English girl you don't take so much care. I thought we were pals.'

'You shouldn't have trusted her.'

'If you can't trust a friend, who can you trust?'

'In the armed forces you learn to trust the enemy. You both keep to a code of conduct.'

'Thank you,' Morton said, hoping no irony strayed into his voice. 'I shall remember your advice.'

'Señor Benjamin Morton, I have spoken to you at some length to get the measure of you as a man. Also, because reports were written about you from a particular standpoint, I wanted to hear your story in your own words. If you were under my command, I would be able to make a straightforward and disciplined man of you. But, alas, you are a convict in a special prison. Now, I was appointed Governor for two reasons: the first was to sort out the many irregularities that had come to light; the second was to bring order to the chaotic finances of the prison. Many people are being paid for work they do not do. For instance I found there was a bandmaster but no band. I found a blacksmith and grooms but the last horses were sent away in 1973, and I don't know what horses would do here anyway. In short I have cut down on the staff. I am also cutting the number of prisoners. I cannot grant a pardon but in certain circumstances I can release prisoners by executive order. I have decided – '

And he initialled the slip of paper on the outside of the file.

' – that you shall be released. I see no reason why you should be fed and housed at Bolivia's expense for fifteen years. I also feel that your arrest and trial and sentence displayed a sad lack of discipline. Have you any questions? None? Señor Morton?'

CHAPTER 3

The new Governor had been processing one potential escapee from the prison in the morning, another in the afternoon. So that evening a jeep took Carballo and Morton and turned them loose in the plaza and raced away.

Carballo said to the *gringo*, 'Do you speak Spanish?'

'Well enough. I can say *cojones* and *puta*.'

'That was no use in the special prison.'

'And I can spit at the memory of that old *hijo de puta* Camoeres.'

'Don't!'

Morton stared at him. It had just been something to say, an overflow of relief at getting free. Fourteen years and ten months to go and he'd been chauffeured into town and turned loose. He said, 'What are you worrying about? Camoeres is dead.'

'Someone could be listening.'

'You think they would take us back?'

'This could be a trap,' Carballo said.

'I don't understand. Why would they release us if they wanted to take us back?'

'Because they are like that.'

The old man turned and began to walk away. Shit yes, Morton said, in Bolivia they are like that. They are crazy enough to do anything. But the jeep wasn't hiding at the corner. It had disappeared. Nobody loitered near them.

'Wait.'

The old man slowed and turned.

'What are you going to do? Do you have any money?'

'Do you think I would ask the Governor for money?'

'I have money,' Morton said, the glory of that making a smile break on his face. 'They took away my pesos and my dollars but they didn't know this was money.'

He took the card out of his pocket. As he twisted the card, a tiny flying pigeon on it moved in a strange way and changed from silver to orange to green. Carballo thought it was a bit of magic, a trick.

'That is money?'

'I go into any bank and they give me money when I show them the card.'

Carballo fingered the plastic.

'This?'

'How long have you been locked up?'

This was the trap. This man. But he looked in his *gringo* face and thought of his *gringo* accent and took a breath, a long painful breath.

'For twenty years.'

'Jesus. *Twenty years?* Jesus Christ almighty. You've got to be out of your fucking mind.'

Morton spoke in English and Carballo stared at him. He said in Spanish, 'How do you survive twenty years and come out sane?'

'By saying: I will live until tomorrow. Never longer. Always tomorrow. And one day I knew tomorrow would come.'

And are you sane? Morton wanted to ask. Why were you put away? It must have been for something tremendous – or did the *muchachos* frame you as they framed me? What had you been doing? Is there a story?

'The banks are closed,' Morton said. 'But in the best hotels I can pay with the Visa card.'

'The card with the pigeon will do that?'

'You have a lot to catch up on.'

It could be another trap. Morton could be part of it, leading him on, making him commit himself. Then Morton would snap his fingers and uniforms would darken round him and he would be taken away. Not to the special prison, but to the other place.

They went to a hotel like a rich man's mansion, with silent servants dressed in brown and white, dark antique furniture, a glass case of stuffed birds, silver salvers. The salvers were displayed on a shelf, like cups for sports triumphs. Perhaps the waiter who served drinks the fastest won a silver tray. Morton asked for two rooms and showed his card with the pigeon on it and the lackey behind the desk bowed his head when he saw it. Morton showed his British passport and the lackey liked the look of that too. *Gringos* gave lavish tips. All Morton had for luggage was an aluminium case. Carballo had nothing. Morton explained that their luggage was unfortunately lost and they would need to buy clothes when the shops opened. All this was done with the confidence of a *gringo*. Two months in prison hadn't eroded that. But after twenty years there was a certain amount of rebuilding to do.

There was a modern world to learn about. In the special prison there had been television and the warders sometimes dropped old newspapers. Even so the world was strange. The card with the pigeon – the credit card, Morton called it – which was as good as money. The box no bigger than a cigarette packet that the lackey played with and said how much the rooms were in dollars. So *many* dollars, but Morton simply nodded. The look of the young people in the streets, boys and girls together, the colours of the clothes that you never saw from newspaper photos. Why were so many boys deaf? It was like an epidemic. They walked the streets with earplugs and wires leading to hearing aids that hung from shoulder straps. And girls wore dark glasses at night, like the blind. And shirts with imperialist slogans: *Coca-Cola mas y mas.* And had hair like candy floss, pink and green.

When they ate, Morton said they should order steak. After you had been in prison, a man needed meat. Carballo looked at his steak. It was enough to feed a family and he couldn't stomach it. With steak, Morton said, red wine. He ordered Viña San Pedro, and Carballo sipped half a glass, while Morton drank the rest of the bottle. It made him a little loud and he laughed. 'A celebration,' he said. 'What did we eat last night? Rice and chillies and some beans. And the night before? Rice and beans and some chillies. And before that? Listen, I never want to see rice again.'

'It's what the people eat,' Carballo said, 'when they have anything to eat.'

'Right,' Morton said. 'Come the revolution, the people will eat steak, like us.' They were quiet a moment while what he'd said hung in the air between them. Morton went on in a softer voice, 'What I would like to do is find the bastards who put me in prison and stuff rice down their throats until they choked.'

Revenge, thought Carballo. Morton had only been two months behind bars and he thought of revenge.

When they had finished eating, Morton said, 'I'm going to take a long hot shower and then I'm going out. It's good to be free, come and go as you like, yes? But I want to check that we really are free, that nobody is following us or watching us.'

And maybe, Carballo thought, you want to find a woman. Perhaps even go to a certain house to thank the girl who was truly responsible for our freedom.

'Tomorrow,' Morton said, 'we can talk.'

'Talk?' Carballo was alert again.

'Do you know why I was put inside?'

'No,' Carballo said. Morton had been shut away from the long-term prisoners. Newcomers brought an unsettling breath of the outside world and were quarantined for their initial months.

'Or what my work is?'

'No.'

'Tomorrow,' Morton said.

There was a mountain rising up behind the church of San Benito and in the sunlight it was pinky-orange. Carballo had passed a girl with hair that colour and eyes with spider legs drawn round them, a wild thing. He walked at his old man's pace across the railway line, along cobbled streets, round the church with its seven domes that were like humps a giant had pressed down. He kept the mountain in front of him. It had been plundered by open-cast mines and heaps of discarded earth were sores that never healed. First they had mined silver, then tin, and there was still metal staining the earth. It wasn't worth mining just for iron. This was one of the mountains that had caused the distortion of the television picture, waving lines and visual echoes. In the special prison they were permitted to watch the news, except when it showed riots and strikes. Carballo had watched the news reader turn into a trio, watched an old movie actor be sworn in as President of the mightiest country in the world, watched a Prince ride off to be married in a glittering pumpkin. Camera crews had flown to Africa for the drought and to Belfast for the bombs and Beirut for the screaming faces. What was it like to be one of the camera crew? Was it better than life in the special prison?

The morning was cold and he crossed to the sunny side whenever he rounded a corner. The air was thin but he had grown used to that. Just don't exert yourself. When he turned to look back he saw tiled roofs like orange waves lapping up to his feet and churches rising up like islands.

Yes, and on the television he had seen not one but three Mendozas. Or Mendoza with two ghosts hovering at his back. He had scrambled higher up the ladder and now was commander of the national police force in Sucre. The Supreme Court was in Sucre and Mendoza was being interviewed about the problems of security. This had been after Colombian guerrillas had taken over the Supreme Court in Bogotá, and when the building was finally stormed, Colombia had lost most of its senior judges.

'This will never happen here,' Mendoza had said, with a steely glare at the camera, 'because Bolivia is a country where law and order prevail. We have no terrorists.'

Look in the mirror next time you shave, Carballo had thought.

Morton had only been two months locked away and he wanted revenge. How did he imagine it felt to be twenty years locked away from the living world? Sometimes thoughts of revenge grew so hot you had to turn your mind to something else or you'd lose your reason. But that was a thought he'd never had – that he was crazy. It was the world that was crazy, with movie actors playing President and peering to see if the script said they should blow up civilization that day, princes in golden coaches, children dying for want of food, priests and rabbis and mullahs blessing war, state terrorists growing sleek and powerful.

Some men survived the special prison through fantasies. I spent the night making love to Marilyn Monroe. How was it? She said it was fantastic, the best ever. Carballo had had his private dream: revenge. He had planned it, the men he would destroy, what he'd say to them first, watching their faces, listening while they pleaded. It was a fierce vision that had sustained him through ten years, twelve years, fifteen years. As the years passed Carballo came to realize that it was nothing more than a fantasy, his Marilyn Monroe. He would end his life behind the walls with the barbed wire along the top.

Now he looked down on the roofs of the city and knew he was free. Morton felt hungry for revenge? After two months?

Carballo sat down at Morton's table and knew at once that something had happened.

'What's wrong?'

Morton stared at him but his eyes were seeing something else.

'It's a trap. They've come to take us back.'

Morton had to close his eyes to clear his vision and when he opened them he shook his head.

'Ernesto – may I call you that? Ernesto, I've been to visit someone I'd seen before I was arrested. He's dead.'

Morton had said he was going to buy clothes but all he had on new was an alpaca sweater. Then he'd gone to see his friend.

'That's bad,' Carballo said.

'For him particularly,' Morton said. He gestured at a waiter to order coffee while Carballo tried to understand what kind of man it was who made a joke of someone dying. Graveyard humour he knew, but not about a friend. Morton was British and perhaps that explained it. They were a mass of contradictions: Poets and capitalists, inventors and fighters, visionaries and imperialists. Their famous sense of humour was a way of coping with this conflicting nature.

'Who was your friend?' Carballo asked.

'I didn't say he was a friend,' Morton said. 'Not a personal friend. Do you want a cake? I haven't eaten cake since you know when, since I was arrested. And Luis Isaura was the reason I was arrested. The man who died. I'm a photographer, *freelance*.' Morton had forgotten the Spanish for that. 'I work for myself, sell my photos to magazines and news agencies and picture libraries. I don't photograph royal weddings or politicians making speeches or girls with no clothes. I photograph the people, you understand, Ernesto?'

I understand, Carballo nodded.

'People working, people relaxing, people loving . . . and people dying. Can you understand *that*? I'm a voyeur, a spy in people's lives. Sometimes you hate yourself because you are recording not helping. Then you tell yourself you have a job to do.'

Strange. Carballo had thought of television and wondered how the crew came to terms with what they saw. Now here was a man who had done much the same and his eyes had a staring quality, searching always for the next horror.

The waiter brought coffee and a square of cake for Morton. It had pink icing with a fancy curl done in orange. It was like the mountain outside the city or the girls' hairstyles.

'You make a lot of money with photographs like that?' Carballo asked, thinking of the plastic card and the cost of their hotel rooms.

'Not enough. Not much by the standards of Western society. But in South America I count as one of the rich. In a sense that's why I'm here. A publisher in London said, "All right, Red Ben, enough of this easy life, out and see the Coca-Cola colonies and come back with a book that'll scare the socks off the US State Department." So that's what I was doing: Mexico, El Salvador, Colombia, Peru and finally Bolivia, the biggest insane asylum in the world.'

He broke off to eat the cake, which tasted better than it looked. And in the silence he tested the temperature of Carballo's reaction. Because this was a gamble, being open about himself to gain Carballo's trust. The other man was no ordinary criminal. He hadn't been locked away for twenty years for sordid murder or theft. If you're in the special prison, it's for a special reason. There had to be a story there, something for the book.

'And do you know what happened to me? Here in Potosi? I wanted to photograph the tin miners, not just the ones who go down the mines but the ones who are too sick to go any more. The country earns its dollars from tin, yet the miners starve. And worse. It's so damn hot down the mine they take their masks off, breathe the dust, get sick.'

Morton laid a hand over his chest. Was it too much of a performance? No, he had the old man's attention.

'But the state feels guilty about the short and squalid life of the miners. So I receive a visit from a policeman. He comes to my hotel, dressed very smart in a suit and tie, gives me a flash of his identity card but his thumb is over his name. 'Señor Morton, we have very beautiful churches in Potosi, also nice Spanish houses, not to mention the old Royal Treasury and Mint. Why don't you take pictures of beautiful things for a change?' He's come up to my room and all the time he's looking round, taking in my clothes, my bag, my photographic gear. So what happens two days later? I went to the house of Luis Isaura. He's coughing his chest out and is as thin as my finger and has dark circles round his eyes like a clown's painted face. His wife is there and his four children. I photograph the whole family round the sickbed with the cross nailed to the wall above the dying man. When I get back to the hotel, the pigs are waiting for me with three-quarters of a kilo of cocaine planted in my camera case. Three-quarters of a kilo makes me a dealer not a user. And I'm a foreigner. And I can't afford a fancy lawyer. So you know where I ended up.'

Yes, Carballo nodded.

'And you know where I went this morning with my camera? Only I was too late. Isaura is already under the ground. That's one tragedy. The next one's in the making. The eldest son Alberto has had to go down the mine. He's not sixteen yet. Because their house belongs to the mining corporation and if no miner lives in it the family has to get out.'

Yes, Carballo nodded again. That's how it is.

'Which is disgusting. Alberto will be dead by the time he's thirty. And what is criminal is that the mine is state owned.'

Carballo said: 'Owned by the state, not owned by the people.'

He had listened intently and now he looked away. If Morton had been hoping for immediate confidences, he had been disappointed. Carballo seemed to be working something out, he was withdrawn, judging Morton as a man, judging the references he had so carefully laid out. This reluctance to repay one confidence with another Morton found encouraging. There was something there, something big.

For twenty-four hours Morton didn't see Carballo and thought he might have lost the old man and his story. It never occurred to him to go to the Isaura household. Carballo had been checking. And that night he slept rough, to see if it was still possible to do it. The answer was yes but . . . He hadn't been staying at the Ritz all these years but lying another night on the pavement near the market wrapped in newspapers would kill him. He was an old man now, and used to the comforts of prison.

Morton had the sense not to blurt out: Where were you? What were you doing? He sat on a bench in Plaza 10 de Noviembre and saw Carballo coming, shuffling his feet like any other old man. No, he's special, there's a story in those old bones.

Carballo let himself be taken to a restaurant. Funny, the Englishman only liked to talk when there was something to eat. Words came out of his mouth, food had to go in.

'You don't photograph royal weddings,' Carballo said. 'How about the people's weddings?'

Morton waited for more.

'Young Alberto Isaura is getting married in two weeks' time. You said he was not yet sixteen. He wants to get married in a hurry so that when he dies he'll have a son old enough to take over in the mine, keep the house.'

They looked at each other. So Carballo had been checking his story, so far as he could. That was good. Morton felt his excitement grow. This was going to be big. He felt no resentment and nodded to Carballo: I understand, I respect your carefulness.

'If I'm here when he gets married, I'll be the official photographer. No problem.'

'But you're thinking of leaving?'

'Ernesto, this isn't my home, they could come and arrest me any time for taking the wrong sort of pictures, and also the pigeon doesn't lay golden eggs for ever. You?'

'This isn't my home either. I don't have a home any more. I don't know I even have a country any more.'

'We're the same, both foreigners.'

'We're not foreigners, we're internationals. You're like me, I think, you don't accept the nation-state.'

It's coming, Morton told himself, but don't look too eager.

'I accept nation-states,' Morton said. 'I have to. They exist. Borders, police, taxes, you can't ignore that.'

'You don't have to accept,' Carballo said. 'You can struggle to bring about change.'

'And if they catch you, they put you inside and throw away the key, because they are that kind of bastard.'

'Twenty years,' Carballo said. 'And only let you out because no one knows why you were locked up in the first place, or who you are, or who to ask about you. It's the saving grace for a country like this: it's too crazy to last much longer.'

The waitress brought soup. Morton looked at it without enthusiasm.

'That's rice at the bottom, isn't it?'

'Yes,' she said.

'Take the plate away, strain the rice out of it, and bring it back.'

She stared at him.

'Go on. Do it.'

'She's saying to herself: *Gringo, yanqui imperialist,*' Carballo said, staring at her retreating back, her neck stiff, the soup plate held out in front.

'And so the revolution comes one day closer.'

'Does that worry you?'

Morton didn't answer the question. They looked at each other the way a man and a woman sometimes look, no word exchanged but an agreement between them, an unspoken contract.

The waitress came back with the rice strained out and Morton grinned at her, such a big grin that she smiled too and he thought: That's put the revolution back a day. When she went away she even got a bit of a wiggle in her walk.

'I've been thinking,' Carballo said. 'Well, thinking for twenty years, but particularly thinking since we began to talk. I was thinking how we could help each other. How we each had something to give the other. How we might even get the world to stop killing itself for five minutes and listen.'

The waitress had forgotten the wine. Morton didn't call out for her. He willed himself to be inconspicuous. Now it was coming and he didn't want to get in the way.

'My name is Ernesto,' Carballo began. He took a deep breath

and then got down to it. 'My *real* first name I mean. When I heard they were going to give me new papers and by chance the first name they had chosen was Ernesto I almost screamed No. But then they'd have asked why and I couldn't have given the reason or they'd have said: You're getting your memory back so what's your real surname and why have you been imprisoned? So I kept quiet and accepted Ernesto. Anyway, who had ever called me that? My family, some friends, but not many. The public never, so Ernesto didn't matter. But if they'd gone on and hammered away at my surname, well, that mattered.' He ate some soup and laid down the spoon to watch Morton and said in the same even voice, 'If I said I was Ernesto Guevara they would have scratched their heads until someone would have said, "Hold on, that's the man who was known as Che."'

And he watched Morton's eyes dip to the table as he tried to take this in and rise again to hold his eyes.

'Che Guevara?'

The old man nodded. 'Che, because I come from Argentina.'

'But Che Guevara is dead.'

'Not quite. Close several times. Wished it more than once. Even begged for it once.'

'Che Guevara?'

'Yes.'

The waitress had remembered the wine and poured out two glasses and left the bottle on the table. She smiled at Morton but the *gringo* ignored her. The *gringo* didn't even see her. That was the arrogant way they had. And why was he taking the old peasant out for a meal? Trying to steal his land, lifting his glass to him now as if the deal was signed.

'Well,' Morton said, 'a toast: Che Guevara coming back to life.'

'You don't believe me.'

Morton was cautious. 'I have to get used to the idea.'

'You don't believe me,' the old man repeated. He could tell from the tone of voice.

'Che Guevara was reported dead. I was only a teenager at the time but I remember. The papers were full of it and it was shocking to me. Well, to my generation. The Rolling Stones were our music and Che was our politics and then – bam! There were photos. I don't remember now how they looked. But a corpse, you understand, with wounds and blood.'

'You don't believe me.' He wore a jacket and he always had the collar turned up. Morton had thought it was because of the bitter cold. But when he folded it down now Morton saw the scar that ran diagonally across his neck. It was an old scar but it still looked angry: mauve skin and a fine line of white. How many stitches would a wound like that take?

'I got that in the final battle, before I was taken prisoner. There was another wound I got at the same time.' He laid his hand on a leg. 'There are many other scars but they are souvenirs of the interrogation cells. Those two are the ones I got fighting.'

Now Morton didn't speak. He'd wanted Carballo's story to be big and here was a sockeroo. If. No, impossible. It was just that the old man *believed* it, was one hundred per cent sincere.

'Well, what happened? The papers all said you were dead, Fidel said you were dead, the Bolivian army said you were dead, everybody.'

'Not everybody. There was a sergeant who said he'd seen me lifted out by helicopter. Castillo was his name. Do you know what happened to him?'

'No.'

'He was sent out on patrol again. This was a couple of weeks later. Go on patrol to see if there are any more *subversivos* still loose. But no *subversivos* were anywhere near. They had been killed or had scattered. But Castillo wouldn't keep quiet about Che being taken away in the helicopter so he ended up dead.'

'The army killed him?'

The waitress came with plates of chicken and fried potatoes and salad. Neither of the men had finished the soup but they had let it grow cold.

'Don't you like the soup? It's better with rice in it. Hey, *caballero*.'

Morton glanced up at her and the grin might never have been on his face. He looked angry or puzzled. Or scheming. Like he was planning to do something. A bank robber?

'Thank you,' Morton said, but not as if he really saw her. She went away. There was no point in putting a wiggle in her walk.

The *gringo* was like a man who wasn't there. The husk of him sat at the table but his real self was somewhere else.

'I don't remember much of the early days,' the old man said. 'I had lost a lot of blood and I was in a state of shock. Have you ever been shot?'

Morton shook his head.

'The nervous system registers such a huge impact it is overloaded. It transmits nothing. I had been struck by three, maybe four bullets. A knife enters the body and the nerves signal the brain urgently: pain. A bullet invades the body with explosive force and I have noticed again and again that a man's first reaction is surprise, even disbelief. For me the pain came later but there was so much confusion I cannot say how much later. My body was leaking to death and I kept losing consciousness and I would drift awake and see images that were strange, no part of a guerrilla's life. For nearly a year I had been making the revolution and living in the jungle. Suddenly I was inside a helicopter, inside a tent, inside a barracks. Faces were close. Some were soldiers' faces. Some were doctors' faces. I could tell the difference because a doctor's eyes look with more detachment. The soldiers' faces showed emotions: triumph, hatred, excitement. They had caught Che Guevara. This was what their entire existence had been directed towards. They weren't concerned with making the world better, improving the life of the peasants. Their aim had been to kill me. Instead they had captured me. That was a mistake. They should have shot me straight away because that is a fact no one can argue with. The back of the neck bullet.'

Morton didn't move an eyelash. Incredible man, discussing his own death. No heat, no fear.

'Instead I lived through a day and a night because the senior officer was concerned with destroying our little group as a fighting force. I think that was the reason. That first night two soldiers came into my hut in a period when I was conscious. They were drunk. Celebrating I suppose. They had come to jeer. They were young officers, the worst. One had his pistol out and was shouting, "Let's kill him now." The other was restraining him, not because he was a secret sympathizer but because the order to kill me hadn't been given, therefore it would be disobedience. The fact of murder wasn't important. Obeying your superiors was what mattered. The first time my life was saved was when I had been flown where army doctors could see me. The second time was when one drunken officer struggled with another. Survive is the first rule of a guerrilla's life. I had survived in Cuba. I had survived here for eleven months. I was surviving again. It was an instinct, like sex or food.'

He broke off and closed his eyes. The words had been locked inside him and this was the first time he had allowed himself to open up. He took long slow breaths, wheezing deep inside his chest.

Che suffered from crippling asthma, Morton suddenly remembered. How did he cope with that? And then it struck him: I thought of him as Che.

The old man picked at a piece of chicken and laid down his fork. 'You'd think after all these years I would be hungry. My body has adapted to life without food. Like a peasant's life.'

'Do you want to get out of here?' Morton asked. It was a dreary restaurant, one whitewashed wall streaked where rain leaked in. The waitress stood watching. You could see she wanted to stand closer to hear what the old man talked about, on and on.

'There were distinct periods in my imprisonment.'

They were back in the main plaza again, side by side on a bench that caught the sun. People tried to sell them ice creams and pastries and cigarettes and shoeshines and lavatory brushes. Ignore them and they went away.

'Directly after my capture there were urgent questions. I was fresh off the battlefield, I had been the leader of the enemy forces, I had information I could give. You know the sort of thing: names, camps, communications, plans. I said nothing and when they insisted I told lies. My comrades were still in the field. I couldn't betray them. They changed their story and said the other *terroristas*, as they called us, were dead. That was a trap. If my comrades were all wiped out, why the stream of questions? They wouldn't show me the bodies. They said they had been buried where they were killed in unmarked graves. In a few days they produced a photograph from a newspaper of a corpse. It was no one I recognized and I told them that. They said I was lying and got angry. I think this was the first time. You answer their questions and they despise you for being weak and spit in your face. You refuse to answer and they grow angry and spit in your face. Anyway, this was in the initial period. My life had been spared because of the information I could give them.'

'But you didn't give any,' Morton said, like a schoolboy who needed to believe in a hero.

The old man opened his mouth and hesitated. *Of course not*, he was on the brink of saying, a routine denial. But perhaps Morton had a way of checking, even after all these years. 'I don't know. I honestly don't know. With a raging fever and pumped full of drugs and in and out of consciousness, I have no way of knowing. The first days were critical but after that it grew to be less important. Most of our group had been killed. The wounded prisoners were shot, except for me. A few – three or four – got away. The hunt for them grew wider but it was wild country and the army was lost. They gave up the hunt. That was the end of the beginning. The army officers went away. They flew to La Paz to collect their medals. Some big fascist – General Ovando was his name, I think – announced I was dead and buried. Somebody else said I was cremated. The truth was incredible but in Bolivia the impossible can happen six times a day.'

A man came with a roll of cloth in his arms. It might have made a suit except it was shiny blue. Morton shook his head at the man. Every time you moved in that suit you would shimmer like a tropical bird in the sun.

'My life was saved again and this time by a Minister in Barrientos's government. I was moved to a military hospital and I learnt it was on the orders of the Minister of the Interior. Extraordinary, Arguëdas was a secret Marxist and risked exposure to save me. I was smuggled out in a coffin and if any questions were asked – '

'*If*?' Morton interrupted, incredulous. 'You were Che Guevara, a tremendous prize, and you'd slipped out of their clutches. There would have been uproar!'

'Well, was there?' When Morton didn't respond he went on: 'Perhaps they didn't want to be thought such incompetents they'd let Guevara escape. Or perhaps the story was put round that this time I really had died, as Ovando claimed. I was too far gone to find out. In the new hospital I was kept under intensive care, hovering on the brink of death. It was the closest I came to it. Living rough for eleven months, asthma, bullet wounds, loss of blood, a fever I had contracted – survive, I whispered to myself. Pain was good, it meant I was surviving. Then I was recovering. I was moved out of intensive care. Then out of the military hospital to a sanatorium. Then an army camp. Another camp. A cell in some army headquarters. I had no papers of course and right from the first move I lost my name. I was Patient X. Then why wasn't I allowed to go free? I asked when I found myself in the cell. Because you have no name. You cannot tell us who you are. We don't know what to do with you. That period ended on the day another doctor came into my cell and murmured: "I know who you are." His name was – is – Doctor Quiroz. Remember that.'

It was the first hint that something different was going to unfold. Morton wondered how he was going to recall all the details.

'I was delivered into the care of Doctor Quiroz. It was like delivering the lamb into the care of the tiger.'

'Che.'

The old man stopped short. No one had called him that for years, not since he'd become Carballo.

'There's too much for me to remember. I'm going to buy a tape recorder so I can have a permanent record of your story. You know what a tape recorder is?'

'So you are convinced I am Che Guevara?'

Morton hesitated, balancing the facts according to accepted history and his gut reaction to the old man's stream of words. 'I am convinced. It is a question of convincing the rest of the world you are alive.'

Morton bought two C-60 cassettes to go with the recorder and they went to his room at the hotel. Two men could sit on a bench in the plaza and gossip all day, enjoying the sun. But speaking into a recorder got you noticed.

'If I'm going to have you telling your story, it's stupid to have you start half-way through. Could you start over again? As much detail as you can manage, right from your last battle with the army. Where was that?'

'In a canyon.'

'Do you know the name of it?'

'I don't remember. I don't think it had a name. We had marched through a thousand canyons by then. Somewhere not too far from Vallegrande where the army had its local base. They had patrols out, they were hunting us as if we were wild animals . . .'

The second time he told it for the tape recorder and his voice was tiring. He'd lived through the bad times once in the telling, and he wasn't lifted up a second time. Until he reached Quiroz, the doctor.

'I am a doctor, did you know?' the old man said.

'I had forgotten.' Che had been a legend, a fighter, not a healer.

'I graduated . . . when? Thirty-five years ago. But I could never practise in Argentina because the secret police wouldn't leave me alone. I worked my way up the continent and sailed for Cuba on the *Granma* with Fidel. I was the doctor for our revolutionary force. Fighter too. With one hand I killed, with the other I patched up bodies.'

For a moment he broke off and Morton felt an awkwardness.

'The soldiers we killed were nothing to the number of peasants Batista killed. We had to kill the few to save the lives of the many. And never, as a doctor, would I behave as Quiroz did. It was as if a worm had got into his brain and turned him mad. And the others . . .'

Che had to break off, breathing heavily, concentrating on getting oxygen into his lungs.

'I conquered this.' He laid a hand on his chest. 'There were no medicines so I treated it as a psychological problem caused by uncertainty and worry and fear.'

'But – '

'No buts. I will survive. Tomorrow will come. And by tomorrow pain and fear will be in the past. That's how I defeated the asthma. Pain I treated as a question of time. Project yourself into a serene future. That's what you do.'

Morton knew he would never have had the strength of will.

'Even in the blackest time, when I cried out for death.' He paused a moment while the cassette kept turning. 'Now,' he went on in a calm voice, 'I shall speak of the torture.'

'How do you want to photograph me?'

'I'm thinking about that,' Morton said. It wasn't enough to have Che standing in front of the cathedral or feeding the pigeons in the plaza like any old tourist. They tried some: asking a policeman a question; having his shoes shined; grinning like the big mask in the Moneda; standing with his arms folded against a wall with a huge slogan – CONTRA EL HAMBRE Y LA MISERIA; another piece of graffiti – PCML and a clenched fist with a manacle on its wrist.

'Something different,' Morton muttered. Because this was his breakthrough chance. It wasn't just for his book – though that would come later. This was the big one he could sell to the *Washington Post, Sunday Times, Le Monde, Corriere Della Sera,* all that circus. Break out of the radical protest ghetto. Or maybe one big killing with *Time.* Whatever he decided finally – and Che had agreed to leave it to Morton because after the initial story, all the world's press would repeat it anyhow – he needed a really stunning photo spread. And he needed proof. After Hitler's diaries, he would need cast-iron proof.

They struck lucky with the pictures. Outside a cinema was a life-size cardboard cut-out of Ronald Reagan taken from an old movie. No, Che would *not* pose, never, the imperialist, the bomber of women and children in Central America.

'Che, Che, this is the one. Believe me. Look, like this.'

And that's how it was: Reagan with his easy grin not caring a damn that Che Guevara is at his side with his hand raised, bunched into a fist, with one finger pointing like a pistol at his temple.

'That's brilliant, that's fantastic, another one, that's ace.'

Looking through the viewfinder Morton was so excited he fell into the patter of professional photographers, forgot to speak Spanish.

And he had the proof. Not just the photographs and tapes but other proof. And he was sure it was going to prove positive because Che fell in with it so eagerly.

'After all these years? You think so?'

'I have a good friend who will check. If anybody can do it, she can.'

It was going to mean a change in travel plans. And a fortnight to bring everything together. With his credit card he bought an airline ticket and got cash for Che. They hugged like old comrades in arms in the dawn before Morton left.

Morton was a risk, Che knew, not someone you would trust to storm a continent. But what choice did he have? Here was the bait and a long line to throw out. Would the shark smell the bait?

CHAPTER 4

It was the names he loved, great names. Frostproof, Myakka City, Hookers Prairie, Kissimmee, Polk City. The reality was something else. The reality was shopping malls, Burger King, gas stations, Days Inns, fried chicken. The whole of it was pressed down under the weight of the sun. There was a weird light as if the sun was filtered through gauze. But the heat wasn't filtered out. Massive heat, the wet kind, so that when you got out of the car your pants stuck to your bum, never mind the air-conditioning. That was the trouble with Florida, too many lakes and swamps for the sun to suck the water from. That was why you got the light that seemed to come through a veil.

Listen to me, Morton told himself, *the trouble with Florida.* By a second visit every journalist was an expert.

Disney World way over to the right, then Groveland – or was it Grovel-and? He stopped past Tarrytown at the gas station just before the Interstate and filled up and asked for the phone.

'Hi, Martina Mancilla speaking.'

'Hi yourself. It's me.'

'Me?' she yelled down the phone. 'Who me? You wake up in the morning and look in the mirror and say, "Good morning, me." That's okay, that's allowed. But on the telephone? We're going to play guessing games? Huh? You still there, Mister Me?'

Morton grinned. That flash of temperament, that Cuban accent.

'M.M., I love it.'

'It's *you*,' she shrieked.

'Sometimes,' Morton said, 'I think you're a bit crazy. I know the perfect country for you.'

'Me crazy? You got to be crazy to think that. The only crazy thing about me is to care about you. How long is it I don't hear from you?'

'You haven't lacked for company.'

'I haven't lacked for company,' Martina mocked. 'Listen to the man. That why you phoned? Warn me to empty the ashtrays and change the sheets and fetch in more beers?'

This is how she always was: yell the house down first, kiss and cuddle up later.

'Castle Lager,' he suggested.

'Castle Lager – shit. Don't remind me. That was the worst time ever.'

'Come on. It wasn't all bad, not all of it.'

'You kidding? I never want to see that country again until the revolution. That pig policeman, you know what he did?'

'I know, Martina.'

'Grabs two handfuls of my shirt and says, "From now on, man, you keep these out of our country." '

'I remember. I was *there*.'

'Called me a fucking Cuban bitch. Probably a lot of other stuff I didn't understand. Told me – '

'Martina . . . M.M. . . .'

Get her started like this and there was no stopping her. The only hope was to head her off at the pass. She was squinting as if the sun was in her eyes. Morton leant over and laid both hands on her bikini top.

'Is this what he did?'

'Only he squeezed.'

'Like this?'

'Harder.'

'You mean like this?'

'You think you got property rights there? Trying for an oil gusher?'

She let out a long sigh and settled back in her chair.

'Oh Ben.'

She reached out for a pair of sunglasses, big round ones with white and yellow striped frames. After she put them on she tilted her head down so she could look at him over the top of the glasses. So why put them on? Effect? She was crazy.

He liked it.

'What happened to us, Ben? What went wrong?'

'Nothing went wrong. We're pals. When we meet it's great, fantastic. But you live in Florida, I live in London. You've got your work, I've got mine. Our careers bring us together, that's a bonus. Truly. Working with you, being with you. Then it's the airport departure gate again. Your flight is gate seventeen, mine is gate forty. Nothing's happened between us. Here we are together again.'

She listened to him, listened to the meaning behind the words.

'You still with that dopehead, the swinging bazooms?'

'I sort of moved on.'

Morton had a half-smile at the memory. He'd told Martina about her because no two people could have been more different. 'The swinging bazooms', as Martina called her, had been a big Jewish earth-mama and if she ever got up enough steam to run, her sweater looked as if there was a boxer in there trying to fight his way out. She was chick pea salad, smoke pot in the nude, steal from Harrods food hall, lay your head on mama's nice soft pillows and bring on the revolution. Whereas Martina Mancilla –

'You sort of moved on and discovered Latin America. This year's fashionable cause, huh? Well I guess it must be okay for a *gringo* who wears a suit and carries a briefcase and has a limo pick him up at the airport and drop him off at the Sheraton. But how about you, Ben? Denim like it was still the seventies, camera case, Clint Eastwood stubble. Fifteen years they gave you, huh?'

'Special prison too. Hundred to a cell.'

'A hundred?'

'Cockroaches.'

'How about the option of a fine?'

'They laid three-quarters of a kilo on me. The system is you pay twice the street price and they let you loose. I don't have that kind of money. I don't know the kind of people who do. I'm just a poor *gringo* who likes jeans because they're classless.'

'You think? Since Calvin Klein?'

'Oh shit, M.M., you know what I mean.'

She smiled, white teeth showing against her olive complexion. She must have been pure Hispanic with no black slave blood in her. She was small and living in the land of plenty hadn't put a blob of fat on her.

'Ben,' she said, 'why you come here?'

'To see you,' he said.

'See me, sure.' She'd calmed down, her voice reflective. 'No little ladies on the stop-over in La Paz? Or in Miami? You missed me that much after all those months apart? Is it that kind of seeing me? You want to go inside right now and do it? Must be pretty urgent to bring you all this way. Or maybe see me for something else.'

She was looking through those big dark glasses at him. His eyes dropped. Her bikini was yellow and white striped – could be part of a set with the glasses. Her slim body had a gleam as if it had been oiled. Her belly had just the right contours, and from the navel a scattering of dark hairs led down, a pathway.

'You know what I'd like?' Morton said.

He looked up at her face again. She had gone serious, her lips parted a fraction so he could see her tongue lying in wait.

'A swim,' he said.

Her house was two blocks from the beach but they had to drive.

'Drive – what do you expect?' she yelled at him. 'This is America. I'm an American and I salute the flag and screw the tennis pro and drive two blocks to the beach. Okay?'

'If you want to be American, you should drive an American car.'

'If you want to prove you're American, you drive a Japanese car.'

Although it was two blocks, hers was the only house. It had been painted cream and blue, had weathered and was due for a smartening up. If she stayed. The land had been bought up, subdivided, roads and water laid on. Already along the beach half a dozen frame houses had been thrown up. During the last winter people had come every weekend to view the lots. 'I'm by the creek,' Martina said. 'Perhaps that'll save me. Woman asked if the creek breeds a lot of mosquitoes and I told her straight, Nope, the alligators ate most of them. Woman like that – what does she know, huh?'

The beach was good sand even if the water looked off-colour. Morton liked blue sea and this was brownish. She swam much better than he did but then she lived two blocks from the Gulf of Mexico and he had Kentish Town on his doorstep. But the great thing about swimming was you were free, floating in a different element. You were as far from a prison cell as it was possible to get. She came from behind him, underwater, swirling round him in a flurry of limbs, an octopus from a sci-fi movie, ending up cradled in his arms, laughing.

'So what's this thing you want to talk about?' she asked.

'This thing?'

'Ah come on, you trying to pretend I'm some cheap Cuban whore you're aching to get into bed? This thing I see in your face, in your hesitations. You want to tell me and you don't want to tell me both. Come on, Ben, shape up. If you're not going to tell me then put it out of your mind and we'll play. But if you are going to tell me . . .'

'Okay,' Morton said.

They sat side by side on the sand, Morton with a towel covering his English shoulders, Martina sniffing because salt water made her nose run. Round her neck was a small gold crucifix. She never took it off, not to swim, not to make love. Morton checked they had the beach to themselves, except for a black family way down. She saw him checking and he knew what she was thinking: melodrama.

'Martina, this is going to be the biggest story of the year. Not just this year either. This will get the biggest, blackest headlines you ever saw.'

There was a silence.

'I mean truly big.'

'Sure, Ben, I got it. Big. So first of all we fool round the house and then we have a nice swim and then we sit on the beach. Must be a bombshell of a story.'

'The story is waiting in Bolivia. It's not getting away, not going stale. And it can't break until we break it.'

'We?'

'An even split. Okay, I'm bringing the story and I've got the photos but there's something you can do and I can't: you can prove it's true. Okay so far?'

She had her arms on her knees and her chin resting on her arms. Little dark eyes watched him.

'You make a big production out of this.'

'Yeah.' He nodded. 'When I was in the special prison, they locked me away in solitary so I never got to meet the other prisoners. When they let me out, they freed another prisoner at the same time, an old feller. He'd been locked away like for ever and he had no money and no family so I sort of took care of him. Right? He got to know me, told me his story because he trusted me, wanted me to come out and publish it so the world would know. Okay?'

'Ben, get on with it.'

'He'd been locked away nearly twenty years and nobody knew who he was any more. If they had, they'd never have let him out.'

'Who is he?'

'He'd been tortured for years. He'd be put into hospital to recover. Then they'd get him into the interrogation cell again and throw another party. It's amazing he survived.'

'Ben, I take another swim now. When you reach the part with the old guy's name, you call me in.'

'Che Guevara.'

She sniffed again. It was the sea water, it was disapproval. Her face showed nothing.

'That Che Guevara?'

'Yes.'

'Big hit with Fidel in Cuba, big flop in Bolivia?'

'Yes, that one.'

'Che Guevara, eh? Ben, he's dead. They killed him absolutely dead.'

'Yes,' Morton said, 'and now he's come alive.'

'I tell you most sincerely, dead. Even the worms that ate his corpse, dead.'

'I've got proof.'

'Photographs prove shit.'

'Agreed. So this is where you get to earn your fifty per cent.'

*

Wasn't it always the way? Ben Morton, radical, chronicler of misery, witness to the world's oppressed, jet traveller with his bleeding heart packed in his camera case, bringing it out to make sure it was in good shape like a pot plant that needed watering. Show him the big chance, greed took over. He didn't say: *Fantastic day, Che's alive.* He talked of the big story and the big bucks. 'I'm talking telephone numbers,' was his actual cliché. Another funny thing, he seemed to have left his London self behind and was growing into some character from a TV show. Money corrupted. Even the smell of money corrupted.

They had gone back to the house and listened to the tapes. They had looked at photos. Morton had spent twenty-four hours in Miami, finding a professional photographer, persuading the guy to let him use his dark room.

'This job is one hundred per cent secure, M.M.'

'Secure?'

'Yup. There is no leakage here.'

'You mean these are the only prints in existence. Why don't you say so.'

'I've done all the development and printing myself, and I've got the negatives right here. No assistant has kept a print because he thought it looked interesting or he recognized Che.'

Well, Martina thought, he wouldn't recognize Che even if it was Che. He'd see an old peasant whose body seemed to have shrunk. Lack of calcium in the prison diet would account for that. The head seemed a little out of proportion. Straggly beard, wisps of hair, grey. Maybe some dark strands in among the grey. Cheeks sunken. Diet again. But the eyes were interesting, the expression there. Suspicion, well wariness. Certainly guarding some central core of himself against any attack. Hugging a secret close to him.

'La lucha continua,' she said in a lapse into Spanish, looking at the graffiti on the walls.

'The slogans don't change,' Morton said.

'The problems don't change. The reality is the same. The poverty, disease, hunger and ignorance are no better than they were a generation ago.'

'Right,' Morton said. 'Make a super spread, that one. I never noticed the dog cocking its leg against the wall. Sort of a comment. What do you think?'

'I think,' Martina said, 'you've brought back pictures of Latin American poverty.'

'Ah, come on.'

'Let me finish. I'm a features editor, I'd spend two minutes looking at these, two minutes maximum. Our readers don't need reminding of Third World squalor, spoil their breakfast. The tapes? Five seconds only until I realized they were in Spanish. Tapes in English I can maybe judge – this is the features editor talking, you understand. I ask myself: do the tapes sound faked, actors speaking lines? But foreigners talking – forget it. Can't judge dagos. That's no proof. Excuse me.'

She wasn't apologizing for scepticism. She went to the window and pulled a cord to tilt the blinds against the afternoon sun. For a moment she fingered down one of the slats to look out. She sighed.

'Think I should go out and warn them about the alligators?'

She turned and came back and sat on the chair opposite Morton.

'What's that?' she asked, reaching out a hand.

'Don't touch.'

She stopped. His voice had been sharp. She looked at his face a moment and then down at the coffee table. Next to the tape player and the fan of photographs he'd placed a white dinner plate in a polythene bag. It was a cheap plate, the kind you buy from a pile in a market, or eat chicken with fried rice off in some flaky whitewashed *chifa*. Definitely not a new plate, because of the chip out of the rim.

'There is our proof,' Morton said. 'Che's fingerprints. His right hand on the upper side, his left hand on the underneath. Latent prints, you understand, as I didn't have an ink pad. But they'll come up all right. And I washed and dried the plate first so it's only his prints.'

'His fingerprints? The guy agreed? Did he know what he was doing?'

'Oh yes. I explained to him how I needed absolute proof or else it would be no better than another sighting of Martin Bormann. He was eager.'

'So what happens?'

'Your chance to shine. It's something of a gamble but I figured it out like this. You were a reporter in Havana before you got out. You were a good crusading journalist – what we'd call investigative – and since you wrote critical stories about local security committees and – '

'Okay, okay, I know what I wrote.'

'I'm giving you my reasoning.'

'Ben, I'm way ahead of your reasoning. The evidence is on this plate, you say, and the proof, if it exists, is in Havana. Guevara's fingerprints on file. And since I was a journalist there, I know people with access and someone will be in a position to check.'

'Where are fingerprints kept? Security headquarters? Interior ministry? You must have a source, or an old lover, or a second cousin.'

'You're convinced, huh?'

'Damn right. If you'd seen him, heard his story, seen his readiness to have photos taken and give his fingerprints as evidence, you'd be convinced.'

Well now, she thought, who's gone crazy? An old man in Bolivia? A bourgeois picture-taker who imagines he's radical? Or the Cuban exile, a *Marielita* who came out on the boat-lift?

'Tell me again.'

'What?'

'Everything. All the details. Right from the start.'

'What for?'

'You want me to take this seriously? You any idea what you're asking me to do?'

No, of course not. Did he imagine Cuban exiles could fly in and out of the country just like that? Did he know there weren't even direct flights from Miami to Havana? It was greed again, got his brain working and then blinded him to the difficulties.

When Morton had finished telling his story the second time, Martina said she wanted time to think.

'Think? What about?'

'What you've told me.'

'Okay, think if you have to.'

Morton sat still. Nothing in him moved. He sat and stared at her.

'You like another swim?' she said.

'I'm okay.'

'I mean, go to the beach and have another swim, go jogging along the sand, anything, just go out and leave me alone for an hour so I can think. You stare at me like you can watch me thinking, my brains are all over my face.'

They were in bed with the lights in the room out, but the curtains open and the starlight and moonlight showing up the shapes of furniture, the shapes of bodies.

Against his white body she was dark, except for the strips her bikini covered. She was on top, bending down, kissing his mouth, breaking free but her head still low and her face in shadow so he couldn't see her expression, whispering and crooning his name and muttering in a Spanish that was strange to him and then she was upright with her head thrown back and you'd think she was screaming in terror with her eyes wide open and her mouth stretching and he thought she was like a jockey, riding him hard, as they galloped to the finishing post and, 'Yes,' she cried out, 'yes . . . yes . . .'

She slumped down, her head on his chest, feeling the thump of his heart, sticking to the sweat on his skin. The man was still inside her but the swelling was going. He was good but not as good as he thought he was. Wasn't that the way with men? In a while, when he'd got his strength back, they'd do it again and he'd think of her. The first time was for lust, the second time was for love.

He'd wanted her and God knows she'd wanted him. It had been a drought recently and joking about screwing the tennis pro was just that. What tennis pro? And the guys who came to look at the building lots were middle-aged with families. Once she'd driven into Yoreville and gone to the Orange Grove just to get picked up, just to feel like a woman. But all in all she was safe here. Secure, that was Ben's word, no leakage. Poor Ben.

No, don't make fun of him. He was right – they'd had some times. It had been Jamaica where they'd first met, covering the election where Manley went out and Seaga came in. And one of the new Prime Minister's first acts was sending the Cubans packing. Not that she had been expelled. She already had her American passport, accelerated procedure because it was essential for this fine political refugee from communism to be able to earn her living as a Spanish-speaking reporter.

And now Ben had thrown this curve-ball at her.

Well.

'Ben?'

He didn't answer. She lifted his arm off and walked out of the bedroom down to the living-room. No need for clothes, no need for lights. It was her house and she knew its pathways at night, like a blind person would. In the living-room she went to the window and turned the slats to let in whatever illumination came from the sky. There was no street lighting. When that came, it would be time to get out. With street lighting she would be part of suburbia and there would be gossip. 'Who's that funny little woman on her own?' A reporter. 'Thought she was a divorcee from Chicago.' Comes from Cuba. '*Cuba* for God's sake. Why isn't she in Miami, Little Havana, with the rest of them?' Guess she likes to be private. 'Not have people spying on her, you mean?'

That would be the time to move on.

She went to the coffee table and fiddled with the tape player, rewinding the cassette and playing it back with the volume turned low.

' . . . understand that the psychology of torture isn't well documented. The victims often do not survive. The torturers, understandably, don't want to talk. And in any case they are at a loss how to explain themselves. How do you explain Quiroz opening a vein and draining off blood as if it was a blood donor session but with the bottle slung up in front of your face so you could see it filling. And when it was full, another bottle, and then another. It was mesmerizing watching your lifeblood being drained from you. Eventually, of course, you would die, which wasn't his intention at all. The cat must keep the mouse alive. Before death came unconsciousness. During that period Quiroz would give me a transfusion, all my own blood back again. Technically easy for him because he was a doctor. But psychologically, how could he play with me? How?'

She switched to fast forward. And how could the old man

recite the terrible things that had been done to him in such a calm voice? It had happened years in the past, which was a help. But to recollect was to relive. Horror, fear, pain, obscenity. No wonder he planned revenge.

'Was it always the same questions?' Morton was asking on the tape.

'Sometimes they'd think of a new question. Suddenly they might ask about Fidel's brother Raul. Maybe his name had come up in a newspaper story. But the questions were really only important at the beginning. That was when they thought there was information to get out of me. Then when the doctor rediscovered me, knowing who I was, and introduced me to the policeman, questions then were important only as an excuse. The acts of torture were the real purpose. A session with me was like a weekly game of tennis. Exercise, a social occasion, a drink . . .'

On, not this part.

She believed the old man was telling the truth. Even his calmness carried conviction when you considered it. If he'd screamed and shouted that he couldn't bear to remember, that would be like acting, trying to engage an audience's emotions. These were facts, a recital of the truth. In fact a lengthy catalogue of torture turned out to be a little boring. Only the parts that cried out to the imagination – like the blood-letting – were effective. She had to admit that to herself. For the rest, what did it matter if they put the hose down his throat or up his rectum? This was the twentieth century, not an age of innocence. Pain wasn't pain when it was happening to someone else.

' . . . was a bottle of detergent, for washing up dishes . . .'

No, not that. It was as if he had a macabre shopping list: electricity, drugs, fire, water, blunt instruments, very sharp instruments, physical and sensory deprivation, mental uncertainty.

' . . . Doctor Quiroz had at times pretended he was conducting medical experiments, like Mengele . . .'

Nearly. The part she wanted to hear again was only a little further.

' . . . which was when the change came, with the third man. Yes, it was a different atmosphere then.'

'Did he attempt to conceal his name from you?' Morton asked on the tape.

'I thought I heard voices,' he said from the door.

She switched off the player and looked up at him. He was pale apart from his dark jungle, like Bolivia in the middle of the continent.

'I couldn't sleep for thinking about it,' Martina said. 'I had to play it again.'

'You're convinced,' he said.

'I'm convinced he has to be checked. Che is dead. That is a historical fact. Now he is alive. That would be a miracle and must be checked.'

'But still, you are beginning to admit the possibility – '

'Oh Ben.' She reached out a hand to touch him. He was naked, like herself. Stop pissing me off, stop all this persuasion, this is our only night because I'll be gone in the morning. That's what she wanted to tell him. But there was no need to use words. She let her fingers do the talking.

Mexico, she'd told Morton.

Yes, Morton had said. Merida was close to Florida and close to Cuba and there were flights two or three days a week.

Mexico City, she'd said. Because she knew a diplomat at the embassy there. He might arrange a visa for her to enter Cuba.

But you were born there.

Sure, but I am a *Marielita* and now I have a US passport and things are not easy. But this diplomat is a friend from the old days and he'll smooth things over if anyone can. If not, I could charter a Chris Craft. That would cost a fortune and mean a north coast landing and a cross-country journey to Havana.

Morton wondered if the diplomat friend was an old lover.

He stayed in her house, sleeping in her bed. It was a strange and disturbing experience because she had black sheets and they were impregnated with the smell of her, of the perfume she used. What brand was it? He'd buy her another bottle as a gift. He searched her dressing-table and found half a dozen bottles, but none had the right smell. Taken it with her. That diplomat, that old friend.

He poked round other rooms in the house, looking for a typewriter. There wouldn't be a typewriter in the desk drawers but he looked anyway. There were a dozen letters, some typed, some handwritten. He read a few: a friend who'd got a job in San Francisco, someone in New York who'd met a mutual acquaintance identified only by an initial letter, a love letter from a man in Palm Beach. He was passionate about her and Morton couldn't follow the Spanish completely. 'We shall eat the apple together!!!' Was that a reference to the Garden of Eden? Morton spied on her without shame. Hadn't she gone to Mexico City to screw some diplomat?

When he found her typewriter he couldn't settle to write the story. The facts were there but the words wouldn't come. He was more of a lens-man. Let her write it and he'd iron out wrinkles in her English. Better.

Perhaps it was the ambassador himself she was screwing.

Jealousy didn't suit Morton. He considered himself above it. It made him restless. He went to the beach to try to tan the body that looked shamefully pasty beside hers. He walked the two blocks carrying a towel, Hemingway's *The Old Man and the Sea* and a bottle of Coppertone. The glare made him squint when he read. The water was still off-colour. The sun was too hot and he couldn't oil his back. He walked down the beach to where the same black family was having fun. Two teenage girls played with a frisbee. Could one please oblige and put some oil on his back to stop him burning? They stopped and stared at him as if they were deer and he was a hunter coming through the trees. Great-looking girls, flat stomachs, small tits but it was quality not quantity that counted and God he was getting randy already. Disconcertingly it was the father who came and oiled his back, which wasn't what Morton had intended at all. It made him feel like a honky who couldn't stand the heat.

On his third evening alone he drove into Yoreville. He ate the shrimp supper at a place where the waitress didn't think his English accent cute.

The fourth day he didn't stray from the garden. He took the cordless phone outside in case she called. Why wasn't she in touch? Yes, no, getting close. He took the envelope stuffed with photos and studied them again. Now he wasn't so sure about the one of Che shooting Reagan in the forehead. The old actor was awfully popular. Be okay for Britain, Europe, the rest of the world. There was another one he was growing to like: in the cathedral, two nuns kneeling, Che standing in front of them. The nuns appeared to be bowing their heads to him. There was a religious light that showed up the suffering in his face.

In the late afternoon the phone rang for the first time. Wrong number.

He drifted out again that evening. He drove towards Yoreville but stopped off at the place on the edge of town. It had all the class of a small warehouse or supermarket. Orange trees were painted on the wall and a car-park stretched round two sides. Inside there were three rooms and he chose the bar because the music was less insistent there.

'Hi, my name's Diane,' the waitress said. 'What's your pleasure?'

Looking at her face and the beady eyes and the lines at the corner of her mouth that came from too much forced smiling, Morton drew a breath and took a chance: 'You.'

She wasn't hostile or enthusiastic. She simply studied him. 'I don't see anything to get excited about.'

'Haven't you ever heard of the special relationship?'

'You English?' she asked.

'Me and the Queen are like that.'

'That accent,' she said. 'Say something more.'

'What time are you finished here?'

He'd meant to go back to Martina's house in case she rang. Then he meant to leave Diane's motel room after they'd celebrated the end of her evening shift. Then he meant to leave early in the morning. It was after nine when he got back, a humid wind blowing in off the Gulf, making the palm fronds scratchy. He checked the answering machine and though someone had called, they'd left no message. He was going through to make coffee when the doorbell rang. Parting the slats on the blind he saw a car parked out in the road and thought it was people asking about building lots. Don't forget the alligators, he told himself as he opened the door and the two men came in fast, filling the vestibule. One man jammed a pistol under Morton's chin so tight he gagged and wanted to spew. The other checked the living-room, the kitchen, then to the back to check the bedrooms.

They wore masks, Mickey Mouse masks.

What are you doing? What do you want? Morton couldn't get the sentences out because the gun was choking him. Jesus Christ, I don't believe this. This is too dumb. Are they looking for Martina, money, what?

The guy came out of the guest bedroom and nodded: okay. Okay what? Mickey Mouse masks, guns with silencers, not a word spoken, no demands for money. This can't be . . .

Morton was shot twice: once in the throat, a finishing shot to the temple. He was thrown against the wall and slumped to the floor. There was blood spattered on the paintwork and the carpet but not much; his heart no longer pumped his blood out.

About quarter of an hour later the Messmer family, cruising in their Buick looking for the placard that said Lot 73, saw two men come out of the only house on the block.

'Ma, look, it's Mickey Mouse,' said young Gary. 'It's two Mickey Mouses.'

'Two Mickey Mice, stupid,' said his brother Tommo. They'd visited Disney World only yesterday and it wasn't so far away.

'Hey, Mickey, Mickey,' Gary yelled from the car window. 'Mickey, over here.'

The two men were momentarily startled. Then they both waved and one of them did a little caper on the path as they moved down to their car.

'Looks like it could be a fun place to live,' Mrs Messmer said to her husband.

CHAPTER 5

Che went to the restaurant where Morton had asked for the rice to be strained out of his soup. It was called El Dragón, which was as stupid a name as any for a room like a barn with a high ceiling and whitewashed walls and naked lightbulbs hanging from long flexes. Che chose always to sit with his back to the rainstreaked wall. You were safer with your back to the wall and also your eyes weren't staring at something like a tubercular lung.

Just as the restaurant turned out to have a name, so did the waitress. It was Lucrecia. He didn't ask her surname. Probably Borges. Only in Bolivia, he decided, would a restaurant hire someone whose name immediately roused worries about the food.

'The cook,' Che asked. 'Does he have a name?'

'Of course he has a name,' Lucrecia said. 'Everybody has a name.'

She was quite indignant about that. What did the old man imagine – the cook was a number, a slave, maybe a zombie? She walked away without telling Che. She stacked dirty dishes on one of the other tables, dropping forks and spoons on the wooden floor, before standing in her best position beside a photograph of the Pope kissing an airport runway. After a while she relented and brought the newspaper to Che. Men liked to read about the football scores and the divorces of film stars and wars.

'His name is Adolf.'

Che nodded a thank you for the name and the paper. He wasn't greatly interested in the news but it made a change from looking at the food on his plate. The main stories were about local politicians, the wedding of a rich capitalist, a strike of street cleaners, and the defeat of the Bolivian navy football team by the Peruvian navy football team. The score had been 7–1. 'This is a national humiliation,' Admiral Ayaviri was quoted after the match. 'The Bolivian flag has been insulted.' The Peruvians should not have scored seven goals, he seemed to be saying, because seven was a declaration of war. There must be an agreed scale for such military encounters. Four goals would equal the withdrawal of an ambassador. A couple of goals would be a stiff diplomatic note. Best would be a goal apiece, a frank and friendly exchange of views.

The only thing that Che really liked to read in the newspaper was the date on the masthead. All three parts of it gave him a lot to think about. 1987 was the most amazing collection of numerals. He stared at it every day, checking to make certain he was not mistaken. Suppose in 1967 God had said to him: You have a choice – you may shoot your brains out now with this rifle, or you can endure twenty years of prison, cold, hunger, fear, loneliness and torture more agonizing than is humanly bearable. Just suppose that and give me your considered answer in the next twenty seconds before the soldiers overrun your position. I have one question, God: If the torture is not humanly bearable, how do I survive it? What did God reply? He said: Good question – I shall be curious to know the answer.

He knew the answer now: You do not survive twenty years, you only live until tomorrow, never longer, because you know tomorrow will come.

All things considered, he would prefer to have blown his brains out in 1967. Still it was too late for that now. The trouble was that God had not issued him the warning. It was not that God did not exist, it was just that he was too busy elsewhere to warn one defeated guerrilla what was going to happen. God had more and more people in the world to try to look after, billions upon billions. What was one guerrilla? Indeed what were a few hundred thousand Ethiopians, a few million Jews? Right now God was occupied planning years ahead, making sure that the airports were built in time for the Pope's visit so he could kiss the runway.

Che had thought of things like that in prison. It had helped. He wasn't crazy. He was the sanest person he knew. It was the rest of the world God should worry about.

Another part of the date was April. The newspaper confirmed it. In truth he hadn't been twenty years in prison, only nineteen and a half. But twenty was a satisfactory number. He would stick to that story. Of course he could go back and ask the new Governor if it was all right for him to make up those few months. No, the Governor would think it was irregular. Also he would be in a bad mood because of the navy's defeat at football, constantly taking off his gloves to smoke. Also he'd want to know where ex-prisoner Carballo had suddenly acquired the money to buy new clothes, and to say that the pigeon bought them did not sound convincing. To a navy officer it would sound insubordinate, even mutinous. No. Forget it.

April always had given him a lot to think about. In April, twenty years ago, he'd gone on the offensive. They'd been training long enough. If you did it too long, the training became an end in itself. But his purpose had been guerrilla warfare and Bolivia had been perfect because it was at the heart of South America and guerrillas could be trained and sent back to their own countries to bring about their own revolutions until the whole continent was convulsed.

His theory had been right. Still was right. He knew that. The revolution had failed but that wasn't his fault.

He'd thought of that in prison too. A lot. Which brought him to today. Each lunchtime at El Dragón he had checked the progress of the date and this was the day agreed with Morton. He had work to do. Today, in Che's mind, was Act One.

'Your friend the rice,' the waitress said. She said it like a lady poet of a certain age announcing the title of her latest work. She paused because that was necessary with the old man. His mind was always off on a journey.

'Yes,' Che said. 'What about him?'

'You don't bring him here any more.'

'What of it?'

'Nothing,' she said. 'I just wondered where he was.'

She noticed how the look on the old man's face hardened and the eyes stared into her own eyes. There seemed a dark concentrated fury in his attention. It was how a policeman looked, or a lunatic, or a murderer.

'Why do you want to know?' Che asked.

'No particular reason,' Lucrecia said. 'No reason at all, really. Now I come to think of it, he was American. Quite handsome in his own way, I suppose, for a *gringo*.'

'He is English,' Che said.

'Oh well,' she said and picked up his plate with its half-eaten food. An Englishman, a lord, that explained his funny way with the rice. The English were mad. It was a well-known fact.

'My name is Doctor Adolf,' Che said. 'I telephoned earlier.'

'Of course, Doctor,' she said. 'Won't you take a seat through there. The Doctor is seeing the last of his patients now.'

Che lowered himself on to a leather-look chair. A table held a collection of travel brochures for holidays in Rio and Colombia and Florida. Florida was where Morton had said he was going to see the Cuban woman who could verify his fingerprints. And today was the day Morton was going to publish the story. *Bombshell*, Morton had said in English. Che understood. Fragments of hot metal striking the target, striking others too. This was the day Che began his revenge. He picked up the Eastern Airlines brochure and looked at the shots of silvery sand, palm trees and concrete hotels. The people on the beach all smiled. According to the evidence, the United States had no black population, no Jews, no Hispanics, no Italians. The women were blondes and wore bikinis and had good teeth. The men were muscular and had flat stomachs and good teeth. The master race could have fled there from the ruins of the Third Reich. Look closely and you might see Uhler taking his vacation.

His mind seemed to be running along Nazi tracks today. Blame it on the cook at El Dragón. Che had chosen to use his name. Also . . . also . . . there was a memory stirring. When he'd left the training camp at Baracoa in 1966 he'd flown from Cuba to Prague, Frankfurt, Zurich, Dakar and Rio, dodging and weaving until his eventual destination of La Paz. One of the passports he'd used was in the name Adolfo Mena. Forget the surname. His unconscious had seized on the first name and here he was, Dr Adolf, in the waiting-room, wearing his new clothes, with a haircut and a beard-trim. He looked so smart, Dr Quiroz would never recognize him as that bundle of skin and screams.

The nurse came in and gave him a brisk smile. She wore a crisp white uniform with a blue blouse underneath and Che wondered whether she was a real trained nurse or just a receptionist dressed up. And whether she did anything else for Quiroz and whether she shared his tastes.

'I'm sure Doctor Quiroz won't keep you waiting long,' she said.

Oh, he told her in his mind, another few minutes don't matter. I've been waiting a long time. For years. I've been waiting since you were barely out of the *jardin de niños.*

He said, 'Please,' and raised a hand to ward off any apology. 'Doctor Quiroz is a distinguished physician and naturally someone so important is kept busy. It is an honour he is going to do us. At least I hope so.'

'I'm sure he will. What was it again? The Conference on Pain?'

'That is its short title.'

'In Buenos Aires?'

'Yes.'

'I've never been there.'

'Perhaps this will provide an opportunity.'

She looked at him very directly and her expression didn't change in the least. 'Someone has to stay here.'

'To answer the phone?'

'To direct patients to other doctors.'

'Surely Mrs Quiroz . . .'

'Doctor Quiroz is unmarried,' she said and left him.

Well, no wife. That was good. No family interruptions. Only the nurse. He heard a bell sound and in a moment she put her head round the door.

'Doctor Quiroz is free now.'

In the corridor Che laid a hand on her elbow.

'And there are no more patients? It's just that I shall be some time with Doctor Quiroz explaining the sort of paper we hope he will deliver.'

'No, no one else.'

'Then you can leave us alone to talk.'

He saw her hesitate.

'I shall in any case be inviting Doctor Quiroz to dinner. I hope he will do me the honour.'

'He may already have an engagement,' she said.

With her? Was there disappointment there? Then she was going to be in for a much greater disappointment, the ghastliest shock of her young life. Che felt an excitement rising in him and wondered if Quiroz had felt the same thrill before coming to see him in the cell in that special place. A pressure behind the eyes, a quickening of the pulse, breathing that was faster and shallower, a glow to his cheeks as the blood flowed to the skin's surface. There was no tumescence, otherwise he marvelled at the similarity with sexual anticipation.

She opened a door without knocking, something no proper nurse would have done in Che's experience, and said, 'He must be washing his hands. He'll be with you shortly.' She left him without a smile.

Better and better, Che told himself. The windows were closed and shuttered. They had velours curtains and he drew them across. Heavy curtains would muffle a shout, even a scream. A dozen steps to the desk. There was the bell-push that instructed the nurse to bring in the next patient. Using his penknife he sliced through the wiring. There was the telephone and he cut that too. And an internal squawkbox so doctor and nurse could talk directly. He hesitated but left that alone. No alarm switch that he could see, and only one door.

When Quiroz returned, Che was standing in the middle of the room as if he couldn't bring himself to sit until invited by the so distinguished doctor.

'Well, sir, pray forgive me for keeping you waiting,' Quiroz said. He had a certain formality that could be confused with courtesy. 'Enchanted to make your acquaintance, Doctor Adolf, yes, certainly.'

They shook hands and Che felt a shiver at touching that flesh. He wouldn't touch it again, not if he could help it. But if it became necessary . . . if he himself had to become a torturer . . . He felt the tension in him growing.

'Please, why don't you take a seat? Doctor Adolf? Doctor Adolf? Let me see, I don't believe I have ever had the pleasure . . .'

'Oh, I'm not famous,' Che said. 'In fact for years now I have been quite out of the public gaze.'

'That is what the world needs, my dear colleague, doctors who honour their profession without thought for themselves, only their patients.'

'Uhh.' Che caught his breath. Almost lost control. Very nearly. He knew his blood pressure was rising.

'Now, what can I do for you, sir? Genoveva said – a charming girl, don't you agree – something about a conference at which it has been suggested I speak. Well, well, frankly I'm surprised to think I have any reputation in Bolivia, let alone in Argentina.'

'I assure you, it is my intention that your reputation will be known to the whole world.'

Something in the words or possibly the voice made Quiroz pause and cock his head to look more closely.

'Haven't we met before?' he said. 'I don't boast that I never forget a face because I see so many. Yet . . . there is something about you that grows more familiar. The voice too. But I don't recall any Doctor Adolf.'

'No, well Adolf is not my real name. Excuse my simple trick for getting into your surgery. Would you recognize Doctor Guevara?'

Quiroz raised a hand to his face and smoothed a trim little moustache while his eyes wandered over Che's features: nose, ears, mouth, strip of beard, end of a scar on his neck visible above his collar. Then his hand dropped fast to his desk and jabbed at the bell-push.

'It doesn't work,' Che said. 'I cut the wires. The telephone too.'

He was on his feet and moving close to the desk so that when Quiroz reached for the squawkbox the pistol was aimed straight at Quiroz's chest. It was a Walther P.38, a policeman's gun, though it had come from the Isaura family. Every few years the tin miners manned the barricades and this had been the trophy of one uprising. By the time that Isaura had got the gun away from the policeman several shots had been fired. They hadn't been able to get more ammunition but three bullets should be enough. It was not Che's intention to use any if he could help it.

'Don't do it,' Che said. 'I can't miss your chest from here. I may not hit your heart but I'll puncture your lungs. You're a doctor, you appreciate what pulmonary wounds are like.' A sucking wound that opened with every breath, Che thought, I've seen them and so have you. But he let the other doctor's memory do the work.

'I thought you were deceased,' Quiroz said, his formality still intact. 'You passed out of my mind years ago and I assumed you were dead.'

'God plays funny tricks,' Che said. 'Isn't that true? First he allows you to practise your evil on me, and now he is allowing me to take my revenge. That is strange of him. Do you believe God is love? When you look at the world, do you think that? Do you see the evidence? And then consider yourself – God made man in his own image. If that is true you are indisputable evidence that God is a sadist.'

There was a silence until Quiroz said, 'So what is your purpose, Doctor Guevara?'

'Such formality! What was it you used to call me? The Case, The Experiment, The Specimen? Have you forgotten?'

Quiroz gave a slight shrug.

'I want your co-operation,' Che told him.

'Co-op – '

A buzzer sounded and a light on the squawkbox flashed on.

'Who's that?'

'Genoveva.'

'Hasn't she gone yet?'

'She never leaves until I give permission.'

Che moved round the desk until he was at Quiroz's shoulder. He moved the Walther so its snub nose was in Quiroz's ear. 'Be careful now, very careful.'

Quiroz's hand extended in slow motion and a finger pressed down the switch.

'Yes?' He barked it out, short and nervous.

Che leant forward. 'Be natural. How do you usually call her?'

'Yes, Genoveva?' Quiroz said. And still it didn't sound natural.

'You've no more patients tonight,' she said. 'I don't know how long you'll be with Doctor Adolf.'

'You're having dinner with me,' Che breathed.

'We're having dinner,' Quiroz said. 'We have a lot to sort out.'

'I see,' she said. 'All right, Doctor.'

'Perhaps later . . .' He broke off as the pistol dug deeper into his ear.

The nurse said nothing to this.

'Say you'll see her in the morning,' Che breathed.

Quiroz turned his head enough so his eyes held Che's.

'Say it.'

'I'll see you tomorrow morning, Genoveva.'

'All right, Doctor. Good night.'

Quiroz released the switch and the light went out. Che found there was sweat on his hands. On Quiroz's cheek too, a trickle ran down. Che took a step back and with the release of tension he felt a laugh forcing its way up. Ridiculous. God had a macabre sense of humour. As he began to laugh he saw the surprise on Quiroz's face and the surprise turning to a smile that opened twin cracks at the corners of his mouth and then he began laughing. There they were, a pair of old pals enjoying this huge joke.

Che stopped abruptly. With laughter came sympathy. He wasn't here for a comradely reunion. He went to the door, locked it, and pocketed the key.

'Enough,' he said.

The laughter stopped in Quiroz. *Enough*. It had been a command ending the first act. He said, 'What . . .'

'What do I want?' Che said. 'Is that what you were going to ask? But then you grew afraid of what I would answer? Do I understand you right?'

Quiroz lifted a hand to brush away the trickle of sweat. The way it ran down his cheek made it look like a tear.

'What a shame there is no Conference on Pain,' Che said. 'Your paper would be a joy to hear. You would be uniquely qualified to speak, drawing on your own observations. Other medical researchers have had to make do with lesser mammals, dogs or rats. But you – well, you had your very own human rat to prod and pull to pieces, to watch and listen to. It would be a strange experience to hear your report on my responses. What would be your conclusion? "Pain is good – it is a warning mechanism that the body is under attack and needs to be defended." Is that what you'd say? Make pain somehow a moral force. How would you explain the pain of terminal cancer when nothing can be done to defend the body against attack? Tricky that. Perhaps you would need to conduct more experiments. Once, Doctor Quiroz, I was so intimately involved with your research work. But as you notice, latterly I have become more detached, taking a philosophical perspective of pain.'

Che leant across the desk and pressed down the switch on the squawkbox.

'Genoveva? Genoveva?'

There was no answer.

'We really are alone. You know, in prison other men used to fantasize about sex but I used to dream of this moment. Do you find there is possibly an echo of sexuality in the situation? Just the two of us. The torturer and his victim, although I'm not certain which is which. It is a shame the girl has gone or she might have taken part in an experiment. Are you flinching? An experiment of great scientific importance. Or at least value to me.'

'I suppose,' Quiroz said, 'it is no good offering you anything? Whatever I possess to go and leave me in peace.'

'But you *do* offer me something,' Che said. 'Oh, you mean money. I am told that just by the trick of being alive I am going to be showered with a great deal of money. That will be a problem – what to do with it. Never mind, that will not be your problem. No. Now you are the expert on pain. Tell me frankly, Doctor, did watching an experiment involving hideous pain give you pleasure? A sexual *frisson* perhaps? Pain as pleasure – there is another notion for the paper you are not going to give.'

Che left the desk to wander round the room. He opened a wardrobe where white coats hung, pulled out the metal drawers of a cabinet, tried the hot tap in the sink. In between he glanced to see Quiroz didn't move from his chair. The pistol was always between them.

'Just a short while ago there was a most interesting occurrence,' Che said. 'A great pillar of society went to a brothel in this city and at the moment of climax he died. So would you say he enjoyed pleasure or pain? You must have asked yourself questions like this because you have a most enquiring mind. To your patients you show only the cramped virtue of the professional. But a few of us are privileged to know how your spirit soars into areas ordinary men would never dare enter.'

'Is it sex you are after?' Quiroz asked. 'Perhaps the girl. She is most accomplished for someone of her years. Or do you need a safe-conduct out of Bolivia? I could – '

'I'm not leaving the country. I have work to do here. You are only the first.' He opened another closet and found outdoor coats and leather boots. 'Tell me, a doctor such as yourself would surely carry out blood transfusions. It's just an idea I have of you. Dear señora, I can hear you saying, I do not like the idea of such a distinguished lady going to a common hospital. I see I'm right. Then you must buy blood. Peasants, miners' families, poor people who have no other way to get money must sell you their blood.'

'Would you prefer them to starve? I do them a favour.'

'Only I can't see the equipment. Suppose I wanted to give blood now. Would you do it?'

Quiroz frowned. Guevara giving blood?

'Come, on your feet. Show me where your equipment is. But no tricks please. Remember this.'

As Quiroz stood up, Che stepped in and laid the muzzle of the gun on the tip of the man's nose. Quiroz's eyes squinted at the barrel and he swallowed. Che could see his Adam's apple bobbing.

'All right.'

Together they went to a battleship-grey cabinet, and packed in a carton were a number of half-litre glass bottles, containers for blood. Beside the carton was a brace to clamp the bottles, a small hand puffer, a rubber constraint that went round the arm, and tubing.

Che's breathing became difficult. He took a slow and painful breath, and another, imposing his will on his body.

'Do you remember that time?' he asked.

Quiroz looked at him. Che could see the understanding dawn in him.

'I don't think you're going to give blood, are you?' Quiroz said. His tone of voice said he already knew the answer.

Che kept the fiction going a moment longer. 'I want you to assist me. Bring all the equipment over to the examination couch. I would offer to help but my part is essentially to hold the gun.'

Quiroz moved the brace, the tubing, the rubber constraint

which was like the inner tube for a kiddy's toy. They had been jammed inside the cabinet as old gardening tools might be and Che doubted the sterility of the blood the doctor used. When Quiroz picked out one of the glass containers, Che said, 'How many bottles are there in the carton?'

'A dozen.'

'Bring the whole carton.'

Quiroz stretched upright and squared his shoulders.

'I refuse. You plan to carry out some experiment, to torture me in revenge for what happened many years ago. It was a different world then, you must agree, standards have changed.'

Che listened to the pleading in silence. Then he gestured with the pistol for Quiroz to pick up the carton.

'I will not. I think you intend to kill me.'

'Untrue,' Che said. 'I adhere to the ideals of Hippocrates, unlike yourself. I have killed as a guerrilla but not as a doctor, never using medical knowledge. The fact is this: you are going to kill yourself. I shall be present merely to observe that justice is carried out.'

'You plan to kill me,' Quiroz insisted. 'It is better that you shoot me now and be done with it.'

'Do you know what you are saying? Suppose I shot you in the stomach. You are imagining a quick death with a bullet through the brain. But imagine what it would be like to have two or three bullets through the intestines, liver, colon. You would die a lingering and agonizing death, on the floor, smeared with your own blood, vomit and excrement. I offer you a far more pleasant alternative. By the way, you're certain to know your own blood group. You can leave a farewell note bequeathing your blood to the hospital of your choice. And I suppose you're Rhesus positive. Oh, it doesn't matter. Just a thought.'

Che lowered the pistol until it was aimed just below the rib-cage. Quiroz picked up the carton but seemed to have lost the use of his legs.

'Come, come, Doctor Quiroz, courage. I assure you from personal experience the sensation is not too bad. The worst you will suffer is a headache. Your heart rate may increase as if your heart is trying to find where all the blood has gone.' Che prodded Quiroz towards the couch. 'Later the heart slows.'

Quiroz held the carton in front of him like the waitress had held Morton's offending soup. The doctor wouldn't be flattered at the comparison. The doctor was a gentleman.

'Now set up the equipment.'

Quiroz's hands were shaking. Che wondered if there was sweat on his fingers and whether he would drop the container he was clamping. His face was frowning as if he was concentrating so he wouldn't make a mistake. No, he's trying to remember all those years ago what I looked like when he drained the blood out of me and I lost consciousness. I never pleaded for my life. And I only once pleaded for my death and that wasn't the occasion.

'I will change the bottle when it is full,' Che said. 'But can you manage to attach the tube to a vein on your own?'

Quiroz stared at him, appeared to be judging the distance and his chances of rushing the pistol.

'Don't try,' Che said. 'I have shot men before. I have shot soldiers because they represented a system that was corrupt. And you are corrupt. I would have no hesitation in shooting you. Come on. The worst you will experience is the headache. Also, there is the sensation that you are shrinking, within yourself and away from the world. That must be partially a psychological response. I am no psychiatrist, but that is what I would diagnose. Now take off your jacket.'

Quiroz removed his jacket.

'Don't think of throwing it at me. The shirt – do you want to take that off or will you manage by rolling up the sleeve? It's entirely up to you. Personally I think it would look better if you kept your shirt on. Your tie too. We must consider Genoveva's feelings in the morning.'

'You're mad, do you realize that?' Quiroz said.

'Do you know, I've wondered about that,' Che said. 'Often in prison I would plan revenge for the pain I had suffered but more particularly for the indignities to the human spirit. I must be mad to contemplate such things, I told myself. But then no, I realized that such revenge was a necessary part of rebuilding myself. You drained some of my spirit out of me and this is how I get it back. Nevertheless, since I was imprisoned and there was no likelihood I would ever be released, wasn't it mad even to consider this? I wondered. Still, hasn't it been clinically proved that if you question your own sanity, you are undoubtedly sane?'

'Mad.'

'Well, encountering you in the flesh has awakened many painful memories,' Che said. 'So tonight perhaps I am a little crazed, and you are alive. The difference is that in the morning I shall be sane.'

'There,' Che said, 'that wasn't so terrible, was it?'

He wasn't expecting an answer.

CHAPTER 6

They must smell death. Was that it?

They stood and stared. The Vultures, Bodinetz called them. Death was the attraction, the stench of carrion. Perhaps they really could smell it, sure as sugar they couldn't see anything. Single-storey house, ordinary woodboard, salt air making the cream and blue paintwork tired, standard issue four palm trees, bed of cannas that had been planted and forgotten. Two uniformed cops but any time you wanted to see those you only had to drive into Yoreville.

Nothing special about Larry Goodman and Jack Gonzales except for the fact they were waiting outside. Hell, they were going to beat the Vultures off? They'd pulled two white patio chairs up and perched in them like you sometimes saw the old ladies sit, talking a bit, waiting mostly. It should have been a warning to him: they weren't sitting inside.

'Guys,' Al Bodinetz said. 'Enjoying the air?'

'Practising being film stars,' Gonzales said, nodding his head.

Bodinetz looked back and two of the Vultures had cameras to their faces. Jesus Christ, these were just the amateurs who kept to the street, wait until the professionals came. Al Bodinetz really loved the happy snappers from the press. Over here Sergeant, back a step Sarge, hey Bo put a hunter's foot on his chest, bit to the left so we can see more blood. Jesus, what kind of freaks became pro cameramen, spent their lives recording death, disaster and destruction? Don't say the same kind of freaks as became cops. El Al had jaw muscles that jumped when he got angry.

'Shall we get inside?'

'Ahhh, Bo,' Goodman said, 'it's not too good in there. Thought we better warn you.'

'You want to stay outside is okay with me,' Bodinetz said. 'Don't want you throwing up on the evidence.'

'We turned on the air-con – '

'Sure, we got a hot one today.'

'Scrub the air some but honest, Bo, it's – '

Bodinetz had his fingers on the door handle. 'Folks who found the body?'

'Name of Peters. We've got their phone number you need to check anything.'

'You let 'em go, for Christ's sake?'

'Had a plane to catch. They were only here on an inspection visit. Just their boy threw a ball, broke a window. Mrs Peters came to say sorry and pay for the damage and looked in.'

'And they've gone?'

'You bet. Reckon they won't be moving here after all. Detroit seems safer.'

'Okay.'

Bodinetz opened the door and took a step in and came staggering back like the Refrigerator slammed him.

'Jesus, *Jesus*, why didn't you warn me? I never ever in my life . . .' He gave up searching for words to describe it. He'd been right: the Vultures *could* smell it.

'We tried to warn you,' Gonzales said. 'Would you listen? Well would you? All we are is guys and you're the brains.'

They'd had the media. God, they'd had the media. A guy dressed in a white polo shirt and a black beard as if he was a real artist had taken photos through the front door of a shape under a wrap, of Sergeant Bodinetz looking grim (The Law Enforcer), of the Vultures in the street. There'd been a creep with acne and a steno pad. Another bigshot came with his recorder and turned one little murder into the betrayal of innocence, the era of looking-glass moral values, other stuff which slipped by Bodinetz, saying to himself, so that's what we've been fighting all those years, me and Gonzo and Larry. 'This is not the first of these acts of violence. Since the coming of Disney World, the discovery by the college crowd of St Pete, the mushroom growth of condos, we seemed to have swopped real worth for its shadow.'

'Yup,' Bodinetz had said as the reporter tilted the microphone his way. 'Time was when all we had was a handful of traffic violations, maybe a couple of drunks round Fourth of July – what we called the patriotic boozers. Back a bit before that, the good old days, all we got was people dropping stuff, you know, empty cigarette packs, used rubbers . . .' The reporter didn't like the tone of this interview. 'The people have a right to know – ' Was this really someone from the local AM station? Bodinetz said, 'Don't give me the Constitution. I'll lock you in the room with the corpse. That's what your listeners want to hear about. He's had his brains blown out. There's blood and shit everywhere. Been dead a week and more. Think of that, a week in this heat.'

They'd got all the windows and doors open and the air-conditioning unit working for good measure. After a couple of cigarettes the official photographer agreed to go in and take positional photos of the corpse and finally it was loaded into a body-bag and removed. There would be an autopsy and whenever Bodinetz thought his job had bad times he reminded himself of one job he would like less.

An oldtimer from Yoreville PD – one who remembered when dropped cigarette packs were the big worry – came for forensic evidence. 'At a guess you got maybe a million clues here. You want me to start on them?'

'Forget fingerprints for now.'

'Sure. I'll come back when I've got elimination prints off the deceased.'

Bodinetz loved it, the oldtimer and his *deceased*. Benny, the oldtimer, was unfolding a pair of thin cotton gloves that had started out as white.

'You fellows come inside, you keep your hands in your pockets,' he said. 'Else you'll end up getting arrested for murder.'

Only cops wear gloves now, Bodinetz told himself. Violent criminals didn't have the patience to pull them on. Could be they'd find prints on some of the surfaces, could be they'd strike lucky and identify someone. Anyway by now a dozen men had tramped through the vestibule. There was going to be enough forensic evidence to convict half of them: not just fingerprints but the impression of a heel in blood that was still viscous (must have reacted with some chemical in the floor polish, Bodinetz didn't know), sand and grit, hairs, Wrigley's wrapper, cigar ash from the reporter with the recorder who'd braved the smell, vomit from when he'd realized too late it was a mistake. Nevertheless other stuff could be interesting. Benny had the habits of years, professional and no messing.

Bodinetz checked the Peters family's story. Yes, Mrs Peters had tried the door when there was no answer because she wanted to leave a twenty inside, feeling the guilts about the window. The kid who threw the ball was – in Gonzales's telling of it – very cocky, full of shit, twelve-thirteen, his voice already broken, could have thrown the ball on purpose.

Benny had finished in the guest room and called in Bodinetz to consider certain things. The bed had never been slept in but a small overnight bag had been dumped there. The bag was brand new – go on, smell it – but around it were old and unwashed clothes. Really old, ragged in the case of the slacks. It looked as if the clothes had been crammed inside the little bag and been tossed out by someone searching for something.

The main bedroom was a woman's place: clothes, cosmetics, jewels, chunky rings, king-size bed, both sets of pillows used. The man had slept here, his clothes dumped on a chair, unwashed clothes but new. See, Benny pointed out, pair of shorts with a staple that had held the price tab.

In the bathroom, man's shaving things, toiletries, only one toothbrush. Benny slipped it in a plastic bag to examine later. There was little chance of clear fingerprints but a better chance of dried saliva on the bristles and if it was her toothbrush that would give her blood group. Well, it would be *something*.

Watching them you'd think Benny was the detective and Bodinetz was the rookie but it wasn't like that. Benny's expertise was seeing physical things. Bodinetz saw connections.

'You're thinking they had a bust-up,' Bodinetz said, 'the woman shot him and got out?'

'It's staring us in the face, isn't it?'

'She killed him by the front door, took time out to throw his dirty clothes round, packed a toothbrush but not her jewels. Is that like any woman you know?'

Benny had the air of a man who didn't know many women.

In the living-room was the interesting discovery: an aluminium camera case holding a long lens, UV filter, folder of cleansing paper, hood, single sealed roll of black and white film. There was no camera, no prints, no negatives. Benny found an end of celluloid, it could have been shaved off a negative. Nothing showed on it.

'Robbery?' Bodinetz asked, taking opinions.

Gonzales and Goodman had followed into the room. Benny was bending over a portable tape recorder on the coffee table. There were no cassettes. There were a television, a video recorder, a record player. Goodman took a hand from his pocket to point at them, one, two, three. Robbery? He said nothing.

'Right,' Bodinetz said. 'Very selective robbery: camera and photographs, maybe cassettes, what else? We don't know.'

Benny was at the corner table where the telephone and answering machine were. He said, 'Somebody's rung.'

A red pinlight glowed. He rewound the tape and pressed playback. They listened to tape hiss, a couple of clicks, nothing.

'Those clicks,' Bodinetz said, 'somebody rang but didn't leave a message.'

'I do that all the time,' Benny said. 'Hate talking to a machine.'

'Another thing,' Bodinetz said, 'what's happened to the recorded message? You know: This is the Browns' residence, we're busy screwing in the bedroom right now, but leave your number and I'll get back to you . . . You know. It's been wiped.'

Bodinetz went to the window to get some fresh air. The stench was bad in here, just off the vestibule. It would be a couple of weeks before it faded. Some people said when a violently killed man was locked up like this, the house never lost the smell. It was always in the background, like a swamp stink. Some days you'd scarcely notice it, then the weather would change. Best thing with a house like that was to smash it down, build it again. You could call that the Kissinger doctrine, Bodinetz decided, polished to perfection in Vietnam.

'They did more than steal his camera,' Bodinetz said, 'they stole his identity. No driving licence, no credit cards, no tickets or letters, no tag on his camera case, no address book. They think we can't find out who he is, then they're pretty dumb. They try to hide it, makes us go at it harder. Right?'

Gonzales sighed. It was going to be another of those marathons: if-I-can-do-without-sleep-so-can-you-guys.

'So who's the woman?' Bodinetz said. 'We start with her.'

'I'll call the development corporation,' Goodman said. 'Find out who bought this place.'

He was at the phone when Bodinetz said, 'Hold it.'

'Okay, let Benny do it, he's wearing gloves.'

'No, hold it.'

The hell with fingerprints. Bodinetz picked up the phone and punched the Redial button. Whatever the last number was, they'd get it again.

'Nobody say anything.' He covered the mouthpiece anyway.

He held the phone a little apart from his ear so Goodman could hear the ringing tone. At the other end the phone was answered and a male voice said something incomprehensible, using a strange slurring language. Bodinetz looked at Goodman, frowning, wishing they were taping the voice so they could identify it later. Then the male voice said in slow and careful English, 'This is the Cultural Section of the Soviet Embassy. Hello? Hello?'

Goodman broke the silence. He said, 'Russian Embassy? Didn't the President close the fucker down?'

Gonzales said, 'That was the Libyan Embassy.'

Goodman said, 'Should have kicked the Soviets out the same time.'

Benny said, 'Let 'em stay.'

Goodman turned on him. 'You some kind of closet Red?'

Benny said, 'How many Russians have they got there? Hundred fifty, two hundred? So a couple of hundred people see what ordinary America is like, not what the propaganda is. When they go back to Moscow they spread the word.'

Gonzales said, 'You call Washington ordinary?'

Goodman said, 'He's some kind of nut. I told you.'

Gonzales looked round and said, 'Hey, where's El Al got to?'

Al Bodinetz was outside in one of the chairs, enjoying the fresh air. He waved a beer can at them. 'I'm destroying evidence. More in the fridge, you guys want one.'

Goodman pulled a chair round to face him. 'Russian Embassy, huh? You want my opinion, it's too much.'

'Well now,' Bodinetz said and took a pull of beer. 'What do you prefer? Dropped Pepsi cans? Unauthorized skinny-dipping? That our level, you say?'

'Come on, Bo. Sure we do traffic violations. Also we do drug busts, we do rape and murder and extortion and kidnapping. This is kind of different. This is over our heads.'

'Beginning to smell of government,' Gonzales said. 'We should bring in the *Federales*.'

'Right, get some class down here to solve this one,' Bodinetz said. 'That what you mean? College boys with button-down minds. Run it through their button-down computers. Use the print-outs as prayer sheets 'cause they're too holy to wipe your ass with.'

'It's one for the Bureau, Bo,' Gonzales went on. 'There's a murder, an empty house, cleaned of identity, and the last phone call was to the Soviet Embassy.'

'Murder plus that interstate call make it a federal crime,' Goodman said.

'You think?' Bodinetz squeezed the beer can until it buckled. 'What's wrong with you guys? We've got a murder here and it's our job to wrap it up. What we're paid for, right? The last call that was made on that phone was to the Russian Embassy in Washington but as of now nobody can show it was connected with the crime. Prove that and it's hands off. But all you know it could be someone ringing up to ask if it's true the Bolshy Ballet is touring in the fall.'

Silence.

The air was hot and humid and Gonzales disappeared, muttering about raiding the fridge for a cold one. The Vultures had gone from the street.

'Larry,' Bodinetz said, 'we solve this one and there'll be promotions all round.'

'We solve this,' Goodman said, 'and it turns out Ivan is controlling a spy ring, how do you explain doing it on our own?'

'We do that, dummy, the President will be shaking our hand, not asking why we did it.'

Gonzales came out with beers for them all, popping one and taking a swallow. Behind him came Benny.

'Nice party you got going here.'

'Just collecting our thoughts,' Bodinetz said.

'Here's something more for you to think on,' Benny said. 'Thought someone ought to ring the development corporation before they went home for the night. Seems this place is rented by a woman name of Martina Mancilla. Been here three years.'

Bodinetz sighed. Here was one oldtimer working while the rest of them sat round and drank beer and argued about doing it. And the woman's name. 'Martina? What was the rest? Mancilla. Sounds like one for you, Gonzo.'

'She's not Puerto Rican,' Benny said. 'Fellow from the company said he had to check her before she could sign for the place. Before she came to Yoreville Beach she'd been in West Palm Beach and before that Miami and before *that* Havana.'

Bodinetz straightened up. 'Havana, Cuba? That one?'

'Do you know any other? She was open about it. Came right out and talked about how tough life had been under Fidel, standing in line for bread, censorship, security committee on every block. She got political refugee status.'

'So why does she ring the Russian Embassy, if she's a refugee from communism?' Goodman asked.

'Well,' Benny said, 'we don't know she did. We only know *someone* did. Ever thought the dead guy might have done it?'

The trouble with Bodinetz, as Benny would have told him if he didn't value his own teeth, was the fellow was lazy. He had the brains but he wasn't hungry enough to sweat for it. A beer outside under the palm trees, anybody could see that was better than getting to work in that stinking house. But he was getting a gleam in his eye at the thought this might be the big one. Headlines, TV news, handshakes, medals, Hollywood buying the rights. And Bodinetz would never have agreed he was lazy. Detached would be his description, looking at a problem from a little distance. Until his attention was fully engaged, like now.

'Come on,' he said, 'we've got work to do.'

*

I've opened the door on a whorehouse. That was the first thing that came into Benny's head. You would never pick out the stench of the dead body for the overpowering tide of perfume. On the table under an oval mirror was a plate with a puddle of liquid evaporating. Beside the plate was an empty flask of Ma Griffe. More evidence vanishing. He didn't know Ma Griffe from Ma Bailey but she packed a powerful smell.

He glanced in the kitchen and saw the crusts from pizzas and styrofoam coffee cups. He checked the living-room and found sandy footprints on the carpet and grey drifts of cigarette ash. Give them twenty-four hours and the police could turn any nice house into a ghetto. So much for protecting the scene of the crime. But this wasn't going to be one for forensic evidence. If they broke this one it would be Luck or Intuition or Confession or Examination. LICE was the great police secret weapon.

In the guest room he came on Bodinetz and Gonzales.

'Where's Larry?'

'Fetching breakfast.' Bodinetz looked rough, as though he hadn't slept. Or he'd sat in his car, jammed into the bushes, to see if anyone tiptoed back during the night.

'Well . . .' Benny didn't care for telling things twice but he didn't want to spend longer here than he had to. 'Brought you these. Perhaps you ought to wait till you've got breakfast down you.' He opened his case and took out glossy prints.

Bodinetz studied them. There were close-ups, profile and frontal, of the face. It had been cleaned up and looked better than he expected. Other pictures were of the full corpse. It had been slit and closed again.

'Autopsied already?' Bodinetz was surprised.

'Right,' Benny said. 'I told the Medical Examiner to hurry it along because of being a Russian spy.' When Bodinetz looked up sharply he added, 'Well, not yet I didn't.'

'Anything interesting? Anything more than the guy was killed by bullets and during his last day ate a hamburger?'

'Time of death flexible. Five to ten days.'

'Jesus, can't they do better than that?'

'On TV they can.'

'What else does the corpse say?'

'Stomach contents include tuna, bread and beer. That indicates time of death as afternoon or evening.'

'Not if he's unmarried,' said bachelor Gonzales. 'Tuna sandwich and beer sound okay for breakfast if you got no one to fix it for you. Like you're on vacation and your woman gets out.'

'Could be,' Benny said. 'He's not local. You can't tell from the photos but from the skin tones he's not local. No tan, or only the beginnings. On his shoulders – you look hard, you can maybe see – are sun-blisters.'

Bodinetz looked. He couldn't see sun-blisters. The skin on the shoulders was mottled, as if a disease was taking hold. He sighed. 'Wish to Christ Larry would get back. I need my coffee.' Couldn't use the jar in the kitchen. Beer was okay because that was sealed in a can. Open jars and packages, you never knew what you could get. People kept poison in the weirdest places. You'd think you were sweetening your coffee and you got two spoons of DDT. Sometimes – not in this case, he didn't think – but sometimes the very crazies would put a spoonful of some poison in the coffee jar on purpose, to kill someone, anyone, it made no difference.

'If he's been on the beach,' Benny said, 'someone will have noticed him.'

'He's pale,' Bodinetz said, 'he's skinny and he's friendless. Also he has no means of transport. Didn't he have a car? His Latin mama pick him up at the airport?'

'Or whoever shot him drove his car away.'

'Means two of them. One to drive their own car, one to drive the dead guy's.'

'Or one guy came on foot,' Gonzales said.

'From where? Along the beach? The road? With his gun in his pocket?' Bodinetz shrugged – idea stank. Two guys had come, shot the pale skinny wimp who'd answered the door, taken selected items but hadn't touched the money in the wimp's hip pocket, wiped the answering machine's tape, called the Russian Embassy – mission completed, comrade – and got out, taking the dead guy's car. So he couldn't be traced. Car would be rented and the rental company would have his name and details from his driving licence.

And then there was the funny thing about the clothes. Bodinetz had laid them out in a line on the bed.

'Look,' he said to Benny, 'let me try this out on you. These are all the clothes that were scattered round that little case. All old, all dirty. He'd been wearing them almost to destruction, like he'd been in isolation someplace, a desert island where there were no shops. Then he got rescued and was able to buy new things. But the old clothes had become part of his life and he couldn't just junk them. You know how it is with an old pair of Levi's.'

'Well . . .' Benny tried not to get carried away when Bodinetz was in one of his picture-it-like-this moods. Funny thing about Bo – how could he look like a slob of a cop and yet invent whole worlds from a bent toothpick?

'Well what? You think they're his gardening clothes? Doesn't matter, that's not my point. Let's start here. Slacks, hip pocket torn, one knee ripped, stains, dirt. Look at the label inside.'

'Embassy,' Benny read.

'What else?'

'Made in Turkey.'

'Don't tell the United Garment Workers,' Bodinetz said. 'It's bad news all the way. The shirt.'

'Palm trees, hibiscus, parrot. You can buy a dozen like it at Tropix in Yoreville.' Benny looked at the label, peered closer, and read slowly. '*A. Vargas. Modo de lavar. Usar sabão neutro . . .* How much more?'

'Bottom line.'

'*Ind. Bras.*'

'That's not Spanish,' Gonzales said. 'Portuguese. Comes from Brazil.'

The shoes had badly worn heels, scuff marks on the toes that had made tears in the leather. Inside, by the instep, was a printed trade mark. Half of it was worn away so Benny read: *Veld* and *Trekk* and *Suid Afr*.

'Is that South Africa?'

'I guess,' Bodinetz said.

He held forward the label on the underpants.

'St Michael. Made in UK.'

'Socks,' said Bodinetz. 'No indication where they're from. But there's this.'

This was a dark-brown sweater with a tan design woven in.

The wool was soft and shaggy. The label read simply: Made in Bolivia.

'That's a world tour we've got there,' Bodinetz said. 'Not one damn thing American except maybe the socks which we can't tell. Everything well used except for the sweater. Perhaps he *was* on a world tour, buying things that caught his eye wherever he went. What do you think?'

'You don't even move from the States, you pick up a lot of foreign clothes.'

'Come on, not *everything*. Perhaps he's not a United States citizen. The sweater is new, so he just got in from Bolivia. Also, also I would say this. You see a shirt you like in Rio, you buy it. But look at the underpants. Plain blue. Nothing fancy. He's in Britain as a tourist, he'd buy something nice, a reminder. Like a parrot shirt brings back Copacabana, the brown and tan sweater reminds him of Bolivia. Underpants no. You buy basics before you leave home.'

'You guess he's British? One pair of pants?'

'And for his colour. So white.'

'If he's been in South America,' Benny asked, 'why hasn't he gotten tanned?'

'What was he doing there?' Bodinetz wondered.

'People are amazing,' Bodinetz said. 'Come to Florida on account of the weather and the first thing they do is buy an air-conditioned condo, drive an air-conditioned car, go to air-conditioned restaurants. They don't like the climate, they should've stayed in New Jersey. You know what I feel like I am? A fucking tourist.'

They were sitting in the Chevy with the air-conditioner going. Bodinetz stared through the window at the big golden arches and the Hispanic family walking out with their bag of eats and wondered if Martina Mancilla looked like the wife: pink slacks, red and yellow shirt. Gaudy as the parrot on the Brazilian shirt.

'It's a world class secret,' Bodinetz went on, 'that's why we're sitting here? No one in the station must know?'

'Cocaine,' Benny said. 'In the camera case.'

'He's a user,' Bodinetz said. 'Guy with a shirt like that.'

'The traces are in the compartment for the camera itself. You could squeeze a couple of pounds in there. That would make him a dealer, or a carrier. And he's been killed. It's not ours any more, Bo. You can see that.'

A glorious sunset was fading in front of Bodinetz.

'I don't accept it's anything more than stuff for his own use. Think of the call to the Russian Embassy. You saying he's supplying the ambassador?'

'I tell you I don't know what to think,' Benny said. 'The case is beyond Yoreville Police Department. LICE won't solve it. It runs off in too many directions, it's too big. That's the reason we have an FBI.'

In his heart of hearts Bodinetz knew the reason for creating the FBI was to make jobs for college boys.

Within twenty-four hours the college boys had provided an identity for the dead man.

'No problem, Al,' said Glen Shortley, a beefy young man who prided himself he had class. Class? Bodinetz thought. Couple of letters too many in that word. 'When you're our size, with our facilities and our connections, well, we're just made for a case like this.'

A commercial. Was the FBI up for sale? Reduce the budget deficit?

'Miami is the nearest gateway airport,' Shortley instructed the hick local cop. 'I know what you're going to say, Al, Tampa is closer. But it's not a gateway for South America. Miami is the one. So our people got on to the Immigration people straight off.'

Our people. Like a wonderful family, run the Kennedy clan close.

'That was good thinking you did in the clothing dimension. Good deduction, I'd say. Ever thought of applying to the Bureau? I could put in a word with our people. We asked for a check on all Brits who'd flown in during a ten-day period and they hollered like we'd reached out and grabbed a handful. So we said, Stay cool, we want to pull a male Caucasian, British, twenty-five to thirty-five, arriving from South America, query alone, query from La Paz. What's so terrible about that? You want to know how long it took to flip through the cards, would you believe half a day? It would be five seconds if they'd gotten computerized but have you ever tried telling those people what century this is?'

'The twenty-first century,' Bodinetz said.

Shortley looked startled, then for a moment confused. He was having to check, which made Bodinetz feel a lot better. Then he grinned to show he was a regular guy who appreciated a joke.

'They gave us fifty-one names, British, male, right approximate age, coming from South America. So then we get the visa application forms and compare photos and zap! We got him.'

Zap? Bodinetz considered this. LICE was no good, what Yoreville PD needed was Zap.

'Benjamin Morton. British citizen.'

'Name don't mean shit,' Bodinetz said. 'Benjamin Franklin I've heard of.'

Shortley blinked. There was something odd about Al's priorities. He wasn't serious. This was murder, drugs, vanished Cuban, stolen evidence, a Russian connection. This was international and Al Bodinetz was Yoreville and out of his depth.

'This is going to be very big,' Shortley said. 'We are going to need co-operation from London. Our people over there are getting on to it.'

Good show, Bodinetz thought, jolly good show. Out loud he said, 'Something so big, you should fly to London and shake those Brits up yourself.'

For a moment Glen Shortley was baffled, a look that went easily with his pudgy features. He grinned. 'Al, you have the gift of getting right to the heart of a problem. It's a *gift*, believe me, and Yoreville PD is lucky to have you.'

In his guts Bodinetz had never believed in the cocaine business. Or rather, he'd believe it was cocaine or believe it was spying but not both together. He'd read that the French secret service had sold drugs to pad out their budget. There had been totally believable stories of the CIA doing it in certain areas. But the Russians? They were puritans about drugs where they weren't about supplying sex. Also they weren't sophisticated enough to run a dope outfit. The outfit would run the Russians.

Any guy who owned a parrot and palm tree shirt was in line for having a tiny packet of the white go-powder for personal use but not for being a wholesale carrier. So it pleased Bodinetz when Customs couldn't be shifted: on that Eastern Airlines flight from La Paz via Lima and Guayaquil (Guy who?) they were particularly tough. Customs had had problems with certain airline personnel in the past and this was ass-kicking time. Body searches, baggage inspection, sniffer dogs – crew and passengers and aircraft got the whole menu.

Certain important executives had been irate at the delay and indignity and swore they would write to their Congressmen. You do that, the Customs people enthused, and inform those fine and concerned lawmakers how hard we're fighting against drug smuggling.

So how come there were tiny traces of cocaine in Morton's camera case?

'Another damn puzzle,' Benny said.

'Man, don't sweat,' Bodinetz advised him. 'Let's go out and find a couple of Budweisers with our names on them. Shortley and his people are at the controls now and everything is A-okay. Good as solved. Fact, Shortley probably doesn't even need this.'

Benny looked at the deep-blue book Bodinetz produced from a pocket.

'Passport.' Bodinetz held it up between thumb and forefinger. 'Used to belong to the deceased, as you call him. I played a hunch and called round the banks and here I am, holding this clue. Morton was bumping up against his limit on his Visa card so he got a small loan and left this for security while money was being transferred from London. Think it would confuse the college boys if I showed it to them?'

CHAPTER 7

Lucrecia, the waitress at El Dragón, was standing near the photograph of the Pope kissing the runway. She didn't know which airport it was. Somewhere in Brazil, possibly. Rio de Janeiro, possibly. The Pope had visited Rio and kissed the runway and she hoped he hadn't picked up any disgusting Brazilian disease doing that. It was a dirty habit, kissing runways, but if you were Pope you had a more direct communication to God and could always ask him to stop the germs making you sick. If you were God it would make sense to agree. No point in having a Pope if he got ill every time his plane landed.

Now if she, Lucrecia, had kissed the runway she would certainly have picked up some disgusting Brazilian disease. Or, since planes flew to Rio from the most distant parts of the world, she would have picked up some equally disgusting African disease or Chinese disease or German measles. Perhaps a plane had flown from Russia. Was it possible to catch communism through kissing? Not in her experience.

She'd had a boyfriend once, León, who was a member of the Marxist-Leninist Communist Party, which he said was the only pure revolutionary party. She had caught something from him and it wasn't communism and it wasn't pure. Holy Mary, that had been a time. León had had the devil in him, as men did if they did not sleep enough with women. León would argue and shout and grow angry with the people he said were his comrades. Even in bed with her he would struggle and a rage would come in his eyes and afterwards he would sleep.

Women could bring peace to the world, Lucrecia knew. But it would mean finding every violent man and subduing him in bed until he slept. Yes, that was what a woman did: she subdued a man, the urgency went out of him and he lay back exhausted.

The old man sitting at the table, not eating his rice and omelette, he looked subdued today. Had he imagined he was a young man last night and exhausted himself? He had been the same yesterday, the spirit drained out of him.

'*Caballero, caballero.*' She stood by his table until he looked at her. 'Is the omelette not good? You don't like it? Adolf can make you something else, with chilli sauce to wake you up.'

'I was looking at the picture of the Pope,' Che said.

'That is funny. I was thinking about him myself only a minute ago. But I imagine millions of people all over the world are thinking about him this very second. It must be terrible to have millions of people thinking about you.'

'Why?'

'Why? Well . . . ' She had to think about that. She didn't want to disappoint the old man just as he was waking up. 'Whatever you do they are thinking about you. You go to the toilet – excuse me for speaking like this – the Pope goes to the toilet and millions of people are thinking about him.'

'But they don't know he is going to the toilet.'

'He has to go to the toilet some time during the day. Everybody does. So they know he is going to the toilet, perhaps this very minute. Now, are you going to eat this or not?'

She took away his plate when he didn't answer. The old man had not been exhausted by a woman, she decided. He was just an old man, a little out of this world, imagining the Pope didn't go to the toilet.

Though now she thought about it, she'd never seen any pictures of the Pope eating or drinking. He was always kissing the runway or blessing crowds or driving in the Popemobile. Was it possible he didn't need to go? No point in asking the old man. He was reading his paper again.

You worked on a plan, something went wrong, you modified your plan until things began to go right.

There had been an ambush – one of the first, in Cuba, so many years ago Che had forgotten the name of the place. They were in hiding on either side of the track, behind rocks, waiting for the army patrol. When the leader of the patrol reached the big boulder, that would be the signal to begin shooting. The army did not patrol in tight formation because they lacked discipline but by the time the leader reached the boulder most of the soldiers should be in their gunsights.

It turned out to be a mounted patrol, which was the first thing the guerrillas weren't expecting. There were as many as thirty soldiers on ponies, but the guerrillas never saw them all. The patrol was led by a sergeant. Sometimes it was a corporal, rarely a lieutenant. It would take a *macho* lieutenant to lead his men from the front and they were scarce in Batista's army. Their *machismo* ran more to shooting prisoners and raping peasant women.

The sergeant rounded the bend and was half-way to the boulder. A dozen of the patrol were in sight now, some of them smoking, some with their rifles slung over their shoulders. The leading horse suddenly reared in fright. It could have got wind of the hidden guerrillas, or seen a snake, or heard a strange sound. But it reared up, the sergeant yelled out, 'Take care!' and the stupid soldiers began shooting in all directions, imagining they were under attack. They were blundering into an ambush without knowing it and by chance began shooting first.

Che fired at the sergeant but only wounded the pony, which staggered, throwing the sergeant. After that it grew confused, as battles did, which was why afterwards there were such conflicting claims. Certainly two or three of the soldiers were shot down. Then the rest of the patrol arrived as reinforcements, not along the track but through the bush. The guerrillas, outnumbered and lacking the crucial element of surprise, had withdrawn. The army ponies were hampered by the rocks and didn't pursue.

The plan had gone wrong in Cuba because they hadn't known the soldiers were mounted and spread out and how many there were. But Che had learnt from his mistakes.

Now this plan was going wrong.

The paper should have carried big black headlines: 'CHE GUEVARA ALIVE'. Morton had taken the photographs, the cassettes and the plate with his fingerprints to verify his story, dramatic because it was so hard to believe. So why wasn't there the tiniest mention, two days after the date he'd agreed he would publish? Had he not been able to persuade the Cuban woman, or had she been unable to check his fingerprints? Were negotiations taking longer than he'd thought? Haggling over money? How could Che tell.

The other thing that was going wrong was the death of Dr Quiroz.

In Che's mind the timetable was clear. First came the disclosure that he was alive. Second, the discovery of Dr Quiroz's body. Third, and hard on its heels for maximum impact, the phone call to the newspaper that he Guevara had killed Quiroz, a revenge killing, and that he was planning revenge on his torturers and betrayers.

The death of Dr Quiroz had made the front page of the newspaper, though the photograph was of Genoveva, who was certainly prettier. She had discovered the body when she came to the surgery in the morning and was 'distraught'. The photograph showed her dressed in black, like a widow, and as always mourning clothes thinned her features and gave a haunting beauty to her girlish face. She must have changed from her nurse's uniform to the mourning clothes for the special benefit of the photographer. It was fortunate she was prepared. Not everyone keeps widow's weeds at their place of work. But perhaps the black dress had formed part of some ritual with Dr Death.

It was the police who were the wreckers. The simplest mental tasks always had been beyond them and it was unrealistic to expect they would change to fit in with his plans. Why hadn't he taken into account the stupidity of the Bolivian police?

The police imagined it was suicide.

The police did not suspect murder.

The police were not hunting for the man who would announce himself as Che Guevara.

Che went further. Despair cast a lurid light on his thoughts. If all the self-important officials in the whole world could be gathered in one stupendous Conference on Bureaucracy, the Bolivian police would stand out as the geniuses of stupidity. They were baffled. They even talked of several 'unique and grotesque features' of the suicide. They would never be anything but baffled since they had to twist facts until they fitted their bizarre view. The little widow Genoveva said the good doctor was so 'happy' and had 'everything to live for. Why, he had just been invited as guest of honour to a world congress being held in Argentina. Alas, we ordinary mortals never understand the pressures that build up inside deep and original philosophers. I have been cruelly robbed by his death, and so has the world.'

The Conference on Pain? The police didn't bother to check whether it even existed.

The bottles of blood had been stowed carefully in the carton. Apparently the suicidal doctor had managed that. All except for the final bottle, only partially filled, still attached to his arm.

They knew nothing. They didn't even know that they knew nothing. The police were mad.

And if Che telephoned the newspaper now with his story, he would be dismissed as a crank, a ghoul with unhealthy delusions.

The old man seemed so upset, Lucrecia came and put a dish in front of him. He folded the newspaper and looked at the dish and up at her.

'I didn't order this.'

'You don't have to pay. You should eat something to keep your strength up. The cook wasn't looking and never saw me take it.'

'What is it?'

'What is it? It is rice pudding. What does it look like?'

'It looks as if it has been eaten once already.'

'Eat, enjoy. It is good for you. They give it to babies. The milk and the rice are good for young bones. Old bones too.'

'Yes.' Che stared at the dish. 'Milk contains Vitamin D, particularly calciferol, which stops the bones of growing children from softening. The rice, however, is polished and doesn't provide much nourishment.'

'Bravo,' Lucrecia said. 'You know all that, do you? Then you should know even an old man must have food.'

She stood above him. To please her, Che took one spoonful.

'How do you know such learned things?' she asked. She said it as an accusation: crazy old man making up nonsense.

'I am a doctor,' Che said. 'Or I was a doctor, once.'

'I see. Gave it up, did you?'

'I did other things.'

'What other things?'

Tell her he was Che Guevara? Would she believe him? 'Well, I was a government minister. Not here. In another country.'

'Very good. Anything else?'

'I suppose you could say I have been a banker.' Certainly, why not? He'd been head of the Cuban National Bank, travelled all over the world. It was about this time that Fidel issued a decree making him a native-born Cuban, never mind that he had been born in Argentina. Thus he was eligible to become President of Cuba. Lucrecia would be interested in a decree like that. As a true Bolivian she would appreciate its soundness. 'Also,' he said, 'I have been a soldier.'

'You have had a busy life.'

'It's not over.'

'Then you must keep your strength up,' she said again.

He took another spoonful.

'I don't like eating under the eyes of the Pope. That is what it is.'

'He's not looking at you.'

'I think he's watching me. Take his picture down.'

'I couldn't do that. There has always been a picture of the Pope there. In some restaurants you see a picture of the President, but a Pope lasts longer. Except for that one, whatsisname, the one who only lasted a month.'

Che got up and walked to the photograph.

'You mustn't touch it,' she said.

'I'm not taking it down,' Che said. 'Just turning it round. Let the Pope have a rest from watching me.'

The photograph was in an ornate gilt frame, hanging on a wire from a nail. He turned it round to face the wall. The reverse side held another photograph of the Pope. He wasn't kissing the runway. He was celebrating an open-air mass in front of hundreds of thousands, millions, more than had ever listened to Che or followed him into the wilderness. His holy arms were raised, like a footballer who had scored the winning goal.

That night, visiting the Isaura family, he asked to borrow the pistol again.

'You did not even use it last time.'

'It wasn't necessary last time,' Che said. 'Death should be appropriate to a man's life. So this time I shall use it. I shall strike a blow for the freedom of ordinary men and women everywhere.'

'You may take it,' Alberto said.

'This time I may not be able to return it,' Che said. 'I'm not certain.'

'Take it,' Alberto said. 'And your friend, the Ben, the man with the camera?'

'He has not come back,' Che said. 'I don't know what has happened to him. I have heard nothing.'

'I shall be married on Saturday. I would like him to take the photographs.'

'Potosi must seem a long way away where he is.'

Wherever that may be, Che added to himself.

'You said you are striking a blow for freedom,' Alberto said. 'It is a revolutionary act then?'

Was it a revolutionary act or a personal act? Possibly, if you were Che Guevara, there was little distinction between them.

'This is a corrupt and bankrupt society,' Che said. 'It is the poorest country in South America. The people have no food, no schooling, no medicines. You may hear people talk of social justice but that is because they are talkers. A man cannot eat social justice or wear social justice or use it to learn to read. What the peasant families need is not a concept but actual things. Food, a house, a school, safe water. What I am doing is removing one of the barriers that prevent the people seizing what they need.'

'It is a revolution we need,' Alberto said. He was sitting forward in his chair, his eyes sharp in the lamplight. 'And for a revolution we need a leader.'

He means me, Che knew. He thinks an old man can rally a class, a country, a continent.

'No,' Che said. 'For a coup you need a leader. But then you exchange one dictator for another. For a revolution you need a committed working class. You, and your workmates, and your families, and all the oppressed and hungry in every village and town. You don't need a leader, you need people power. Then you will be invincible.'

Should I tell him I am not Ernesto Carballo but Che Guevara?

Would that inspire him? Would he laugh? Would he insist I stay and rally the miners?

Alberto was not happy. Che could see that. He was like a man who was sexually aroused and then rebuffed by a woman. He was watching as Che wrapped the Walther in a length of cloth and tied it round his waist under his shirt like a moneybelt.

'Stay,' Alberto said. 'We need you.'

Che shook his head. There was a time, when he was younger, when the pleading would have been irresistible. A revolution needed fire in a man, and the flames in him were too low now.

'When you hear of my act,' Che said, 'let it be the spark that lights the blaze in you.'

Che walked back through the alleys, listening to his heels on the cobbles. The freezing night air helped to clear his mind. He had decided now. He couldn't wait for Morton for ever. He would travel to Sucre and declare to the world that he, Che Guevara, was alive. It would need to be planned properly, taking into account the stupidity of the police. A dramatic event, having maximum impact.

Then, when he had the ears of the world, he would kill Mendoza.

CHAPTER 8

It was the evening of the Latin American Solidarity Committee's 'Sing for Freedom' concert and it had a most unexpected ending. For an encore Debbie Becker invited Raul Lopez to go to bed with her. She didn't put it like that. No indeed. Just as the bourgeoisie had their conventions, so the radical left had their own way of expressing things. She said to Raul, 'How about coming to my place for a cup of coffee? Nicaraguan beans.' Raul had been in the seat on her right and they'd got talking in the intervals, the long delays between groups. To her girlfriend Pauline who sat on the other side she whispered, 'You mind if we split?' Pauline said, 'You going to forge closer links with Latin America?' And Debbie raised a fist and said, 'Solidarity.'

Now Raul wasn't greatly surprised. In Cuba, despite the revolution, things weren't as open as this. But his time in London had taught him that the fruit was so ripe it just fell off the tree. Not always, it had to be admitted. But at social events like the Sing for Freedom, at marches like the Rally Against American Imperialism, at demos like the Sit Down for Peace in Central America – well, you could hardly go wrong. Not if you were Raul Lopez, Cuban citizen, slight Afro fuzz to your hair, face the colour of good olive oil even after the coldest winter since records began.

'Jesus, isn't it cold though,' Debbie said as they left the hall.

People always made remarks about the cold or the rain or the wind. No wonder they'd emigrated by the shipload to conquer warmer parts of the globe. Raul had been in London three years and he hated the weather. There were other compensations: the restaurants, the theatres, the clothes, the television, the women.

She said they were in good time to catch the last tube and her house was close by Kentish Town station. The tube was democratic but he wanted a taxi. For a moment it seemed the Northern Line was a principle with Debbie. If Raul insisted it was because he knew that late at night a woman was impressionable and a taxi was darker, more intimate, more of a conspicuous display.

'You own a house?' Raul asked.

'I share it,' Debbie told him.

There was something of a silence while Raul wondered who she shared it with. In the end she broke into his thoughts.

'But Derek's away for the weekend. He's gone to visit his family.'

'And left you on your own?'

'For Christ's sake,' she said. How could she explain? He was a Latin and quite frankly their sexual mores were a century out of date. Derek was away and wasn't she entitled to a weekend off herself? In the light from passing streetlamps Raul could see she was frowning.

'You are absolutely correct,' Raul told her. 'He does not own you. Slavery has been abolished. It's just that a man – any man, even the most progressive – can become jealous.'

'Will he ever know?'

Lopez could not believe this was happening. It was too fast. It seemed settled already and he preferred the excitement of the chase, of not being quite certain. To try to rouse the woman was what roused the man. Then came the time when she opened her mouth when she kissed and closed her eyes. That was the magic moment. Then it was sure.

She really did have Nicaraguan beans and she made the coffee while they found out things about each other. Such as that she worked in advertising.

'How can you?' he asked. 'A socialist like you?'

'Advertising is the boil on the arse of capitalism,' she said. It wasn't a saying he had heard before and she had to repeat it.

'Then why do you do it?'

'Bread,' she said. 'It pays for this. You'd be surprised how many socialists work in advertising, crossing their fingers and worrying about their political virginity.'

'It's your house?'

'Yes. The bloke who lives here just shares the expenses.'

And the bed. But they didn't let that thought darken the mood any more. She went and put a record on, Joan Armatrading. Joan shared her secrets with the world and it was odd how they had the same doubts, the same wars with men, the same reckless loneliness.

'I work for the International Sugar Organization,' he said.

'How long have you been in London?' She was standing by the stereo as if she was uncertain where to sit.

'Three years.'

'You must get homesick. I'd love to visit Cuba. Do you know Fidel?'

Extraordinary, he found, how people assumed that if you were Cuban you were friends with Castro. This woman was English so did she take tea with the Queen?

'I've seen him make a speech.'

'What was he like?'

'He is still learning how to make a short speech.'

When she laughed her big breasts shook under her blouse. It was as if they were restless and wanted to break free. He stared at them and she saw his gaze. She came away from the record player and stopped in front of him. The smile went out of her face and that was the sign. When a woman's face grew serious, she was ready. He got to his feet and that was how it began, as simply and directly as two animals coupling.

'That's her,' Moulter said, 'that little beauty. It was taken last year.' With a felt-tip pen he drew a black line round her. It was a squashed circle, a noose round her neck. 'That's Debbie Becker for you.'

Moulter had a face on which sarcasm settled heavily. Its complexion was ruddy, like a farmer's or a big whisky drinker's. When he clamped his jaw shut, you knew it would take a crowbar to prise it open again. For a moment there was just the sound of his breathing. Tanner reached across the desk for the photograph and found that Moulter's fist lay on it like a ham.

'I'm only going to look,' Tanner said. 'I won't steal it.'

'What do you people want with Becker?'

Tanner looked at the half of the woman's face that wasn't

under Moulter's fist. It wasn't beautiful or restful. Her mouth snarled in a scream. You'd go to the pub with her and she'd bite your head off if you came out with the wrong views on Lesbian Motherhood.

'You see,' Moulter went on, 'your lot are a bit tight. Scratch our backs, they say, and we'll scratch yours. Only trouble is, the moment your backs are scratched, you saunter off on your own. Information is a two-way street. They don't understand that at the Bunker.'

Philip Tanner nodded, though he didn't agree. The Bunker, aka the Furorebunker, aka the Glasshouse, inhabited a newish block not far from Waterloo Station. What was information to the Special Branch was intelligence to them. Intelligence was your bank account. You tried never to spend it. The people with the biggest bundle of intelligence were the most regarded in Whitehall. It brought you a larger budget and more power. It meant knighthoods for 'C' and his deputy, and lesser glittering prizes for departmental controllers. But when you reached lower levels, the everyday level where Tanner had to deal, you weren't called Sir Philip and you didn't have a CMG after your name. It was necessary to bargain with men with big fists and a mouth that clamped so tight the lips were invisible.

Tanner said, 'A British citizen, name of Morton, got himself killed in America. He was having a little rest and relaxation with a lady in Florida who has subsequently disappeared. Efforts had been made to hide his identity and what he was doing. There seems to be some connection with the Russian Embassy in Washington, though nobody knows what. That is why we have been dragged in. Flash of lightning across the Atlantic: new British spy scandal threatens special relationship. I have been to Five and they are totally ignorant about Morton, par for the course. Passport Office gave the address on his application form and it turns out to be the house of that woman, Ms Becker.'

'Ms, that's right, Ms,' Moulter said. 'Sums her up perfectly. Morton's other names?'

'Benjamin Edward.'

'Date of birth?'

'2nd March 1952.'

Moulter spoke into his phone, presumably to the young man

in the outer office. While he waited he picked up the photo to glower at it. Look at those white knuckles, Tanner thought, how he wants to put his fist into some face, the woman's, mine, anybody's. He grunted and put the phone down.

'Nothing known against your Benjamin Edward Morton.'

'That was highly efficient.'

'So it should be, the money it cost. I hate computers but not as much as I hate computer people. They are overpaid arrogant ponces, but there's no law against that unfortunately.'

He tossed the photo across the desk and Tanner picked it up. It was a night shot, taken by flash, high contrast with few softening shades of grey. Debbie Becker was shown from the waist up. She had a broad face with cheekbones that made her look almost Slavic. You could see her teeth as she screamed. She looked violent and abusive. There were shoulders to either side of her, faces behind, no one in front. Debbie Becker was the front line. Somebody at the edge of the frame held a placard. 'SMASH,' Tanner read. He didn't know what was to be smashed. The usual, he supposed, the system, the Tories, imperialism.

'What was the demo?' he asked.

'Bloody picket line, wasn't it,' Moulter said. 'Bloody Wapping. Mind you, it could have been a picket line in the coal strike or a demo in Grosvenor Square. Same bunch turn up.'

'And you just happened to have a photographer handy?'

Moulter had a large manila envelope and was dealing photos like playing cards. 'Help yourself, see what it was like, bloody England 1986. They were taken by a *Sun* photographer.'

'I didn't know the *Sun* worked for the Special Branch now.'

The *Sun* didn't know it either was the meaning of the sudden crack in Moulter's face. His mouth opened in a mirthless smile.

'You rang Murdoch and said the safety of Her Majesty was at risk?'

'One of the girls from the goldfish bowl – I chose her myself for her long dark hair and chubby cheeks – she put on a scouse accent and a CND badge and went to Wapping and asked to buy a set. 'To show me mates in Liverpool.' Moulter was a surprisingly good mimic, even to the sassy cocking of his head.

'And Becker – is she notorious, a threat to national security?'

'Not specially.'

'You went and got photos of her.' Tanner sorted through the glossy prints. There were general shots of the massed pickets. 'SMASH MURDOCH NOW' was the full message. 'SUPPORT THE PRINTERS', 'MURDOCH TELLS WAPPING LIES', 'STUFF MURDOCH WHERE THE SUN NEVER SHINES' were on other placards. In one shot a horse plunged into the crowd, the officer in the saddle wearing a helmet with a visor that looked medieval. What did a police horse think of its work? SUPPORT POLICE HORSES NOW.

'You could say there was a spot of trouble,' Moulter said. A woman came in with two cups of tea and a sugar bowl on a tray. Moulter's eyes followed her until she left. She wore a tight skirt and dark stockings with seams. Moulter seemed to be checking the seams were straight, wondering where they ended. 'Yes, bit of a fracas,' he went on. 'Not sure who won really.'

One hundred and fifty of the protesters on the picket line were treated in hospital, and one hundred and seventy police. It had happened a year ago but Tanner remembered as if it had been last Saturday. There were only losers that night. Broken bones, a heart attack, wrecked TV cameras. And all the time a press photographer with a long lens was shooting Debbie Becker in the front line of the pickets.

'Well, why did you get the photos of her?'

Moulter took two spoons of sugar and stirred his tea. 'I would say it was a riot that night. A lot of the mob faced charges – threatening behaviour, offensive weapons. Becker was one of them. She was charged for shouting abuse at the police and fingerprinted. Later, when the police collected all the metal bars, bricks, spanners and other hardware, they found a thumbprint on a whisky bottle – Haig, I think it was. A half-bottle, one of those flat flasks.'

'She was drunk?'

'The bottle had contained petrol, though it hadn't gone up in flames. Becker wasn't a printer, she was a Trot, a Militant supporter. So that's why we thought we should know a bit more about her. Throwing Molotov Cocktails begins to sound like the revolution to me.'

Moulter drank some tea and Tanner waited and nothing more came. He sensed there was nothing more to tell. Moulter had refreshed his memory reading Debbie Becker's file and nothing else had been recorded against her for a year. She was one of a few thousand disaffected citizens – dissidents they would have been called if they'd been Soviet citizens, and everyone would have applauded – who courted minor martyrdom but weren't very serious.

Tanner asked, 'Was she living with Morton at the time? Or had they broken up?'

'With that mob, you don't go into their sex habits or you'd have time to do nothing else.'

'What happened about the petrol bomb?'

'Case bloody dismissed, wasn't it. She said she'd bought the whisky and drank it with her little playmates and ever so carefully placed the empty in a litter bin like a good little girl. And if some bad man had taken the empty out and filled it with petrol, she couldn't be held responsible. Had anyone seen her throw the bottle? No. Had anyone even seen it in her hand? No charge to answer. For abusive behaviour towards the police, fined fifty quid plus costs. Refused to pay, preferring to rot in a capitalist dungeon. However, much to her fury, the fine was paid on her behalf and no, before you ask, we don't know who by.'

'Can I keep this photo, the one where she's shouting?'

'Going to put it under your pillow at night?'

Tanner didn't put the glossy print of Debbie Becker under his pillow but he did look at it that night when he got home. He'd slipped it in his briefcase and if he'd gone back to the Bunker he would have noticed it and taken it out. But sod the Bunker, he told himself, and went to a movie instead. It was a French film and he was disappointed. French films used to be sexier, or he used to be younger.

Home was a terrace house in Tulse Hill – almost Dulwich – and he took the photo of Becker out and put it on the mantelpiece between a postcard of Corfu and a card from the AAAA Minicab Company. Who'd paid her fine? Did it matter who'd paid her fine? The Workers' Revolutionary Party had a number of rich supporters and one of them could have paid fifty pounds plus costs out of the small change in his pocket. Tanner went to the kitchen and washed a glass and came back with a whisky and soda. He stared at her again. A murdered man had lived with her, presumably been her bed partner, and here she was shrilling for the blood of the bourgeoisie. Tanner couldn't make that mean anything.

When the phone rang he looked at it and wondered if it was his wife. He always wondered that. It never was.

'Hello?' No name, no number. Somehow that was felt to be more secure.

'Phil?' It was Hershey, his Controller.

'Speaking.' He was known as Phil. It was a class thing. Nobody ever said Prince Phil. Maybe the Yanks.

'You didn't come back to the office.'

That was obvious. Tanner didn't say anything because there didn't seem anything worth saying. Sod them, they felt they owned him.

'I want you to come in tomorrow,' Hershey said. 'The Foreign Office finally got off thc potty and sent us Morton's passport. It's worth your looking at. I'm afraid he may be interesting to us after all. How about the girl he lived with?'

Tanner looked across at her photo, mouth gaping. You saw pop fans with mouths like that, and dead fish, and Ulster politicians. Debbie Becker was caught screaming her hate and that's how she would be immortalized in the files. She might become a nun or Prime Minister or Prince Andrew's second wife, but some nosy security copper would open her file and see the rage in her.

'No, I don't think so,' he said. 'Home-grown agitprop girl. Shout for the revolution, sell *Militant* at King's Cross, spread a bit of groupie comfort. Nothing serious.'

'Well, I don't know,' Hershey said. 'Come in tomorrow morning, look at his passport. You weren't going away for the weekend, were you?'

'Come on, you don't give a Donald whether I had anything lined up.'

'A Donald?'

'Duck.'

Tanner put the phone down. He liked to make up a bit of rhyming slang from time to time. It kept Hershey guessing.

*

'My name is Phil Tanner,' he said.

Cold eyes stared into his. Perhaps not cold. Cold showed some sort of feeling. The eyes were without expression, a cop's eyes, because that is how a cop works. Those dead eyes mean I don't give a shit.

'I am thirty-nine years old,' he said. 'Thereabouts.'

The eyes stared at him, saying nothing, believing nothing. It was such a petty lie.

'All right, I'm forty-three.'

If you're going to lie, make it a Goebbels one.

'I am . . .'

He still couldn't say it: 'separated'. Everybody was a separate person but 'separated' was different. 'Separated' brought too much luggage with it. 'Separated' meant you had failed. 'Separated' was putting wallpaper over the cracks, not admitting the truth. 'Separated' was a waiting-room while lawyers duelled over money and turned you both into enemies. *Denise and I are separated.* He tried it inside his head while the eyes watching him lost their dead look and frowned.

Out loud he said, 'I am separated from Hershey.'

The eyes watched him, showing patience, seeing if there was more to come.

'I am . . .' What word to use? 'Available.'

He looked away from the mirror down to the photograph of Debbie Becker, mouth open, raging.

Perhaps he should scream. Babies scream. Terrified people scream. Haunted people scream. Mad people scream.

Screaming drew attention to you. Screaming was a relief. Screaming was not a cure.

There was the business of getting into the Bunker. It was held to be more secure to approach it from Waterloo Road, sneaking up on it from behind. Here a ramp led down to the underground car-park and the deeper bombproof levels with the communication equipment and the tunnel leading back under the Thames to Whitehall. Before you reached the ramp you had to stop at a sentry box where two jokers checked your car numberplate against the list. They displayed a sign which read 'NO REST FOR

THE WICKED'. We never rest, Tanner thought, so are we the wicked? Or do we disturb the rest of the wicked other side?

From the underground car-park you entered what he thought of as the decontamination chamber. The outer door was automatic and shut with a hiss. You were trapped in something the size of a cell, lino on the floor, smooth walls, strip lights in the ceiling, totally bare except for the video cameras way out of reach. Big Brother was watching you. The second door had a buzzer and you pushed it open when it sounded. Then came the checks. There were two security men though until the F-111s had bombed Libya only one was needed. And long ago when they were called the Depot and had a front door in Queen Anne's Gate and a tradesmen's entrance in Broadway, a uniformed commissionaire had been enough. Those were the days when spies had been gentlemen and sold their country to Moscow in upper-class accents.

Definition of a gentleman, Tanner thought. A gentleman never gets drunk. A gentleman merely gets confused by the champagne.

Philby had been a gentleman.

Tanner was not a gentleman.

Tanner had an identity card he surrendered to Pearce, who was not a gentleman either. How could he look both bored and suspicious at the same time? Pearce inspected the card and perhaps he recognized it was all lies. It should have read: Phil Tanner, aged ninety-three, notoriously separated, lover of all womankind, late-night philosopher, menopausal doubter. The mug shot was real though. It showed Tanner in the Chamber of Horrors. Phil the Ripper.

Pearce ran the card through the scanner to check the magnetic code. His companion watched to see Tanner didn't make a run for it. Pearce had been a corporal in the Marines, Tanner knew. The other security guard was new and unknown to Tanner.

'Bloody typical, isn't it,' Pearce said suddenly. He held on to the identity card. 'Can't get anything right in this country.'

Pearce blinked a lot, which didn't seem right for a Marine. He came to work on his drop-handlebar bike because he couldn't stand travelling by tube. He hated to be touched. He was known to have killed three men in Norway. It was during Nato war-games, Exercise Snowball, and they were in his patrol. The official story was that a grenade had been issued with the wrong fuse.

'You've been reading the *Guardian* again,' Tanner accused.

'No listen, I'm talking about this weekend. Bank Holiday weekend, right? May Day it's supposed to be, so Monday's a holiday. Well, why don't they have May Day on May Day?'

'I give in,' Tanner said. 'Why don't they?'

'No, I mean, in every other country May Day is the first of May. In Russia they have the big parade in Moscow, all the missiles, the tanks, the workers parading, soldiers, kids, the leaders taking the salute in Red Square, everybody drunk. That's proper May Day. So what do we get in Britain? We get a travelling May Day, the first Monday of the month. Why do we have May Day on the fourth of May?'

'There's no answer to that,' Tanner said.

Pearce put the ID card on the counter and slid it across. Tanner picked it up, careful not to brush against Pearce's hand. The unofficial story was that one of the men had tried to touch him.

'Working this weekend?' Pearce asked him.

'Looks like it.'

'Bloody typical, isn't it,' Pearce said. 'On May Day.'

Tanner had a suspicion that in Moscow the KGB didn't declare public holidays and dance in the streets. No rest for the wicked.

On the sixth floor Tanner was subjected to more scrutiny. It was always done in dead earnest. No one ever made light of it or said sorry. No one ever called him 'sir'.

Hershey met him at the outer office door. More security. There were no secretaries at the weekend.

'Good of you to come in,' Hershey said.

'You told me to,' Tanner said.

They smiled without much meaning. Hershey had a one-sided smile like someone who'd just visited the dentist and been given an injection. Tanner didn't like to look at it but what other part of his body could he look at? Hershey's hands had blood on them. His knee was poised to gouge you in the vitals. His shoes were smeared with the dirt he walked through.

'No, I mean it sincerely,' Hershey said. 'Messing up your May Day weekend.'

'It's all right. I've already watched the Moscow parade on the news last night.'

Hershey considered this. He said, 'Ah.'

'Looking for old friends.'

'Of course,' Hershey said.

They went into Hershey's own office with its view of blocks of council flats in Camberwell. That's what Hershey's horizon is, Tanner thought, that's what we're protecting. It's so the muggers can sleep safe at night. If you went into the other regional Controllers' offices you saw wall-maps of their areas. Hershey preferred the spiky Buffet prints that had been popular in the 1960s. To have maps of both North and South America would have seemed like boasting. Also it disturbed visitors from the United States, as if Britain was secretly planning to retake the colonies.

They drank coffee that Hershey poured from a Thermos. He'd brought it from home because the canteen was shut at weekends now and the Italian sandwich bar round the corner was out of bounds. Hershey picked up a large buff envelope from his desk.

'The passport?' Tanner asked.

'The passport.'

Tanner took the envelope and shook out the passport. On the cover was MR B. E. MORTON. It was handwritten by some Dickensian penpusher. Tanner opened it: Her Britannic Majesty's Principal Secretary of State for Foreign Affairs says we'll send a gunboat and wipe you dirty wops off the face of the earth if you don't unhand our hero. The usual.

'Not another East German special is it?'

'It's genuine,' Hershey said.

Tanner rubbed a page between his fingers and checked the watermark against the light. He didn't know what he was looking for but he knew he should see something. Across a white band he saw dog roses and leeks and artichokes. No, not artichokes, thistles. National emblems. Like the state flower of Colorado was the columbine. Where had he picked that up? And why?

'Looks kosher.'

'I told you it was.'

Then he noticed down where the passport number was printed a handwritten note: '*See page 5*'. Tanner skipped to page 5. There was a boldly inked stamp: '*British Consulate-General – Pretoria.*' In menacing capitals was written: 'THIS PASSPORT TO BE WITHHELD BY UK IMMIGRATION AND RETURNED ONLY AFTER HOLDER HAS CONTACTED CONSULAR SERVICES DEPARTMENT, FOREIGN OFFICE, LONDON.' Someone's initials. A neat green line had been drawn through this and at an angle was different writing, more casual: '*Passport restored to bearer 15 May 1986.*'

'So what the hell's all that about?'

'Go on,' Hershey said. 'Look further.'

Tanner turned the pages. Morton was a photo-journalist and a traveller. Spain, Portugal, Turkey and Greece could be holidays. Next page: '*Ceskoslovenske Vizum.*' A week in Prague in 1984, as a tourist unless you were of a suspicious nature. An American visa and several stamps, including one recent one: '*US Immigration 06Q MIA C – 13462 April 13 1987.*' Other pages had stamps for El Salvador, Nicaragua, Brazil, other countries that were illegible. Flipping through the passport was like searching someone's hotel room, fingering their possessions.

Go on. He sensed Hershey intent on him because he hadn't reached the meat yet.

'*RSA Immigration – Durban. Re-entry prohibited.*' Repeated in a second language. Morton had been having fun and games in South Africa.

'He was kicked out?'

'Yes.'

'Why?'

'We don't know. The Foreign Office doesn't know. The British Embassy doesn't know. All the Consul knew when I telephoned him yesterday was that Morton was declared *persona non grata* and the Embassy in Pretoria informed. Someone from the consular section flew to Durban to monitor the expulsion. That restraint order on the passport was so the BA could recover the cost of the ticket, or he'd lose his passport for ever. Apparently he refused to pay in Durban, shouting abuse about fascist Afrikaner police. He also said he did not want to return to London, that wasn't on his itinerary. He had no choice with his passport cancelled. And then confiscated when he arrived in the UK, which is normal in circumstances like that.'

'Been a naughty boy had he?'

'We assume.'

'Then changed his mind after a bit in London and paid to get his passport back?'

'To the tune of five hundred and eighty-five pounds. A second person was also deported, his woman companion. She did pay, using her American Express card. She decided against coming to London and she got off at Harare.'

'She didn't go through Heathrow Immigration. Do we know her?'

'The Consul had to call me back. He made enquiries and found out she was an American citizen. Martina Mancilla. That's right, that one. Her house that Morton was found dead in.'

There was a sound from the outer office where no secretary sat on a holiday weekend. If it had been a big operation, Hershey would have called her in. He'd have called in half the troops if he had anything firm to go on. It wasn't really serious yet but Tanner was beginning to get a feeling – how could he describe it? Like the feeling there was someone behind your back, watching you. There were things to find out, people hiding in the shadows, connections to be made. The sound came again from the outer office, like something chinking on the desk. Hershey crossed to the door and pulled it open. Pearce stood outside, holding a tray, shuffling his feet. Something definitely spooky about him, Tanner decided. He was working in the right place.

'I brewed up for you,' he said, 'seeing as it's Saturday.'

He carried the tray in and veered away from the desk as if that was too important for anything but state secrets. He put the tray down on a table under the Buffet prints. There were two cups of tea, a sugar bowl and a plate of custard cream biscuits.

'Do you think he was spying on us?' Hershey asked when they were alone.

'When he blinks that means he fancies you,' Tanner said. 'Bit of a Ron that one.'

'A Ron?'

'Ron and Nancy.' Tanner was at the window staring at the view. Hershey joined him and they stood like passengers at a liner's rail at the start of a long voyage. Was it going to be a rough trip? What were the other people like? Who'd have a shipboard romance? 'On a clear day,' Tanner said, 'they tell me you can see as far as Moscow from the top of those flats. There are no hills until you reach the Urals.'

Hershey said nothing.

'Well, that's what they say. I wondered if we couldn't rent the top flat and buy a bloody great telescope. We could see what they were up to in the Kremlin and it'd save us a lot of money. Which we could spend on something useful, you know, whisky, research trips to Bangkok, that kind of thing.'

'The telescope,' Hershey said, 'as well as the Kremlin, does it see into Dzerzhinsky Square? Does it see a cabinet with files on Comrade Agent Morton and Comrade Agent Mancilla?'

'Ah,' Tanner said. 'Bit cloudy for the telescope today. That's the trouble with this low-tech stuff.'

'What did Special Branch have to say?'

'They know nothing. They couldn't even find Morton's address. No telephone or gas or electricity account. He must have been shacking up with someone new. Marvellous thing about a free country, how you can just disappear.'

'How about the woman he was living with before?'

'They have photos of her on a picket line, but nothing serious. She's a Trot, a groupie. No law against either in a free country, except it's not so free for her.'

'She must know something about Morton.'

'Unless there's nothing to know.'

'Do you believe that?' Hershey asked. Tanner hesitated. 'Expelled from South Africa with a Cuban-born woman, phone call to the Russian Embassy from the house where he's murdered, Trotskyite girlfriend.'

'The phone call is the bugger. Without that . . .'

'We haven't finished digging yet. There are people we should look at more closely.'

'That's a job for Five.'

'Call them in? Is that a serious suggestion? Have them tramping through the door, calling for our files, asking questions?'

Tanner nodded though he didn't know why. His long weekend was disappearing down a black hole.

Hey, now this isn't a bad place. Tanner had never really looked at Kentish Town before, he had no friends living here. Now as he turned into Leighton Road and searched for somewhere to park, he thought it had a lot of life. He had to drive four blocks before he could find a space he could reverse into, bumping the wheels up on to the pavement. He walked back and turned up Lady Margaret Road and then down Falkland Road. There were police barriers blocking off traffic and people walking in the road and up Leverton Street he could see stalls and crowds and hear music and cheering and laughter.

There was a group of men outside the Pineapple holding pints. From the shine on their faces they looked as if they'd been holding pints all afternoon. But not in England. When people wanted the pubs open, they were shut. Bloody typical, that's what Pearce would say. More cheers. Someone had a yard of ale and was tipping it back, the beer sloshing out of his mouth as if he couldn't force another drop down his throat. Later he would go and vomit and the lads would clap him on the back and buy him another pint.

Tanner checked street numbers. Her house was further up. He still had no plan.

He walked up the middle of the road, through the street party, the theatre of the absurd. It was something out of Merrie England. They should run coachloads of American tourists. Man with a flute, another with a fiddle, a juggler, a clown painting clowns' faces on little kids, stalls selling trinkets and dog-eared books and ice cream cones and vegetarian samosas and pottery and posters of pop stars and day-glo orange drinks in polythene bags with a straw and rag dolls and badges saying 'Remember Chernobyl – forget nuclear power'. A ghetto-blaster was raising the dead and a skinny boy was break-dancing on a square of lino. Coloured bunting zigzagged the street. A black man with the build of a middleweight boxer asked Tanner how he was doin', man. Tanner told him he was doin' fine, just fine.

'No *really*, man, no shit, how ya doin'?'

'Like I said,' Tanner assured him, 'I'm doin' fine.'

The black man raised a hand and put a powerful grip on Tanner's shoulder. In his other hand he held a bottle of Captain Morgan, half a bottle now. The other half of the bottle swept over Tanner in a sweet wave as the man laughed.

'You doin' fine, huh?'

'Everything's ace.'

'Then how come you ain't happy, man?'

The fingers bit into Tanner's shoulder, the rum breath overwhelmed him. The black man was decked out for a carnival, though it was no more than his everyday style. Around his neck was a padlock on a chain. Tucked behind his ear was a dart. Elephant hair bracelets made his triceps bulge. His head was shaved apart from a strip down the centre where it stood up as if a million volts were juicing through him. And never mind it was a cool May evening, he wore nothing on top of his T-shirt.

'I say, how come you don't look happy?'

Because, Tanner told himself. Because I'm s-e-p that word. Because I'm slowing down. Because I don't have that gut-conviction any more. Because I don't feel I'm defending democracy and freedom, I'm more standing guard while the cat eats the canary. Aloud he said, 'I'll be happy when I've found a piece of the action.'

'Man, drink,' the black man said, thrusting the bottle up to his face. 'This here is action juice.'

Tanner took a sip. He hated the taste of rum. He hated a rum hangover.

'You not a drinkin' man? Man, no wonder you got long face. Enjoy.'

Tanner took a longer swig and the black man grinned and released his grip.

'Right man.'

'Hey,' Tanner said, 'where d'you get your T-shirt?'

'This? You like it? Here, I'll swap with you.'

Under his leather jacket Tanner wore a blue and white gingham shirt. The black man wore a T-shirt showing King Kong holding the hapless blonde in one hand, dwarfing the Empire

State Building. The legend printed across his chest was: 'THIS IS THE BIG ONE BABY – THE FALKLAND FAIR.'

'Right here?' Tanner asked.

Debbie Becker wore jeans and a peasant blouse embroidered with daisies that had been a souvenir of a week's autumn fling in Yugoslavia. You had to prepare for an English winter, lay in a stock of sunshine, paint yourself with a tan to last through to Christmas at least. Also she fancied a week with Jonty, the director from the production company that was shooting her Chien Chic campaign. This was the consumer society gone out of its mind. Millions of people starving in Africa and she was writing dog shampoo commercials. It turned out that she didn't see as much of the sun as she'd expected but she saw a lot of the bedroom ceiling. She came back pale but with the daisy blouse with its frills at the cuffs and collar. The TV commercials went on to win a prize.

Usually she wore a bra because only women with small breasts could get away without one. 'You know what your knockers are like?' Derek had volunteered one night when they were sitting up in bed eating pizza. 'They're like melons only soft. Squidgy melons.' At the weekends she was a little freer. If she went to Dingwalls or to a peace protest or a small-hours party, she let herself go braless. It turned some men on and that was okay, they were her kind of fella. But during the week, at the agency, no thanks, she wasn't putting on a show for account executives, or worse, giving clients ideas. The clients were always from Birmingham or Warrington, and were spending the night in 'town', as they called it, and they were randy from the moment they stepped off the Pullman at Euston.

Screw the clients. But not her.

Raul had gone. It hadn't been a thundering success. In fact he was a lousy lover. He was also vain, glancing in the dressing-table mirror before he came to bed, folding his shirt neatly, hanging his trousers over the back of a chair while she waited for him. Where was passion? Where was tearing his clothes off? Also he had talked. Now, she enjoyed a man who talked, good basic stuff, and she would talk right back because a woman talking dirty really got a man going. But Raul had been like a commentator at a sports event. 'Oh, you are really big on top. You know what papayas are called in Brazil? They are called *mamaos*, like these, yes? And I am big, yes? I am a small man but a big man too. And we go well together like a well-oiled machine, and I think I am going to come now, no, no, not yet, not quite yet . . .' And then did. Never mind her.

So Raul had come and gone, come three times and gone. And she'd done the houseperson things like shopping and washing her knickers and she'd had a glass of wine and she'd gone out and eyed the stalls in the Falkland Fair which would be going on all the long weekend and she'd looked in the Agitprop section of *Time Out* and rung up John and Cherry about going on the march to the South African Ambassador's residence on Monday and rung up Pauline to tell her Cuban revolutionaries were male chauvinists under their foreskins.

But tonight was an unaccountable blank. Saturday night too. She supposed she could ring up Dick. He'd given her the big spiel once or twice. And there'd been that time when he was smashed and he'd squeezed one of her nipples and wandered off in search of more booze. But the thing about ringing Dick up and suggesting a film or a drink at such short notice was that if he was already going out you felt a complete prick. You were a failure, on the shelf.

That wasn't how an equal person was meant to feel but she couldn't help it. That was how she felt. As a woman, you trusted your feelings. As a man too she supposed. Except a lot of men were unreconstructed pigs and had feelings you didn't trust.

Shame about Derek being away. Not that she was getting possessive. But let's face it, she was twenty-nine and it was nice to have someone around. That's why bourgeois people got married. It was just all that ownership crap which went with marriage that turned her off.

After mature consideration she decided she wouldn't ring anybody up. Perhaps she'd just go out and see what was happening at the fair. Enough noise anyhow, good that people could enjoy themselves, the class barriers down, racial problems forgotten. Then she might pick up a kebab from the Greek take-away – remember to say *souvlaki* – and have an early night. One or two wrinkles starting at the corners of her eyes so an early night wouldn't be all bad.

Bloody thirty next birthday.

Then, looking out of the window, she saw an extraordinary thing. A black man and a white man were stripping. Some street theatre? A wrestling match? No, they were swapping shirts. The white man had something of a battered look to him. The black man was hunky with one of those washboard stomachs where you can see the muscles rippling. Happening just down the road from her. Then the black guy gave the white fella a slow-motion punch to the shoulder and they grinned and split.

That's the Falkland Fair for you, she told herself. Brings people together.

Now the white man was looking at her house, not seeing her through the net curtains, staring and moving on.

Battered, yes. Seen life, experienced, older but not too old.

She went out.

'Debbie,' she said. 'Deborah if you want to go all posh. Never Debs. There was this upper-class twit at the office called me Debs, like I was someone he'd picked up at Queen Charlotte's Ball.'

'What did you do?' Tanner asked.

'Do? Spilled my coffee in his lap, ouch. Told him to bugger off, didn't I?'

She spoke in a mongrel accent, sliding between Cockney *dint I* and Sloane *orf.* She was uneasy in both, a homeless exile. Over her shoulder Tanner could see the kids on the inflatable, bouncing and whooping to the call of old Beatles tunes. Funny, he thought, how the Beatles have become folk music. It was here in the crowd that he had bumped into her. It had taken him a moment to recognize her because her mouth wasn't open in a scream. He'd said 'Oops' and smiled. The usual pick-up, he'd thought. That was easy, she'd thought.

'By the way,' she'd said, casual but bright, as if the thought had just come to her, 'do you fancy a coffee?' Those trusty old Nicaraguan beans.

'Nice,' Tanner had said and brought out a smile, his face crinkling like a used sheet. She'd planned it, he knew. She must have picked him out, perhaps seen him change shirts, so he better have a reason for that. She wanted him for the night? Was that it? Did she do this every night or just because of the fair? He looked at the smile she gave him in return. She's deeply unhappy with the state of the world and the state of her own life. She thinks if she tries enough men she'll find one who suits her.

'It's not far,' she'd said and moved away.

Though in the end she'll decide all men are the same. Fair enough. She's offered them all the same thing.

Debbie's house was in the middle of the row. Now they were called town houses but it was a nineteenth-century artisan's dwelling, two-up two-down, with a bathroom tacked on the back and central heating put in.

'Nice place,' he said. Must stop saying *nice*. Wretched English pursed-lips word.

It was something to say and she made some reply like twenty-two years and it would all be hers provided the world lasted that long. He wanted to study her, make a judgement about her. He didn't know what she wanted. It was sunset and she couldn't want to go to bed yet. Perhaps she wanted him to ask her out for a meal. She was lonely. You couldn't shout for the revolution day and night, not after you were twenty-four or twenty-five.

'Jesus, it's cold,' she said. There was a fan heater against the wall and she knelt to switch it on. 'I turned off the central heating because it's stupid to have it on in May. If the heating is on through May, it's going to be on all bloody year.'

'That's known as a tropical climate. People who sweat it out in the tropics have fantasies about an evening like this.'

She rose to her feet and looked at him with her big brown eyes. He hadn't intended 'fantasies' to be taken the way she was taking it. She smiled and said, 'I promised you coffee.'

He could have followed her to the kitchen but he took the time to look around. The furniture was a mix-up as if she'd started with Habitat Basic, then indulged in a Dali settee in the form of a pouting pair of lips, and then splashed out on an antique display cabinet. Lighting was from spotlights but any day now she'd splurge on a chandelier. There were steel mobiles and wind chimes and stuffed budgies on perches to dodge through. Half a dozen gaudy scatter cushions made an animal's lair in one corner. One wall had three restful Hockney prints, another had two Soviet posters about peace. The Russians appeared in favour of it. One showed a little girl looking into the heart of a flower, the other showed a happy family contemplating a sunrise future. Tanner didn't understand the slogan but he understood the dove with the olive twig that fluttered in each. Then there was the bookcase.

'Unless,' she said, poking her head round the door, 'you'd prefer a drink. There's a winebox in the fridge.'

'Coffee's fine,' he said. 'Wine wouldn't mix with the rum.'

'You've been drinking rum?' She came in and went right up to him and reached on tiptoe as if she was going to kiss him. 'I can smell it. You should have met Raul.'

'Who's Raul and why should I have met him?'

'Because he's Cuban. They know a thing or two about rum.'

Tanner should have said something. He hesitated and she'd gone back to the kitchen. Raul Castro? That one? Oh come on, he can't have slipped into Britain unnoticed.

He looked now at the books on the shelves. A lot of people were interested, concerned or angry with things in the world. Protest politics formed a part of their lives. It was when it swamped them to the exclusion of everything else that Tanner took note. Third World poverty, the American bombing of Libya, Didion on El Salvador, apartheid, the coal miners' strike, the Malvinas (Jesus, the Malvinas! Tanner remembered being in Buenos Aires, being part of the crowd that brought traffic in Avenida Nueve de Julio to a standstill, shouting for Argentine victory in the Malvinas and if they *had* won, Argentina would still have a military dictatorship), the Cuban revolution, Che Guevara's *Bolivian Diary*, the Palestinian struggle, Vietnam, the 1917 revolution . . . Did she read no fiction? Ah, fiction was in the bookcase on the other side of the boarded-up fireplace. But now she had come back with a filter-jug of coffee and mugs on a tray.

'Will Mae West mind if I sit on her lips?' he asked.

'It'll give her great pleasure, I suspect.'

Come on now, Tanner told himself, angry. Stop acting the playboy of the night. Debbie knelt on the carpet beside the tray as if she knew her part, the Bohemian, the free spirit.

Tanner said while the subject was reasonably recent, 'Your friend Raul – what does he do?'

'I don't know about "friend",' she said. 'More someone I met. He's at the Embassy. Or some international organization.'

'Not Raul Castro?'

'Raul Lopez.'

'Got an important job, has he?'

'So you're the jealous type,' she said, slipping away from the subject.

She poured coffee and handed him a mug. She wouldn't talk about Lopez because he was another man? Or because he was something else? Tanner kept a professional eye on the Cuban Embassy and Lopez wasn't one of the diplomats. Of course, they often passed someone off as a driver when he really had other duties. Or he worked for an international body. She hadn't even said he lived in London. But the time for questions about Raul Lopez – name noted – had passed. There was even a slight tightening of her brows because of the questions. The revolutionary left were pathological about being probed, as if a secret policeman hid behind every moustache. Tanner couldn't think why.

'You don't live round here, do you?' she said.

'You mean you haven't seen me before.'

'First time I saw you was really wild. You were swapping shirts with that black guy. I was watching through the window. It intrigued me. Why did you do it?'

It had been Tanner's idea it would authenticate him, make him local.

'Why?' It was on the tip of his tongue to say because he wouldn't swap jeans. Why did he have this unprofessional urge to bring hints of sex into everything? Because when your wife left, you had doubts about yourself. 'This is a great area, interesting, and I was thinking I might look for a house here. The T-shirt was just a spur of the moment impulse. Remind me of the place.'

She knelt upright and pulled his leather jacket open for a closer look, though she must have seen T-shirts like it a dozen times already.

'This is the big one, baby,' she read. 'Well, that's certainly advertising yourself.'

As she smiled, she turned aside. And before he could say

anything, the doorbell rang. Or rather chimed, Avon calling. And the evening changed because it was no longer just the two of them, it was the six of them.

'Da-di-da-di-*da*-da, da-di-da-di-*da*-da . . .'

A four person conga line isn't long but that doesn't matter if you're drunk. Two men, two women, four grins. The back three had their hands on the hips in front. The leader held aloft two whisky bottles, half-bottle flasks, Haig.

'Hello, comrade,' the Haig man said, seeing Tanner. 'Who's the new one, Debbie? When the cat's away – '

'Shut up,' she said. 'You're drunk.'

'And he looks experienced.'

'You experienced Debbie yet?' the last woman of the conga asked.

That was pretty funny and they fell about at their own wit.

'Why is it gloomsville?' the other man asked. 'Have we come at the wrong moment?'

'Coitus interruptus, Tom.'

More hilarity.

'They need a drink.'

'And I happen to have in my hands,' the Haig man said, 'this Scotch whisky. Booze in the bottle isn't doing anyone a favour. What we need is a party. Glasses, ice, action. Got to finish the whisky in the bottles so that on Monday we can throw a different party. *Throw* – get it?'

'Shut up.'

Tanner flicked his eyes just in time to catch the look that Debbie gave the Haig man: you drunken slob, he's not one of us.

'Pardon me, I'm sure,' the Haig man said. He was just drunk enough that he couldn't resist a glance at Tanner.

'What's going on?' the woman at the rear said. 'I don't understand. Will someone *please* explain.'

Tanner said: 'Aren't you going to introduce me to your friends?'

'Now, you say she has some kind of relationship with a Cuban, possibly one with diplomatic immunity?'

'Yes.'

'And her house is stuffed with revolutionary literature?'

'Yes.'

'And she had friends to match?'

'Tom, Nicky, Jill and Heidi. No surnames.'

'Heidi I like,' Hershey said, smiling as if half his mouth wasn't there. 'Makes me think of a roll in the edelweiss. They were planning a different kind of party on Monday for which they'd need empty bottles? And her prints have been found on petrol bombs in the past?'

'Only one.'

'Only one. If it was your clothes that caught fire, one would seem plenty.'

Tanner didn't respond. The thing about Hershey was that he went straight for the jugular. He was the Controller whose star had risen fastest during the Thatcherite years. He was direct, never had doubts or hesitations. His self-confidence hadn't been dented by a wife walking out.

'And tomorrow afternoon there's a march planned on the South African Ambassador's house?'

'Tomorrow a number of political rallies will take place but none with that potential.'

'The bomb-throwing classes,' Hershey said. 'Is that what you'd call them?'

How could Tanner answer? Say no and he sounded a wimp. Say yes and he endorsed Hershey's view of a world where things were simple, coherent, unambiguous.

Tanner could hear the sounds of an English suburban Sunday, distant church bells, an agnostic lawnmower, a radio while someone cleaned the Rover. Bomb-throwing classes were undesirable aliens in Surrey. Through the window Tanner could see Mrs Hershey wearing a gardening apron. She was a homebody who bottled chutney for the Women's Institute. She'd brought coffee, smiled and left the men to their talk. Now she was on her knees, her Sunday devotions to rid the garden of weeds. No dilemma there. You're a weed, out you jolly well go.

'But you found out nothing more about Morton?'

'Even if I'd had her on her own, it would have been difficult. Questions made her suspicious.'

'Decision time,' Hershey said. He *liked* making decisions,

Tanner understood, that was what made Hershey feel good. 'Have you told whatsisname in Special Branch about the surprise party tomorrow?'

'Obviously I reported to you first.'

'Warn him what to expect. Do us a bit of good. Secondly, South Africa. Morton and the Cuban woman were booted out and we need to know why. Fast.'

There was a pause while Tanner and Hershey stared at each other. On Sundays Hershey wore a blue blazer with a crest on the pocket. Tanner didn't know its significance: university, club, sports team. Tanner wasn't one of the blazered classes. Suddenly he grasped that was all: decisions communicated.

'Fly to Durban? Is that what you mean?'

'Fancy a sea cruise to get your strength back?'

CHAPTER 9

The Pope couldn't come to Potosi. The airport was closed and there was no runway for him to kiss. 'They are building a new runway,' the waitress at El Dragón told Che, 'except that they aren't. The airport has been closed for years because there is no money to finish the runway. Maybe next year, the year after.'

Che shook his head. He wouldn't wait that long. He had to go to Sucre.

'How long does the train take?' he asked.

'A very long time,' Lucrecia said. 'The railway is on strike.'

In Bolivia there were always strikes, Che appreciated. The strikes were not angry manifestations of a properly organized proletariat, they were more public holidays. For a few days the people did no work. They painted slogans on walls, they shouted a bit, they ate ice cream. Then they went back to work and nothing was changed.

'Then I will take a bus. When do they leave?'

'Maybe next week, after the strike.'

'A truck?'

Trucks were the most basic form of transport. Peasants travelled long distances, twenty-four hours, thirty hours, in the back of trucks. The Pullman class of truck had planks for seats. In others men and women stood, swaying like cattle while children crawled over their feet.

'But the *campesinos* have blockaded the roads. It is the strike. Can't you understand?'

'They will let me through.'

'Because you have been a government minister and a banker and a soldier? You are the kind of person they are striking against.'

They will let Che Guevara through, he thought.

He said, 'Did you know that Sucre was named after the army general when they were fighting for independence?'

'Fancy,' she said. 'Now do you want to order? Perhaps some chicken and rice?'

'Santa Cruz was another general. In those days a great military leader who fought for the people's freedom had a city named in his honour.'

'You had no luck as a soldier?' she asked. 'Not even a village called after you?'

There were streets with his name but not a whole city.

'Would you like me to name this table after you?'

He stared very hard at her. She didn't laugh at him. She seemed sincere.

'That won't be necessary,' Che said.

'How about La Paz?' Lucrecia asked. 'Was he also a general?'

'Not La Paz. History shows that few successful generals have been known as Peace.'

'The cook has made noodles too,' she said.

The truck didn't leave until after dark. Nothing unusual about that, nothing to do with the strike. In Bolivia buses and trucks travelled at night so that the day would not be lost. Or possibly, Che was not sure, people did not want to see their own country, to witness the injustice that cried out for revolution.

There was desperation about the departure of the truck, like the last helicopter from the roof of the US Embassy in Saigon. A crowd of a hundred besieged the driver, who announced he knew a route that avoided the peasants' blockades along the highway. Two policemen prevented a riot and tried to prevent profiteering. A discreet bribe to the driver got you a seat on a plank in the back. He also allowed on three *gringos*. They seemed exotic creatures with bright windcheaters and headbands and backpacks. There was a young couple with Australian flags on their packs and a tall painfully thin man who was probably American. The driver stood on the tailgate, fighting off the crowd but pointing to the foreigners: 'You, you, you.' Because of his age or because of his suit Che was taken into the cab. He sat jammed against the doorhandle. On the other half of his seat was a Quechua woman, chubby face and rounded body, as if smoothed by much handling. It was the driver who put her in the middle where she suffered in silence each time he reached between her knees for the gear lever.

'We go,' the driver announced.

They passed through a shantytown where soldiers stood at street corners. Potosi was one of the first places the army patrolled, because its mines produced high-grade revolutionaries. They would die young in any case and they could easily acquire dynamite and detonators. If the tin miners had joined him twenty years ago, Che thought, if his contacts hadn't been betrayed . . . Well, he'd brooded on that in the long stretches in the special place.

'You think that's a casino,' the driver said, putting a hand across the woman's breasts to point. 'In fact it's an army camp.'

Wrong, it's the special prison I have just been released from, Che told him, but not out loud. It's for special criminals the state fears, guarded by men who are blinded to reality, bossed by the admiral of a country with no navy. Che stared at the high wall crowned by barbed wire. It stopped the outside world getting in as much as the prisoners getting out.

On the outskirts of Betanzos the truck hissed to a halt for an army checkpoint. Soldiers clambered up the sides to peer in. What could they see? A truckload on its way to the gas ovens? The soldiers didn't even have flashlights – the army was too poor to issue them.

'Where are you going?' a sergeant asked though the window.

'To Sucre,' the driver answered.

'It's not possible. The highway is blocked further ahead.'

'I know another route through Esquiri.'

'Do you have permission to go that way?'

'Yes.'

'Show it to me.'

'It is verbal permission.'

The sergeant was puzzled by this but stepped back and waved the truck on. They made progress through the darkened town and when the highway headed north the driver slowed, hesitating about the turn-off. It was a couple of kilometres further when he swung right down a road to nowhere.

But not quite to nowhere. It was not far to the region where Che had begun and ended his revolution. Hills and valleys, Che remembered, scrub and jungle and rocks and rivers. Keep going, march until the road gives out, then march some more. You won't meet many humans but there'll be *yaguasa* and *marigui* and *boro*, bites and itches your constant company, foul water to drink, fever to shake you, roast mule on feast days. He felt his gorge rising.

Che gazed out of the window at darkened hills and a star-studded night sky.

'We're in the middle of nowhere,' the driver said.

'I smelled a chickenshed,' Che said.

'Chickenshit. There is nothing here, nothing.'

'Do you know this part well?' Che asked. He might even have seen the driver when he was a kid, playing in the dirt of a village, throwing stones to make the chickens squawk.

'No,' he said.

But there was something here. A fist hammered on the roof of the cab and the driver braked. A man and a woman and a boy got down, with baskets and a sack of potatoes and a bicycle wheel. They stood at the side of the road and watched the truck leave. They were castaways in the darkness.

The truck lurched over bedrock. The headlights showed curve after curve, rocks on either side, trees in the gulleys, hills up and down. The driver kept in second gear, sometimes in first.

'I am dying,' the woman said. They were the first words she had used. 'Is it far?'

'There is a roadblock on the highway near Otuyo,' the driver said. 'Once we have detoured round that we rejoin the main road.'

'I am dying,' she said. 'I have road sickness. I will not live.'

'Say to yourself: I will live to tomorrow,' Che told her, 'not longer. Say tomorrow because tomorrow always comes.'

'I do not want to live to tomorrow.'

The driver said nothing. He hunched over the wheel, staring ahead. It was a dirt road, badly potholed, washed away at the corners, puddled by the first of the winter rains. Coming up a hill, over the crest and round a curve, the truck shuddered to a halt in front of a makeshift roadblock: a fallen branch laid between rocks, two or three swinging lanterns, shadowy figures.

Why here in the darkness of nowhere? It made no sense to Che. This must be the only vehicle all night.

The figures with lanterns came close and Che saw they weren't peasants or soldiers but men in scruffy jeans and old sweaters and cast-off jackets. A lantern was held up to the window and the man checked the driver and the woman and Che.

'*Ya!*' he said. It could have been a greeting or a threat. Then he backed off and shouted up to the passengers, '*Control contra la coca.*'

On this dead road? It wasn't even close to Santa Cruz where the smugglers went to blow their money, or the *yungas* near La Paz, or the ranches up north in the Beni. But you could never tell with the drug squads. And if they searched him, Che wondered, would they worry about Isaura's pistol? Confiscate it?

'I am going to be sick,' the woman warned.

Che unlocked his door and stepped into thick grass while the woman leant out and threw up over the wheel of the truck.

'What is it?' a man with a rifle demanded.

She retched again and he stepped aside.

Two men left their rifles on the ground and clambered up on the back of the truck. They had flashlights and ran them over people's faces and bags. Looking beyond the roadblock Che could see no Land Rover or jeep. Where was their transport? Then he heard the snort of a horse and caught the sweet smell of its sweat.

Che edged further into the darkness, stepping back between boulders that had tumbled down the hill. This was no drug squad. These weren't undercover police. Or the army. He moved quicker as he heard Anglo-Saxon shouts from the back of the truck. Turning for a moment he saw the wire-thin American having his watch slipped off his wrist while the second thug manhandled his pack to the side of the truck and tipped it over.

Higher, Che told himself, those rocks up there brooding in the starlight.

A woman's scream made him turn again. The Australian girl was a blonde she-cat as she struggled against the man who was tugging a money-pouch on a thong over her head.

'Leave off, you bastard,' she yelled in English.

'She's good, that young one, she's got life,' shouted the man who had spoken to the driver. 'Bring her too.'

Screams rose louder than ever. The passengers weren't coming to her aid. They were under the rifles of the bandits and why should they risk anything for a *gringa*? From the stories that were told, foreign women were no better than whores anyway. How many bandits were there? Six, eight? She would be dragged in the bushes and each man would take her in turn. Or perhaps they would carry her off and rape her a second time when they were safely away. Then she would be disposed of.

Now there was new shouting and a heaving of bodies and Che realized the Australian boy was fighting for his mate and already one of the bandits on the ground had angled his rifle up, trying for a shot. The Australian, a peasant, someone was going to be killed by these dregs who preyed on ordinary people. Che struggled with the buttons on his shirt and then with the cloth round his waist. He drew out the pistol, the Walther P.38. Three bullets would be spread thin among eight of the enemy. And they were armed with rifles. But surprise and darkness and uncertainty had always been the guerrilla's friend. He drew long slow breaths.

'Stop!' he called out. 'Stop!'

He had the gratifying sight of the struggles subsiding and faces lit by lanterns turning towards the unseen voice. The leader of the bandits was walking forward with his rifle held to his side like a lance. Che picked up stones and lobbed them left, right and above.

'This is Major Ordonnez of the Second Battalion of the armed forces of Bolivia. You are faced with overwhelming odds and I order you to lay down your arms.'

As the stones clattered their way among the rocks like so many army boots, he loosed off a shot. He aimed not at the leader, whom he would certainly miss, but at a big boulder. To the rattle of stones and the explosion of the shot was added the whining ricochet.

'Men, be prepared to charge. Go left and right and surround them.'

The bandit leader raised his rifle to his shoulder and Che fired again and a third time and then events swept ahead of him.

There was the roar of the truck's engine as it started and crashed into gear and battered through the roadblock. It vanished from sight, trailing screams from the passengers who were thrown to the floor. A bandit leapt from the tailgate and then the whole gang of them fled into the night. Che heard shouts, whinnies, the smack of hooves. Then he heard nothing.

Ah yes, Bolivia, Che told himself. He picked his way cautiously down the hill. Only in Bolivia could a bandits' ambush be defeated by an army of one man, supported by stones and armed with a pistol with three bullets.

In the morning Che saw the aeroplane. He had climbed up a hill to see if there was any sign of a village or a *hacienda* or even a hovel and there the plane was, a little below him, tucked into a fold in the hill. A grapevine was trained above the row of portholes, papaya trees stood guard by the steps leading to the door, smoke curled from a chimney on the flight deck, a clump of bananas gave a bit of privacy to the toilet seat which had come from the plane. There was a disciplined kitchen garden with lines of beans, tomatoes, pineapples and earthed-up potatoes. A scarecrow stood sentinel. As Che gazed down, the scarecrow waved.

The scarecrow was called Bill and was the second sanest man in Bolivia after Che. He'd been flying back from the States when the plane ran dry and he ended up in the dip in the hill. 'Bastards had cheated me when I filled up,' Bill said. Alternatively it was a sign from God that he should give up the drug run and make his home here, which he had done. 'Got every damn thing a man could ask for,' Bill said and recited a pioneer's needs: 'Got food and a woman and two kids and no damn government telling me when to blow my nose.' His Spanish had the direct vigour of his native Missouri. Che caught sight of a woman at a porthole. She was a Quechua woman. 'Got somc name of her own but I call her Dakota, after the plane. Where you headed?'

'Sucre,' Che said.

'Why the hell?'

'There's a man there I want to kill.'

'What you want to do that for?'

'He had me prisoner once and he tortured me.'

'Pretty well sums up the world.'

Dakota cooked him *salteñas* for the journey. Bill gave him a gourd of water. He went back over the hill to the dirt road and began to walk. The more he thought about Bill and Dakota, the more it seemed they had had a revolution all of their own. Socialism in one family you could call it. Not far from their home was another fold in the hill. It was just the right size to crash a plane in. Che thought about that.

It was May Day when Che reached Sucre. He'd walked for two days, got a lift on the back of a bicycle, then a mule, finally a tractor. When he rejoined the highway, he found the strike was finished. The government had settled it in the traditional way by doubling everybody's wages. He flagged down a truck and reached Sucre in a couple of hours and found himself in the May Day parade.

This was not Moscow. There were no missiles, no tanks, no self-propelled artillery. Some two or three thousand people were drawn together and they marched behind a band with a thumping bass drum. You could *feel* the beat of the drum five blocks away. The peasant families from the truck Che had travelled in pressed him to join. Two men carried a banner: '1° DE MAYO – UNIDAD Y LUCHA.' So he marched down the hill and past the market and into the Plaza 25 de Mayo. The May Day parade filled the square. There were placards identifying railway workers, bus drivers, nurses, construction workers, street sweepers, teachers, postmen, airline crew. There was a group of stooping veterans from Bolivia's last war, a half century ago. They all wore medals though it had been Paraguay that won. There was a netball team from the girls' school and the local football team. Small boys mobbed the ice cream sellers who honked on bulb horns.

A truck was parked at the top of the square outside the pizza palace. It was draped in swathes of red, yellow and green. A huge banner proclaimed: 'RECUPEREMOS LA DEMOCRACIA PARA EL PUEBLO.' A man on the back of the truck delivered a speech. '*Compañeros . . .*' he cried, '*compañeros . . .*' He spoke too close to the microphone and the loudspeakers howled. He launched into a scornful tirade against the government which had only settled the strike so they could enjoy the May Day holiday. He made a bloodthirsty attack on the idle rich, assorted generals, corrupt bosses and the cocaine barons. Enough, he bellowed and the loudspeakers howled again. The people would suffer no longer.

The orator raised his arms like Christ being crucified. The crowd cheered.

At the eastern corner of the square was the white wedding cake of a cathedral. Che pushed his way through the crowd and went inside its massive doors and took a seat near the altar. This was ringed by lights like the mirror in a star's dressing-room. Che sighed, a long asthmatic wheeze. The people had cheered the speech. They had cheered that speech last year and the years before. Nothing changed. In a world that cried out for deeds, there were only words.

Today, he decided. Not one day longer.

Afterwards, when he faced the court martial, nobody could find fault with what Lieutenant Bellot had done. Indeed he had even tried to be a hero, if you consider inviting someone to shoot you in the head a heroic act. Nevertheless he was stripped of his chevrons as an encouragement to others.

In the morning Lieutenant Bellot had gone out with a sergeant driving the jeep and two conscript boys in the back to make up the numbers. They had travelled as far as Tarabuco to make certain May Day was passing off peacefully. It was. They stopped on the way back in the valley where the peasants had blockaded the road. Bellot carried out an inspection of the oil drums, old timber and battered car panels that were stacked under a tree, ready for the next blockade. Carry on sergeant, he ordered, back to Sucre. They were almost in the shadow of Cerro Churuquilla with the first outlying houses only a hundred metres away when an old man stepped out from a wall and waved the jeep down. What sort of an old man? An old man sort of an old man, that's all. He wore a suit that looked newish but grubby and carried a newspaper. Was it a subversive newspaper? Certainly not. It was

Presencia. This caused a muttering of indignation at the court martial because it was a staunchly Catholic paper.

The old man stood in the middle of the road so the choice was between running him down or halting. The sergeant chose to stop and the old man walked to the side of the jeep where Bellot sat and out of the folded copy of *Presencia* he drew a pistol and put it to the Lieutenant's temple. The evidence given to the court martial made this sound ludicrously simple but indeed it was. Bellot's eyes opened wide and he swallowed. The sergeant waited with his hands on the steering wheel for further orders. The conscripts in the back sat with their mouths gaping.

'You two soldiers,' Che said, 'drop your rifles over the side on to the road.'

The Lieutenant swallowed again and said in a small but steady voice, 'Abuawad, Bohorquez, keep hold of your rifles. That is an order.'

'If you do not drop your rifles, the Lieutenant will be shot.'

'If you abandon your rifles, that is cowardice in the face of the enemy and *you* will be shot.'

The two privates looked from their officer to the old man, back and forth. Che said, 'If the Lieutenant is shot, it will be your fault. Contemplate your punishment then. Better drop your rifles.'

They did.

'Now the ammunition.'

Abuawad said, 'There is no ammunition. They do not give us bullets in case we lose them.'

'It is true,' the sergeant said.

Looking now at their belts, Che saw they had no ammunition. Poor Bolivia, it couldn't afford bullets for its soldiers' rifles. The sergeant was armed only with a bowie knife. But the Lieutenant, the heroic Lieutenant . . . Che transferred his pistol to the ear of the nearest conscript.

'Lieutenant, you will very carefully take your revolver out of its holster. Holding it by the barrel you will extend its handle to me. Is that understood?'

'As an officer bound by an oath of loyalty to the Commander-in-Chief, I refuse.'

'As the officer responsible for your men's lives, how will you explain to your Colonel that they were killed? First this one, next his comrade with the spotty chin, then your sergeant. Perhaps you won't have to explain because you will be the last to be shot. Since it is inevitable I get your revolver, do it at once and save four lives.'

'Do it,' was the sergeant's advice. He was ten years older than the Lieutenant and spoke his worldly wisdom in a firm tone and didn't call Bellot 'sir'.

Che accepted the revolver and told the sergeant to turn the jeep round and drive back in the direction of Tarabuco. Then he clambered over the wall and disappeared among the spindly eucalyptus on the hill, pausing to discard Isaura's useless Walther and check his new .38 Colt Special. Yes, bullets.

Before he left Potosi, Che had thought it was obvious: shoot Mendoza and get away in the confusion. On his way to work, on his way to church, on his way to a restaurant, on his way to his mistress – no lack of choice. Che had only to establish his pattern of movements. Best would be if Mendoza could be enticed to the Supreme Court and shot to death on the steps, because he had boasted on television that terrorists could never repeat in Bolivia what they had done in Colombia.

But when Che had been forced to walk for two days after the truck's ambush, he had leisure to think: simple shooting would be too clean a death. To catch the world's imagination, a ghoulish death was necessary. *Sit up and take notice: I Che Guevara am seeking revenge for the hideous wrongs done to me.* Let the press print it, the radios broadcast it, the television show ghostly pictures. Let the news spread. Let certain people hear the message.

So, in the afternoon while the army chased all over the hill, which had twelve stations of the cross leading up to a gigantic statue of Christ, Che made his one station and completed his preparations. Then he presented himself at a certain house in Calle Trinidad. It was well-protected, with wrought-iron grilles over its windows and two watchdogs baring teeth like bananas. He pressed the bell and a maid answered.

'I have come to see Comandante Mendoza. I have no appointment but tell him this and he is sure to see me. Tell him I have come from Potosi with a disturbing message about Doctor Quiroz.'

He was certainly no peasant so the maid invited him to wait inside. He could smell beeswax from the old dark dresser and hear the clink of crockery from the kitchen and see the glass eye of a stuffed antelope's head winking at him. There were more people about than at Dr Quiroz's surgery, but then he wasn't intending to do it here. He stood quite still, feeling the slow regular beat of his pulse. He was not frightened or worried, not even excited. It was quite simply time he did certain things. He had the sense that it was time. His body and mind were alert and ready.

He was shown into the Comandante's study. The maid closed the door behind her and Mendoza looked up from the papers on his desk. It was a public holiday and instead of his uniform he wore a pale-blue shirt open at the collar and fawn slacks.

'Yes,' Mendoza began, 'you have come with . . .'

His voice faded to silence as he stared, his brow corrugating in a frown, his cheeks paling. Then he lunged for the central drawer of his desk and came out with an automatic pistol.

'You dare come to see me. How did you get out? Quiroz said you were locked away for ever. Or dead. I forget the details.'

'Well, that just shows the absurdity of the human condition,' Che said. Perhaps this philosophy was a fraction sparse. He explained, 'The Governor of the special prison is dead and the new Governor knew of no reason to keep me locked up. So he set me free. And the message I bring you about Quiroz is that he also is dead. I thought you'd like to know.'

'Don't move,' Mendoza said.

'Why should I move? I have come to see you. Don't worry, I have come unarmed.'

Mendoza knew this was a lie. He came round the desk and patted Che's body all over: back, chest, under his arms, his legs, his crotch. It wasn't a lie.

'You must be mad to come here. I could shoot you now and that would be the end of it.'

'Shoot a totally unarmed man? How would you explain that away?'

'I wouldn't have to. I am the Chief of Police.'

'In any case you won't,' Che pointed out, 'without knowing *why* I am here.'

Mendoza stood back and stroked his pencil moustache. Does he keep his brain there? Is he stirring it into action?

'You have one minute. Explain.'

Che shook his head. 'Go on, be a hero. Shoot an old unarmed man. He was Che Guevara, you'll protest, the notorious terrorist. But Che's been dead twenty years – and people will begin to wonder about you.'

Mendoza stuck his pistol into Che's stomach and searched inside his pockets for scraps of paper, messages, letters, evidence, anything.

'I do have something to show you,' Che went on. 'You're quite right to search. But it's not here.'

'Where?'

'It's better if you change into your uniform. We'll need your official standing.'

'Why?'

'Because it's nearly sunset.'

It was, but that simple logic didn't impress Mendoza.

'Why does that matter?'

'You'll see.' Che smiled.

It was ten minutes' walk to the cemetery. Above the gate was the warning: *Hodie mihi cras tibi*. Going through the entrance there was a chapel on the right, its door standing open. It had a calvary with a neon halo above Christ's head. On the left was the gatekeeper's lair and he shouted out, 'We're closing.' Then he noticed Mendoza's razor-sharp uniform, black boots and pistol in its shiny leather holster. 'Sorry, Excellency.'

'Lock the gate as normal,' Mendoza told him. 'This is official business. I'll knock you up when I want to leave.'

'Sir, I don't live . . . Yes, sir. Of course, sir.'

'Mind you wait to let me out.'

There were families coming out, students muttering aloud from exercise books as they crammed against next day's exam, small boys who fetched ladders to reach the upper levels of graves. For while rich families – Hochstatter, Benavides, Herrera,

Pacheco – had vaults like houses down the central avenue, ordinary folk were interred in apartment blocks six or seven storeys high. There were whole suburbs of battery houses for the dead.

'You're showing me a grave? Whose?'

'It's not far.'

They walked through an area of normal burial plots before shortage of land had made the highrise catacombs necessary.

'Do you have any family buried here?' Che asked, chatting to stop questions. 'Perhaps you visit with a bunch of carnations every Sunday.'

'This is ridiculous.'

'Over there,' Che said. They had the place to themselves. They skirted a bed of straggly roses and stopped in front of one of the towerblocks. Che had felt the sense of rightness when he found it that afternoon. One of the niches were covered by a plaque that commemorated Gerhard Heeren, died on 23rd August 1949, mourned by *'tu esposa y hijos Hermann y Heinrich'*. A swastika was the emblem. The next niche was gaping, ready for a coffin to be slid in soon, maybe tomorrow. Bricks and a bag of mortar in a bucket waited. A grille stopped thoughtless folk stowing rubbish inside the niche. Che pushed the grille up and probed inside with his hand and came out holding the .38 Colt Special.

'Do nothing foolish,' Che advised. 'Don't try to jump me. Don't try and get away. Even if you shout, the gatekeeper is too far away to hear. Nobody will come running to help.'

Mendoza looked appalled. Che removed the pistol from Mendoza's holster.

'Perhaps you have a whistle. Blow it and I'll blow your brains out.'

Mendoza drew himself to his full height and straightened his shoulders. 'You said you had something to show me. I see you are not a man of honour.'

Che took long slow breaths to calm the rumble in his chest.

'Oh, I am,' he said. 'I am honouring a pledge I gave to myself a long time ago. I promised I would see you behind bars.'

The sun had retired behind the hills and there was a greyness settling on Mendoza's face. He felt the prodding of Che's revolver.

'Now,' Che said with the briskness of a man who has made

plans, 'you are to get into the niche. Yes, you are. You might object that you refusc in which case I shall shoot you in both knees. This is not only extremely painful but you will be entirely unable to struggle against me when I push you in head first. Frankly, I prefer you to go in feet first so that your head is at the entrance. That way we can talk face to face. So why don't you slide in.'

He spoke like a man with logic on his side. Indeed he held it in his hand. Mendoza checked the revolver and checked Che's eyes which were like a cat's at dusk, wide open, flat, alert. Come, come, the revolver urged. Mendoza hesitated, aghast at his choices. He had no doubt Che would shoot him in the knees if he declined to obey, and in the belly and the brain if he made a fight of it. There are some situations where a man is denied all dignity and freedom. Mendoza nodded and turned slowly. No one climbs joyfully into a grave. When he had wriggled his feet to the end he twisted his face to the living world as Che pushed the iron grille shut.

'Why do you do that?'

'I've told you. It is redeeming my pledge. Now you are behind bars.'

'And you want to talk to me? Is that it, Guevara? You are in the mood for conversation? What about?'

'Well, for instance, do you have a wife? Tell me something of your life.'

'I am married. My wife comes from an excellent family.'

'Your wife's name?'

'Florinda.'

'That is beautiful. You have children?'

'Two daughters. Angelica is at school still. Cristina is married.'

'Such beautiful names. Sons?'

'No.'

'No one to carry on the family name after you've gone?'

'What do you mean?'

'No boy to carry on your traditions?' Che leaned closer, like a priest putting his ear to the grille of the confessional. 'Tell me, is torture a skill that is handed down from father to son? Or is it a rare gift you are born with, like Mozart's musical genius? Is it a gift from God?'

'What do you want?' Mendoza whispered. 'Is it money? Here.' He struggled until he could push his wallet through the grille.

'I accept,' Che said simply. 'I was running short but I don't like to beg.'

'Now let me out.'

'No,' Che said. 'No. That is not my plan.'

'Do you want more? I keep some money in the safe at home.'

'I am not greedy,' Che said. 'I was never rich. Never stole or accepted bribes or demanded payments from peasants. Do you imagine I was like the old-style politicians who shouted for justice and grew fat? I fought for the starving. That is what revolution is about. So simple. Tell me honestly, don't you think it is necessary? Forget all the theories and just use your eyes. If I were younger . . .' He thought of Lenin saying that at thirty revolutionaries should be taken out and shot. He couldn't remember how old Lenin was when he made that pronouncement. 'Revolution is like sex and is best left to young people. They have the passion necessary for it. But perhaps you feel the same about torture? Do you feel torture is like sex? Certainly the opposite is sometimes true. You must have found that.'

'I must get out,' Mendoza said. 'I need to go to the toilet urgently.'

'If I were you, I would control myself, but of course I am not you.' Che was silent a moment. He felt a strange satisfaction talking to Mendoza, their positions as prisoner and jailer reversed. He supposed it was a sense of power. 'Do you remember the time you and Quiroz and the other man strapped me in a coffin and buried me alive with only a tube to breathe through? You should remember – it was your idea of fun with a revolutionary. Quiroz was always more interested in experiments to extend the boundaries of human knowledge but you were determined to show the power of authority.'

Mendoza got a hand on the grille and rattled it.

'Impatient?' Che asked. 'All right.' He laid down his revolver and broke open the bag of mortar. 'My original plan was to shoot you straight off but then I thought of this.' He poured mortar into the bucket, mixing in water from a can. He slapped mortar on the bottom of the niche and laid one brick, two bricks, three bricks, filling the gaps between with more mortar. Mendoza began shouting to stop, then screaming gibberish as the second course of bricks was put in place.

'You're not making sense,' Che said.

'Guevara, stop. I'll give you anything you want.'

'Anything?' Che seemed to consider this while he laid the next row. He paused. 'Generous, but by and large I am content. I have more than I honestly believed possible. I am alive and free and I have you in there.' He began laying the fourth course of bricks. This took his full attention because they fitted snugly against the top and he had to be certain mortar filled every last crevice.

Mendoza's voice was muffled but he screamed and screamed. 'You're mad. Don't you understand? You're mad.'

Well no, Che didn't think he was mad. Far from it. He paused, the final brick in his hand. He could see white teeth, the glint of a gold filling, a pencil line moustache, one eye. Frankly he thought Mendoza's eye looked mad.

'Doctor Quiroz donated his blood,' Che said. 'From you, the breath of life.'

'You're inhuman. Think of my wife. Think of my family.'

'Think of the families of all the poor and starving. Do you ever think of them? This is more than personal revenge, it is one small act of revolutionary justice.'

He laid more mortar and as the final brick was being slipped in he heard Mendoza babble, 'Insane, insane.'

Che eased the brick in place then slapped mortar everywhere an airhole might have escaped him. Finally he stepped back, considering the tomb.

'So,' he breathed.

All he could hear was a mumble, like bees in a hive.

CHAPTER 10

'Anything to declare?' the Customs officer asked.

Only my genius, Oscar. 'No, nothing.'

'Any books? Paperbacks? Magazines?'

'Books?' Tanner queried. Of course, this was a country which had once banned *Black Beauty* as likely to corrupt public morals. 'Something to read on the flight.'

But the Customs officer had lost interest and nodded him through. 'Enjoy your holiday.'

Tanner passed through the Exit doors and was engulfed in whooping and hollering as if he were a chart-topping pop star. It wasn't for him but for the middle-aged woman who was at his heels. There was the sort of ecstatic reunion you only get in places that feel isolated, a long way from the rest of the world. There was kissing and hugging and the pop of a camera's flash. Tanner thought it was a good diversion, great cover so no one would notice his arrival. Until he saw a man standing all on his own holding up a big cardboard placard on which was written in bold block capitals: 'MR TANNER.' Fantastic, Tanner thought, why not a brass band and interviews with the local press. What do you think of South Africa so far, Mr Tanner, and what business brings a British spy out here?

'I'm Tanner,' he said.

'Welcome to South Africa, sir. Welcome to Durban, sir.'

He'd dropped the placard to his chest now. He was going to be like a sandwich board man advertising Tanner's presence. Tanner took the placard and turned it round to conceal his name. Then, in case the man's feelings were bruised, he shook his hand.

'What's your name?'

'Naidoo,' the man answered. 'Most Europeans call me Freddy.'

'May I call you Mr Naidoo?'

He got an uncertain grin in reply.

Durban Airport had no nonsense about multi-storey car-parks or courtesy buses to a distant field. The car was in a near-empty lot in front of the terminal building. Naidoo paid at the booth and turned the car on to the Durban road. Where's the army? Tanner screamed in silence. There should be roadblocks and checks on the cars coming into the airport. There's nothing to stop someone walking right into the check-in hall carrying a Kalashnikov. Remember Vienna. Remember Rome.

Naidoo concentrated on the traffic on the freeway and they drove in silence through industrial suburbs. All airport roads are the same, Tanner decided, all pass the same used car lots, the same derelict land, the same low-tech factories.

'Where are we heading?' Tanner asked. 'The US Consulate?' Foreign Office cuts meant there was no longer a British Consul. 'Consular facilities' were available but that was no damn use in a case like this. Normally Tanner hated making use of the American allies. Too much bowing and scraping involved and Tanner ended up feeling he was the poor country cousin.

'Mr Mathews doesn't work out of the Consulate. There is a flat he has rented. He calls it the State Apartment. I think that is his joke, sir.'

'Keen sense of humour, has he?'

But Naidoo felt it wasn't his place to discuss Mathews's character. Naidoo, born in South Africa, was Indian and the American was European. Such was the logic of the country. Or perhaps there was something about the road ahead that he didn't like. He made a squealing unsignalled turn to the right which left a wail of protesting car horns behind them. They took an unmade road past a factory that was being demolished, bouncing over railway lines, through a mudslide, along a line of rotting tin sheds.

'So are we being followed?'

Naidoo checked his mirror again. 'No.'

On Maydon Wharf the factories reared above high walls and barbed wire. The gates were manned by black guards with khaki uniforms and businesslike truncheons.

'The factories are working, are they?' Tanner asked. 'Not on strike or closed down?'

'Oh yes, they're working. People need money so they work.'

'No sabotage?'

'I don't know about that, sir. It's the censorship, you see. All we get is rumours.'

'Doesn't Mr Mathews know?'

Naidoo gave his unhappy grin, not liking to be questioned.

Now they were following the Victoria Embankment which curved round the harbour. Between the palm trees Tanner could make out rusted coasters, a laid-up tug, an oil tanker. Oil tankers had their name and registration port painted out before they visited South Africa, so he'd heard.

'And is Mr Brunton going to be at the State Apartment?'

'We're almost there,' Naidoo said.

Is it South African evasiveness, Tanner wondered, that he always answers a different question? And security is a joke if you're met at the airport by Freddy Naidoo, well-known chauffeur and consular help, holding up a bloody great placard. Tanner had shaken hands with him and that must have been noted.

There was an area between Smith Street and the Embankment without any defined character. Tanner noted residential blocks, offices, small businesses, snack bars, shops that sold fishing tackle and typewriters and ironmongery and picture frames. The kind of place, he decided, where the less ambitious dentists had surgeries. The building Naidoo stopped outside was rundown and too small for a lift. He talked softly into the speaker by the street door, which buzzed to admit them. Naidoo said, 'First floor, sir,' pointing the way, but wasn't coming himself. His sheepish grin said it wasn't his place. When Tanner reached the first landing, the apartment door was already open. It was locked behind him like the stockade gate when the last trooper is in and the redskins are thundering close behind.

'Welcome,' a voice said. 'Glad you made it.'

'Did you think I was going to be hijacked?' Tanner asked a young man. From the neat haircut above a bland missionary's face to the well-ironed shorts and matching jacket, he was one of the quiet men of American overseas service.

'Come on in, son, make yourself at home.' By the window

was a battle-scarred veteran of half a dozen secret wars. He gazed between the slats of the venetian blind a moment longer then gave his attention to Tanner. He was no more than ten years older but he had the air of someone who always called people 'son'.

'You're Ed Mathews, are you?' Tanner asked.

'I surely am and this here is my boy Dick Verucci. And you are Phil Tanner. Okay, that's given us all names. Identities are important. Repeating your name is, in my experience, the best way to remember it.'

'Can I get you something?' the 35-year-old boy asked. 'Beer, Coke, coffee?'

Tanner ignored him. 'Where's Brunton? I was told he was flying down last night from Pretoria specifically to meet me.'

'Well now, Bill Brunton has taken to his bed. He said he was "indisposed". It's a privilege to be working alongside Bill because I don't usually mix with folks who use words like "indisposed". No sir. I'm a small town boy and we used to say a guy was piss-sick. But Bill is British, he's got a picture of the Queen in his office and a photo of himself in a tall hat outside Buckingham Palace when he went to collect his award. He's something big in the British Empire, if anything is big in your empire these days.'

He's putting it on, Tanner decided. He's a lot shrewder than his act. 'The smaller the empire, the more the awards.'

'That's the way of the world, son.' Mathews came forward smiling, with his hand out for a shake. 'So on behalf of Bill, I welcome you, son. Come, sit down while Dick fetches us a beer and I'll try and put your mind at rest on just what the hell's going on.'

Tanner looked round and decided he was in a short-lease flat. The previous tenant must have died and the agency had made no effort to refurbish the place. There was overstuffed furniture that was all wrong for subtropical heat. Where the fireplace would have been in a cold climate there was a tarnished mirror in a wrought-iron stand, with a mantelpiece above with two empty vases and a clock that had stopped at 7.20. On one wall was a Tretchikoff print of a girl with a tear rolling down her cheek. On another was a pair of crossed assegais. An air-conditioning unit in a window whirred but either it was useless or it had been switched on only a short time before. The place smelled musty but above all it smelled of being a safe house.

Verucci came back carrying a bamboo-handled tray with two stubby bottles of Castle lager and a can of Diet Coke.

'Here's health,' Mathews said, 'and success.'

Verucci went to sit on a straight wooden chair against the wall. He was doorman, barman, watchman. He fingered the slats of the venetian blind and looked not only down at the street but up to the roof of the building opposite.

'First off,' Mathews said, 'I bring you sincere apologies from Bill for not being here to shake your hand in person. Between ourselves, Phil, I think your fellow countryman's hand shakes enough all on its own. What would you say his medical condition was, Dick?'

Verucci never took his eyes from the window. 'Alcoholic.'

'Dick was dating a nurse once, right, son? Dick knows. Well, I guess it's not too difficult to diagnose that Bill holds a damp glass a little too often. Can you blame him? If I had to stick it out with all that's going on, I might go the same route.'

'So you've not been in Durban long?'

But Mathews had a different question he answered. 'Well now, it is my personal opinion that Durban is not a place to work, Durban is a place to come for a holiday. Like, in the States in winter, people fly down to Miami. Or Fort Lauderdale. Or Saint Pete. Have you been there, son? Do you know Saint Pete and the resorts near it?'

'I'm familiar with Florida,' Tanner said cautiously.

'Did you hear that, Dick? I love that "familiar with". Ah, you British,' and Mathews shook his head in admiration of the quaint way the Brits spoke.

'But I've never been to Yoreville.'

Mathews grunted. 'Me neither. But I heard from someone who had visited and he said it should be called Boreville. Six days you watch the grass grow and on the seventh you mow it. At night there's nothing for the kids to do but play with their acne. You know the kind of place I mean?'

Tanner nodded. He knew the kind of place and it was called Surrey. Hershey escaped from it every day.

'So, if you were of a suspicious mind – and Phil, basically I guess we all are in our kind of work – if you're the kind of guy who nags a bit and scratches beneath the surface, if . . .' Mathews seemed to lose track of where the sentence was going. He drank some cold beer and wiped the condensation off his fingers on his shirt. 'Why is a Cuban woman living in a place like that? Possibly because she can come and go as she likes, nobody notices. She can entertain the Queen of England or Frank Sinatra and nobody would know. Or Fidel Castro. But what an out-of-the-way hole for a reporter to choose. When a big story breaks, she's miles from an international airport.'

'We were told she did features not hot news,' Tanner said and to himself: Why is he telling me this? It's nothing new.

'She's done reports for some of the Spanish-speaking stations in Miami and Texas. She's done magazine articles in both Spanish and English. Researchers have tracked some of these down. She's done stories out of Central America. She did atmosphere pieces out of Mexico during the Soccer World Cup. She did a story on Brits holidaying at Daytona and how they drank champagne when Fergie and Randy got wed.'

'The Rastas in Jamaica,' Verucci suggested.

'Son, I was coming to that. She wrote about the Rastas in Jamaica. She was there at election time and she never reported on Seaga kicking the Cubans out on their ass. Not that we can find. She was here in Durban and never wrote about how she was expelled. She got off the plane at Harare and we *think* her route took her to Lusaka and on the weekly flight to Angola. We can find nothing printed about Luanda, city of courageous comrades fighting the fascist American puppet Savimbi. For a reporter she's pretty shy about writing her own story. I'll tell you what it's like. It's like she was censoring herself, doesn't want to draw attention to herself. Anything that would arouse any suspicion she was radical, she cuts it. She wants to be taken as the freedom-loving gal who got out from communist Cuba. You know as well as I do what we call that in the trade.'

'Good cover.'

'Right. And generous old Uncle Sam even made her a citizen and gave her a passport.'

There was an interruption while the air-conditioner developed a rattle. Verucci, repairman, came away from the front window and went to the side window, switched it off and on without success.

'Show it who's boss, son. Hit it.'

Verucci hammered the unit with his fist and winced.

'Switch the bastard off.'

Tanner found himself studying Mathews's jacket, which he hadn't appreciated before. It was of drip-dry Dacron and could best be described as a tropical tartan of blue and pink and yellow. It would pass as part of the decoration in a disco. In the silence after the air-conditioner died the noises from outside grew more distinct – traffic, the bang of a car door, the tinkle of a street vendor's bell.

'Without the air-conditioner, son, I'm going to need another beer.' While Verucci soft-footed away to the kitchen, Mathews unfolded a sheet of paper. 'Now there's a new wrinkle. This just reached me this morning on the telex from Langley. It's the translation of an article, byline Martina Mancilla, that is at this time being splashed in newspapers in Eastern Europe – *Neues Deutschland*, *Rude Pravo*, if that's its name. Not my field, son. Not yours either, I think.'

No, Tanner thought. Nor this set-up, this safe house. Not my field. Verucci brought two more bottles of Castle, though Tanner had scarcely touched his.

'You're not a drinking man, son. I thought the British appreciated a wet glass.' Mathews was long-sighted. He held the sheet of paper at arm's length to refresh his memory. 'Suddenly Martina Mancilla has come out of the closet. She's gone public in the communist press, not just the radical Western media. Why? It's a real headscratcher. She's written about Che Guevara, red hot papa of a whole continent, killed by Yankee-inspired gangsters twenty years ago.'

'May I see?'

Mathews tore off the coding strip at the top and passed him the sheet. 'Company digest, you understand.'

Tanner scanned the sheet. It was a précis of a translation of an article that had appeared during the past week in the 'state-controlled media' (as the CIA analyst pointed out) in East Germany, Poland, Czechoslovakia, Bulgaria, Vietnam and Cuba. In the West it had been printed in *L'Humanité*. Ostensibly the hook for the article was Che Guevara's death in Bolivia when the army tracked him down twenty years before. But the anniversary wasn't for another five months. Why should there be such a rash of premature publicity? The analyst suggested it was co-ordinated by the Russians and that the French communist newspaper was particularly receptive to articles sent from Moscow. Why? Why now? And why had the writer disappeared?

'Have my bosses in London seen this?'

'They surely have, son.'

'Do they think it's significant?'

'Well now, Phil, significance is kind of hard to pin down in our trade. We have people in Langley – as I'm sure you do in London – who have built whole careers out of the significance of the Pope coming from East Europe or the significance of constipation in successful generals. Is it significant that the writer of that article was in South Africa last year together with a man who has been murdered? Ask a question like that at Langley and you can fill your appointments book with meetings for months ahead.'

And is it significant that the murdered man had just returned from Bolivia?

'May I?' Tanner asked, folding the paper and putting it in his pocket.

'Son, be my guest. We're working on this together.'

'I'll go to my hotel and take a shower,' Tanner said. 'Then I've got people to see. London gave me a list of three or four names.'

Mathews didn't ask who they were. He probably already knew. His disco jacket shimmered when he got to his feet. He draped an arm round Tanner's shoulders.

Careful, Tanner cautioned, don't ever do that to Pearce.

'You want a taxi, son?'

'I thought Mr Naidoo could take me.'

'Good boy, Freddy. Yes sir, he's smart. Could do well for himself if this becomes a more go-ahead society.'

Outside there was no sign of Naidoo and the car. Tanner looked left and right and he'd disappeared. A taxi stood at the corner and he walked up to it. The driver was a woman with straggly blonde hair and a face that had seen better days, or nights. She looked at Tanner without enthusiasm as he bent to the window.

'Are you free?'

She went on chewing gum while she stared. She'd seen all kinds of men and had never been impressed.

'Where to?'

Tanner hated cabdrivers and particularly loathed cabdrivers who asked where he was going before they agreed to take him. He opened the door and got in beside her.

'It's the Hotel . . .'

He dipped into his breast pocket for the slip of paper with the name.

'Don't try and be a hero, will you? You understand me, hero?'

The back of the taxi was no longer empty. Easing his head to the left he saw a tanned face with white blotches of tiredness under the eyes. A gun against his ear stopped him seeing the man to the right.

'You were hoping to find Naidoo. Some nasty racist policeman suggested his papers weren't in order and he left in a hurry. Welcome to Durban, Mr Tanner.'

When they spoke they used Afrikaans. Tanner listened, trying to pick out words that would help him understand who they were and what they wanted. He'd asked once and been ordered to leave off being the hero. Security police, CID, immigration, death squad. South Africa hadn't quite got the hang of death squads yet. It was in Latin America the police and the army took their uniforms off for a night on the town. Latin America was his patch. Perhaps he'd brought the disease with him.

They were travelling along the Embankment again. Across the harbour there were oil storage tanks and behind them the bluff threw a protective arm out to sea. It was a bit of green jungle except for a scattering of army huts. After half a dozen blocks the taxi swung back towards the city centre.

The gun was no longer at his ear so he turned to look at the two men in the back seat. They wore ties and lightweight jackets. It's a conservative society, he thought, where appearances are important. Also, even in this hot climate you had to wear a jacket to conceal the holster. One man was young and Tanner decided he was along just to handle the artillery. The older man with the blotches of tiredness under his eyes stared at him. Tanner's gaze dropped to his lap and saw the white knuckles of his fists and was reminded of Moulter. Why do security people have so much anger bottled up inside them?

They knew who he was and where to scoop him up. They'd picked him out at Durban Airport where Naidoo had obligingly held up a placard with his name. Or Ed Mathews had given them a whisper. On balance Tanner favoured the tip-off by Mathews. *You want a taxi, son*? If you were resident in a country, you reached some sort of accommodation with the local cavalry. It didn't matter that Washington and London denounced apartheid, unofficial liaison between the security forces remained good.

The taxi turned again and was held up by traffic lights. Tanner had a view of overblown municipal architecture. The man with tired eyes spoke to him for the first time since the taxi had got going.

'That's the city hall. They say it's modelled on the one in Belfast.'

'I've never been to Northern Ireland.'

'I thought you people ran the dirty tricks outfit there.'

'It's not my field.'

'Tell me, hero, is South Africa your field?'

Tanner looked out at the crowds and thought how in Europe people would be eyeing each other, their clothes, their faces, the way their bodies moved; and how here each seemed to walk enclosed in a separate world. The security cop was just having a show of temperament and didn't need an answer.

They passed a theatre built in Stockbroker Tudor style, offices, residential blocks. They were entering a district with more the feel of a resort: restaurants, shops with beach toys and postcards, the ET pawnbroker's shop. Tanner looked for a police station but these were a different kind of cop. They drew up outside a tired apartment building a block back from the seafront. The beach was hidden but there was a glimpse of palm trees and a bank of clouds on the horizon that merged into the hot glare of the sky. He smelled the sea and rotting fruit and exhaust fumes.

The third-floor apartment had the air of a failing business. It reminded Tanner of a meeting he'd once had in San Salvador. It had been during the time Britain had had no official presence. The Embassy had been closed because of the civil war – staff had been kidnapped, the Foreign Office was squealing about handing taxpayers' money over to fund terrorists. There was only an honorary Consul, a retired warhorse from the diplomatic service who locked himself away behind steel shutters at night and advised Tanner never to leave his hotel. Information on the war? Read the *News-Gazette*. Sound, though the editor's a Yank. Rosencrantz, Applebaum, Neanderthal, some outlandish name. Like an introduction, old chap? Instead Tanner had found his way to a Syrian whose business was importing oriental rugs. Tanner's theory was that any hot major or upwardly mobile colonel would immediately splash out on a fine new carpet to go with his fine new *hacienda*. US aid had been stepped up again and dollars were sticking to the fingers of any army officer who was awake enough to haul himself out of bed in the morning. All he wanted was a man who could signal London who were the coming stars in the army. It was a severe shock to Tanner's theory to find the business wasn't thriving, dust had settled on the office like fall-out, the telex was silent, the water cooler empty. There was a token Salvadorean secretary and she probably had to double as the Syrian's mistress. Business was terrible, the Syrian said, but then Syrians always said that. Anyone with cash to spirit abroad was buying up Florida. How about the new rich – the military high brass? Terrible, the Syrian wailed, raising his shoulders and his voice. They chose his most expensive stock but fingered the butts of their revolvers when he reminded them that payment was overdue. Perhaps, Tanner hinted, he could pay a little something for a list of such customers, their rank, their prospects. The Syrian had brightened wonderfully and tried to sell him a rug. 'Top quality, sir, absolutely tip-top quality. See how close the stitching is.' He had bent back the rug. 'Six months' work, sir. All hand stitching.' Though even Tanner could recognize the regular machine pattern of a Pakistani factory.

This apartment had the air of a lost cause – this year, next year, some time, but not never. The windows were fogged by the salt air and the towerblock across the alley gave the room an underwater gloom. It was furnished with office chairs, a desk, filing cabinets, a telex machine, a computer terminal. Tanner wondered whether the bedrooms were used for crashing out exhausted on busy nights or interrogation or fornication. The younger man had driven off with the taxi and it was just the two of them now.

The other man tore a sheet of paper out of the telex and spent a long time reading it. Once he glanced at Tanner and resumed his reading, so that Tanner had the ugly feeling the message was about him, a catalogue of past sins, a verdict, a sentence.

'Sit down, hero.'

Tanner lowered himself on a plastic-seated chair that squeaked at the contact with his trousers. He could feel the sweat sticking his clothes to him. There was no air-conditioning.

'I am Major Van der Merwe,' the man said, putting himself behind the desk. 'I come from Jagersfontein. That's a town in the Orange Free State. You know, here they tell jokes about policemen called Van der Merwe who come from the Free State. Have you heard?'

'Nobody's told me a joke since I arrived.'

'Not too many jokes these days.' He got out a packet of cigarettes, offered them to Tanner, and lit one himself. 'Van der Merwe was patrolling the Marine Parade one evening when he came across two drunks. They had their arms round each other's shoulders and were staggering and pointing up at the sky.' He paused and scowled at the tip of his cigarette. His Afrikaner accent was much heavier as he told the story. 'Van der Merwe said, "What are you two doing?" And one of the drunks said, "Constable, constable, you can settle the argument. Is that or is that not the moon up there?" So Van der Merwe gazes up at the sky a moment and then he says, "*Ag*, man, you mustn't ask me – I've just come down from the Free State."'

Tanner waited for the punchline but that seemed to be the end.

'Well, it's like you have Irish jokes in England.'

A phone was ringing in another room. The Major ignored it and the ringing stopped. Somebody else answered it? Got fed up? Van der Merwe picked up a sheet of paper from his desk.

'So are you enjoying your stay here? Immigration people at

Louis Botha Airport say you described the purpose of your visit as Holiday. I suppose meeting the CIA resident means you haven't had time to visit the beach yet. Do you want me to fix a police photographer to snap you riding in a ricksha?'

'I thought they only photographed corpses.'

'That can be arranged. That's our speciality, hero. Don't you read your own press?'

Again Tanner kept quiet. If the local security goon got a glow out of chewing him up, good luck. But if he called him 'hero' one more time, Tanner might just stick it up his fundamentals.

'Did you notice the meter in that taxi?'

'No,' Tanner said.

'It's permanently set at sixteen rand fifty-two cents. That's intended as a joke. At least I think it is. Sixteen fifty-two was the year van Riebeeck landed at the Cape and we've been paying ever since. You see, we're not like the British who kept coming and conquering us, or the Portuguese who ran away from Mozambique when it got independence. We've been here a long, long time. It's our ancestral home as much as it is the blacks', but it is we who have developed it, not the blacks. We've built up farms and mines and industry and we have universities and a parliament and communications and churches and culture and an independent legal system. Show me, please, one other country in the whole dark continent that boasts all that. Do you think we'll give it up? Ever? If it's going to be destroyed, we'll do the destroying. Let the English go to England or Australia or Texas. And the Portuguese will run again, maybe Brazil is far enough. The Jews can settle in Israel. Where do we run to? This is our country. We have no other. We live here and we shall die here.'

'You don't have to run anywhere. There'll be changes – '

'It would do you good to visit a few other places on your way home. I remember Rhodesia a long time ago and then I see what a nice little totalitarian state it's turning into now. Watch all the white liberals as they twist on their own pricks and claim a one-party state doesn't *really* betray their principles because it means stability which is the basis of life and economic progress. And that ensures a full belly which is the main thing because you can't eat the vote. Which is what the government of this pariah country has been saying since the year dot. Well, isn't it?'

Tanner felt a deep disinterest in answering. He supposed all South Africans were combative like this, obsessed with their situation. Tanner had met Trotskyites who were the same, obsessed with the wickedness of the rest of the world.

A plump but pretty black girl came in holding a tray with cups and a coffee jug. I seem to have gone from pre-lunch drinks to after-lunch coffee and left a hole in the middle, Tanner thought.

'Have you heard about the South African President visiting London?' Tanner said. 'He was asked how he liked his coffee. "Like our South African women – hot, strong and sweet." "Black or white?"'

Van der Merwe didn't smile but he nodded. Perhaps he was committing the joke to memory, and later to some file. He picked up another sheet of telex paper.

'I was going to be rude to you, because that's how a lot of us feel these days. You all want to make gestures to the Third World dictators. You want to be paper heroes. You don't have to live here, clear up the blood, have your children take the consequences. You want my co-operation? I was going to make you crawl and if you wouldn't I'd send you packing. But now,' he tapped the paper, 'now it seems I owe you a favour.'

Tanner took several sips of his coffee, though it was just as muddy as the brew in the Bunker's canteen. Me? he wondered. Done him a favour? Tanner suspected a hoax, more wit and wisdom in the Free State vein.

Van der Merwe licked his lips and read from the paper: '*May Day Demo Mobs SA Ambassador's Residence.*' His voice rang out like the dominie denouncing sin. You could hear each word began with a capital letter. 'I guess England suffers a plague of such people: agitators, strikers, trouble-makers.'

'It's the same all over. Where's the story from?'

'Reuters, London.'

Tanner still wasn't prepared for what was to come. He was more struck by the journalistic style. The heading began in tabloid cliché and then swung into the upper classes: Ambassador's Residence.

'Can I see?'

Van der Merwe kept hold of the sheet. 'Our Embassy sent it. Came while I was out picking you up. It seems the British

Security Police were expecting trouble. They were waiting round the corner and when the mob arrived they sent in a snatch squad. They grabbed a woman and some of her screaming *boeties*. She had two petrol bombs in her shoulderbag. Correction, alleged petrol bombs. Pardon me. If our police shoot rioters they use real bullets. If your communists burn down our Ambassador's house they use alleged petrol bombs.'

Tanner no longer wanted to look at the message. He had images of the Falkland Fair and kids with clowns' faces and the King Kong T-shirt. This is the big one baby.

'After the Reuters story, the Embassy added a postscript. It seems the British Security Police were tipped off by a courageous Intelligence Officer.' Van der Merwe pretended to consult the sheet. 'By name, Philip Tanner. How did you know?'

I went to this white township called Kentish Town, Tanner screamed in his mind, disguised in a kaffir's shirt, infiltrated this terrorist group, drank toast after toast to the success of the revolution until the bottles were empty and ready to be filled again. What the shit am I doing mixed up in all this? She was just a big friendly girl with big friendly boobs and now she'll lose her freedom, her job and probably her house while I sit here with some hayseed cop and can't even tell him to get stuffed.

'Okay, you have your sources, I have mine. Should I thank you? Perhaps not. Perhaps my thanks are tainted.'

Sandwiches had been brought in, a choice of overcooked beef or cheese and tomato. The black girl smiled at Tanner when he thanked her. She had a restless bosom like Debbie Becker's and a bottom that waved like a flag. There was no art in it, no provocation. She was as shy and natural as a forest creature.

Tanner got up and walked to the misted window and opened it. Warm muggy air gusted in.

'We get winds like this,' Van der Merwe said, 'but not normally so late.'

'Have you seen this?' Tanner asked, bringing out the telex from the CIA. There were times you had to give a bit in order to receive a bit.

Van der Merwe read it with deep concentration, furrows

between his eyes. He read slowly or he read it twice. Tanner turned away to study the building opposite. Just another concrete block, balconies with pot plants, swimsuits pegged to lines. On the balcony below Tanner saw two Pepsi bottles with straws, abandoned as if the people had been called inside by more urgent needs.

Finally Van der Merwe made a comment: 'Martina bloody Mancilla.'

Tanner recognized the tone of voice. It was the way he thought of Denise, who had upped and left him adrift and never made contact.

'Bitch,' Van der Merwe muttered, to prove Tanner right. 'This from the CIA fellow?'

'He'll show it to you,' Tanner said. 'First he has to decide whether it's significant or not. He has this big thing about significance.'

'Your people in Pretoria were asking about her and the Englishman she was with.'

'Morton, Benjamin Morton.'

'They hinted something had happened to the fellow.'

'Didn't you know?' Tanner was surprised. Everybody seemed to know about everything; it was about as secret as an Israeli cabinet meeting. 'Morton is dead. He was murdered in Mancilla's house in Florida.'

'Bitch. I should have locked her up, both of them. Because they were foreign journalists, the practice is to kick them out. What's this rubbish about Che Guevara? Why's the CIA interested in him?'

'Some people would answer the CIA is interested in everything. In this case they are puzzled why all these papers are suddenly printing a twenty-year-old story.'

'When she was here,' Van der Merwe said, 'she screamed that we mustn't touch her because she was writing for the American press. That's why they were here – getting stories and interviews and pictures for the *Miami Herald* and the *Christian Science Monitor*. She was a whore and a liar and no kind of a Christian. I don't care if her passport was American, I can smell a Cuban. We've had Cubans next door in Angola for years. I did not trust her. I wanted to lock her up. Nothing brutal, you understand. A small cell and no sleep and she'd have talked to me. But no, Pretoria says, put them both on a plane, get rid of them. Don't make more enemies in the Western media, as if we still had any friends to lose.' Van der Merwe gave his attention to the précis once more. '*Ag*, man, I was right. She's come into the open, breaking her cover for some dead Cuban revolutionary.'

'He wasn't Cuban. He was Argentinian but he got around.'

'Wherever he was born, he ended up under the ground long ago. Why write about him now?'

'Bormann is dead. Hitler is dead. Stalin is dead. People still write about them.'

'You know what she said to me? "Don't you fuck with me, you fascist Boer." I hate women with dirty mouths. Where do they pick it up? What kind of people do they mix with?'

People like me, Tanner supposed. It was the way the world was going but he suspected Van der Merwe looked even on Durban as some corrupt steaming fleshpot. The girl brought more coffee. Tanner wondered what her name was. She caught his eyes on her and she dropped her eyelashes. A bit of artfulness there after all, he decided. He felt tired from the flight, from the gun at his ear, from this high-strung cop. It would be bliss to sink on to a soft breast and sleep. There used to be a law against it in South Africa but he rather thought it had been dumped. How could you ever pass a law against it? Van der Merwe was watching him. Perhaps it was subversive even to think about it.

'What had Morton and Mancilla done wrong?'

'It was Mancilla more than the man, but they travelled as a team. She went to see Moses Ntuli. She was quite clever. She interviewed a number of other people, even some whites. Her mistake was to see Ntuli a second time.'

'Who is he?'

'ANC. He's a communist. Before his passport was taken away he travelled to Zimbabwe and then on to Prague and East Berlin. And how do we know that if we have no embassies there? Because South Africa isn't entirely friendless. Information reaches us, sometimes from people who shout at us in public.'

Tanner closed his eyes, focusing his mind. 'We have a worry that Morton could in some way have been part of a spy network. He's visited Prague too, according to his passport. And a call was made from the house where he was murdered to the Soviet Embassy in Washington. But we have no hard evidence. It's all smoke, no fire.'

'She saw Ntuli on her own. Morton stayed in their room at the Elangeni and she took a taxi and met Ntuli at the university campus both times. They walked slowly, talking. A white woman walking and talking to a black man gets noticed, but not at the university. The second time she passed him a paper. We have photographs of her doing it but we never found the paper and we have no tape of what they discussed.'

Tanner took a long breath. In the Sahara once he'd seen a mirage and it had been like this, without substance, floating above the horizon, never getting closer.

'You don't know what they talked about?'

'Names of contacts, hit list of enemies, sources of arms? The trouble is Ntuli still refuses to utter one word.'

Tanner gazed at Van der Merwe. 'Still refuses?'

'He's our guest.' He didn't smile. This was Van der Merwe from the Orange Free State where there weren't many jokes.

CHAPTER 11

Che thought more about Lenin than in all the time he'd been locked away. Behind bars, in the Experiment Chamber, in some darkened recovery room, he'd never thought of Lenin. Creating political awareness, building an active proletariat, sweeping away the bourgeois spider's web that trapped the revolutionary spirit – these things had not been at the forefront of his mind. To survive until tomorrow: that was important.

Now he thought of Lenin's plan for thirty-year-old revolutionaries. Line them against a wall and shoot them. Extreme language to make a point. You grew old, you lost urgency, you lost certainty, you faltered, you failed. As he was doing.

He walked down Calle Argentina, past the post office with its broken windows. He was stomping along, an old man in a hurry, frowning because his plan was drifting out of control again. Anger was a knot in his stomach. He screamed in his head: *Useless old man, crazy country, stupid people.*

What did he have to do? Write it in words of fire? Nobody had discovered the corpse of Comandante Mendoza. He had checked again, his third day of strolls in the cemetery. The cement and the bucket had been removed but the newly filled niche in the cell-block of the dead had caught no one's attention.

He crossed the Plaza 25 de Mayo, past the statue of Marshal Sucre. Bronze lions guarded it, their backs used as slides by small boys who polished off the gifts of pigeons. A fountain was playing, its spray catching the morning sun and turning to jewels.

Of course, Lenin hadn't sentenced himself to death. There had to be exceptions. Would he have had Che shot? Perhaps. At thirty-nine he'd been too old to lead the liberation struggle in Bolivia. At fifty-nine he couldn't grab the ears of the world, not even with two executions.

It was too early for ice cream sellers but boys who should have been in primary school hawked trays of caramel pastries. Shoeshine men clapped the backs of their brushes to point out the shabby state of his shoes. There, Che thought, is the division of the classes: between people who own shoes and people who can only afford sandals. I am rich, I wear shoes. Send for the firing squad.

He sat on a bench and let a thin-faced kid polish his shoes. When he'd finished, Che praised his work. The shine was better than the President's Cadillac. The boy straightened his shoulders and grew two years taller.

Morton's money had bought the shoes. What had happened to him? Morton had been so confident he would sell his story for mountains of dollars. He had used a particular expression. Che, he'd said, do you understand the English phrase: to make a killing.

Morton is dead. The thought slipped into his mind and he knew it was true. He didn't understand why he was certain but he was. He had a sixth sense, an intuition, and sometimes it frightened him. And sometimes, in the Sierra, it had saved his life. Morton didn't have the guerrilla's instinct. He had taken a risk checking the fingerprints and the people he'd checked with had killed him.

Che blanked out his mind. He watched students streaming across the square, mostly boys, some girls. They weren't joking or shouting and he recalled the students he'd seen cramming in the cemetery. Exams were a pain.

The thought wriggled back: they'd killed Morton because he knew Che was alive. These same people would come and try to kill him, except they didn't know where he was now. Here it was, three days after he'd bricked up Mendoza, and his body hadn't been discovered. All right, since the body was still in there, he would make use of it.

Whistles blew across the square and a pair of policemen halted the traffic at the intersection, raising their arms like petty Hitlers. A bus manoeuvred across the road and stopped. Five men and a boy got out. They carried two ladders. Che watched as they leaned one ladder against the side of the bus and all of them climbed up on to the roof. The second ladder they put against the neck of a lamp-post that arched over the road. Four men held the ladder while the fifth swarmed up with his bottom jutting out like a monkey. The lamp standard was flimsy and swayed as he changed the bulb. The small boy's job was to watch in silence. He was learning the trade.

Crazy country.

Che's eyes edged away from this spectacle to the radio station on the corner. On the roof was a cut down Eiffel Tower that served as its aerial. A sign said it broadcast on 92 FM and gave its name: Radio Colosal. Only in Bolivia would a radio station have such a name.

Lunch at the Snack El Carreton. In the evenings they had the television on and the night before Che had watched the Bolivian National Song Contest. This had been broadcast from La Paz and by some atmospheric freak the TV set could pick up the picture or pick up the sound but not both at once. The waitress had fiddled with a knob to listen to a girl lament about betrayed love and then tuned the set to watch while she sang. Che had preferred the Silent Song Contest.

At lunch there was no television and Che asked for the radio to be switched on.

'The reception is poor during the day,' the waitress said. 'We cannot receive La Paz.'

'The local station,' Che said.

'Ah, Radio Colosal. You wish to hear the news no doubt. I have a newspaper if you want the football results.'

'I want to listen to the radio.'

The waitress sniffed and turned on the radio.

'What is your name?' Che asked.

'Serafina,' the waitress said.

'That is a pretty name.'

The waitress sniffed again at an old man paying such a compliment. She left Che to enjoy his soup with a bone in it and listen to the radio. First there was national news – the cost of rice was going up, a general denied the army wanted to seize power – then local news. He spooned up the soup while he listened: new coach for the football team, an improved water supply, a big order for the cement works. Propaganda, Che thought, nothing but good news. No report that the Chief of Police was missing or that his body had been found in gruesome circumstances.

After the news came a station identification: 'This is Radio Colosal from Sucre, capital of the Republic of Bolivia.'

Che sighed. The President, the ministries, the whole government had long ago moved up to La Paz but the people of Sucre hadn't noticed. They still thought they lived in the capital.

'What is this?' Che asked.

'What does it look like?' Serafina said. 'It is ricc and salad and chicken. Look, there is a piece of chicken.'

'I'm not hungry.'

'You must eat or you will have no strength.'

'Do you have a sister called Lucrecia?'

She stared at him through narrowed eyes. First he paid her compliments. When that didn't work he asked for her sister. It was disgusting in a man his age. She backed away to the bar at the end of the room. There was a shelf with dusty bottles of Kohlberg wine and an empty bottle of Johnnie Walker for show. A calendar showed a girl in a bikini perched on the scoop of a bulldozer. Why wasn't the Pope kissing a runway?

The radio played Western pop and in between listeners phoned in to a man called Agustino.

'What is your name?'

'Napoleon.'

'Napoleon? Great. Terrific. A most illustrious name. Tell Tio Tino, are you planning to be a leader of our great country? A general, perhaps even President?'

'Yes, certainly.'

'Excellent. Terrific. We're playing a golden oldie from Los Menudos next. Do you want to dedicate it to someone special?'

'To my wife.'

'What's her name?'

'Josefina.'

'And where do you live?'

'The Instituto Psiquiatrico.'

'The Instituto Psiquiatrico? I like it. Terrific. Perhaps Tio Tino should come and consult you. You work on this radio station, you go a little *loco*. Seriously though, what are you, Napoleon? A doctor? A nurse? A porter?'

'I'm a patient.'

If he had to choose between an evil man and a fool, Che would choose the company of an evil man. You could point out the injustices of the world and the falseness of his beliefs. If he wasn't persuaded, you could kill him. But with a fool what reasoning could you use?

'Is that Agustino?'

'This is indeed yours truly, Tio Tino. And who am I speaking to?'

'You've been difficult to reach.'

'The price of fame. This is the programme that lets the people speak, and they speak and they speak . . .'

Did Che have to stroke this inflated ego?

'My name is Ernesto.'

'Great. Terrific. I've known many Ernestos and every one of them has been a fan of this programme. My congratulations to your parents on their choice of name.'

'When I was a boy my family called me Tete.'

'Tete? That is cute. Do you want to dedicate a record to someone? Let's see what we have cued up next. Oh, great. It's the new English group Buck House with their latest *boum-boum* hit, *The Royal Wee*. They are *faaaaantastico*.'

'I want to dedicate it to Emilio Mendoza.'

'Who hides behind that name? A pal? A workmate?'

'You don't know Comandante Mendoza, Chief of Police?'

'Hey, hey, hey . . . Tete, that is some dedication. Hey, for a moment there I was lost for words, which doesn't happen too often. *Great* dedication, terrific. Comandante, if you're listening, remember whose show you heard it on.'

'He won't be listening.'

'You can never be sure, Tete. The humble and the great all listen to Tio Tino.'

'Mendoza won't be listening because he's dead.'

Silence.

Che was sitting in the office of the Hostal Londres. He'd asked the owner if he could make a call and the owner had nodded to the phone on the desk. It was something of a *personal* call, Che had said, and the owner had walked out to the reception area. Through the glass panel Che could see his back. He was turning over the pages of the register, reliving happier days when the hotel had been humming. Che had signed his name as E. Carballo and was the only guest.

'Now, now just a minute Ernesto . . .'

The trouble with zeros like Agustino was that they didn't have brains that could handle reality.

'Agustino, you are privileged. The news has been broadcast on your programme.'

'Another first for Tio Tino,' he cried out with a glimpse of his old spirit. 'My sympathy, yes, deepest sympathy is extended to his wife and family. There *is* a Señora Mendoza, right?'

'She may not know he's dead. She may think he's away on police work. And at headquarters too they may not know he's dead. They may think he's away on a long weekend visiting friends. But *I* know he's dead. And now *you* know he's dead. And all your listeners.'

'Tete, Ernesto, please, this is a little confusing. The Police Chief is dead but nobody knows? How can this be? How do you know?'

'I killed him.'

'Tete, Tete, please . . . You've had your joke and in the poorest taste . . . Just a minute.'

Again silence.

'Ernesto, I'm going to have to cut you off. The station manager – '

'Don't do that. I'll tell you where his body is. It is in the cemetery, in the catacombs on the south side, second block. He's buried in the niche next to Gerhard Heeren. Mendoza's grave is unmarked but Heeren's has a swastika on it so they'll have something in common to talk about.'

'You *killed* him?'

'He crawled in the niche and I bricked up the entrance. He died through suffocation.'

'Holy Mother of God.'

'Let the police go and find the body of their late master.

Let them do this now so they know this is not a hoax.'

'But why did you do it? You must be crazy.'

Had Agustino looked at the world outside? Had he noticed the wars and the misery and the ignorance that the rich and powerful did nothing about? Had he walked two blocks from the radio station to where whole families made their homes on the streets? It was not Che who was crazy. He said, 'At three o'clock I will ring again. I have things to tell the world.'

'Who are you?'

Che hesitated and decided his name would draw a bigger audience.

'I am Ernesto Guevara, known as Che.'

'Ooooh,' Agustino groaned, losing interest fast. 'Che Guevera, of course. The brother of Napoleon. Home address: Instituto Psiquiatrico. Married to the Queen of Sheba.'

'Find the body! Learn the truth!' Che smacked the phone down, furious.

He fought for breath, feeling a pain in his chest as if a rope was being tightened. The hotelkeeper had turned at his shout and stared through the glass. What did it matter?

'I'm leaving,' Che said. 'How much do I owe you?'

'Captain Rodriguez!'

'Captain Choque!'

They greeted each other without warmth. Rodriguez was army and Choque was police. The jeep and the black and white car had stopped nose to nose outside the cemetery gatehouse. The captains had got out and faced each other, like their vehicles, a little too close. Their men shuffled at their backs like street gangs arguing over territory.

'Hardly an army affair, I would imagine,' Choque said. He had a well-nourished face and plump hands that fluttered. 'It doesn't affect the integrity of the state.'

'It is the integrity of the police we should perhaps be more worried about,' Rodriguez retorted. 'The Comandante absent for three days and nobody noticed.'

The gatehouse was the perfect backdrop for two dogs to sniff and growl. Its pillars were embellished with scrolls and curlicues and like all public buildings in Sucre it looked grand enough for imperial Rome.

'The command structure of the police in Sucre is so superbly ordered that it continues to function in the absence of any one of its senior officers.'

'So it is true what they say: the Comandante had no duties but continued to draw a hero's salary.'

'Your attitude makes co-operation between the two forces of the state difficult to sustain,' Choque said, at his most pompous. 'I shall ask the Comandante, on his return, to speak officially on the matter to your Colonel.'

'So you imagine he's not walled up inside?'

'A hoax,' Choque said, 'but one that has to be investigated.'

'A crazy old man's boast, eh?'

'Possibly the same old man who disarmed a lieutenant, a sergeant and two soldiers. I debate with myself who was crazy: the old man or the army patrol shitting its pants.'

Captain Rodriguez took a step back at the insult, a hand tapping at his holster. Then they both became aware of the growing audience: their own men, the flower sellers from the stalls under the trees, boys who'd been playing football, housewives, students, a stray dog. Other people were hurrying through the gates. The story was spreading in town. The story might be absurd but life itself was absurd and that didn't stop it being real.

'Come.' Captain Choque raised a gallant hand and gestured his men forward.

'Follow me,' Captain Rodriguez said.

The two captains walked down the central avenue of the cemetery in step. You would have thought they were comrades in arms instead of bitter enemies who'd fought over a girl. Captain Choque had won her and married her. There was no telling which man had most regrets now.

At the mausoleum of the Familia Benavides, Rodriguez paused. 'Which direction?'

'You mean you don't even know where to look?'

'The army has better things to do than spend its afternoons listening to the radio.'

Ahead of them a boy called out, 'This way.'

Rodriguez turned to inspect his troops. 'Straighten your cap, Dario. Forward.'

They walked between old yew trees, dark green with black folds. Glancing over his shoulder Choque saw they were now a sizeable procession. Boys in short pants were marching with stiff arms like doltish army recruits. An ice cream seller brought up the rear. Did he have no respect for the dead? At the first honk of his horn, he'd have that man arrested.

'Captain?'

'Yes?'

'What is it?'

Both captains stopped and turned. It was the soldier Dario speaking to Captain Rodriguez.

'I hear something. Can you hear it?'

Birds sang in pine trees. A hoe struck stone in a rose bed. From far off floated the sound of cars and dogs. But closer, ahead, the rumble of low voices.

'A funeral?' Choque suggested.

'In a cemetery?' Rodriguez said. 'You amaze me.'

'Not far,' the boy sang out. He skipped ahead down a line of palms. The procession straggled after him and as they cleared the trees they had a view of the wall of graves and a semi-circle of figures marking the spot. It wasn't a funeral. A funeral was coloured black. These were passers-by in everyday clothes and people from nearby houses alerted by the bizarre radio programme.

Captain Choque set off at a brisk pace. His uniform, ironed by his wife, stretched tight over his stomach and the trousers had creases as sharp as a guillotine. 'Who gave authority for this gathering?'

Rodriguez, lengthening his stride to catch up, said to the crowd, 'What are you standing round for? There's nothing to see.'

'He's in there,' came a stubborn reply. 'That's what the madman said on the radio: next to the grave of the German.'

The block was a patchwork quilt of graves, plaques, withered carnations, faded plastic chrysanthemums. The grave indicated was on the second layer, at hip height. On the upper levels half a dozen niches were open as if grave robbers had got to them. The rest were bricked or cemented over, and metal plates were engraved with names, dates and heavenly promises. Just this one niche was anonymous, keeping its secret.

Choque and Rodriguez glanced at each other, enmity overlooked in the shared moment. For the first time it appeared this madman's claim on the radio might be true. The Comandante was certainly missing and his subordinates had assumed it was some sexual quest that had taken him away. In the army headquarters in Calle Ravelo, when the radio programme was reported, it had seemed a hoax – but you never knew. Perhaps it *was* an elaborate trick to make the forces of law and order look foolish. A dozen bricks blocked up the niche. When Captain Rodriguez scratched with a thumbnail, the mortar hadn't dried completely.

'Right,' he announced. 'Yes, indeed.'

'Absolutely,' Choque agreed. 'Now it will be essential to follow the correct procedure. Is that fully understood?'

'The correct procedure? You know do you? You are the civilian power here.'

'Yes. Yes, I am.' Choque stared hard at his rival, enjoying this little moment. 'Send for the director of the cemetery. Or the curator. Or even the gatekeeper.'

'Captain, Captain, I am here, sir.'

Choque inspected the man with the thin cheeks and the permanent frown of a petty official.

'Good. Excellent. Now you've heard the rumour that the Chief of Police has been interred here.'

How ridiculous, the tone of voice implied. The gatekeeper had no love of the police, finding them either sadists or puffed up with their own importance. He said, 'The Comandante came here three days ago in the company of an old man. He spoke to me, ordered me to stay at the gate after closing time. Neither of them came out and after two hours I locked up anyway. My supper was ruined.'

'Why didn't you search for them?'

'Show me the man who searches a cemetery after dark.'

'How did the Comandante appear?'

'He was rude to me. How else would the Chief of Police behave?'

'Give a description of the old man – it could be a vital clue.'

'The old man . . .' The gatekeeper considered while everybody waited. 'Well, he wasn't poor, but neither did he have the arrogance of the rich. He was no longer young but he didn't need crutches. He was an old man.'

'Enough,' Choque decided. 'We shall have to open this grave.'

'To disinter a body,' the gatekeeper said, 'you need a magistrate's order.'

Rodriguez, who had kept silent long enough, laid one hand on the gatekeeper's shoulder and turned him so they were face to face. The other hand slapped his holster. 'This,' he said. 'Know what this is? It's all the order you need. Get to it.'

'Me?' The gatekeeper took a deep breath and let it out. 'Yes, sir.'

His heart wasn't in it. He produced a penknife and scraped a small hole in the mortar before the feeble blade bent. Sighing, he fetched a pick from the gravediggers' shed. Choque gestured to Rodriguez.

'Give the pick to Captain Rodriguez. Soldiers are used to digging trenches. They need them to hide in.'

'Have the police grown so soft they cannot even knock down a few bricks?' Rodriguez shrugged. 'No wonder we have a plague of crime. Dario, show the police captain how it's done.'

The sound of the pick was like the worst hammer blows inside his skull on Ash Wednesday morning, Choque decided. Damn soldiers were only good for brute jobs. Anything that required finesse or imagination was beyond them. Dario, with his sleeves rolled up and his hair shaved above his ears, looked no better than a convict. How he made the dust fly! There was no subtlety like aiming for the mortar so the bricks could be prised out. It was a frontal assault on the grave's defences. Then a corner of a brick was bludgeoned out and a hole opened.

The smell crept out.

Choque, concentrating on the widening hole, at first didn't take in the smell, just that his men had retreated and left him on his own. He noticed Rodriguez offering his soldiers a packet of cigarettes. He smoked Colorado, a real sergeant-major among cigarettes, and typical of his lack of refinement.

Finally, a mighty blow sent the top two layers of bricks scattering and the smell of corruption billowed out. Dario stepped aside.

Peering from a distance, Choque saw a grille with fingers jabbed between the iron bars. The fingertips were bloodied, as if the man had been scratching and scrabbling like a desperate mole. Beyond, barely visible, was the pencil line of Comandante Mendoza's moustache. His mouth gaped in a rictus. The eyes were wide, glazed.

'Your commanding officer, sir,' Rodriguez said, breaking the silence.

A woman screamed and then there was a clamour of voices.

The time of waiting was always difficult. In war it was difficult, in the Sierra it had been difficult. Che was restless until it was time to contact Radio Colosal again. He left the hotel and turned away from the Snack El Carreton. The first places the authorities would search would be cafés and hotels. Later it would be churches and the homes of union activists and party leaders. It was better to be on the street, mingling with the crowd. At three o'clock he was going to speak to Agustino so the police would be checking telephones in public places. That was all right. He'd planned for that.

He walked up Avenida Hernando Siles and then began the parallel walk back along Calle Ravelo. The street was busy with trucks, pick-ups and buses belching diesel smoke. Steps led to a Spanish colonial church, high doors open to a sombre nave, and at the far end a glow from candles. On the steps squatted a beggar. He had no arms, just twitching ends to his shoulders, the skin puckered as if it had been drawn together and sewn. What terrible accident had he had? Some giant piece of machinery had sliced off his limbs and his boss had got rid of him because he could no longer work. That was the way it was. A sheet of cardboard served as his begging bowl. When a woman dropped money, the beggar picked up the note between his lips and smuggled it inside his shirt.

Past the market, on, not hurrying, just another old man. The street turned suddenly squalid. Whole families lived on the pavement, had made a village out of it, men with dulled eyes, Quechua women in dark skirts and ponchos and bowler hats, children playing with bottle tops and plastic cartons, babies wrapped in a length of cloth that was swung round the mother's neck. Were the babies born on the street? Were they conceived on the street as men and women huddled on the concrete under a rug? Killing the Police Chief was more than a personal vendetta, it was a political protest. Look at these people, Che screamed in his head. Look at these homeless families. This was what his political act had been about.

How could the rich drive past in their limousines while these people lived without hope? Did the rich not care? Perhaps not even notice? Did they despise the street dwellers, hate them, fear them? Think it was God's will? Believe that nothing could be done or should be done?

If I was half my age again, Che thought, the right side of thirty . . .

People were cooking. Thin corncobs roasted on a charcoal pot. A mess of rice was coloured by chilli sauce. Potatoes were boiled and eaten with salt. People squatted by sacks on which were goods for sale: a dozen chillies, bunches of wild herbs, garlic sold not by the bulb but by the single clove.

A slogan was daubed on a wall in red and bright as new blood: 'GOLPE AL HAMBRE.' Another slogan shouted: 'EL PUEBLO JUNTO A SES MARTIRES.'

Che stared. He and Inti and Ramón and Pacho and the others had been martyrs.

Look at the street dwellers and say a revolution wasn't needed. Twenty years ago he had been betrayed. Had anything changed?

A group of naked women stood in the Parque Bolívar. They cupped their breasts with one hand, clutched towels to their pubic ruffs with the other. Water from the fountain kept their bodies shiny. Their expressions, if you looked at the faces, were dumbfounded more than anything, as if they were surprised to be discovered taking a shower in public. Che stared at them because with statues you could always maintain you were studying the sculptor's art. The park sloped down to the railway station, a massive structure out of scale with its dozen trains a week. Oaks, palms and pines softened the red stone of the building.

From the centre of the city Che heard a police siren, joined in a moment by the bell of an ambulance. Ah yes, the grave had been opened. Time to act.

He crossed the road to the supreme court, a fine white temple to the principles of the law. Here, in this one building, was the whole contradiction of justice in Latin America. Justice was akin to a funfair. There was nothing certain about it. You shied coconuts and if it was your lucky day you staggered off with your prize. It seemed at first sight to be a tremendous prize wrapped in glittering cellophane and fancy ribbons. Strip away all the promising finery and what did you find? A pitiful doll that broke in your hands. Justice? You might as well look for it in the lion's cage as in this legal palace.

Drawn up at the steps was a black Mercedes and where its number should be was a plate lettered *Corte Suprema*. The driver wore a dark uniform and dozed behind the wheel. The windows were closed, which Che hadn't expected. He went to the passenger side and tapped on the glass. The driver opened his eyes, frowning at the sight of the old man. Che, with one hand in his pocket, gestured at the back wheel with the other. He mouthed: You've got a flat tyre. Eh? the driver shrugged. Che gestured again and mouthed 'Puncture' until the driver leant across and opened the door.

'What do you say?'

'Thank you,' Che said, sliding on to the seat.

'Old fellow, you're making a terrible mistake. Don't you know whose car this is?'

'And don't you know what this is?' Che showed the pistol that was half out of his pocket.

'I am the driver of the Chief Justice of Bolivia. This car is at the disposal of His Excellency . . .'

Che pulled the pistol fully out of his pocket. Encouraged by this sight, the driver started the engine and drew smoothly away from the supreme court. A face behind one of the glass doors watched. What would he say afterwards? What would be his excuse for letting Che Guevara walk up to the Chief Justice's car and force the chauffeur to drive off?

'Take the Cochabamba road,' Che said.

'Do you imagine you can hijack this car all the way to Cochabamba? You'll be stopped long before then.'

'If we are stopped, you won't do anything foolish? Just say I'm one of the judge's servants. That should do the trick.'

'Who are you? What do you want?'

'A little ride, a little talk. I may have to tie you up but you'll be unharmed.'

'You'll never get away with it,' the driver said with some relish, 'never. It's against all reason.'

The car swung through a square where the spray-can artists had been at work. 'GLORIA A LOS CAIDOS,' he read. And 'VIVA LA REVOLUCION'. Who were these radicals? he wondered. Did they ever plan to *do* anything but paint walls?

'Are you a robber?' the driver asked. 'Do you hold up banks?'

'It's the banks who rob.' But Che was engulfed by a wave of tedium at the prospect of trying to realign such a man's political viewpoint. The pistol was the better argument. 'Do you know what this makes me? At this moment it makes me the Chief Justice of Bolivia. Remember that.'

The car left the city centre for the ring road that ran round Sucre. Here was the chaos of poverty: boys kicking a tin can, girls of seven or eight minding babies, men with trays of combs, women selling single cigarettes from open packets. Stopped at a traffic light, Che watched a woman dig into the earth bank and take out three potatoes. The earth wasn't her larder, it was her shop, for she sold the potatoes to another woman. The Mercedes bumped over disused railway lines on to the Cochabamba road. Ahead, just before the bus terminal, there were flashing blue lights on police cars slewed across the road.

'You won't forget this,' Che said, half showing the pistol again. 'Tell me, do you have a wife? Children perhaps? With a man your age, the children would still be living at home.'

The driver didn't answer but Che noticed a moustache of sweat.

A taxi in front of them was slowing for the roadblock. To stop was to lose the initiative, Che knew. The driver had already lifted his foot from the accelerator.

'Keep going,' Che barked at him.

On an impulse Che leant across and gave a blast on the horn.

That was the way to behave. Two policemen lifted their heads and seeing the car of a supreme court judge approaching, waved it on. One saluted as they passed and Che returned a languid wave.

'On,' Che ordered. He had his eyes on the nearest range of hills. No further. The car was equipped with a radio-telephone but he was ignorant of its range.

'What do they call Sucre?'

The driver stared at him, not understanding these social niceties, understanding only that the belt cut into the flesh of his wrists and that if he tugged against the steering wheel it bit harder.

'You've heard they call Venice the Pearl of the Adriatic. Personally I don't think anyone ever said he was going on a visit to the Pearl of the Adriatic but you get the idea. Possibly they call Sucre the Bejewelled Crown of Bolivia. What do you say?'

The sparkling white city lay below them bordered on three sides by hills. The statue of Christ rose above eucalyptus trees on the slope of Cerro Churuquilla, a tiny figure on a distant calvary. The driver, hunched sideways on the seat, cast one glance at the view and stared at Che again. He was not happy, not a talker.

'I tell you what I would call Sucre,' Che went on. It scarcely mattered to him that he had to provide both sides of the conversation. Over the years he'd got used to it. Indeed he'd preferred the talks he'd had with himself to the talks he'd had with others. Such as Dr Quiroz. Such as Comandante Mendoza. Such . . . Come, he told himself, concentrate on the task in hand. 'What was I saying? Ah yes, Sucre. I would call it the White Bandage of Bolivia. Don't you think that is poetic? Go on, look, really look. See how it binds up the wounded land. Observe the grey pus of the slums oozing out at the edges.'

'How long will I be tied up?'

'Not long. For your sake I hope it's not long. I have to make a call on your telephone. To you it may seem extreme to be kidnapped simply so I can telephone a radio station but I couldn't do it in the city. Not safely. Police and army everywhere.'

They were maggots crawling under the White Bandage. Come, Che chided himself, forget the fantasies. It is time.

He couldn't dial direct on the radio-telephone. He spoke to the central exchange, giving the number of Radio Colosal. This would set in motion a frenzied effort to trace the origin of the call. But he was safe up in the hills.

'Hello.'

'Is that Agustino?'

'Yes, yes, this is Tio Tino.'

'Do you recognize my voice? Che Guevara.'

'You're late. We thought you weren't going to call.'

'We?'

'I'm at the cemetery. We've established a mobile unit near the grave.'

'You see,' Che said, 'I was telling the truth, wasn't I?'

Straining his ears, Che could hear a voice in the background.

'Tell me your phone number,' Agustino said, 'in case we get cut off.'

Che gave a dim smile. It was like dealing with a child who was wheedling for a treat. Now there were several voices raised.

'And this is going out on the air? You're broadcasting, not just speaking to me on the telephone?'

'This is going out live.'

'My side of the conversation too?'

'Yes, so I must warn you – '

'What are those voices? And that knocking I can hear?'

'It is because of Comandante Mendoza. They cannot move him.'

'Cannot? Explain yourself.'

'It is not the kind of thing we put out on the air.'

'Your listeners rely on you. They can only see through your eyes. Are you going to disappoint them?'

'They cannot move the body of Comandante Mendoza out of the niche. It is a delicate matter to explain. The, er, gases have built up inside him and his stomach has distended so much that even when the grille is pushed right up it jams. I mean his stomach jams. It has blown up like a balloon, bursting open his shirt buttons.'

Agustino had no tone of voice for dealing with the grimmer

side of life. He stumbled over the words. Then his voice brightened to the Tio Tino who babbled out requests. 'But it's a lovely sunny afternoon here in the cemetery and there's a terrific crowd of curious citizens. In a moment I will talk with some of them. Ernesto? Che? That banging you mentioned . . .'

'Yes?'

'They are knocking off the grille that's causing the obstruction.'

'There is an easier way.'

'I'm sure an easier way would be appreciated.'

'Puncture the stomach and release the gases.'

Silence. Che tried to picture the scene: the pout on Agustino's face, a score of police with their hands fidgeting with their guns, the expectant crowd, one cursing workman banging at the iron grille with a hammer, birds singing among the gravestones, white puffball clouds gambolling across Tio Tino's blue heaven. Now there was some sort of argument at the edge of the microphone's effective range. Che picked out a phrase or two: 'mosaic thought patterns', and 'bloody loony'. The second voice had the angry frustration the commonsense man feels when confronted by the expert's jargon.

'You still there?'

'That's what they do to horses when they're blown,' Che explained. 'Puncture the stomach. It should work for a pig too. Where did you think I'd gone? The confessional?'

'Here, give that to me.' Che heard a new voice, pompous beyond its years, one of the Comandantes of tomorrow. 'Now listen here. This is Captain Choque of the National Police. The corpse of this highly respected – not to say dedicated and selfless – public servant has been discovered in the place you indicated. Now, if you truly killed the Comandante as you claim, then I order you to surrender yourself to the nearest police officer.'

Fantastic. Worthy to wear the mantle of leadership.

'Hello? You haven't run away?'

'I've been considering how best to give you my answer.'

'What is it?'

'No.'

'In accordance with the Presidential decree of – '

'Both your parents must have been stupid. They were stupid ever to conceive such a son. Since birth you have been raised in stupidity, which has been finally refined by your police training. So keep quiet while I say this. I am Che Guevara and far from being killed nearly twenty years ago, I am alive and capable of acting. The world was told gross lies about my death. The world was kept in ignorance of my imprisonment. The world knows nothing of the tortures and indignities I have suffered. Now is the time for the world to sit up and take notice. I have embarked on a course of revolutionary justice. I cannot be revenged on all who were implicated in my imprisonment. Most assumed I was just a common political prisoner and closed their ears and eyes. But the men who knew I was Guevara and deliberately tortured me for their own gratification – these men I am now executing. The first was Doctor Quiroz in Potosi. The authorities, more thick-headed even than you, convinced themselves it was suicide. The second is Comandante Mendoza. There will be one more. I have not the time or the appetite to search out the minor sadists. But the third man – I shall track him down wherever he has hidden. He should prepare himself for death. Let him see to his will, pension off his mistresses, kiss his children goodbye.'

Choque cleared his throat and announced, 'I order you not to kill this gentleman, whoever he is.'

'Or whatever he has done. Of course that is how you think. You are the same species of animal as he is, only you are the family cat and he is the tiger. Now listen closely. When the third man is dead, I shall speak again. Not to you. Or to the prattler on Radio Colosal. I shall speak to the world. I shall go to the United Nations and demand my voice is heard because the truth must be known. There is a man who condemned the revolution in Bolivia to failure. This Judas betrayed honest fighters for social justice and it is only right that he end his life in shame, reviled by mankind. I swear to do this. You have the word of Che Guevara.'

Emotional, histrionic even. Too bad. There had been no holding it back any longer. Che found he had closed his eyes to concentrate on his message. When he opened them, tears of rage blurred his vision.

Captain Choque, out of his depth, was mumbling, 'You have murdered the Chief of Police. You will be captured. Better to give yourself up now. There is no possibility of escape. You are surrounded. Every road out of Sucre has already been sealed. Every man's hand will be against . . .'

Che held the telephone away from his ear.

'Listen to that. Who does he think he's speaking to? Perhaps his General is glowering at him.'

Captain Choque's voice droned on. He was a fly beating against a windowpane. Che gave a sharp tug, wrenching the cord out of the radio set, and the fly was cut off. He tossed the phone into some bushes.

The driver's face was a marvel. His eyes darted everywhere, taking in Che's expression, his hands, the scar at his throat. They were wide-open eyes, round with fear. His skin had paled and sweat left slug-trails down his cheeks.

'Afraid I'm going to kill you too?' Che asked. 'What kind of man do you imagine Guevara is?'

When there was no answer, Che got out and began to walk. Excitement was running through his veins. He could feel it like a motor driving him on.

CHAPTER 12

They crossed over the uMgeni, a mean-spirited solid bridge that prevented you seeing the river, and drove north through Durban's suburbs. Tanner saw neat houses with black maids cleaning windows, neat flowerbeds with black gardeners standing with hoses, black nannies rocking prams with invisible babies. He thought of saying black shantytowns weren't as bad as the overseas media made out but he looked at Van der Merwe's face and decided no. The sun hadn't yet risen on that Orange Free State sense of humour.

'Hotel okay?' Van der Merwe asked.

'Lonely.'

'Didn't have to be. Plenty of Jo'burg Widows stay there. They come for a month and their husbands only join them at weekends.'

'Those the ones eyeing me in the corridor? I thought they came from your department.'

'Want to be surprised? My department runs more to Zulu maids. People think: only a coon, she won't understand. They gabble about everything except sex. People don't talk sex in front of the blacks because everybody knows blacks are hot at screwing. They know that like they know it's foggy every day in London. They've never experienced either. My advice is stick to the Jo'burg Widows because they're grateful. Also you've got novelty value. You're a limey but you're not queer. They think London is full of homos buggering themselves in the fog.'

'Well, it is legal,' Tanner said. 'But it's not compulsory.'

They passed between sugar-cane fields. Tanner had seen a lot of sugar-cane in Latin America and was not impressed. It was endless boring green. The sugar-cane covered rolling hills, soft as a thigh. Got sex on the brain. Better chat up one of the JWs tonight. The car turned off the highway before a town signposted Verulam.

'Pity you missed that,' Van der Merwe said. 'It's the fourth largest town in Natal.'

Great, Tanner thought, super, absolutely bloody spiffing. I'm here on a paid holiday with the secret police as guide, chauffeur, mentor and pimp. Go for a JW. Here's the fourth biggest town. Later we visit the third biggest barbed-wire factory.

'It's all Indian. It's going to be Bombay when it grows up.'

And right now we're on our way to visit the first most dangerous commie terrorist in the continent of Africa. Just as a favour between sister services. Just to see if he'll talk to an emissary of the Great White Queen from across the seas because he sure as hell won't spit out any secrets to his jailers.

'How long have you had him?'

Van der Merwe glanced at Tanner because their talk hadn't touched on work yet this morning.

'Ntuli?'

'Yes.'

'Year, more or less.'

'What's he convicted of? Talking to an American reporter without permission?'

'He's not convicted of anything.'

'Well, what's he charged with?'

'Nothing.'

Tanner looked out at the passing scenery. The car was climbing up a curving road. The sugar-cane had given way to a patchwork of maize, beans, pumpkins and the beaten earth of cattle pens. Each hillside had a collection of thatched round huts. Black children came running with their hands outstretched, shouting for coins or sweets.

'KwaZulu,' Van der Merwe said. 'Or a piece of it.'

'Doesn't *habeas corpus* apply in South Africa?'

'There are a number of laws and decrees under which he could be arrested and held. Basically, when you boil it right down, it comes to this: if we want to hold him, we can. For ever.'

'His life doesn't belong to him, it belongs to you.'

'Mr Tanner, some people would say your life belongs to God. Others that it belongs to the state or the Führer. Or to your class or your race or your tribe or your gang. Only a tiny privileged percentage of the world has the luxury of claiming their lives are their own. You think your life belongs to you? Believe me, there are areas of this country where I could put you down and you'd rapidly realize your life belonged to other people.'

Now Tanner saw bungalows with corrugated-iron roofs and Indian families, huge mango trees, gangling pawpaws, bananas pushing each other over. The land had a familiar feel. He could be on a country road between Rio and Santos, even somewhere in Cuba. But the atmosphere shimmered with alien vibrations.

'There is a hell of a difference to my life being forfeit in a black shantytown, or a back street in Kingston, Jamaica, or an alley in Harlem. The state is meant to serve the interest of its citizens, not deny it. Still,' and Tanner thought to soften the criticism, 'I do understand your predicament.'

'Predicament? That what you call it? Wait till you're confronted by Moses Ntuli.'

The road was still climbing and the air was noticeably fresher after the humidity of the coast. They'd passed out of the piece of KwaZulu. Round a corner was a big farmhouse set back from the road. A paddock lay to one side with four horses standing in the shade of eucalyptus trees, a girl perching on a white fence.

'You tell me what you'd do if you had to deal with Ntuli,' Van der Merwe said. 'What route you'd take to the promised land.'

As the car drew level the horses broke into a canter and the girl twisted to watch them pass.

'And don't tell me you wouldn't start from here,' he went on. 'I'm a Van der Merwe, don't forget. They tell Irish jokes against me.'

They left the tar for an unsignposted dirt road. They passed through a wattle plantation in silence. Van der Merwe slowed as the car approached a gate by a guardhouse. There was a double wire fence with a dog-run in between. Dobermanns kept pace with them.

'What's this place called?' Tanner asked.

'I'll tell you what the detainees call it: the provisional capital of free Azania.'

*

The door closed behind Tanner and he heard the key turn. He felt that surge of panic that people who have been imprisoned in Latin America feel: this time the key will be thrown away. Cells I have known, Tanner thought. Sometimes visiting, sometimes as a prisoner. Show me a cell and I'll tell you the regime. A prison is a distorting mirror of the world outside the gate. In Sweden expect a social cure: curtains, television, toilet, conjugal visits. In Latin America expect degradation: grime and a bucket. In Colombia, falling foul of the *narcos* in Caquetá, Tanner had been locked up for three nights and there hadn't even been a bucket: you shouted for the warder and offered him money to let you go out into the yard. If you had no pesos for a bribe, you used the floor and were forced to clean up in the morning. And in South Africa?

Before he looked at Ntuli, he looked at his environment. The cell was larger than he expected, built for two or three or four inmates. Breezeblocks, whitewashed. A single window at chest height, barred and without glass. That wasn't for the sake of economy. The prisoner must not be allowed to break glass and use a splinter to open an artery. The prisoner's life doesn't belong to him but to his captors. The gospel according to Van der Merwe.

In the ceiling was a light protected by a wire security cage which looked distinctly familiar. Get away, he scolded himself, all wire guards look the same. Nonetheless he was struck by the similarity with the light fittings in certain rooms in the Bunker. Could the same manufacturer have been doing a flourishing export trade with South Africa?

In the corners of the ceiling, spiders' webs with dead flies.

A basin with a single lidded bucket next to it.

The floor was concrete, easy to hose down.

There was no mirror, no reflective surface where a man might stare at his own face. He would see only his captors, would forget what his own features were like, so that if he caught a glimpse of himself reflected in some pane of glass he would have become a stranger. Isolated from the world, Ntuli would begin to lose his identity and so his sense of purpose. A man draws strength from companions, even his own reflection; alone he weakens.

Dropping his eyes on Ntuli at last, Tanner abandoned this flight of fancy.

Ntuli lay stretched on a concrete bunk built out from the wall. There was a mattress, a pillow, two blankets, and Ntuli lay on top of the blankets. He wore a khaki boilersuit, much laundered, so the cotton fabric was fraying at the seams. It was buttoned to the neck as if he was used to the coast and at this modest height he felt a chill. Tanner took him in at a glance and didn't know how to address him. Moses? Ntuli? Mister? There was going to be no right way to speak to him because he was a political detainee and Tanner was a visitor blessed by his jailers.

'My name is Phil Tanner and I've come from England because I think you might be able to help us. Oh, I work for a department of the British Foreign Office,' he said, using the well-worn phrase. There was no response. I'm not believed, I'm not trusted, Tanner decided, I'm on stage and the other actor has forgotten his lines. He got going again. 'A British subject has been murdered in the United States and we are following his movements in the past year to try to get a clue why he was killed. That should help us pin the murder on the person or persons responsible.'

Person or persons, for God's sake. Tanner was cross with himself for lapsing into officialese. Next he'd be spouting about the deceased's next of kin and – what was it Van der Merwe had complained of? – the alleged murder weapon.

'His name was Benjamin Morton. Ben, I suppose he was called. I don't know whether or not you met him but Martina probably talked about him. He and Martina were travelling together. They were close friends. You know the Martina I mean?'

The impressive thing was Ntuli's stillness. Was he drugged to the gills? Perhaps they had given him a shot of something to smooth Tanner's way. His eyes were open, gazing at the ceiling. Well then, was he sick? In a trance? Dead?

'Martina Mancilla, of course. She was here in South Africa interviewing . . .' Tanner hesitated over the right description. 'Interviewing a whole lot of people. She saw you a couple of times, I believe. Did she talk about her Ben at all?'

Ntuli wasn't dead. His chest rose and fell slowly. Then Tanner understood: Tanner wasn't here, he didn't exist. Where he stood there was a hole in space. He felt a rage growing in him: he wasn't one of the jailers, the interrogators, the torturers. He was nothing at all to do with the regime; he was simply out from

London to do a job he didn't care for but which needed doing. He had the urge to grab Ntuli by the boilersuit and shake him until their eyes met and he was forced to acknowledge . . .

Tanner took a deep breath to stifle the emotion.

'Martina and Ben were staying together at the Elangeni. They were lovers. She must have chatted about him. It's a woman's way to talk about her man. Even a woman as committed as Martina doesn't shove her man into a separate box. He is a vital part of her life and she naturally brings him into conversation. So you must have heard about him.'

Ntuli's silence was becoming arrogance. He appreciated why Van der Merwe had said, You tell me what you'd do if you had to deal with him. Ntuli didn't answer questions; he didn't appear to hear; he didn't acknowledge Tanner's existence. Tanner found his own position ridiculous: he was standing, a supplicant begging a favour, while Ntuli lay on his back, at ease.

'Ben Morton travelled around South America and then went to Florida. He stayed at Martina's house. He was found murdered there and Martina has vanished. You know her, you've met her, which I never have. Do you think she could have killed him?'

Tanner became aware of silence. There wasn't just an absence of noise in this cell, it was silent outside, silent in the whole camp. A prison always has a background of noise because of the number of men locked up and the warders guarding them, let alone the sounds of machines and plumbing and dogs. This whole place seemed to be holding its breath while it listened to him make a fool of himself. Van der Merwe had said he would leave Tanner to do his questioning on his own but there would be a hidden microphone and a tape recorder. No secrets in this confessional.

Tanner swallowed. 'I doubt she would have killed him. It wasn't some lovers' quarrel that turned violent. The thing that strikes me – and it should worry you – was that she has disappeared. Could the people who killed Ben have kidnapped her? Were they political opponents? Comrades who became enemies?'

If there was no chair to sit on, how did Van der Merwe manage? Obviously Ntuli must be taken away for interrogation. But Van der Merwe had pushed Tanner into the cell and locked the door and left him to this humiliation.

Did they punch Ntuli? Five minutes was enough for Tanner's patience to run out and for the urge to violence to well up. Talk, you black bastard. Or he should take him out for a drink. Crack a bottle of KWV brandy, tell a few jokes, be rude about the system, fantasize about the girl who brought the coffee at Van der Merwe's place, her softness, her rolling walk. If you can't beat 'em, join 'em. And if you can do neither, cut your losses and get out.

'Don't you care that she's vanished?' Tanner found himself pleading without any conscious decision. It was chattering to fill the emptiness. Think of all the way she'd come, and the risks she'd taken to see him twice, and she must have talked about something, and now she's gone and her lover is dead and didn't he find himself moved to help in the tiniest bit? 'It might help me find her and Morton's killers if you said what you'd talked about, gave me the names of contacts, where . . .'

Damn. That was a stupid mistake. Asking for a list of names was just what Van der Merwe would have done. It had an effect on Ntuli, as if Tanner had let his disguise slip. He was frowning.

'I think,' Tanner ploughed on, 'she brought you a message from some outside organization and for some reason that organization has silenced Morton. Are you the kind of person who protects murderers? I can't believe it. Maybe the others – ' and Tanner waved a hand to include the hidden listeners, ' – have that idea about you because of the confrontation between . . .'

Tanner didn't finish because Ntuli swung himself off the bed and in three strides was in front of him. They stood face to face, much the same height. The irises of Ntuli's eyes were brown, the whites had yellowish patches as if they were nicotine stained. Ntuli had the appearance of a big man who had lost weight. The muscles of his neck stood out like ropes. He was younger and stronger than Tanner and stared in a way that said: I could break your neck before anyone came to your aid. Tanner supposed Van der Merwe was at the spyhole in the door, watching, content to let the Englishman feel the force that was in Ntuli.

With deliberation Ntuli raised his arm and pointed a finger at the window. When Tanner didn't move, Ntuli's eyes shifted to the window. Go, his eyes said, there's something there for you to see.

Tanner crossed the cell to the window. He saw the double boundary fence, trees and hills beyond, a clear blue sky. Not that. It was close, right in front of the window. A hole was dug in the ground, the earth piled to one side. The hole was narrow and a little longer than a man, say the length of a coffin. At the end were two planks nailed in the shape of a cross on which was daubed in white paint: 'Moses Ntuli 1956– '. The year of his death wasn't filled in.

When Tanner swung round he found Ntuli lying on his bunk again. He gazed at the ceiling. Tanner had existed for only a brief moment.

'Not a word, as you know.'

'So what would you do?'

'Let him go.'

'He would be swallowed up in some township and the violence would move up a gear or two.'

'How about if he stood for parliament at the next election.'

They drove in silence.

'He talked in the beginning apparently,' Van der Merwe said. 'He gave away nothing important but at least he answered when he was spoken to. Then they sent to Pretoria for a new man who had a reputation for always getting information. He'd probably been questioning children. With Ntuli he had no success. Just the opposite. He won't even ask for a glass of water now. When I first came here he was referred to as the Trappist monk. You notice he keeps his boilersuit buttoned up.'

'Yes.'

'To hide the scars.'

'I see.'

The girl no longer sat on the fence. The horses were still in the paddock and cantered away.

'I got the shit-hot interrogator recalled to Pretoria. He was a colonel but I told him to his face: You've turned Ntuli into a clam; the more you hit one, the tighter it shuts up.'

Some black kids outside a kraal waved at the passing car. Tanner waved back.

'By the way,' Van der Merwe said, 'you've been getting phone calls at your hotel, so I'm told. Unofficially, of course.'

'You don't know who it is, unofficially?'

'It might be a courtesy,' Van der Merwe said, 'if I dropped you off at the apartment Mr Mathews uses.'

Tanner's thoughts went back to the waiting grave. Whose idea was that? It didn't sound like the colonel from Pretoria, not immediate enough. Had they made Ntuli dig it himself? That's what the Nazis had done with the Jews. As a courtesy, Moses old chap, you can choose the depth.

The rest of the drive was in silence, nothing spoken to interrupt their thoughts. What does a man in Van der Merwe's position think about, Tanner wondered. The future of his country? The tactics of his next interrogation? The wobbly spine of the visiting Brit? Or the mishmash we all think: the stupidity of the boss, the carelessness of the juniors, money, relations with rival services, relations of a more intimate kind?

Nothing to say to each other, like a whore and her client, business done, desires defeated. Only which of us is the tart, which her punter?

There must be bigger camps than that because there had been thousands of arrests. Where were they, these big prisons, what were they like? What did people think, seeing hundreds of black political prisoners behind wire? Or did they not see them like Ntuli had not seen me? That was just a little place set among rolling green hills. Old Billy Butlin would have recognized it. The huts set in regimented lines, the concrete paths, the floodlights in clusters of four on tall poles, the loudspeakers on the corners of buildings. Wakey wakey campers, rise and shine, a new day, a new world to build, a new revolution, a new round of interrogation, a new pain built on the old one.

Butlin had made a fortune persuading people that old army barracks were the place to have fun. He'd ended up Sir Billy. Perhaps in some future people would holiday in that prison camp. It needed a man of vision to see its potential. Arise Sir Moses.

*

'You know what this country makes me feel like sometimes, son?' Ed Mathews was standing at the window when Verucci let Tanner into the room. 'South Africa makes me feel like the eunuch in a harem. There's not a damn thing I can do but if anything goes wrong I know I'm for the axe. Welcome to the State Apartment.'

Mathews turned round with his arms stretched wide in extravagant greeting. Tanner found his hand enveloped in a two-fisted grasp, like a secret ritual he should recognize. Mathews nodded down towards the street.

'I see you are on friendly terms with the overworked Major. How do you find him?'

'I don't,' Tanner said. 'He finds me.'

'Well, that is his job.'

'And friendship doesn't come into it. It's a working relationship between two professional organizations, that's all.'

'My, my, you two sound like you've been having a spat. If you were boy and girl, I'd say you should get to bed and work things out.'

Tanner recovered his hand and went to sit in the only chair that wasn't overflowing with cushions. It was the look-out chair that Verucci had used yesterday, peering between the slats of the venetian blind, watching for watchers, and when Tanner had walked out of the apartment, making the signal.

Tanner looked out and saw Van der Merwe had driven away. He wondered if there was some little watcher out of sight, or whether the apartment was bugged.

'Got a beer in the icebox with your name on it,' Verucci said. He had a soft voice, perfect for breathing secrets down a sleeve-mike. His anonymous face had arranged itself into a half-smile. You don't squander a whole-hearted smile in this job, Tanner thought. The smile kept going while Tanner asked himself questions: Why hasn't Mathews asked where I've been? Why doesn't he ask how Van der Merwe knows me? The answers were obvious.

'You better have one with my name on too, Dick. Go get 'em.' Mathews eased himself into one of the fat chairs and sighed. 'That Van der Merwe, you could be mistaken about him. He's not a bad son of a bitch, he's just perplexed. He doesn't know what to do. They none of them know what to do. Phil, I've been two years in this country and I've seen their frowns grow deeper by the day. There was a time – some years back, say under Verwoerd – when there were certainties in his world. The laws were carved in granite. The white man was boss and the black man was under his boot. Segregation was complete. Nothing would change. God had settled the Afrikaner nation in this country, his chosen people. Anybody questioned the status, he was a radical, a commie, a denier of God's law. Then the little changes started and the certainties were gone. Like a girl can't be ninety-nine per cent a virgin. Black entertainers were applauded. Black athletes competed against whites and licked the hell out of them. Black politicians in other countries had to be talked to. Blacks had money to spend in white shops. The little changes were accepted, the rigid structure suddenly had holes. Blacks and whites share the beaches and pools now. Blacks go to cinemas and restaurants and hotels that used to be all-white. There are blacks and whites sharing the same beds even. So what comes next? There's no stopping it.'

'He said if the country was going to be destroyed, the Afrikaners would do it themselves.'

'Had he been drinking? Well, the guy's socko, genuinely puzzled by events he can't push his way.' Mathews didn't bother with a glass. He up-ended the bottle and closed his eyes. 'Have you heard the Mathews theory of current events? I'm famous for boring people with it. In its crude form it states that there aren't a thousand separate problems in the world but they are all part of one big problem and everything hangs together. That's why people in our profession should work together. It's Us against the All-problem.'

'You mean . . .' Tanner, feeling at a loss, searched for the most extreme case he could imagine. 'You mean the CIA should co-operate with the KGB.'

'Not should, son, *does*. The Russians go into Afghanistan and are in shit with the Muslim world. We arm Israel and are in shit with the Muslim world. Hey now, we can make common cause there. So we tell the Russians: We're going in to blast Gaddafi so why don't you keep your boys out of the way. And they did.

Result: not one grieving Soviet mother. What's more, they didn't even warn Gaddafi. That's a sick man there, sick in his head, and the Russians damn well know it. Gaddafi is a part of the All-problem. And now, Phil,' and Mathews sighted across the top of the beer bottle at him, 'now we've gotten news of another part of the All-problem and that's what I've been busting to reach you for.'

What had seemed an aimless lecture to Tanner wasn't that at all. It was a preamble that brought Mathews to exactly the point he wanted to make.

'In London, you tip off the security boys and they drop on a fire-bomber. In South Africa, you are chauffeured off to see a detainee you would never have interviewed otherwise. The American reporter who talked to that same detainee suddenly breaks into print in the communist media with an article about Che Guevara's death in Bolivia. The British citizen murdered at her house had just returned from Bolivia. And yesterday, in Bolivia, a most surprising piece of the All-problem saw the light of day. Dick? You want to say your piece?'

Verucci was wearing a different jacket and matching shorts. Yesterday's had been a conservative blue. Today's was a discreet tan. And when he spoke, that was discreet too, soft enough to be coming from the next room.

'Glad to, Ed.' He turned a degree to face Tanner. While Mathews swamped his chair as if he was on a throne, Verucci perched on the edge. 'Phil, I know you are acquainted with the work our National Security Agency does because they have such close links with your GCHQ at Chel-ten-ham.'

'Fine people,' Mathews growled, of the NSA or GCHQ.

Verucci paused a moment to see if Mathews had any other contribution. 'There are some who say their work is even more important than ours. Now, although I certainly don't go that far, there can be no doubt – '

'Right, Dick, he *knows* what they do. It's his job, Dick. You don't have to convert him.'

'Right, Ed. Now the NSA employs many thousands of people who analyse their daily intercepts and since relations between our two organizations are so close they naturally pass across what they consider – '

'Dick, if you don't give it him, I sure as hell will.'

'They can't listen to all the radio stations in the world but this was being broadcast on a security frequency, being rebeamed as it were up to La Paz in Bolivia. Apparently the authorities there don't know – '

'Jesus,' Mathews said as he hauled himself out of the chair. 'You'd think he was running for Congress. Give me the damn report. Where is it? Right, Phil, you read this.'

'It's only a Company précis,' Verucci warned.

'Terrorist slays police chief and doctor,' Tanner read at the top, *'claims he is Che Guevara.'*

'If some weirdo claims he is Guevara,' Verucci said, 'no one pays any heed. But if there's been a big splash just a few days before about how Guevara is absolutely and certainly and without any shadow of doubt dead, then that looks like smoke and adds rather than subtracts to the likelihood that Guevara is alive.'

'Those analysts.' Mathews shook his head in wonder.

'What is your judgement, Phil?'

Forget the cock-up theory of history and the conspiracy theory. This was the reversal theory. Fair enough, they inhabited a looking-glass world. Tanner put the beer bottle down. It seemed to be empty. His judgement, eh? Rational thought processes didn't seem of much value. He'd come to South Africa to sniff round for Morton's possible spy connections when he'd felt in his guts it was a waste of time. Now here was a wild story being given credence by a clumsy denial. But it did suggest a motive for the murder of Morton. If Morton had met the man who claimed he was Guevara. If he was Guevara. If, if, if.

Madman? Hoax? Publicity stunt?

'He's going to kill a third time,' Tanner said, checking the précis. 'Another of the torturers. Can we work out who that is? And he talks of exposing the person who betrayed the revolution. What does that mean?'

'I kind of hoped you'd know,' Mathews said. 'You're the ace on South America.'

Well, Tanner had been the junior in charge of paperclips

twenty years ago. Yet he recalled there had been gossip, speculation about the scrappy end of the guerrillas. And South America was a continent of impossibilities and magic and tricks and illusions. But Che alive? Even in Bolivia, that weirdest dream of all?

'Strictly this is nothing to do with me,' Mathews said. 'South America is not my field. But I can tell you what the Company's thinking is on this without having to ask Langley. Suppose Guevara turned out to be alive. We sure as hell would want him rather than let the Russians get him in their hands.'

What had happened to the great KGB–CIA mutual admiration society, Tanner wondered. But he didn't ask. A phone was ringing in another room and Verucci had gone to answer it. He put his head round the door.

'Phil, it's for you. London.'

The long arm of Hershey, Tanner suspected.

'Another dose of jet lag, huh?'

Tanner nodded.

'Couldn't help overhearing your side of it. You told him you felt fried?'

'Friared.'

'Well now, son, you've lost me. Friared?'

'You've heard of Robin Hood? Bloke who helped him was Friar Tuck. Think about it.'

Why couldn't he take the direct flight from Durban next day? But Hershey had put on a brisk voice and said his holiday by the sea was over. A seat had been booked from Johannesburg that evening and Tanner had been too tired to argue. He tried to sleep on the connecting flight from Durban but it was more of a feverish doze. He was next to the wing and the jet engine roared inside his head. Maybe I'm sickening, he thought, headache, clammy hands, tightness in the chest.

He hadn't kissed Van der Merwe goodbye but the Major knew he was going, no doubt. At the check-in desk they'd asked for identity papers, muttering about security regulations, and turning back he'd seen the clerk speaking into a telephone. Well, so long as they didn't stop him getting out, that's all he asked.

He opened his eyes once on the flight and saw mountains in the distance with snow on a line of jagged peaks. It wasn't the view that had pulled him out of his doze but the smell that had insinuated itself into his weariness. The woman beside him used perfume to define her territory like a dog cocks its leg against every tree and lamp-post.

'Anaïs Anaïs,' Tanner tried.

She turned her head slowly. 'I beg yours?'

'Your perfume. Anaïs Anaïs.' He'd no idea what it smelled like but he'd long admired the name.

She inspected his hair and clothes and he seemed to fail some kind of test. 'Miss Dior,' she said. Her nostrils widened as if she'd detected something unpleasant and she looked away. The hell with her, Tanner thought. She wore a two-piece outfit in a silky green material with bold blue meanders. She looked as if she'd sprayed herself all over with hair lacquer. At night she'd spend ten minutes taking off her make-up while your ardour cooled. A JW going back to the gilded cage. The hell with her again.

At Jan Smuts Airport Tanner passed two unsmiling men whose eyes kept pace with him as he walked through the Domestic arrivals. He made his way up an escalator and on and on and became aware of the man skipping alongside to keep up. Another of Van der Merwe's chums, Tanner thought. No, not that bright pink face. Jehovah's whatnots. The man was hissing, 'I say,' and tipping him a wink. Not interested, and Tanner lengthened his stride. 'No, I say, old chap.' Oh boy, Tanner realized, one of ours, a Foreign Office wonder playing at cloak-and-dagger.

'Who the hell are you?'

'Meadowcroft. From the Embassy. Chancery, actually.'

Chancery types were the worst in Tanner's view. Winchester and Oxford, introverted and superior, knew it all. 'I still don't know you,' Tanner said, 'actually. Show your pass.'

Meadowcroft produced a plasticized card in the palm of his hand, as if he was touting a dirty postcard.

'I'm going to pick up my ticket from the BA desk. Then you can have a chat.'

'Don't bother, old chap. You're not booked on the London flight.' He leant forward to impart a secret. 'Rio tomorrow, lucky fellow, then a connection to Bolivia.'

From the Embassy in Pretoria Tanner spoke on the secure line to Hershey in the Bunker.

'I told you London because we were speaking on an open line. You never know who's listening.'

'What bloody difference does it make?' Tanner wanted to know.

'I don't want the Americans wise to our being in the hunt.'

There was a picture of Balmoral Castle on the wall. Tanner stared at it. Imagine having that as your time-share holiday villa. 'Pardon me for being naïve. I thought they were our allies. They let us use their facilities in Durban. We let them turn Britain into the world's biggest ammunition dump. They pay half the cost of GCHQ. They send over for some branch of the Royal family every year. Why hide I'm going to Bolivia? Why, come to that, do I have to go?'

There was silence and Hershey said, 'Got it out of your system? All right. You have no idea of the uproar here and in Washington.'

'Some crank goes wild and – '

'Belt up and listen.' There was a savageness in the voice that shut Tanner's mouth. 'You're not thinking. Have you forgotten Morton who came back from Bolivia and was murdered? Have you forgotten the telephone link to the Soviet Embassy in Washington? Because the cousins haven't. We know – just *know* – that the State Department is having a sudden brainstorm over this. The President cancelled a routine press conference and the reason is he didn't want to answer questions. Can you imagine the grilling? How about this Che thing? Do you believe it, Mr President? What are you going to do? Ahhh, gentlemen, I don't seem to see the answer on the teleprompter. Are you going to fumble, Mr President? Send the Delta Force in?'

'You're making this up.'

'There is nothing about the White House I could make up that remotely approaches reality. Right here in London we have the media hounding the Foreign Office. Some fool is trying to have an emergency debate in the Commons. Guevara, alive and on the warpath. That opens a lot of old wounds. Can't you understand? The President has called a meeting – we hear, only hear – of the National Security Council.'

'Moscow's reaction?'

'I don't know. We're listening but we haven't heard anything yet. They've made no comment. You'd expect an instant denunciation. Western trick, so on. But they've said nothing. When the Soviets are silent, Phil, what does that mean?'

It's quiet out there tonight, sir, too quiet. I don't like it. Is that what I'm supposed to say, Tanner wondered.

'So,' and the urgent tone changed, became relaxed, or cautious, Tanner couldn't define the difference. 'So Phil, assuming this story isn't a madman's fairytale, I want us to have him. Afterwards we can share him with the Cousins. We'll be able to drive the hardest bargain ever, and Langley will be in our debt for years. But first we have to get him in our hands.'

'Our hands?'

'Your hands.'

'Mine. I see. What back-up do I get?'

'Your hands.'

'Bloody hell, have you any – '

'*Your* hands.'

'But have you no idea of the American presence in Bolivia?'

'I think so. Indeed yes. As your Controller I know better than you. A tremendous presence. The station in La Paz. Certain ex-CIA men who are beyond Congressional control but have kept their links with the Agency and are freebooting down there. Plus the US army doing drug raids in the lowlands. And I know this: there are so damn many of them, you'll hear the thunder of their boots a mile off. You have this advantage: they won't know you're there or what you're doing.'

'But . . .' Stunned, Tanner gaped at the picture of Balmoral. He took a deep breath of Highland air. One lone foot-soldier against the secret armies of the world? It was like a parody of Britain's reduced status among nations. Him, on his own, to trawl the whole of Bolivia? One day the lung-biting cold of the Andes, the next the tropical fevers of the Amazon basin?

'Can you explain why? Suppose Guevara has survived. What's our interest in him? I mean Britain's interest.'

'Student of politics suddenly, Phil? South Africa stirred your conscience?'

'You're asking me to do the impossible and I just want to know it's necessary. Is that so bloody unreasonable? If I was in London I'd have a chat with Polly. I'm a long way from base so I'm asking you.'

'The Political Evaluator would tell you to hold your tongue and get on with your job,' Hershey snapped. He didn't hold with office nicknames.

'Is that all you've got to say?'

There was a pause. What was Hershey doing? Frowning at the Buffet prints? To Tanner's eye it was the Buffet prints that were always frowning.

'South America is the continent of the future.' Hershey was speaking as if he'd sorted out a jumble of reasons. 'That's what some people say, though God knows it's a pretty grim future for all of us if it's true. But someone has told it to the Prime Minister and the Prime Minister has told it to the Foreign Office and the Foreign Office has told it to the Palace. And with the PM pushing and the FO pulling, they've agreed.'

'You're talking about a Royal visit to South America?'

'Yes.'

'I've heard nothing about it.'

'This isn't Washington,' Hershey said. 'We still contrive to keep a secret or two. We've been asked our views – at the very highest level – and the Director-General was against it. But the Prime Minister has refused to pass on his advice. My view was preferred.'

'What are you letting the Royals in for?'

'The plan is a circular tour starting in Caracas, then to Bogotá, La Paz, Brasília and joining the Royal yacht in Rio. That'll be good for Britain in those parts, restore our prestige after the Falklands war, and be good for exports, which is all anybody cares about nowadays.'

'I've just bloody been out there. Why wasn't I told?'

'Because it was too highly classified for you to know.'

Until now, Tanner thought, until now.

'So the idea that Che Guevara might be alive,' Tanner said, 'and rousing the downtrodden masses to revolt during a Royal tour . . .'

He didn't finish. He was silent, thinking about it.

'Phil, we cannot take that risk. The Queen would be advised to call the tour off. We don't want that. Bad for exports. Phil, if that is Guevara, we have to get him. And no whisper of it is to leak out. Think of the stink it would cause: Brits kidnap Che so Queen's tour can go ahead. So you're deniable.'

'Deniable?'

'You know the word, don't you?'

Then Tanner understood. He heard greed in the tone of voice. Oh yes, Hershey would be glad to trade Guevara to the Americans, if the price was right. But deep down there was a more personal reason. Hershey wanted Guevara snapped up so a Royal tour could progress without a hitch. Good for exports. Even better for Hershey. Look what I can do using just one man against all the odds. Imagine what I could achieve if I was Director-General. Tanner was being sent in to gratify his ambition.

Tanner stared up at the picture of Balmoral. Why couldn't the Queen just pop off to her country cottage? Save so much trouble.

CHAPTER 13

How many hours of my life have I wasted in planes? Tanner wondered. How many days have I wasted doing crackpot jobs for a pushy boss? And how many nights have I wasted on my own?

The 727 dropped lower and lower. In the distance was Santa Cruz, no skyscrapers, just a sprawl of houses and commercial blocks and the smokestacks of small factories. Closer, like a horse galloping in panic, was the shadow of the plane. It raced over grassland, skipped mosquito ponds, jumped over lone palm trees. Tanner saw his first Bolivian. He drove a motorbike across a field, scattering cattle.

'We shall shortly be landing at . . .'

First in Portuguese because it was a Brazilian plane, then in English, lastly in Spanish. The airport at Santa Cruz was called Viru Viru, like some tropical disease.

The plane made a circuit of the airport. It could have been specially laid on so Tanner could study the American presence, the ungainly transport aircraft, the big helicopters used for airlifting troops, the jeeps and fuel tankers, the wooden cabins erected as command posts. The Americans had been allowed in to help the Bolivian army find and destroy the cocaine labs in the jungle to the north. It had been a temporary measure but those cabins and the barbed-wire compound had taken on a permanent air. It was too far off to see if the Americans had planted flowerbeds. That was when you knew they had settled in for good.

What amazing luck it was for the Americans. They had men, transport and radio communications right on the spot. They could fly in fifty CIA agents and nobody would be any the wiser. If they got to Guevara first he could be smuggled out to Langley and nobody need ever know.

How could the KGB compete against that? What logistical support could Cuba offer?

What the hell could one lone Brit do?

The plane made its final approach and touched down well away from the American compound. There was a roar of reverse thrust and the plane turned down a taxiway to the terminal building.

Welcome to Bolivia, Tanner told himself, welcome to schizophrenia. Up in the Andes, in the Altiplano, it was cold and gasping. Here in the lowlands it was steamy and dripping, the air thick with humidity. Moisture greyed the sky and hazed the sun. Just walking to the terminal raised a sweat.

Welcome.

How many hours of his life had he wasted in airport lounges? There were three hours to wait before the mid-afternoon flight to Sucre. He thought of taking a taxi into town for lunch but he remembered Santa Cruz really only woke up at dusk and the better restaurants, the air-conditioned ones where he wouldn't melt into a puddle, didn't do business in the middle of the day. He hadn't much appetite anyway and even less when he inspected the sandwiches in the café.

He settled down with a cup of coffee and the local newspaper. He was disappointed. There was nothing new about Guevara. He was no longer even the lead story. Instead there was the scandal of a police raid in Cochabamba which yielded a bishop and a young woman. The bishop wore nothing. The girl wore his crucifix. The press happened to be passing, purely by chance, by a tremendous coincidence, at the very moment the police obligingly pushed the unhappy couple on to the street. A smudgy photo showed the bishop covering his genitals, the girl putting a hand over her eyes and nose. It was like the old joke: I don't know about you but I'm recognized by my face. The bishop, the article mentioned, was an outspoken critic of the government. Ah, motive.

Tanner noticed them. It was the first time. Or to be strictly truthful it was the woman he registered. She was crossing from the counter carrying two cups.

He turned back to the paper. There was a Guevara story after all. He had missed it under the fold. Or a pseudo-Guevara story. The bricking up of the Police Chief was being claimed 'by a hitherto unknown group calling themselves the Hand of Allah, punishing Zionists and their lackeys who lick the boots of the imperialist Washington clique'. Oh boy, oh wowie, he'd heard everything now. Arab crazies disputing the honours with Bolivian crazies.

She sat down only two tables away. There was a man there whose back was turned to Tanner. He couldn't see the face but the rear view was jolly: roly-poly body, a bald head. Even without a glimpse of his face it was obvious he was much older than the woman. But not father and daughter: she was *latina* and he wasn't.

The last paragraph said the police were making headway in solving this gruesome crime and were confident of making an arrest at any blah blah blah. Or looked at another way, they were hopelessly adrift.

What a face she had: full lips, almost Jewish in their sexuality, consuming eyes, very white teeth against her tan skin. She wore blue cotton slacks and a canary yellow T-shirt with the legend across her breasts: 'DANGEROUS COCKTAILS.'

The authorities in Sucre, Tanner read, were discontinuing their morning press conferences. There would be no further announcements until the arrest was made.

Sometimes you feel another's gaze on you. It's as if a message passes down the sightlines, taps at another's being, and enters. Sensing Tanner's stare she lifted her head and her eyes met his and didn't drop. The café should have sounded to the crack of steel on steel. It had happened to Tanner before, but not often. The last time it had been that cliché: across a crowded room. Eyes meet and an unspoken dialogue begins, challenges are issued and accepted, challenges to battle or to love. Sometimes you couldn't tell the difference.

She stared with such fierceness that her companion noticed and turned to look at Tanner. He had white eyebrows and rosy cheeks and must be thirty years older than the woman. Make that thirty-five. It was a peasant's face but a peasant from Central Europe not from South America. It was accustomed to snows and north winds and a shot of raw spirits to keep the blood from freezing. At that moment he had no particular expression but Tanner could picture a jolly chuckle or a cruel sneer sitting equally well on his features. He was a cunning peasant and out of place among the sober business suits, the uniforms, the beards and jeans.

The cunning peasant turned his back and spoke to the woman. Tanner couldn't hear what he said. He couldn't even make out the language he used. Now why should Tanner assume he wasn't speaking Spanish? There was no logic behind it. But what did logic count for in the field? They swore by it in London but London was half a world away.

He got up and walked to the smoked glass that overlooked the runway. The last stragglers were climbing the steps to the Brazilian plane, which was continuing on to La Paz. The only other aircraft parked in front of the terminal was a 727 with Lloyd Aero Boliviano painted down the fuselage, presumably the plane he would take to Sucre. It was refuelling from a Caltex tanker under the bored eye of a soldier. An engineer was walking along a wing. He stopped to peer at something, one of the flaps or the stencilled warning: 'NO STEP.'

A light aircraft touched down on the runway. This struck Tanner as unusual. Private planes used the old airport actually within the city limits rather than the flash new international airport out in the countryside. The plane taxied out of sight and then Tanner understood: it was going to the American compound.

My God, I'm slowing up, he thought. Can't take it any more, should ask for a transfer, ask for my pension. When you no longer want to take a risk, when you look for the comfortable way, then you're finished in the field. I'm over the top and coasting, no wonder Blank got out. She sensed it. A wife smells the decay first.

Blank was how he'd come to think of Denise. He was trying to trick himself. Take away her name, take away her identity, perhaps the pain will subside.

Damn her. Bitch.

Come on, do something. Stop brooding. Act. There were still two hours before the flight was called.

As Tanner turned away from the window he saw the woman's head drop. She'd been watching him.

Tanner took a taxi all of three hundred metres. He could have strolled across from the terminal building but to go on foot was to be conspicuous. There were two sets of guards. Outside the gate were Bolivian soldiers. Inside were Americans. Tanner got the impression the two groups never communicated with each other. Everybody watched him get out of the cab and gesture to the driver to wait right there.

The Bolivian soldiers fingered the trigger guards of their rifles as Tanner walked up to the gate. They made no effort to challenge him. I'm a *gringo*, Tanner reasoned, privileged species, they wouldn't dare. Through the wire two American soldiers stared at him impassively. They were black and chewed gum. There was a guard hut to one side of the gate and framed in the window was an officer, white. I never left South Africa, he thought.

Fixing on the bigger of the soldiers Tanner said, 'I've come to see the colonel.'

The soldier transferred the gum to his cheek and asked, 'Which colonel?'

They had more than one for this operation? Tanner looked across at the two wooden cabins. Perhaps they kept a colonel in each one.

'Whoever talks to the press,' Tanner said.

He was admitted to the enclosure but only as far as the hut with the young officer. Must be his first posting, Tanner decided, he looked so earnest. The officer studied the card Tanner offered. He ran three identities but it was his cover as a reporter he found most useful, except in countries where the army routinely shot journalists. The card announced he was a member of the *Asociación del Cuerpo de Prensa Salvadoreño*. It was a gaudy red and green card with a drawing of an erupting volcano and a photo of Tanner facing a firing squad. The card said his *Nombre* was Philip Tanner and his *Medio* was International Press Services, London.

'I guess it's Colonel Farr you want, sir,' the officer said and picked up his phone to speak to someone. They've set up their own communications system, Tanner registered, they're really settling in.

A black soldier escorted him to one of the long low cabins. It was painted white and windowboxes of geraniums gave it a homey air. He passed through an outer room where a plump girl in army uniform looked up from a typewriter, and went into the Colonel's office. He was standing behind his desk as Tanner was shown in. To have remained seated would have been rude. To stand up as Tanner entered would have implied too much deference to the press. This was a very political colonel, Tanner decided.

'Down from Salvador, Mr Tanner,' Colonel Farr said, studying the press card. 'You're a long way from base.'

'It's into a dull patch there, Colonel. London ordered me to do a swing down south and dig up some stories to justify my salary.'

'International Press Services? I don't think I know you.' He was running a thumbnail across the card's laminated surface.

'We're newish. We mainly supply papers in the British Commonwealth who find Reuters and UPI too pricey.'

'How's Frank Seidelmann these days?'

'I don't think the name's familiar.'

'Press Section, US Embassy, San Salvador.'

That was rattled out like gunfire. Tanner met the Colonel's gaze with more calmness than he felt. 'I've been to many briefings at the Embassy. It's like trying to get into Alcatraz.'

'Then you must know him. Frank makes a point of knowing every newsman, and what they write.'

'Could he be Joan's husband? I never did find out his name.' Tanner gave his all-boys-together grin, which got no answering response.

'Frank is unmarried. Well, maybe he's moved on. He was there in my time.'

'You were one of the Fifty-Five?'

'I got to think I was number Fifty-Five in person. Kept shipping me out to Honduras when they reached the limit. Crazy way to fight the communist menace.'

He sighed and gave back the press card. Fearful of being sucked into another Vietnam, Congress had set a limit of fifty-five on the number of American servicemen in El Salvador. It just meant, in Tanner's experience, that they used more CIA personnel and other assorted weirdos.

'Colonel, it was really about the drug threat here I was interested in.'

'Operation Purify.'

'Operation Purify,' Tanner agreed and brought out a notebook and pen.

Colonel Farr invited him to have a chair and rang through for coffee and Tanner let a little bit of himself relax. It was the girl from the outer room who brought coffee in polystyrene cups. She was US army but a *latina*, Puerto Rican Tanner judged.

'She doesn't relate to making coffee,' Farr said after she closed the door. He gave another sigh. Life was treating him roughly: Congress hobbling his Salvadorean activities, girl soldiers who were uppity. What relations does she enjoy? Tanner almost asked. But considering Farr's ascetic body and hollow cheeks and puritanical lips, he thought better of it. Operation Purify – maybe it was Farr's choice of codename. Cleanse the world of communists and drugdealers and fornicators.

'Colonel, could I ask how long you've been in this posting?'

'This facility was offered to President Paz ten months ago and I have been in charge for the past three months.'

'And how much longer will you be here?'

'That is not for me to determine.'

'Where are you from?'

'Arnold, Nebraska.'

'Different from Santa Cruz de la Sierra, Bolivia.'

'As you say.'

Tanner was scribbling in his notebook. He was conscious of the Colonel watching him. He tried to picture him growing up in a small town in Nebraska. Wide streets, clapboard houses, snow to the windowsills in winter, oven heat in summer. Did they have windowboxes in Arnold, Nebraska? Was that the Colonel re-creating a memory of childhood in this alien corner? He wondered briefly where the Colonel and his men and women lived. The airport cabins were for working, not sleeping. He couldn't see them accepting the hospitality of a Bolivian barracks.

Tents would flood during the tropical storms. Easiest would be to hire an entire hotel in town.

'Could I ask your age, Colonel?'

'Thirty-seven.'

'First name?'

'Bill.'

It was an abrupt answer. Tanner looked up and saw Farr's frown. He didn't approve of personal questions.

On one wall was a map of Bolivia, the usual one prepared by the military. The departments were shown in various pastel shades so that it resembled a child's jigsaw. Farr walked across to the map and tapped it with his finger.

'This is the headquarters of Operation Purify. Santa Cruz. I must stress it is a joint operation with the Bolivian authorities to destroy the menace of drugs. It is not Uncle Sam coming in to dictate, it is by mutual agreement.'

'Sure,' Tanner said. And if they didn't consent, Washington would chop off their aid.

'Drugs have become a global problem and require a global response by the democracies of the world. In many instances drug dependency has been deliberately encouraged by our country's enemies. They know that a country whose youth is weakened by drugs will not have the will to resist.'

'Great,' said Tanner writing wildly. 'May I quote you, Colonel sir, as saying that the Bolivian cocaine barons are communist?'

There was silence and when Tanner looked up, innocent questioning in his eyes, he saw a furious frown on Farr's face.

'No, you may not. This interview is to be regarded as non-attributable.'

The Colonel launched into his recital. One hundred and fifty soldiers, pilots, drug enforcement officers and FBI liaison men under his overall command. Spotter aircraft operating from the airfield at Trinidad, up here. Tremendous tract of jungle to cover in the Beni and Santa Cruz departments. Inaccessible country bordering Brazil. Wild Indian tribes. Sluggish rivers that eventually drained into the Amazon. No roads. You travelled by boat or you came in by air. Estimated there were over two thousand airstrips and the problem the authorities faced was checking each one from the air and making a judgement whether the buildings among the trees were genuine ranches or sheds for cooking cocaine. If an airstrip looked suspicious, a raid would be authorized. Colonel Farr supplied the helicopter transport and communications and back-up, the Bolivian army supplied the troops.

'Successes?' Tanner asked, pen poised.

'It is our experience that the sheds are usually cleared out.'

'Sounds like a little bird somewhere is going cheep cheep.'

'At least they're being forced to move on. Their operations are being harassed.'

'How many airstrips a week do you check?'

'Depends. Two, three.'

'And there are two thousand plus? Colonel, it sounds like you have your whole career mapped out here.'

'Sir, if it takes my whole life, it will be time well spent. I am protecting tomorrow's youth. That is the essence of a soldier's life – protecting the innocent. And you may quote me on that.'

It was an article of faith with him. If you happened to disagree and suggest that a soldier's job was actually to kill people, why, the good Colonel might be forced to remonstrate with you. But also he pronounced it as if it was an epitaph to finish the interview, so Tanner judged it was time to get to the point.

'And the other colonel? What are his duties?'

Farr went very still, his thin lips almost disappearing, his eyes black pinpoints.

'What other colonel? There is no other colonel.'

Tanner hesitated and decided he had nothing to lose, he could only be thrown out on his ear. 'The colonel who's just arrived. Gossip has it he came in to track down Che Guevara, *if* it is Guevara, which is a very big if.'

'Where did you hear this?'

'Newsmen never reveal their sources, Colonel, you know that. Is it true he's taken temporary command of your field forces? Have they gone to Sucre? Does the Bolivian government agree to this?'

Wild stabs in the dark. Each question was followed by silence. Now Farr crossed the room, took the notebook from his hand and ripped out the pages he'd scribbled on.

'This interview is concluded, Mr Tanner.'

'Colonel, I have to tell you your behaviour is tantamount to a confirmation.'

Farr pressed a switch on his desk. 'Our British visitor is leaving. Ask Sergeant Wilson to escort him out.'

'If not Sucre, where are you looking for Guevara? In Santa Cruz? In the jungle maybe? Have you any information about who the next victim will be?'

'Goodbye, Mr Tanner.'

'The public has a right to know. It's taxpayers who pay your salary.'

'Not British taxpayers.'

'If you catch him, will you kill him or ship him to the States? What are your orders?'

The door opened and his black escort came in.

'Not if, Tanner, not if. Sergeant Wilson, do not answer any of this gentleman's questions. Put him out of the gate. Do not let him in again.'

'Yes, *sir*.'

He wanted to ask what was dangerous about her cocktails.

She was three places in front of him in the line as they checked through the gate. The man was at her side but she held both the boarding passes.

She knew he was watching her. He was sure of it. There was the stance of her body and the way her head was turned just enough to show the line of her cheek and jaw. Her head was lifted as if she was straining to catch the sound of someone's voice.

Perhaps he hadn't been too brilliant with Farr. But he'd confirmed the American commitment to tracking down Guevara. *Not if, Tanner, not if.* The cool had blown away at the last moment and the Colonel must now be having regrets. Tanner didn't count it as a victory, just a confirmation of the mounting odds against him. The Bolivian police and army. A brace of American colonels and their troops. Assume the CIA residents from La Paz. Others? Such as?

Such as the ill-assorted pair in front. Somehow, while he'd been engaged with Colonel Farr, his subconscious mind had gone hunting on its own and this was what it had come back with: one Russian hood, one Cuban interpreter. Part of him accepted this without question and without proof. But was it likely?

Tanner had arrived Durban–Johannesburg–Cape Town–Rio–Santa Cruz. If someone was coming from Moscow, he'd fly to Havana. Was there an onward connection direct to Bolivia? Tanner thought not. He'd have to look up an airline guide but the route probably went via Rio or even Buenos Aires to Santa Cruz. So. You could look on Santa Cruz Airport as a waiting-room where people collected for the daily flight to Sucre. Unless, like the Americans, you were equipped with your own transport. People sneered at coincidences. They should save their scorn for airline schedules.

They were twenty metres in front of him walking out to the plane. He could see the elastic of her knickers under the thin cotton of her slacks. Her companion was much the same height as she was. He put Tanner in mind of Khrushchev. How about his shoes? Tanner smiled. There was a joke inside the Bunker that you could tell a KGB hood by his shoes. He might wear a lumpy suit but as soon as he got to the West he bought new shoes. Ridiculous when you thought about it. What peasant could stuff his feet into Guccis?

Steady, he cautioned himself. You're building wild theories.

At the foot of the steps she paused and patted her pockets as if she'd dropped something. She half turned, which was quite enough to check whether Tanner was embarking too.

At Sucre rainclouds blanketed the hills on the approach to the airport, which gave Tanner no good feeling about landing. The plane broke through to show dun hillocks and rocks and stunted trees almost brushing the undercarriage. They passed over a ridge where children waved – or were they trying to touch the wings – and suddenly the plane's wheels were on the runway.

Flights I've survived in South America, Tanner thought. There'd been the one in Colombia when they'd wound a rope round the propeller shaft to get the engine turning over. What was the alternative? A day and a night in a bus. Once you'd been on a bus where the driver did a three-point turn in pitch darkness to negotiate a hairpin on a mountain road, you went back to flying.

There were soldiers outside the terminal building and guarding the engineering hangar and a sentry on duty near half a dozen light aircraft. Ah, the Colonel's cavalry. There was a strong police presence inside the terminal and the usual throng of dark-suited men with briefcases and peasants with cardboard suitcases and women guarding baskets of vegetables. The military in Bolivia ran an airline and a blackboard was promising a flight to Tarija.

Outside it was drizzling like a bracing day in the Scottish highlands. One day, Tanner promised himself, he would leap into a taxi screaming, 'Follow that cab.' Today he got into the front seat by the driver and told him, 'Those are my friends in front. They know which hotel we're going to.' The only time they lost sight of the cab in front was at an army roadblock where a sergeant inspected every page of Tanner's passport.

In the main square Tanner paid off his taxi as he watched the other two disappear through the entrance of the Hostal Colonial. He humped his suitcase across the road and mounted one of the wooden thrones the shoeshine men erected for their customers. From here he could keep an eye on the hotel's entrance while the man went through an entire theatrical performance to restore some sparkle to his shoes. There was a newspaper for the entertainment of customers and Tanner used the uninformative story as a pretext for asking questions. It was his experience that taxi drivers in South America were opinionated oafs, self-important because they negotiated traffic jams; but shoeshine men observed the world and its foibles and were as reliable sources of information as barmen but less venal.

So what were the *real* facts about the Guevara saga, not the newspaper fairytales?

Well now, the *señor* could not have positioned himself better. There, across the square to his right, was where the drama began to unfold. Tanner obediently looked at the building with its aerial and a sign for Radio Colosal 92 FM. It is from the studio on the top floor that the radio star actually spoke to the villain.

Now in that direction, but five blocks away, was where the respected *Comandante* lived and where his inconsolable widow is preparing for the second interment. The daughters are also present, tragedy only emphasizing their great beauty.

And there, if you persevere down Bustillos and bear to the right at the end, you come to the cemetery where the unspeakable act took place. The immediate scene of the crime is cordoned off and under armed guard but there are boys who will fetch a ladder, for a consideration, should the *señor* care to look over the top of thc ncighbouring mausoleum.

The police, Tanner said jabbing a finger at the newspaper story, boast that an arrest is imminent.

The police say that, *señor,* and will continue saying it until people forget and instead become bound up in the exploits of the bishop. Perhaps one day they will stumble on the corpse of some unfortunate peasant and swear he was the murderer. Then the police will award themselves medals and that will be the end of it.

'Do the police really believe it is Che Guevara?'

'*Señor,* bend closer. I have cleaned the shoes of a major in the army. Now the army is just as interested in this affair as the police and the major was generous in his talk while I took special care of his shoes. In confidence he told me that the dead police *Comandante* and the dead doctor in Potosi were indeed at one time both living near a special place of incarceration. Guevara is long dead, everyone agrees. But it could be another prisoner from that place who possibly suffered intense interrogation and now seeks revenge. This demented person has assumed the identity of the dead guerrilla for the sake of publicity. That is the opinion of the major.'

'And your opinion?'

'My opinion?' The man removed the pieces of cardboard that had been tucked inside Tanner's shoes to protect his socks from polish. He held up one piece of cardboard. 'On the one hand it is a madman.' He held up the second piece of cardboard. 'On the other hand it is Che Guevara. But I ask myself, would the police conduct house to house searches every night for a madman? Would thirty *Norte Americanos* fly here for a madman? Would the army blockade every road for a madman? I think,' and he laid the two pieces of cardboard together, 'that it is both a madman *and* Guevara.'

Tanner was generous in his tip and was given in exchange the name of the Supreme Court driver who was kidnapped, the address of the Hostal Londres where the prime suspect had stayed, and the hour at which Agustino finished his radio programme and might be persuaded to play a tape of the fateful conversation.

'Mind you, *señor*, you are wasting your time if you expect to find Guevara here. He was already up in the hills when he spoke on the radio-telephone in the car. But the army and the police cannot think of anything else to do.'

'It's a single room you wish?' the clerk asked.

'Yes.'

'For how long?'

'Not long. Tonight, maybe tomorrow.'

Tanner signed the register of the Hostal Colonial. The names directly above his were an I. V. Gurdjiev from West Germany and an American, M. Mancilla. They had separate rooms.

The next morning was crisp and clear, a tonic after the mugginess of Durban and the turkish bath of Santa Cruz. Tanner breakfasted on rolls and coffee and the newspaper. The journalists obviously considered it a dead story. The police were holding no more press conferences and no one had been killed for days. And besides, there was a much juicier affair in Cochabamba where the naked woman turned out to be the daughter of a prominent trade unionist. Somebody recognized her tits, Tanner decided. So the newshounds had quit Sucre and gone to bay elsewhere.

That still left the American presence in Sucre. There were an amazing number of crewcut, fit, young *gringos* out in the streets, drinking beer in the cafés, eating ice creams in the plaza. Indeed the ice cream sellers had never done so well. But what did the American boys actually *do*? That was a mystery to Tanner. Did they know what to look for? Where were they staying? The local authorities tolerated them, but on whose orders?

And the police and army were like an occupying power. Show

your papers, why are you here, where are you staying? Tanner was stopped a dozen times during the day.

He went to the Hostal Londres and flashed his press card to the owner. This man was incensed that the police had padlocked the room Che had slept in. 'It is an outrage. Are they going to pay for the room? I cannot let it to anybody else.' To Tanner's ear he was building himself a bargaining position for the hotel was silent and quite empty. Next door at the Snack El Carreton the waitress gave a vivid account of Che. But she was too vehement and thus an unreliable witness: she hadn't served meals to an old man, she'd had a narrow escape from a monster with blood dripping from his fangs. It was a couple of blocks to the Supreme Court. The driver had been discovered after being six hours tied to his steering wheel. He was none the worse for his ordeal and gave a coherent account of Che's behaviour. Tanner pressed him: 'Do you think he was telling the truth – that he was Guevara?' At this question the driver became tongue-tied and evasive and darted glances beyond Tanner's shoulder. Someone's got at him, Tanner guessed, told him to keep his mouth shut.

But of Martina Mancilla and I. V. Gurdjiev there was no sign all day. They hadn't asked questions at the Londres or El Carreton. They weren't sitting under the palms in the main square. Their room keys hung on hooks behind the hotel reception desk.

It wasn't until the evening that Tanner had an encounter with a dangerous cocktail.

CHAPTER 14

When he reached Santa Cruz, Che felt doubt for the first time. What he was attempting was too fantastic, too far fetched, too wild in its logic. He was seeking vengeance on his torturers but at the same time he was promising the unmasking of the people who had betrayed the revolution twenty years before. Such a revelation was unacceptable. The traitor would be drawn to silence him and Che would achieve his ultimate revenge. It remained only to arrange a rendezvous with the traitor but Che didn't yet know where it would be.

He had reached Santa Cruz by truck, by bus and by walking and now he was exhausted. The humidity of the lowlands made his asthma flare up and breathing was painful. He was resting on a bench in Plaza 24 de Septiembre, amazed at the mushrooming of this boom town. Santa Cruz had grown rich on cattle, oil and cocaine. Above all, cocaine. In the special prison the inmates had told surreal stories about the cocaine wealth. It was asserted there was so much money to be made that now the planes which flew the cocaine no longer bothered to land at isolated airstrips in Florida. Why go to the trouble of bribing the local police to keep clear? No. Now they ditched at sea and left their cargo to float with a marker buoy to guide the pick-up launch. To Che that was unimaginable. A throw-away plane was the ultimate sign of capitalist decadence. The society was driving itself to destruction, hastened by the cocaine it craved.

Santa Cruz had effectively seceded from Bolivia. It was the frontier post of the American drug state. Look at the frontiersmen as they drove their Ford Mustangs and Cherokee Chiefs with the bulletproof glass. Watch how they shook hands with a policeman, leaving a folded banknote in the palm of his hand. Observe their Cessnas and Beechcrafts winging their way northwards. Pause in front of the shopwindows crammed with Scotch whisky and Japanese televisions, priced in dollars. Take care as you walked past the sleek banks with their air-conditioners dripping disdainfully on poor pedestrians. Up in the Altiplano a child counted himself blessed to eat rice flavoured with onions and chillies. Here were restaurants that boasted Steaks as Big as Texas.

A woman stared at Che. Sweat was glistening on his brow. It was loathing that sprang out of his pores. Did she see that? Her eyes were fierce, her hair grey and greasy, her clothes had fused with her body. Did she recognize him? Could she discern the old Che with the messianic look and dark hair and starred beret? Perhaps he had met her one day long ago. They used to come across peasants working the fields. Occasionally they had found favour with a woman because they were fighters. It was not, Che decided, because they struggled for social justice but because they dared to risk their lives. They would go in turn behind a shed and be quick. There was no time for tenderness in a guerrilla's life. They grunted and were finished. The woman would pull down her skirt and go back to hoe.

That shipwreck of a woman? Che looked away.

The plaza was perfect in its symbolism. Behind him was the cathedral of pale red brick. Facing him was the street where the money changers clustered. To his right was a school of English. To his left was the Palace Theatre – its sign in English – which was built in Banana Republic Rococo. In the centre was the inevitable statue. Che hadn't looked to see which hero it praised. Perhaps it commemorated the nineteenth-century Bolivian President who was sent a white stallion by the President of Brazil. So impressed was the Bolivian President that he called for a map of his country and pressed his thumb down on it. 'Whatever part of Bolivia my thumbprint covers,' he told his neighbour, 'I present to you in return for your magnificent stallion.' Only in Bolivia, Che thought, only in Bolivia.

The old woman was making faces at him, mouthing silent curses. He gave her some money. She snatched it without thanks. She spat on it. She laid it on the ground and rubbed it under her heel. She picked the pesos up, smoothed the notes and tucked them out of sight down her bosom. She barked once, like a yappy mongrel, before striding away.

She is training to be Finance Minister, Che decided. That is how to treat foreign bankers.

He refused offers of lime juice and cigarettes and ice cream and shoeshines and a parrot in a tiny cage. But he bought a newspaper.

The bishop said he had been called to the house to hear a special confession. The trade unionist's daughter said she had been told to strip naked so she could be given a total immersion in holy water to cleanse her sins.

Beneath the fold was a headline: '*The body in the wall – Che not the killer.*' The authorities were convinced they were dealing with a demented sadist. Only a madman would claim to be someone who died in a hail of bullets twenty years ago and whose death had been publicized in the media of the whole world. Searches were under way for anyone absent from the lunatic asylums of Sucre, Potosi and Oruro. The police anticipated an early and successful conclusion to their investigation.

Fury made Che's world tilt. An earthquake rocked the buildings back at desperate angles. His vision was a boiling lava flow, a primeval soup that burped grey fumes. Voices became the screech of jungle birds. He could hear the breathing of the currency touts.

What did he have to do to prove he was alive?

Ah, nothing.

His eye was caught by a tiny news item, a snippet at the foot of a column that filled a blank space. Police in Florida wanted to interview a Cuban woman in connection with the murder of an English photographer Ben Morton. He had recently returned from Bolivia where he had been imprisoned on suspicion of drug-dealing. There was evidence of a link to the Soviet Embassy and the theft of various items.

If the madwoman had turned to watch, she would have seen the old man's face relax in a smile. He beckoned a boy over and treated himself to a shoeshine. He wasn't celebrating Morton's death but the circumstances of it.

CHAPTER 15

From the Telecom office Tanner put a call through to the Bunker and waited while the switchboard tracked down Hershey. What a bastard, Tanner thought. There are rough tough bastards, bawl you out and kick your backside if you foul up. And there are the Hershey kind, the smooth bastards, stamp on your toes as they clamber up the greasy pole, call you a good fellow and clap you on the back, but it's only to select the right spot to slip in the knife.

'Hershey,' a voice said in his ear.

'This is your globe-trotting representative, bringing you front line despatches from the world's trouble spots.'

'Where the hell are you?'

That didn't sound too smooth. Somebody had been ruffling his Controller's feathers.

'In Bolivia, following your directive. City called Sucre, spelled like the French for sugar but pronounced sook-ray.'

'I don't need a bloody geography lesson. What's happening?'

'The usual confusion, South American style. They put the army on the streets to shove people round and check their papers while the generals go out to lunch. A certain co-operation is developing with our Cousins. I was stopped by an army patrol who showed my passport to a *gringo*.'

'Problem?'

'I'm a bona fide journalist, why should there be a problem?'

'What kind of Cousin? The military kind?'

'Plenty of those in Santa Cruz. This was the more earnest save-the-world-from-communism type, lost without his brief-case.'

'Understood. From what you're not telling me, I impute no progress.'

Impute – that was a good one, more like the Hershey of old.

'I have a good story on how Uncle Sam is helping to bust the drugs racket.'

'Not interested. That's not the story you're there for. Have you given any thought to how you're going to get the story out?'

'I'll think of something.'

'Now listen to this and give it some thought. Don't let our rivals steal the story. I don't want that. Rather than let our rivals get a scoop, I prefer to put the story on the spike. Got that?'

Tanner thought of Debbie Becker with breasts like pillows gesting?

'Hello? Can you hear me?'

'I hear you,' Tanner said. 'What follow-up has there been on the May Day story?'

'What? What the hell are you talking about? Oh, the girl with the petrol bombs. She's remanded in jail.'

Tanner thought of Debbie Becker with breasts like pillows where a man could rest his head and dream.

'You still there?' Hershey asked.

'I'm still here.'

'I'm having an encounter with a Cousin of a Federal kind. In fact I've been called out of a meeting with him. He's here to find out what progress we're making in certain directions. He wants to clean up the murder in that woman's house in Florida and he wants the Russian Ambassador to have done it so he can close down the Soviet Embassy. Something subtle like that. He calls that his scenario and in return he wants to trample through our files. Also to take in a couple of shows. And he finds my name funny.'

'It's the name of a chocolate bar.'

'Don't you start.'

There was a short silence. Who's listening? Tanner wondered. Police? More Cousins? Hershey was too angry to be guarded and this was an open line.

'Any sign of the other side?'

'The men with snow on their boots?' Tanner asked.

'Yes.'

'I haven't seen them.' The lie came easily. Tanner couldn't think why he kept Martina Mancilla and the roly-poly peasant a secret. It's because this is an open line and you never know who's listening. But that was a lie too, he knew.

'Get back on the trail,' Hershey said. 'I want a world exclusive.'

In the late afternoon Tanner admitted defeat and went to the cemetery. He had a sense of drifting and there seemed nothing better to do. Show his press card and interview the Deputy Police Chief? Buy the Americans a few beers and hope for a crumb or two? Talk to more shoeshine men, offer a reward? Bloody Hershey and his 'world exclusive'.

Tomorrow morning I'll leave, he promised himself.

If, he sighed, I can think of somewhere to go.

There was a slim chance the murderer would return to the scene of his crime. A certain kind of psychopath wanted to gloat over the bumbling police and enjoy his sense of power. If that was the case there were several dozen psychopathic killers on the loose. They pressed against a rope and stared at nothing much. Bored policemen kept an eye on them and smoked cigarettes. For a few moments Tanner joined the sightseers but there were no ghoulish sights, not even a hole in a wall. The authorities had closed off this whole corner of the cemetery and the gaping niche was invisible. When had that ever discouraged a crowd in South America? They came to a disaster not to observe a vigil but to worship death itself.

Tanner turned to check the faces round him.

Tanner turned and there was movement at the edge of the crowd. A figure slipped behind a yew tree. He was sure of it. Absolutely sure. In his memory he called up the small figure and the intense face. It definitely had been, most definitely. He pushed his way through the gawpers and when he reached the yew there was nobody. He wasn't mistaken. He was never mistaken about things like watchers and tails. Almost never. The path went thirty metres before it joined the imposing avenue that ran between the family vaults. When he reached the avenue he looked first towards the gatehouse, then the other way and it was like seeing a film all over again. A small figure, last seen wearing thin cotton slacks and a yellow T-shirt that promised Dangerous Cocktails, slipped out of sight. Now she wore blue jeans and a cotton-knit sweater. But it was the same person.

He began running. He pounded down the avenue to a central rosebed like a traffic roundabout. He paused. A whole family dressed in black forgot their sadness at the sight of this man panting and listening. She'd disappeared. He heard birdsong and the rhythmic thud of a hoe but no footsteps. She'd exited right so he followed down to an area of broken masonry and straggly lilacs. The path turned and ran along the edge of the cemetery where it fell away down a hillside. Martina Mancilla was holding on to the fence, staring down the slope at lines of tiny graves.

He came and stood at her shoulder. She must hear his breathing and feel his presence but she didn't move a muscle. She'd been running hard. He could see her breasts rising and falling. He felt a tension in himself as if he had settled into the starting blocks and was waiting for the pistol crack for the beginning of the marathon.

'Why were you following me?' Tanner asked. He spoke in English.

'You crazy?' She wheeled round and Tanner took a step back as you would from a spitting cat. 'I come down this path and *you* follow *me*. The path goes nowhere so why do you take it? Hey? Answer me. What is it? Mugging? Murder? Rape? You the mad guy walls people up? I shout for help? Why don't you say something?'

When she ran out of breath Tanner said, 'You were running away when I spotted you.'

'Why would I do that? Why would you follow after me?'

'You didn't come down here to look at the dog cemetery.'

'Dogs? Those are babies who were never baptized. So they bury the bodies in this patch of land and their souls are in limbo. That's some church that does that. God of love or what?'

Tanner saw now that each tiny plot had a cross. The air of neglect was disturbing. The grass was long and the graves lacked flowers as if such youngsters had never merited love and weren't mourned. He shook the thoughts out of his head. She was trying to turn the talk.

'You were watching me back there by the rope. Then you ducked and ran.' He grabbed an arm to turn her towards him. 'Why?'

She said, 'You want me to bring my knee up, mister? You won't be such a big strong man then.' Tanner let go of her arm. 'The Incas tore the hearts out of people, so what's changed? This society still demands human sacrifice only it goes by a different name now – starvation. That's why I was looking at the graves. That's what I was thinking.' She looked into his eyes. 'You think I followed you? You are one conceited man. Or . . .' Her eyes moved over his face as if she saw secret marks there. 'Or you have something to hide.'

We all have something to hide, he thought. He pushed the Bunker out of his mind, and the wife who'd betrayed him. But Debbie Becker's face stayed with him.

A whistle was blowing some way back in the cemetery, warning of sunset and the closing of the gates. Together they turned. They walked back in silence as if they were old friends and this was the most normal meeting in the world.

The gates of the cemetery were between massive Roman columns. The people passing through had the sulky look of a crowd that's been cheated. The murderer had not put in an appearance.

'Look at them,' Martina said. 'Look at their disappointment. There's been no more blood. Know what they are? They are eaters of death.'

Such an odd phrase, like a translation. While Tanner puzzled over it she raised a hand towards his face. She was forbidding him to speak any more. Or warding off the evil eye. There was no telling. She walked away.

When he got back to the hotel Tanner understood why she'd been at the cemetery. She hadn't been there to see if Guevara returned. Nor had she really been following Tanner, not in the sense of wanting to know where he was going. She had been watching to make sure he didn't return to the hotel too soon. When Tanner had turned away from the rope as if he'd had enough of the cemetery, she'd let herself be glimpsed. When Tanner had reached the main avenue and had a choice of going to the gate, she'd shown a bit of leg again. She'd been certain he'd follow, and like a dog after a bitch he had. Meanwhile his room was being searched. Her part had been to see that her companion had time to do his job.

Tanner closed the door behind him but kept his fingers on the handle. He might want to leave in a hurry. No, this wasn't a Russian wet affair. No bit of *plastique* on the light bulb. He could sense Gurdjiev's passage through the room. There was a suggestion of another body in the air, a body fed on a lifetime of cabbage and potatoes leaving a hint of itself among the must of the old carpet and heavy curtains.

The room wasn't in a mess. Gurdjiev wasn't that much of a peasant. But there were one or two little things Tanner noticed. If he had been Gurdjiev, what route would he have taken? The easy things first: the drawers in the dressing-table, the bedside table, under the pillow. Then warming to his task: beneath the mattress, under the lid of the lavatory, inside the roll of toilet paper. Harder still: fold back the carpet, feel outside under the windowsill. Looking for what? Something, some hint. Gurdjiev wouldn't know. All he would know was that the lone Englishman stood out as a suspect figure.

Tanner noticed the little things Gurdjiev had lifted and probed and put back. There was the thriller – an Elmore Leonard paperback – which had been flicked through and placed face down on the bedside table. His shoes which he'd jammed in the closet had been straightened. Small things.

It's the maid. But Tanner had no faith in easy answers. Besides, there was the matter of his suitcase. No maid would have known how to unlock his suitcase. No maid would have searched the envelope in which he kept receipts. They had been inspected and put back upside down. He had receipts for the minicab that took him to Heathrow, for the hotel in Durban, for drinks from the bar, for the Gloria Hotel in Rio, for restaurants. The accounts department at the Bunker screamed that the taxpayers met his expenses and needed the proof of the bills.

If I had come across those bills, Tanner reasoned, three continents in a week, what would I think?

So they know, Tanner thought, so what? They would say: Hmm, an English spy also looking for Guevara, but only one man as against several dozen Americans not to mention the whole of the Bolivian army and police. So the Englishman wasn't much of an extra danger.

Nevertheless, watch your back, Phil old son, it's the only one you've got.

He left the hotel and crossed to the plaza where he bought the newspaper that had come in on the afternoon flight from Santa Cruz. *'The body in the wall,'* he read, *'Che not the killer.'* He glanced through the story, which was nothing. If they were going to check on every madman in Bolivia, who were they going to get to do the checking?

Then at the bottom of the page he saw the tiny filler. The only reason it was printed was because Ben Morton had been imprisoned in Bolivia. The police in Florida wanted to interview Martina Mancilla, a Cuban-born woman, in connection with Morton's murder.

Bastards, he exploded and jumped up from the bench. Smooth bastards in London, hairy bastards in Florida. Probably some DA running for re-election and wanting publicity. Perhaps it didn't matter. It was only a tiny paragraph and it might never be noticed. But it might panic Martina and her companion and drive them out of sight.

He checked at the desk and Gurdjiev's key was on its hook. He was out. Hers wasn't. She was in her room.

She stood in the bedroom door with the light behind her and her hands on her hips. It could have been provocative, the pose of a thousand bargirls.

'You won't leave me alone,' Martina said. 'What you want?'

She was frowning as if she could read what was going on in his mind.

'I thought,' and Tanner wondered what it was he really thought, 'I thought we might have dinner.'

The frown grew more intense. Perhaps she could read his mind.

'You think that, huh? You think because you pick me up at the cemetery this afternoon, you can start dating me?'

Tanner tensed. He was about to say, 'Well, sod you then,' and turn on his heel. Something in the way she tipped her head so the light curved down one cheekbone held him back.

'Strange city, two people on their own, it's better to have company than to stare at the wall.'

'How you know I'm on my own?'

'His key is on its hook. Herr Gurdjiev's.'

'How you know his name?'

'I looked in the register. He's gone out without you.'

'He has business.' She considered Tanner so that he began to wonder if there was a dirty streak across his cheek. 'Maybe that's why you ran after me at the cemetery. You wanted to ask me to dinner and I never give you a chance.' On this lie they both kept silent. She lifted her hands from her hips and stretched. It was like a cat waking up and arching its back, readying itself for the hunt. He had known women do that. 'Okay, I change, you wait for me in the lobby.'

They ate at a Chinese restaurant half a dozen blocks from the hotel. In unknown towns a Chinese restaurant was often the only place where the food was eatable. This was awful. It was like Chinese restaurants used to be in small towns in England. There would be sweet and sour pork, chicken and canned bamboo shoots, and the waiter would ask if you wanted rice or chips. Martina looked round and was not impressed and looked at him and raised an eyebrow: so this is the way the English do their courting.

'I thought we wouldn't be disturbed here,' Tanner said.

'What?'

At the back of the restaurant a disco was getting ready to start. A booming voice tested the loudspeakers: *'Uno, dos, tres . . .'*, like a language lesson. Four or five men sat on stools at the bar staring up at a television. Venezuela was playing Bolivia at football. The Bolivians had the advantage of a home game at 4,000 metres, but the Venezuelans scored first. The men at the bar whistled in derision.

'Herr Gurdjiev might look for you but he wouldn't come here.'

'You afraid of him? You think maybe he get jealous and shoot you?'

'Does he have a gun?'

'Don't be stupid. You can't travel by plane with a gun because of the searches.'

'What does Gurdjiev do?'

'Export and import,' she said. 'You know, the usual things.'

'Bolivia doesn't export much except cocaine.'

'Peasant things. Alpaca sweaters, leather handbags, embroidered shirts, stuff like that. It's why I am here. I help him choose, tell him what will sell.'

'And that's where he is now?'

'What do you mean?'

'Back at the hotel you said he was out on business. But he hasn't taken you.'

She looked at him with a certain narrowing of the eyes and Tanner knew he'd gone far enough. The waiter came for their order. He was a Chinese youth with red and yellow stripes in his spiky black hair. Terrific, Tanner thought, a Chinese Bolivian punk, now I've seen it all. Martina wanted duck but they only had pork. Tanner wanted wine but they only had beer.

'Hey,' she said, 'you speak good Spanish.'

'For a *gringo*, you mean.'

'No kidding. What do you do?'

'I'm a journalist.'

'Who do you work for?'

'A wire service,' Tanner said, speaking carefully, 'that no one has ever heard of.'

'So why are you here?'

'I was in South Africa doing a story on Buthelezi when head office ordered me to Bolivia. Guevara, what else?'

She considered this and Tanner wondered whether it was possible she believed it and decided it didn't matter. He hadn't made things any worse.

'South Africa to Boliva. That's a long way to come for a lot of wild ravings.'

'Look at it this way. South Africa was a long way to go in the first place. London making a cock-up as usual. I don't have Zulu but I do have Spanish.'

'So you've looked and haven't found Guevara.'

'Do you believe he's alive?'

She drank some beer. 'He died twenty years ago. That's a fact. Belief has nothing to do with history. You can't change it. That why you were at the cemetery?'

'Visiting the scene of the crime. You?'

She looked at him with eyes that seemed bigger than before, very serious. She leant across and laid her fingertips on his wrist. 'Could be I'm just another of the eaters of the dead.'

That was pretentious crap but Tanner didn't say anything because her fingers were still on his wrist. In Latin America to touch wasn't a sexual ploy, it was part of the heritage. But to let the touch linger had the same meaning anywhere in the world.

The Chinese Bolivian punk brought plates of food, Venezuela scored another goal and the disco thundered into life.

She said something.

'What?' Tanner asked.

'I said,' she shouted, 'do your ladies ever accept a second dinner date?'

It was the noise that did it. It was like a bombardment in a war, a hardship endured together. Suffering shared becomes a bond. Perhaps it's why people talk of a marriage bond, Tanner decided with his wife in mind, because there is so much bloody suffering involved.

The disco was in a room at the back of the restaurant. An open doorway beckoned and when Tanner got up to shut the door he found it had been removed from its hinges. A dozen kids shuddered under strobe lighting. The music blasted from speakers like weapons of destruction. To counter the disco, the volume on the television was turned full on. The men jeered and whistled. Motorbikes arrived outside. Shouting erupted from the kitchen. The punk waiter yelled at a deaf old man.

'To be deaf here is to be blessed,' Tanner said.

'Speak up,' Martina screamed.

Tanner spotted a bottle of *singani*. They drank it with Canada Dry to mask the taste. After the second glass you forgot it was rotgut. By the third glass there was a glow to Martina's cheeks and her head bobbed to the beat of the disco and her lips parted in a grin.

The other thing about the noise, Tanner acknowledged, was that it made questioning impossible. What is the name of your wire service? Where are you based? How is wild man Mike these days? The bearded giant on the *Express* – you must know him. Or is it the *Mail*?

In a gap between records she asked, 'Do you have places like this in England?'

The music crashed in before he could answer. Dingwalls? Derby Day? He pulled her close to shout in her ear, 'Late night session in the House of Commons.'

She squeezed his hand.

The police arrived. The neighbours have complained, Tanner thought. But they were checking papers. They looked at the photos in their passports and then looked at their faces.

'Martina Mancilla?'

'Yes.'

'Peeleep Tanner?'

'Yes.'

Great, we've been formally introduced at last, Tanner thought. We never swapped names. There was no need; we'd each done our bit of spying.

After the noise there was the silent street. Silence is its own kind of conspiracy. It was a natural gesture for Martina to tuck her arm through Tanner's. Their footsteps echoed between the two-storey buildings so that Tanner checked once to see if anyone was following. Cars without lights cruised by. An army patrol ignored them. Shouts and ritual grunts came from behind shutters and a sign announced the KO Karate Klub. In Bolivia, Tanner decided, the spelling is krazy.

It was cold and he put an arm round her shoulder. Squatting against the wall were two bodies. They were huddled together for warmth and company, a blanket over both, the woman still wearing her bowler hat. Did she make love in her bowler? In the street?

'Jesus, it's awful to have to sleep like that.'

'Yes,' she said.

'At least we have a warm room to go to.'

'Yes.'

They walked in step, their hips together, their thighs touching.

*

Astride him she bent back against his knees. Her arms stretched wide, her face lifted, her mouth opened in delight. Tanner had never seen such freedom.

She leant over to kiss him. Her tongue probed his mouth and wouldn't rest. Her tongue was searching, saying there are secrets in here I want to discover.

Lying underneath she raised her legs and crossed her ankles behind his back. He was caught.

When he looked into her eyes, into the dark pupils, he was led in deeper until he was lost.

And finally he grasped her tight, clung and clung like a man in danger of drowning.

Leaning on an elbow Tanner said, 'Lovers are the eaters of the living.'

She put a finger to his lips. 'Idiot.'

He dozed and came awake with the thought: this is known as consorting with the enemy.

If they found out at the Bunker, the internal security officers would have him thrown in a cell for interrogation. Hershey would ask: 'But did you find out anything useful?' and 'C' would say, 'But all women are the enemy.'

It was to Tanner's room they had come, without any hesitations, as if they always slept together. Inside the room, the door closed, he had kissed her for the first time. She'd laid both hands on his cheeks and pushed him away so she could read the expression on his face. 'Yes,' she answered herself. Satisfied, she'd kissed him, then closed her eyes and stood on tiptoe to kiss him again. They'd helped each other undress and she was shivering a little, from cold or anticipation.

'Did you lock the door?' she asked.

'Yes.'

'Check it, please.'

'Who are you afraid of?'

'Who? We're in a hotel so anybody could try the door. Robbers, police. Just check the lock, okay?'

When he'd turned back from the door, she'd been waiting for him, lying on the bed with the sheet and blanket pulled back. She was a present with the gift wrapping open.

'Leave the light on,' she said. 'I want to look at you.'

Now the light was off. In the dark she whispered, 'You awake?'

'Yes.'

Her fingers found his face and stroked his cheek and mouth. It seemed the most intimate of gestures.

'I must go back to my room.'

'Stay the night.'

'I can't. He might come in and check to see if I'm in my room. I'm his assistant.'

'Why should he do that? Why should he need your assistance in the middle of the night?'

She pushed herself away from him. 'Not that kind of assistance.'

'Well then?'

Martina swung her legs off the bed. 'Sometimes he likes to talk.'

'How about me? I want to talk. I want to find out about you.'

Tanner stopped. He'd said that without thinking. He put his hand on her thigh, on the inside. That was the smoothest skin of a woman's body, softer than her breasts.

'I want to see you again,' he said.

She lifted his hand and kissed the palm, her tongue exploring. But she said, 'You find plenty other girls.'

'I said I want to see *you* again. Doesn't that stir anything in you?'

She laid his hand on her breast. 'Come on, we're not kids, you don't have to make a big declaration to keep me sweet.' But he could feel the beating of her heart. 'Listen, your work must take you to the United States. If not, you come on vacation there. I give you my address in Florida and you come and see me. Make that a promise, okay? Maybe, just maybe we have something. Could be.'

'Martina . . .'

'What is it?'

'You can't go back.'

'Why not? They can't stop me. I got US citizenship and my

home is there. I go in and out when I want. That's what it is in a free country.'

Tanner couldn't believe it. Her voice was genuine. But how could she not know that Morton had been murdered in her house? She hadn't killed him but she'd left him there and two men in Mickey Mouse masks had come and shot him to death and left him to rot on the floor. And the police were waiting to question her about that and about a whole lot more.

She turned on the light. 'So why can't I go home?' She looked at him, her intense look again. 'What's the matter?'

The matter? If I tell her, Tanner knew, I have to tell her everything. That's not just consorting with the enemy, that's handing over the keys to the bank deposit box. That's cutting the rope and drifting out to sea. In plain language it's treachery and there's no going back. 'Screwing a woman is one thing,' Hershey would say. 'Screwing the Bunker is something else.'

'You don't speak. You just say crazy things and shut up. Maybe you're no different from other guys, always try and trick a girl.'

She began to dress. She turned her back on him.

'You know what time it is? Have you any idea?' It was the voice of a man brought out of his warm bed in the exact middle of his night's sleep.

'Coming up to nine o'clock,' Tanner said, squinting through the window and across the check-in area. If the clock was right. He looked at his own watch.

'I mean in England,' Hershey began and from his tone was going to say a great deal more. With an effort he brought his voice down. 'What is it?'

'Guevara's surfaced again. I just thought you'd like to know. You can go back to sleep again.'

'Now wait a minute, wait a minute. What's the story? Has he killed anybody else?'

'Soon. He telephoned a radio station in Santa Cruz last night. They didn't tape him but they put it out on the news and it was repeated here this morning. He's on the track of the third torturer and within a couple of days revolutionary justice will be done. He promises one further surprise.'

'Hoax?'

'I've seen three little planes with well-fed Cousins taking off in the last twenty minutes. They don't think so.'

'Where are you?'

'Sucre Airport, Administration Office.' Tanner had shown his press card and made a donation to their coffee fund.

'Plans?'

'I've got a seat on the next flight.'

Through the glass he saw Martina and Gurdjiev come in through the entrance. Martina carried her small case. To Tanner's eye she looked intense and mysterious, strong and vulnerable, vital and infinitely desirable. Some you win, some you lose after one night. Half a night. He forced his gaze away from her. Gurdjiev had only a briefcase. His suitcase was carried by one of a pair of crushers who walked close behind. The one without the suitcase pointed to the check-in and Tanner turned aside.

Of course, that was where Gurdjiev had been last night. Tanner didn't know why he hadn't guessed the nature of the 'business' that had kept him out of sight. The CIA could mount a saturation operation here in a way the KGB never could. But they hardly needed to. In any city in South America the Russians could call on the secretary of the local Communist Party. They were brought up to conspiracy. You need help to find Che? A telephone, a shortwave radio? You want honest proletarians to go on the streets, search the shantytowns, listen in bars? You need a gun? Ask, comrade, we are deeply honoured to bring the day of revolution closer.

'Phil?'

'I've got to go. The flight's being called.'

'Any sign of our other rivals?'

'Listen, can't you find out who the third victim will be? It would be terrific for once not to stumble along two steps behind Guevara. What do we pay all those research people for?'

'They're working on it.'

'Bloody academics, that's their trouble.'

'Takes time.'

'I don't want a thesis, I want a name.' Tanner rang off.

For a moment he had a mental snapshot of Hershey holding the telephone in front of his face and looking petulant. He was in his 'den' with the hunting prints on the wall. He was wearing a Paisley dressing-gown bought by Mrs Hershey at the Harrods sale. Mrs H. was standing in the doorway asking if he'd like a cup of tea, dear. He'd been too abrupt. No, he hadn't. He was the lad far from home.

The two angels had shaken hands with Gurdjiev and Martina and left them by the doors leading out to the apron. An official had taken up his position ready to inspect boarding passes. Tanner turned to a pretty girl who sat on a desk swinging her legs and painting her nails.

'I was longer than I thought telephoning.' He got five dollars out of his wallet. She waved a hand but it was only to dry her nails. With her other hand she accepted the money. 'I'm supposed to be meeting a Señor Gurdjiev. Do you think you could put out a call for him? Ask him to come to the baggage gate. Would you be a darling and do that?'

The girl smiled because of the smile Tanner gave her. He was good at smiles to girls.

He watched Gurdjiev and Martina move away from the glass doors and ask an official where the baggage gate was. They disappeared from sight. Tanner went out and waded into the crowd of passengers. He'd be able to board the plane and get a seat at the back without being seen.

CHAPTER 16

Che remembered a time when mornings were created fresh. In Santa Cruz mornings simply happened. The night was dark and clammy, the day was light and clammy. There was no difference in the quality.

He stood outside the hotel for a moment. It was newish, put up in the first flush of the oil boom. Like most buildings that were hurried up, it had looked tired from the start. Across the street were buildings from a romantic though brutal past. They had boardwalks and overhanging roofs and hitching posts where a man might tether his horse while he went in search of a drink or a woman or a bullet. Those old buildings had seen a lot and would outlast the concrete blocks, provided there was no profit in tearing them down.

Mornings in Potosi had been different. To step outside there was to feel the shock of cold, taste the iron air, see precise outlines cut by the sun. Potosi had been in another lifetime. He had done so much in the weeks since he had been turned loose. He'd plotted and kidnapped and seen off brigands and killed two men and gazed at photos of the Pope kissing the runway and bluffed his way to this steamy city. Not many killed even one man in their lifetime yet he had killed two, with another two to come. Of course there were all the others he had killed but that was during the revolution. In revolution it should not be seen as killing but purging a sick body of poison. This was a private affair, though now he thought about it not so very different. He was ridding the body politic of diseased organisms.

He bought a *salteña* from a woman at the street corner. She sat on an upturned crate with her tray of pastries on another. In Potosi or Sucre she would have worn a poncho and a bowler hat. In Santa Cruz that would invite heatstroke.

Was it vengeance or justice? In this case they were the same. And when it was done he would disappear in some place where he was not even a dusty memory. There he would try and find out what it was men did in old age. They sit and gossip about the old days and take a drink and play cards but what else? Cards bored him and he had never liked to drink and gossip was out of the question. Would he just sit?

'You are supposed to eat it not talk to it.'

'What?' Muttering to themselves was something old men did. If he did that, he would betray himself. There were spies everywhere. He was counting on it in Santa Cruz.

The chilli in the *salteña* made him thirsty. He stepped into the Trieste for a cup of coffee and decided that the long day ahead might as well start here.

'And tell me, has Herr Uhler been in recently?' Not Señor Uhler, Herr Uhler. It established him at once as being an immigrant rather than a native of German stock. There were many German immigrants in South America, some in search of opportunity, others fleeing from one of Europe's upheavals.

'Herr Uhler? Do I know an Uhler? You think I do but the name is not familiar. Describe him to me.'

It was a bouncy middle-aged man Che questioned. The proprietor of a baker's shop called Trieste could be anything. He could be northern Italian. He could be Yugoslav, making his escape from Trieste. Or he could be descended from an older line, from when the Austrian empire stretched to the Adriatic. For Uhler this would be a place to hear German spoken. Immigrants kept that hunger always. He wasn't a voluntary settler in search of a fortune, or a displaced person. He was of another kind, of the wave of Germans who had fled to South America as the Third Reich collapsed in ruins. They followed the Jews they'd driven out and fulfilling God's irony they even went to ground in the same cities.

'Hello?' the proprietor said. 'Are you in there?' He was peering into Che's face.

Che swallowed. It was just he felt at a loss how to describe Uhler except as a torturer.

'He is older than me, though he looks younger. He is short and trim. He wears thick glasses, as if he spent hours reading in a public library. Wispy grey hair.'

'That's not much to go on. Does he talk a lot? Enjoy a joke?'

'Yes, he enjoys a joke but his sense of humour is peculiar.'

'Everybody's sense of humour is peculiar. Some laugh at fat women, some laugh at dogs cocking their legs, some laugh at politicians, some laugh at their own bad luck.'

He laughs at pain. It was in Che's head, in his memory, making his tongue tumescent. He probably began as a boy pulling off a fly's wings, went on to shooting at cats with an airgun, then to shouting at Jews. Pain was a complicated drug. It required the victim to suffer larger and larger doses for it to cause pleasure to Uhler.

Che drank his coffee. It tasted of urine. Uhler had made him drink that. He hadn't looked like a Nazi torturer. No bull neck. He had looked like a mild bank clerk. Psychologists would talk of compensation but there were hundreds of thousands of bank clerks who managed to do without sticking pins into women's nipples.

'Thank you anyway,' Che said. The hot coffee had brought sweat to his forehead. Or the humid morning. Or the memories.

At the Francisco, a plump waiter waved a plump hand in the air. 'Herr Uhler? I know a Herr Uhlmann – Ulli we call him which drives him *mad*, which is why we do it. As he knows. Bit of a tease, you see. But Herr Uhler . . . There can't be anything very striking about him because I remember a striking man. Can't you just imagine, though, suppose he came in I could introduce the two of them: Ulli, meet Ulli the Second. My, that could be a riot, an absolute riot. Provided your friend has a sense of fun. Would you say that?'

No, Che would not say that, not personally speaking. Of course the sense of fun was akin to the sense of humour and some enjoyed themselves dumping buckets of water on your head while others delighted in dumping buckets of shit. Yes then, a sense of fun, but scatological fun.

The plump waiter was decked out in a black jacket and white

tie though it was still early. He had the darkest rings under his eyes that Che had ever seen. He looked as if he was destroyed by insomnia.

'The essential thing about Uhler,' Che said, 'is that he has fun at other people's expense.'

'One of those. Well, it takes all sorts I always say.'

'If he should come in, tell him I was asking for him.'

'Who should I say?'

That brought Che up short. He hadn't considered that. It had just seemed enough that it should be known all over town that an old man was searching for Uhler. 'Just tell him,' he said, 'tell him the Special was looking for him.'

'Oh, Special. Well now. Mind you come back. Sometimes in the room upstairs we organize very special evenings.'

The plump hand was like a handkerchief waving farewell.

Che heard German being spoken but when he turned it was only Mennonite farmers. There were two of them, he guessed father and son. They were in town with their wives as well but you never counted Mennonite wives because nobody did, not even the women themselves. Catching Che's glance they dropped their eyes to the ground. Heads bowed in submission, they murmured to each other. What did Mennonite women talk about? How to soothe teething babies? A new cake recipe? How to get axle grease off dungarees? They wore long dowdy frocks. Bonnets hid their hair.

Che moved beside the men who were walking slowly, arguing in German. No, a discussion because their voices weren't heated. It was just that German syllables made such a clash in his ears. German wasn't one of his languages. His whole life – perhaps even the history of a continent – would have been different if he hadn't needed a German interpreter.

They'd stopped talking, these Mennonite farmers, because of the stranger who'd joined them. Che should say something but his mind was dislocated. Part of him had retreated to East Berlin so many years ago. He had gone as President of the Cuban National Bank and as usual he had taken his begging bowl. That was when he first met Haidée Tamara Bunke. She was assigned to him as interpreter. Later she came to Havana and enrolled at the university. When she transferred to one of the ministries it was easier for her to do her real job: which was to watch over Che and report to Moscow. Ah, he'd been a Stakhanovite then, always a new project that needed his energy. There had probably been a whole Directorate in the KGB assigned to keep track of him. Moscow couldn't tie him down. Fidel couldn't tie him down. Neither could Aleida, his wife. Nor could Haidée. She had come to Bolivia before him. Certain gossips had whispered that was the reason he chose Bolivia as the setting for the revolution. It had made Che livid when he had first heard hints of that. Bolivia was at the very heart of the continent so the revolution could spread in all directions. Nevertheless, it was true that she had come to visit the revolutionary group. She had been living in La Paz under an assumed name. When she stayed at the base camp she assumed yet another name: Tania. She had professed her love for Che. 'Admit' was her chosen word. 'Ramón, I admit love,' Tania had said, as if confessing before a People's Court to a bourgeois deviation. He had believed her.

Stumbling over the kerb, Che looked round to find he was alone. The Mennonite farmers in their dungarees and straw stetsons had disappeared, sweeping their frumpish wives off with them. With Mennonites bigamy wouldn't be a crime, it would be a punishment.

More Mennonites. They all dressed the same, but these were older. He had to ask.

'Excuse me, I am looking for Herr Uhler. I wonder if you have any news of him.'

There were three of them this time and they'd come to town without their women. Other men came on their own and bought their pesticide and fertilizer early then had a few drinks and maybe a little relaxation in the afternoon. But these were from a stricter sect and looked at Che as a fair specimen of the ungodly.

'Uhler? What Uhler is this, please? And what is your business with this Uhler? Explain to us, please.'

'It is a personal matter. If you see him, tell him I'm looking for him.'

'Who are you?'

'Somebody Special. He'll know.'

Walking away Che heard a burst of peevish talk of which he understood only *'spezial?'*

In the main plaza there was a language school. English classes were much in demand. After all, if you were going to export cocaine to the United States, you needed to know how to negotiate and how to offer a bribe. Che went in through an arch and found himself in a courtyard under a high glass roof. An elderly couple were drinking a pot of tea at a small table. Along one side of the courtyard a long table was being set with glasses and cutlery. Presumably that was where the students practised their table manners.

Che climbed metal steps to a balcony that ran round all four sides of the courtyard. Passing closed doors he heard a young male voice speaking slowly: 'How much is it? Do you accept credit cards? Haven't you made a mistake in the bill?' At the next classroom, a female voice: 'No thank you, I am waiting for my husband. He has red hair.'

A certain subtlety there. Red hair hinted at the protection of a *gringo* husband.

To reach the Director's sanctum, he passed through an empty secretarial office and knocked on a chipped cream door. There was the scraping of a chair and a pause before he was invited to enter. The Director had a military moustache to add strength to a chalky face. A pall of smoke hung above him and a pack of Big Ben cigarettes was on his desk. The desk was empty of papers.

'Come in, *señor*. In what way can I assist you? You have perhaps a son who is studying here?'

Che found himself puffing, from the stairs, from the humidity, from asthma, perhaps from the reminder of Tania. As Che fought to control his asthma, the Director revised his opinion of his age.

'Possibly it is a grandson you hope will enter the export trade, for which spoken English is a necessity.'

Especially for certain flights going north. It was time the name of the city was changed to Santa Coca.

'It is not English I am interested in,' Che said. 'It is German.'

'Yes, yes,' the Director said, though his eyes slid sideways as if he had to recall whether German was one of their subjects. 'Certainly, German classes, spoken and written, literature and customs.'

'You have native Germans who teach?'

'Naturally. The accent is never correct without a native teacher.'

'But they will have lived some time in South America too, so that their Spanish is also fluent?' Che pressed.

'Naturally. It is necessary to know the idioms in both languages.'

'I wonder if you number Herr Uhler among your teachers?'

Next door to the language school was a *Casa de Cambio*. A woman behind the desk was a surprise. A bonecrusher at the door wasn't.

'Do you change German currency?' Che asked.

'Certainly. How much do you want to sell?'

'What rate are you offering?'

By way of answer she pointed at a board where the rates for dollars, pounds, yen, cruzados, francs, Deutschmarks, pesos from Argentina and Chile, sols, guaranis and other lesser currencies were listed.

'And for large amounts, are the rates better?'

'How large?'

'How much does Herr Uhler usually change?'

Her eyes became distant and she nodded ever so slightly to King Kong. Discussions about other people's money were bad manners.

On the next corner were the street touts.

'I really wanted to talk to the dealer Herr Uhler goes to.'

'I offer the best rates. You got the money on you? A moneybelt? No problem. Just step inside this door and slip it off. No danger. From the moment you step inside you are fully protected by our insurance policy.'

'So you don't know Herr Uhler?'

The tout took a deep pull on his cigarette while he considered the situation. 'The name . . . I hear many names but I am careful always to forget them.'

'He has an *estancia*.'

The tout beckoned an older man. 'Man asking about Uhler.'

'Uhler? What makes that an interesting name?'

The tout concentrated on his cigarette. He raised a hand and curved it so it resembled a big letter C.

'And who's asking?'

They both looked at Che. 'An acquaintance from the old days.' But Che had an uneasy feeling – the hesitation he had always heeded when he'd been a guerrilla – that any trail they pointed him down would lead to an ambush.

Progress round the square brought him to the third side. Next to the Palace Theatre was the Social Club. Through curtained windows Che could see potted palms and cane chairs. He entered the lobby and the porter at the desk eyed his shabby suit.

'Yes, Señor Uhler is a member.'

Che couldn't believe it.

'No, he is not on the premises at this moment.'

It was the first direct acknowledgement that Uhler was still alive. He might have suffered a heart attack since he last amused himself with Che.

'It is the policy of the club never to divulge a member's address in any circumstance.'

And the eyes wandering over Che's clothes implied it would need a lot more money than such a person possessed to cause a temporary suspension of that policy.

He had lunch. He was no hungrier than at breakfast but it was fuel for the afternoon. He sat at a tin table under a tree in a courtyard and was served the inevitable rice and lump of meat. He remembered the Englishman Morton having the rice strained from his soup and Lucrecia who was a mother duck to him and the Pope kissing the runway.

He had made progress since then. It hadn't been easy. It still wasn't easy.

There were shouts from a group of Japanese. They were gambling at cards, slapping down money, dealing wildly. He had always thought of the Japanese as restrained. The rowdiness was explained by the table edged close to theirs which was crowded with empty beer bottles. Probably farmers in for the day. There was a whole colony not far away and they'd even called the town Okinawa.

Without warning it began to rain. It was one of those tropical storms that drench you in seconds.

The Japanese stood up and carried their card table under shelter. Two of their party followed behind with the table of empty bottles.

Huge drops crashed into the leaves above Che and then abruptly stopped. The courtyard steamed as the sun came out.

'Uhler?'

The faces of the Japanese turned up towards him, four, five, six earnest faces, the last having to twist to look back over his shoulder, clutching a fan of cards to his chest so Che couldn't glimpse the strength of his hand.

'Uhler?' came the query from a tubby-faced man. He looked at his neighbour.

'Uhler?'

Black hair sprang in spikes from the crowns of their heads. It was like the hairstyles Che had seen on some of the young. Three men wore glasses and as their heads moved their eyes were like sea creatures shifting with the current.

'Uhler?'

Their heads were now turning left and right. Yet it was a reasonable question. They farmed cotton and sugar-cane and bananas. They could know other ranch owners.

'Uhler?' A man picked up his glass. He held it up towards Che. 'Uhler,' he said. Suddenly they were all doing it. 'Uhler! Uhler!' Six glasses were raised. Teeth showed in six smiles. 'Uhler!' they toasted him.

Baffled, Che turned away.

*

It could have been the food at lunch, or the five-minute rainstorm, or the deadening humidity that followed it. But during the afternoon he had an uneasiness he couldn't pin down at first. I'm ageing fast, he thought, I had better hustle before I lapse into senility. Or it's the asthma, worse in this climate, very tiring. Or it's this obsessed, buzzing, heartless town.

Except for the usual cripples on the cathedral steps, there were no beggars. There were no sellers of single garlic cloves, such as lined the pavement in Sucre. There were signs in the windows of shops and offices advertising jobs. Santa Cruz was booming and perhaps that was what made him uneasy. Money making, money spending, a consumer society on the American pattern.

It was that. Analysing a little further, he added up the number of Americans he had seen and it was surprising. They stood out because of their height and the flesh on their faces and the shortness of their hair and their wrinkleproof clothes. The black Americans had a lazy power in the way they moved. Chewing gum, Marlboro, after-shave, baseball caps, sneakers. Singly, in pairs, in jeeps, in cafés, on street corners. No women. Hand signals. The army, the CIA, agents of imperialism anyway.

It was to be expected. They were bound to take an interest in Che Guevara. But their arrival meant it was time to stop spreading Uhler's name, time to act.

With the opening of Viru Viru, the old airport had changed in character. El Trompillo still had a sign proclaiming it the *Internacional Aeropuerto* but in fact it was devoted entirely to the air force and to private citizens. It was convenient to the city centre, only a dozen blocks from the main plaza. Che looked for a taxi and changed his mind. People's attention focused on someone arriving by taxi, paying off the driver, turning to go to a certain entrance. An old man hobbling on foot, of what importance was he?

Huge shade trees lined the streets for most of the way. At first there were shops and small businesses, then battered buildings which had been the edge of town before the great cocaine expansion, then a medical centre, a *jardin de niños* where children shouted and played while a woman windmilled her arms at them, bungalows behind fences and hedges, some very fancy houses with the tallest radio aerials Che had ever seen. Towards the end of the street was the Club Aerotecnico, a low ranch-style building set well back from the road, with tables and chairs set out on the terrace. No, he didn't want technical people.

The airport was ahead of him. He turned left and followed the perimeter fence. Beyond it were lines of parked planes, hundreds and hundreds. They seemed to be formed up for an invasion, waiting for a general to bark a command. Bomb them to bits, napalm them, burn their shanties, slaughter their babies, the peasants breed too much.

He caught himself swaying and rested a moment on a bench. Touch of fever, old age, exhaustion? Madness? Just the heat and the pursuit of evil and the clock moving steadily round. He felt his scalp itching. Looking up he saw a cloud of midges descended from a tree. Symbol, he thought. Bloated Yankee imperialists searching the city, thirsty to suck his blood. Puny Bolivian bloodsuckers strike first. Symbol, you can always find a symbol if you put your mind to it. If everything is a symbol, what is reality?

He walked further. There was a low wall, a line of hibiscus, a sign for the Circulo Aeronautico. This looked like a social centre, a swimming pool of violent blue, a line of changing huts, a green and cream building with crates of empties stacked against a wall. It would have been a possibility except it was deserted.

At a roundabout he turned and went down an avenue along another side of the airport. On the other side of the perimeter fence two soldiers shared a cigarette. Perhaps the army always posted sentries there, perhaps not. There was a long line of buildings, hangars, soldiers, a flying school, engineering workshops, fuel tanks, offices for Beechcraft and Cessna dealers, soldiers. A gate in the wire was closed and guarded. In the shade of a hangar was a car with darkened windows. Changes in the world had ceased to surprise him but he noticed the dark windows. When he'd been at liberty twenty years ago men of a certain kind had felt obliged to hide behind sunglasses. Sunglasses were no longer enough. The crimes they were ashamed of now were obviously greater.

At the end of the road was a terminal building with an

unexpected crowd outside it. More soldiers, police cars. To his left was the Associación Pilotos Civiles and that was what he wanted. He turned in.

He walked slowly, as a man of his age was entitled to. He avoided the front entrance, not being a member, and crossed a lawn of coarse tropical grass. It had been cut that morning because the smell of it lingered in the air but in a day or so it would need cutting again. Watch closely and you could see it growing. A pleasant garden he wandered through, palm trees, plumbago, frangipani, bougainvillaea swamping a pillar. He was guided round the back by the tock-tock-tock of ping-pong. Two teenage boys were playing. A man he took to be their father was stretched out in a lounger watching them and then watching Che as he moved directly up to him.

'Caught you too?'

Che frowned.

'The police got you?'

This was not what he wanted to hear. Che looked cautiously past the ping-pong game to where other people sat at tables under the shade of umbrellas. A lot of men, maybe a couple of dozen.

'What do you mean?' Che asked.

'Well, they got me. I flew in this morning to pick up my boys and see one or two people in town. When we got here after lunch – ' and he jerked his head at the airport – 'the police had closed it. No planes allowed to take off. Is that what happened to you?'

It has now, Che thought, it has now.

'Why is it closed?'

'Americans ordered it. That's the story.'

'How can the Americans order it?'

'Demanded, requested, suggested, required, threatened.' The man gazed up at the sky where clouds appeared, boiled and disappeared under the hot sun. 'Perhaps you prefer one of those words.'

'But why?'

'Story goes they are mounting a seek-and-destroy mission against a big cocaine kitchen.' He shrugged.

'So what are you going to do?'

'Play ping-pong. Have a few drinks. Stay the night. Time the boys found out what goes on in town at night. Send the bill to Washington. What can we do?'

What can I do, Che thought. Airport shut, army and police on alert, Americans on patrol. He'd been going to find a pilot who'd fly him to Uhler's ranch.

'You?' the man asked. 'Where were you headed?'

Che swept his eyes over him, his buckled moccasins, his sharp creased trousers, his button-down shirt, his wavy hair worn to his collar. He was a prosperous rancher from the Sierra. What he farmed to make him rich enough for a private plane, that was another matter.

Che said, 'I was going to see Wolf.'

'Wolf? Which Wolf is that?'

The wolf in sheep's clothing, Che thought, as the English have it.

'Wolfgang Uhler.'

The man took out a packet of cigarettes, offered them and lit one himself.

'So you know Wolf. Well, it's not impossible. I'm not saying it's comfortable but if your business is urgent you can do it. My boys and I are headed for Esperanza and that's out of the question. But you could make it.'

Where? How? Che wanted to know.

'I have an idea,' he said. 'I'll go to the Americans and ask them to airlift me.'

The other man went still, the cigarette between his lips, sighting down it like a gun barrel at Che. His body relaxed and he gave a shout of laughter.

'I'd love to see Wolf's face, the US cavalry swinging low over Puerto Vargas, you saluting from the door of the lead helicopter.'

Che smiled.

CHAPTER 17

The aerial view was all a spy could ask. The low huts, the fishbone pattern of parked cars, the volleyball net, the jumble of US army helicopters and light aircraft. Tanner couldn't be certain but he thought he saw a man spading a flowerbed. His imagination or were there more people about? A black and white police car was parked outside the gate. Soldiers waited in a jeep. Waited for what?

The plane turned and began its final descent. On the horizon was the city of Santa Cruz, a haze of pollution showing the benefits of progress. Through the window Tanner saw more jeeps, more soldiers. The engine note sharpened, there was a whine from the wing flaps and a perceptible change in the trim of the 727. Tanner looked down and saw the runway dropping away below them.

I don't believe it, this is not happening.

Drawn up across the runway were two trucks. Soldiers' faces were turned up. Silence grew inside the plane. The sisters in the row behind fell quiet for the first time in thirty-five minutes. Tanner was staring at the receding airport buildings when he was hit on the head.

'Where is the crew?' one of the sisters hissed at him between the seats. 'The stewardesses have vanished.'

Squinting between the backrests Tanner saw tiny features twisted by violent fury at the unpredictability of life. The face vanished and a younger version took its place.

'Do something,' the second sister urged.

'What?'

'You are a man.'

A crackle from the speakers in the ceiling alerted them. A muffled voice began: 'This is . . .' A pause.

The first sister said, 'He's forgotten who he is.'

'This is Captain Rojas.' Long pause.

'It is a hijack. There are wild men on the flight deck. They are instructing the captain to fly to Havana,' said the second sister.

The first sister's face reappeared on top. They're not real, Tanner decided, they're glove puppets.

'They are ravishing the stewardesses.'

'This is your captain. I regret to inform you that this flight is being rerouted to Tarija. We have been refused permission to land at Santa Cruz. The authorities have temporarily closed the airport for security reasons. Thank you.'

Tanner was stunned. The rest of the plane was in uproar.

'What did I tell you? When we get to Tarija the captain will make a dash for Havana,' said the second sister.

Tanner said, 'Tarija is in the south. Cuba is thousands of kilometres to the north.'

'Exactly. It is a trick.'

The stewardesses appeared with brave smiles and trays of warm Coca-Cola in cardboard cups.

The most important thing seemed to be to speak to Hershey, though Tanner admitted to himself it achieved nothing. A comforter, was it, a quick suck from mum? Perhaps it shelved responsibility telling Hershey he was isolated at Tarija Airport while Guevara slipped away to his next tryst. It wasn't Tanner's fault that Santa Cruz was physically blockaded. The army was mounting an anti-terrorist drive, that was the rumour. Or a bomb was being defused. Or there had been a coup. Hard information was hard to come by.

The public phone had a sign saying it was out of order. The airline desk had no phone. The airport administration was evasive and not at all impressed by his press card. A man accepted some dollars and disappeared to arrange matters and was never seen again.

A tap on his elbow brought Tanner round to see the two sisters from the plane. They barely reached his shoulder and the configuration of their cheeks and eyebrows gave them the faces of monkeys.

'We have heard that the airport is closed because General Stroessner is flying to exile there.'

'Is that a fact?' Tanner said.

He excused himself to try to find the airport director. He asked three employees and was told the director was unobtainable, in conference, gone fishing with the army commander. A speaker of the truth at last.

Someone was staring at him. There is an animal instinct that warns when we are the object of attention. Looking round he saw a pair of intense eyes glaring at him across the airport lounge. Martina's body and the lower part of her face were hidden by a stout matron. Just the dark eyes were fixed on him, like twin gun barrels resting on the matron's shoulder. It was the same clash of looks as the first time they'd seen each other. Lovers, competitors, enemies. The eyes looked furious. Should he go and ask her the reason? Did women have reasons?

The two sisters had sought him out again. The younger said, 'Isn't it exciting? A Hollywood film company has hired Santa Cruz Airport for the day. An epic, they say.'

Telephoning Hershey had become an obsession. A psychologist would have told him he was suffering from guilt because of sleeping with Martina and was after absolution. Tanner would have punched the psychologist on the snoot. He decided to take a taxi to the Telecom office in town. The exit door was locked. He rattled the handle and a policeman turned round with his sub-machine-gun at the ready.

'It's because you could be leaving at any moment,' a ground hostess said.

'After there's been a collection among the passengers to pay the airline's bills,' Tanner said.

She smiled then thought better of it.

'*Ciao*.' She backed away.

Bolivia isn't a country, Tanner told himself, it's *A Night at the Opera* without the slow bits.

Against all expectations the LAB flight returned to Santa Cruz late in the afternoon. An airline girl had appeared and simply clapped her hands to board the passengers. Girl off a farm, Tanner decided, used to shooing chickens.

It was dusk at Santa Cruz Airport. He saw Gurdjiev and Martina get off ahead of him and by the time he'd pushed down the aisle and reached the steps they were almost at the terminal building. Troops with rifles across their chests watched the disembarking passengers. They probably had no ammunition but the rifles discouraged Tanner from running. The conscripts looked honest but stupid. Night was coming down fast though the clusterlights on poles hadn't been switched on. Brightness came forward from the windows and he saw Martina and Gurdjiev disappear through the Arrivals door.

He was sure of it. But by the time he'd been processed through the main hall there was no sign of a rolling peasant figure or an intense jungle cat. He dodged through a crowd of police and airport personnel and taxi touts and friends of incoming passengers. There was not only their own plane but delayed flights from La Paz and Assunción too. He searched behind pillars, checked the men's toilet, watched taxis loading. He walked through the car-park with its scattering of vehicles, detouring to peer into pools of shadow.

How the buggers did it, he didn't know. A side door somewhere, a beckoning gesture from an airport worker who was a local sympathizer. Comrade, hush, this way quickly, the fascist pigs and spies are everywhere. They loved Party games.

He found a taxi. Upset at his own incompetence, it didn't occur to him that he might not in fact have lost the others. His mind was on Martina again. Why was her stare so hostile?

The driver suggested Los Tajibos hopefully because it was the most expensive hotel and he could expect a fat tip. Tanner disillusioned him, explaining he was not a *Yanqui* but an *Inglés* and thus very poor. The driver doubted this. He had seen the Queen on television and she did not look poor. Have you not heard, Tanner said, how the Queen's family is breeding so that we must give all our money in taxes to buy them bread?

They passed through the tollgate and joined the highway leading to the city. It was fully dark now and their headlights swept across staring cattle, palm trees, billboards for German water pumps, shacks with women stirring pots by oil lamps, black and white painted oil barrels dumped haphazardly at the side of the road.

'Those are from the blockade,' the driver said. 'The army never takes away its garbage.'

'Today?'

'Today. They had the idea of sealing off the city. Forget La Paz, Santa Cruz is the most important city in Bolivia and the army treats us like a village of sugar-cane cutters. Viru Viru closed. El Trompillo closed. The train to Brazil cancelled. All highways blockaded. Just because there's a demented murderer loose. I ask you, in the Sierra who worries about one more killer?'

'What happened?'

'I'll tell you what happened. I was trapped right here on this highway. The traffic tailed back for two kilometres, cars, tractors, trucks, buses. The army put oil barrels across the road and brought up troops and armoured vehicles. Soldiers were checking papers and searching the trucks, which is not popular. So the people marched. They got out of the buses and trucks and crossed the fields and blowing whistles at them had no effect. They went round the blockade to the road on the other side. The buses simply swapped passengers, turned and went back. So that was the end of the blockade. The army packed it up. They're stupid but they're not that stupid.'

'This was because of Guevara? Perhaps they caught him.'

'They wouldn't know who to look for unless he was wearing a lapel badge.'

At the Internacional Hotel he signed the register and asked for whisky to be sent up. They had no Scotch, only Argentine. Plenty of ice, plenty of ginger ale to drown the taste.

In his room, waiting for the whisky, he put a call through to the Bunker. He slumped on the bed while the connection was being made, a fan moving humid air over him. He wasn't so much tired as bone weary. Sleep no longer healed him. Lying awake or dozing fitfully, his brain went on the prowl. It slunk down dark alleys where his wife screamed at him from the ruins of their marriage. Or it sniffed at the titbits other women offered. Or it hauled itself off to the Bunker to refight old battles against old enemies, or lick its wounds from defeats, or prepare for new struggles.

'Hello, what number are you calling?'

Standard response from the Bunker switchboard. Tanner identified himself and asked to be put through to Hershey.

The trouble was, the battles seemed harder now, the reasons more dubious, and the spoils of victory went to others. Such as Hershey, reaching out for the grand prize. Victory glorified the General, got him promoted to Field Marshal. Defeat meant disgrace for the poor bloody infantry. What the hell was he doing chasing after a once-dead revolutionary who should be booking himself into a golden sunset home? It was so Hershey could preen his feathers and boast he had got Guevara out from under everyone's nose, and *then* trade him to the Americans. Che in his hands would give Hershey a powerful bargaining tool.

'Controller, Americas office.'

It took an age for Hershey's secretary to answer. Powdering her nose, that's where she'd say she'd been.

'Is he in? Phil Tanner.'

'I'm afraid he's still out to lunch, Mr Tanner.'

He'd kissed her once. Her name was Jennie Bone, a willowy brunette whose father was something in international banking. It had been after a session at the pub just before last Christmas. Tanner had thought it might spread a little seasonal cheer but she'd just let it happen, as if kissing was an activity for one. And she still called him Mister.

'His lunch hour or three is it? What time is he due back?'

'I believe he's going on somewhere.'

'Believe? You don't know?'

'It's not an office thing. It's private.'

'I see.'

Terrific, Tanner thought. I sweat it out in the front line while the General lunches at his club and wanders off for a private viewing at some Bond Street gallery. Suppose tomorrow morning, which would mean waking Hershey up again, I rang to say: I quit. Just like that. I'm not going to flog the streets and bars and hotels looking for Che, not going to bribe the local law, not going to tangle with the American colonels in their compound, not going to have my shoes shined six times.

'Can I help? Can I give him a message when he comes in?'

I'm not a soldier, Tanner decided, I'm a whore paid by the

Bunker. Well, suppose this whore rolled off in the middle of all the heaving and grunting and said: Sod you, you can finish the job off yourself. That would be something.

'You can tell him,' Tanner hesitated, 'tell him his correspondent in Bolivia rang. I am at present in Santa Cruz. He hasn't left a name with you, has he?'

'A name?'

'The research department, when it had finished *The Times* crossword, was meant to be coming up with the name of someone I should interview urgently.' There was a knock at the door. '*Entre*.'

'I beg your pardon?'

'Not you, it's room service. *Cerca de la ventana*,' he said, not bothering to look round. 'No name?'

'No. Shall I ask him to call you?'

'Don't bother,' Tanner said, 'don't spoil his day.' He was saved from saying anything more by the telephone being lifted out of his hands. Something cold, like an iced glass of whisky, touched the side of his neck. But when he eased his head round, two men he'd never seen before stood behind him. The iced glass of whisky had turned into a knife.

Tanner dreaded a knife. He had a respect for a pistol but there was always the hope you could twist aside or the mechanism would jam. Most hopes were illusions but there was still a chance. With the knife already pricking his skin, which way could he twist? Besides, his nerves carried the memory of steel slicing the flesh of his left arm when he'd once met a mugger infuriated at finding so few notes in his wallet.

They handcuffed Tanner, took him down the stairs and through the darkened coffee shop and out of a service door at the rear.

'Don't shout,' the man with the knife warned.

'Is it money?' Tanner tried. 'I'm not with a rich multinational that'll pay a ransom.'

'And don't try to draw attention to yourself.'

He was put in the back seat between the two of them.

'Where are you taking me?'

'To see someone.'

The car came out of the alley and started on its journey. It was the usual lurching drive from intersection to intersection, slowing down at each because they used no lights. He'd never asked why the cars went without headlights at night. Saving bulbs? Bravado? They went half a dozen blocks east, then turned north.

'I'm a journalist. There'll be an outcry if you kidnap me. Remember Daniloff last year? Almost wrecked the Summit.'

'Daniloff was a CIA spy,' the man on the other side of Tanner said. 'It is a well-known fact.'

This one had a long serious face with studious glasses. He's the intellectual, Tanner decided, and the tone of the reply had confirmed his fears. These were Gurdjiev's local allies. When the car stops is my best chance, he thought. Follow the intellectual out of the car fast, two-fisted jab to the throat, run. Perhaps one had a gun but a night shot against a dwindling target was notoriously tricky.

The car stopped in the middle of a row of buildings and Tanner's chance never came. The driver got out first and stood on the pavement with a pistol levelled at his chest. The knife was at his kidneys, urging him to clamber out but not to do anything foolish. They went in a rush into the house and the door was closed before Tanner even had a chance to look for neighbours. The knife prodded him to go further and he passed three closed doors and found himself in a dining-room with a heavy carved table, eight high-backed chairs, a display cabinet showing ugly crystal glasses. Hardly the home of your average toiler, was Tanner's judgement, more your bourgeois sympathizer. He was still handcuffed and now a rope round his chest tied him to one of the dining-chairs and only then did they seem at ease.

What do we do now? Play I-Spy? Tanner had a nervous desire to joke.

A peasant? Did I think that? Tanner wondered. Then he's a peasant who's angry because his cow has stopped giving milk.

Gurdjiev had come into the building and his voice could be heard demanding what had happened to Lindemayer and if he'd known there was no telephone he'd have used another safe house. There was exasperation in his voice that he was having to work so hard, and an edge of something else. Desperation was too strong a word. Urgency. There was the bang of a door and a bit of peace.

'That's who you've brought me to see, is it?' Tanner asked. 'Is his name really Gurdjiev?'

There were no answers. Gurdjiev had put the fear of Lenin into his local muscle. They weren't content with handcuffing him and tying him to a chair; two of them sat watching every flicker of his eyelids. The one who'd driven the car gripped a pistol. The knife-man had tucked his weapon back in a sheath on his belt. Did he really walk round Santa Cruz looking like a brigand?

Footsteps approached and Gurdjiev came into the room. Tanner had watched him in public places but had never been in a room like this, feeling his personality. He grasped at once why Martina had deserted his bed last night. At close quarters he gave off the hum of a piece of powerful machinery.

Gurdjiev snapped his fingers at the two men and gestured them out. To Tanner he said a sentence or two in Russian and Tanner responded in English. We neither of us know the other's language, Tanner marvelled, just like a Summit with Gorbachev and Reagan. They settled on Spanish, in which Gurdjiev was as fluent as Tanner, his accent suggesting some years' residence in Cuba.

'No apologies for bringing you here or tying you up. No false regrets, Tanner. You have been nothing but a nuisance, an irritant. On the same planes, following me to the same hotel. I have been forced to waste effort on you, forced to take evasive action at the airport, forced to bring you here, forced to hold you and spare the time to question you.'

That's a handsome declaration of love, Tanner said to himself. And aloud: 'Why waste more time? Why not just turn me loose?'

'The British pride themselves on their sense of humour. The rest of the world doesn't find you funny.' Gurdjiev walked round Tanner, inspecting his knots. 'I suspect it's uncomfortable and it's not even efficient. You could get up and walk out, though you'd be forced to carry the chair with you.'

'So that's why they sit and watch me, in case I run off with the furniture.'

'He did at least have the safety catch off his gun,' Gurdjiev said. 'So.' He clapped his hands. 'You are now out of the reckoning. That leaves only the Bolivian army and police and the Americans to contend with. We needn't waste time considering the Bolivian authorities. I am sure it has been your experience that they are a nuisance but not serious rivals. Therefore we are left with the Americans. They have all the weaknesses of their strengths. You must have observed the truth of that paradox.'

He spoke as if, despite their positions, there was a bond between them. How old was he? Tanner considered the bald head with its border of clipped grey hair and the chubby features that defied the cracks of old age. He must be well on in his sixties, even into his seventies, but still vigorous. Communist societies were notorious for the way their leaders clung on. Was it the same in the KGB or had he been called out of retirement to deal with this crisis? Or, possibly, had he come out of retirement on his own initiative?

Gurdjiev was studying him with frank curiosity. 'Do you deal much with the Americans? They are your allies.'

'A certain amount.'

'Here, I mean. Do you liaise with them? Use their facilities?'

'No,' Tanner said, putting out of mind his interview with the Colonel at the compound.

Gurdjiev nodded. 'You have the look of a solo. Self-sufficient. Not one of the crowd. So you don't even drink with them? You are, after all, a drinking man. *Singani.*'

Thank you, Martina.

'No,' Gurdjiev said, musing. 'I suspect you find them simply too much. They send too many *gringos*, whom nobody will trust. They flaunt too much money, which people will steal. They rely too much on technology as a substitute for brains.'

Gurdjiev smoothed his bald pate, unconsciously stroking his own brains.

'And in this case,' Tanner said, 'they are fuelled too much by hate, the wrong motivation. Would you say that?'

Gurdjiev wasn't playing with motives that night. His hand finished its massage, moved down to scratch his chest and then jab a finger at Tanner. 'You haven't found him, have you.'

It wasn't really a question. Tanner shook his head. 'No.'

'And I don't think you have any idea where he is.'

Tanner leaned forward in the chair until the rope tightened on his flesh.

'It really *is* Che.' There was almost awe in his voice. 'Otherwise you wouldn't be under this pressure to find him.'

'It is someone who *says* he is Che. If he falls into the hands of the imperialists, they will pervert him to their own purposes. Whoever he is, they will brainwash him and use him for propaganda. He will be turned into a convert for capitalism and Wall Street.'

'No.' Tanner felt excitement swelling in him at his understanding. 'Never mind history and logic and evidence that he died a long time ago. You have evidence he is alive. That is why you had to come. You have been given some undeniable proof. Yes, that's it,' and his face lit up at his understanding. 'Morton was in Bolivia, Morton brought out the proof, and whatever it was – I don't know, some password, secret document, fingerprints – that was why Morton was killed.'

'You imagine that?'

Gurdjiev at last pulled out a dining-chair and sat down opposite Tanner. The two of them looked straight in each other's eyes. There was a sort of recognition there, as there is with someone who was once very close and has separated: a part of you in the other's face. They were joined by their profession and separated by politics. Here was Gurdjiev sitting down as if they were on an equal footing, colleagues who could discuss a difficult case.

'What do you intend to do with Che?' Tanner asked.

'He is to be taken to safety. The most important consideration obviously is to ensure he doesn't fall into American hands. And what did you intend to do?'

'Persuade him his best hope of a peaceful old age was to come to England with a guarantee of a new identity and no publicity.'

'Peaceful? Do you think peace was what Chershey had in mind?'

For a moment the guttural pronunciation baffled Tanner. For another moment he stumbled at the idea that Gurdjiev knew the name of his Controller. But why not? Ask anyone who'd suffered a plague in their garden, moles were notoriously difficult to eradicate.

'What does Chershey want with this madman?' Gurdjiev pressed.

'Power play, isn't it. He wants to show how effective the outfit could be under his leadership. How we can outwit the Americans and the Russians and the Cubans and snatch Guevara from under their noses. By the way I would have thought this was a natural operation for Cubans. Why only one?'

Gurdjiev didn't answer the question. He raised a hand that took in the room that was Tanner's cell and the handcuffs and the rope. 'Is this being effective? Outwitting us?'

There seemed nothing to say to that. Tanner shrugged.

'I have wasted enough time,' Gurdjiev said. Some of the urgency returned to him as he bustled to the door. He paused long enough to say, 'He *is* in town, or *was*. Asking questions. I don't know what questions but I will find out. One of our people noticed an old man who sounds right asking questions of some currency swindlers and later he saw him at the bus station. We are tracking down the people he talked to. But at night, in this city, it is not always easy to find the people you want.'

'It never has been, has it?'

'No.' Gurdjiev was already through the door when he stopped. 'How did you know I'd been here before?'

'I didn't.'

Wimps worry, Tanner told himself. Did Churchill worry in 1940? Did Henry V worry before Agincourt? Napoleon before Waterloo?

Worry was wasteful. It wouldn't let him sleep. Worry feasted on the rope round his chest, the cuffs on his wrists, the two men who watched from across the room, the pistol with the safety catch off. They didn't sleep. He never caught them blinking. They smoked in turns so that one always held the pistol. They worried too.

There was a smart move, an unexpected ploy, a trick that could gain his freedom. Tanner tried to think what it was.

He listened to the building. It was old, solid, with very high ceilings. Gurdjiev had gone out. Somebody had left with him because Gurdjiev had been delivering a rebuke. A little later he'd heard the front door open and close again, and from upstairs the creak of a floorboard. He was imprisoned at the back of the house and occasionally he caught the muffled note of a car on the street. He could see mosquitoes drifting from wall to wall, coming lower, circling like miniaturized vultures. His thoughts drifted with them.

I should be taking Fansidar.

I should be so lucky to live to catch malaria.

Little bastards. Stuka dive bombers.

He heard a soft footfall in the passage and the door opened. Martina came in, pistol in hand. The guards stirred, uncertain about the situation, but she wasn't looking at them. She stared at Tanner and there was a hint of hellcat to her eyes. She angled her face towards the guards while keeping her eyes fixed on Tanner.

'Go and take a break. There's coffee in the kitchen. I'll call you when I want you.' The men stiffened and exchanged glances. 'You hear? Leave us alone. I've got a gun and know how to use it if he tries anything. Out!'

Machismo died hard in the men. But she'd come with Gurdjiev and carried his authority. They shuffled out and their mutters retreated towards the kitchen. Still Martina fastened on Tanner's eyes. It was the kids' game of outstaring and he blinked first.

'What's this? The seduction bit?'

Her breath came in a hiss. 'We've had the seduction. A line of smooth talk, wisecracks, charm you wash and drip-dry after each conquest. Don't tell me about seduction. Journalist, huh? While you lie and get me into bed, Gurdjiev is sending your name to Moscow. Tanner, P. Didn't know what the P stood for but the reply was pretty damning. P for Philip, agent in the British SIS, known countries of operation El Salvador, Nicaragua, Cuba, Colombia, Peru and Bolivia. Fluent Spanish. Only previous employment courier for tour operator. House in London. Married. You tricked me, P for Philip, lied to me, cheated me.'

She lifted her pistol, held it two-handed, pointed it at the centre of Tanner's forehead, squinted down the barrel at him with one eye squeezed shut. Tanner held his breath, waiting. There was no sound anywhere.

'Huh? Why don't you say something?'

Tanner understood silence was his only weapon.

'You cheat me, I kill you.'

He almost made one of the wisecracks as she called them. Great performance, Martina, only there's no audience to appreciate it.

She took a step closer, as if she wanted to make sure she couldn't miss.

'You don't care if I kill you?'

Tanner liked his silence more and more. She couldn't kill him or she'd never know what he would say. What he wanted to say was: Sweetheart, you're way over the top. He found he was breathing more easily because it wasn't the fact of working for the Bunker that outraged her, it was the deception.

'You're crazy, you know?' Slowly the pistol came down.

'This thing about tricking,' Tanner said. 'You told me Gurdjiev was a businessman and you were his assistant. You were tricking me, but I knew it. I was tricking you, and succeeded. That's the difference. Be honest – a part of you, deep down, recognized what I was. From the moment we saw each other, we both knew. The only reason I succeeded was because you wanted to be tricked. And that was a very personal kind of want.'

He'd said too much. She came to where he was tied to the chair and put the pistol to his forehead. Once again Tanner found he was bracing himself for the bullet.

'Martina? Martina, are you planning to do Gurdjiev's job for him?'

'Maybe I do it anyhow, just for me. He's not going to kill you, only hold you until he's got Che away.'

'You believe that? Look, I'd feel easier if you'd take the gun away. Has he told you he's not going to kill me?'

'Why should he kill you?'

'Because I know Che is alive. Because I'll talk. Other people don't know it's Che. They've only heard the ravings of a lunatic with macabre tastes in killing. But I know so I have to be killed. They want Che to disappear again. In a coffin this time, with the earth piled on top. South America is good at disappearing people. *Los desaparecidos*. Nobody hears of them again.'

'This is the poison they feed you in London, huh?'

'No, I've been working it out all on my own. Che says he has something to tell the world and Gurdjiev is determined he won't.'

She shook her head but at least she took the pistol away. The muscles at the back of his neck ached and he longed to massage them.

'Che is to be offered asylum in Cuba. That's why I'm here. To deliver a personal message.'

'When Gurdjiev locates Che, you'll go along too?'

'Of course.'

Tanner was numb inside. He recognized the numbness: it was when you were faced with the impossible. She wouldn't be persuaded. Words never did any good. A brute fact smack in the face could work, something that could be seen, experienced, not ignored.

'If . . .'

'If what?'

'If you go . . . Listen to what I say, Martina, listen very closely. Gurdjiev will take you along and he will kill Che and then he will kill you. Because you know about Che, know about the fingerprints Morton brought as proof. It *was* fingerprints, wasn't it? That was why Morton was killed, because he knew.'

She stared at him. There was the shadow of a smile on her face, not finding anything funny, pitying him.

Tanner remembered being in bed with her. *I give you my address in Florida and you come and see me*. To a house full of cops?

'Martina, this is very important. Do you truly not know Morton is dead?'

She didn't answer. The half-smile had gone from her face. She waited for him to go on.

'He was killed in your house. That's why I told you that you couldn't go home. Morton was murdered, shot and left to rot. After all, since you wouldn't be going back, it didn't matter. The killers removed his papers but they missed one clue, a connection to the Soviet Embassy in Washington. You're paying attention? You hear what I'm telling you?'

'You're lying. You're making this up to save yourself.'

Words were liars. She wouldn't change because of what he said but there was nothing he could show her. More words.

'Do you know why I was in South Africa? Because it was thought you and Morton were part of a Soviet spy ring. I was sent out like a scavenger to see if I could pick up any scraps. All I succeeded in picking up was a security cop called Van der Merwe, who sends you his regards.'

'Pig.'

She means Van der Merwe, Tanner comforted himself. But she glared through narrow eyes.

'One scrap I was shown was Ntuli. Do you know since your visit he is a detainee?'

'There will be a lot of martyrs,' she said.

'The Americans are there, of course. Like they're here. Like they're everywhere. One of them was in a philosophical mood and his theory was that everything wrong in the world connected up. He calls it the All-problem and it's Us versus Them.'

There was the murmur of a car's engine outside and the slam of a door. Martina lifted her head to the sound and then looked back at Tanner.

'Us versus Them? That's pathetic, like a child speaking.'

'Too simple? When it comes down to it, a bullet in the brain is a simple thing. And, like it or not, you and I are part of the Us, and Gurdjiev is one of Them.'

The front door closed and Gurdjiev's voice could be heard. He was calling out something that Tanner couldn't catch.

'He's part of the All-problem. Why are you shaking your head? God, you're a stubborn woman. What does it take to convince you?'

He stared into her eyes, wanting to show honesty, sincerity, truth. The handcuffs and the rope turned it to desperation.

'Perhaps you'll believe it after he kills me.'

Gurdjiev came into the room, still full of vigour. His face showed his news even before he spoke.

'He's found. Or rather we know where he's gone. He's been asking for an old Nazi called Uhler who's taken up a late-life career as cocaine farmer. Wonderful.'

Gurdjiev clapped his hands and gave a jolly smile.

'In the morning we pay him a visit at Puerto Vargas. I asked for a pilot who was discreet so they assume it is cocaine business. And the best part . . .' He gave a shout and clapped his hands again. 'The pilot is actually called Baron. What a country! When this is over I shall change my name to Tsar.'

He was in great good humour. Tanner said, 'Martina is going with you to intercept Che?'

Gurdjiev was at the door, calling for the two guards.

'Certainly. But not you. I have no further use for you. At dawn,' he said to the two men who crowded the door, 'take the Englishman to somewhere quiet and kill him. Is that understood?'

They nodded. They had smooth faces, innocent of expression.

'Make it look an accident.'

Martina took a couple of steps until she was in front of Tanner. She looked first at Gurdjiev and the two guards and then turned her back on them to confront Tanner. He looked for a message in her face but saw only confusion. *Do you believe now?* he wanted to plead. *Isn't my death enough?* She was frowning, as one does at a pain. She drew her left hand back and delivered a ringing slap to his cheek.

'That's because you lied to me once. And this . . .'

She leant closer, looming over him and slapped with her right hand, jerking his head round.

'That's because you tricked me once.'

Tanner's cheeks blazed. 'I won't do it again,' he said. He held her gaze. He didn't dare let his eyes wander.

CHAPTER 18

There were primitive souls who worshipped the river. It must be a god, they believed, because it moved yet never ended. And the eddies where the sluggish current heaved over some hidden obstacle, those were the spirits of drowned people trying to escape the river-god's embrace.

Why not, Che thought? Some people worshipped fire, others believed in a virgin who was a mother, so why not a river whose beginning you never saw and whose end was a few thousand kilometres away in an ocean? If they saw the ocean, they would prostrate themselves before that too.

The Pope worshipped runways and they were much less awesome.

The far bank was a low line of green, hazed by steam sucked from the river. Brazil was over there, huge jungle trees dwarfed by the width of the river. The trees hid headhunting Indians and jaguars and snakes and howler monkeys that swung by their tails from branch to branch. There were hairy black spiders the size of your hand. There were spiders that caught birds for their supper. Were there even more primitive souls who worshipped spiders?

The boat kept to the Bolivian bank. It looked much like Brazil but being closer Che saw turtles that slithered down the bank at their approach, blue and yellow macaws with long green tails, drunken landing stages with fishermen's boats swinging at the end of ropes, tiny paths leading to shacks set among banana trees and papayas. Boys splashed in the shallows. Others waved from the bank. Girls on the boat waved back, giggling, because the boys were naked.

After avoiding the army roadblocks, it had taken fourteen hours by truck to reach the river. That was the end of the road, a potholed track for the last three hours. A man on the pier had been shouting, 'Puerto Vargas, Puerto Vargas.' The river was the highway for people who couldn't go by plane. 'Hurry girls,' the boatman had shouted, 'the *carnivalito* has started and the boys are going fast.' That's when the girls had begun giggling. There were eight of them and they tried on masks and snatched them off again. Puerto Vargas was famous, even notorious, for its *carnivalito* and the anonymity the masks ensured.

That wasn't why Uhler had chosen such an isolated retreat, Che knew. It was because the border with Brazil ran along the river and on the far side was the sanctuary of the sister-town of Porto Vargas.

He wondered who Vargas had been: trader, outlaw, missionary, bigamist with a wife in Puerto and another in Porto. Perhaps even the Brazilian President of half a century ago. Politicians got their names everywhere.

The boat swung out to steer clear of a mudflat and round a bend appeared a little river port.

'Puerto Vargas,' the boatman shouted. 'Fasten your masks, girls, and loosen your clothes. It's the *carnivalito* of the Second Easter.'

The Second Easter! That was why the name of Puerto Vargas had been familiar to him. He'd forgotten until now.

In the square the old colonial church had been freshly whitewashed. Men clutching glasses of rum stood outside the café. Banners were stretched between palm trees. 'TWO EASTERS FOR THE GREATER GLORY OF GOD' was long enough for two sides of the square. On another side a banner exhorted: 'PRAY FOR THE THIRD DAY.' On the fourth side the door of the church was open and Che joined the crowd.

'In Puerto Vargas,' Che had been told, 'the people are different. They are heathen Christians.' Looking round the packed church, Che didn't think they looked much different from other Bolivians. Admittedly they weren't Quechua from the Andes or Guarani from the south but Amazonian Indians with some European and Japanese faces mixed in. But when the Jesuits had been expelled the Catholic Church in all this region had begun an accommodation with local customs. So in some places the devout might light candles in front of the holy figure and then worship the candles. Or would strap a murderer to the beam under the bell so that its peals would drive the devil out of his head.

'In Puerto Vargas,' a prisoner called Pedrozo had told him, 'they have the usual Easter and then towards the middle of May they celebrate the Second Easter.'

In the special prison Che had had to share his cell with a succession of prisoners. They were a trap, he knew it. They were informers sent to lure him into giving away the secret of his crime in return for the confidences they offered. A futile ruse. Che kept quiet and stared them out.

Pedrozo had been squatting on the cell floor. 'It began some years ago when an official of the government's drug squad paid a visit to Puerto Vargas. Cocaine was not so lucrative in those days but growing the coca leaves and refining the cocaine base provided a better income than fishing in the River Guaporé. He came by boat and though he wore no uniform people suspected. After all he wasn't a trader or a soldier or a runaway murderer. He stayed several days, walking up tracks, asking who was the owner of such-and-such a building. Finally a maid at the *alojamiento* went to his room and spent the night and reported next day that he was composing an official report: The cocaine trade in Puerto Vargas. Why do you keep staring? I'm not boring you?'

'I have all the time in the world. If I didn't listen to you, what else would I do?'

'It must be a tremendous affair you're locked away for.' When Che didn't rise, Pedrozo said: 'Anyway, that day when he was measuring the length of a grass airstrip, he was captured by some of the men of the village. They didn't kill him, because of the commandment against murder. What they did was this. Using fishing line they sewed his lips together so that he couldn't shout aloud. They carried him back to the village and took him to the church where there was a life-size crucifixion scene. It had a plaster Christ, a hollow mass-produced thing, on a wooden cross. They hid the cocaine inspector inside the body of Christ and nailed him to the cross. Mumbles and groans came from the cross, so the inhabitants of the village were summoned to chant prayers. The priest came and announced that the groans of anguish from the cross were a miracle, a re-creation of the

Calvary, a Second Easter. This alarmed the villagers for they had been taught that on the third day He rose from the dead. This is why each year on the anniversary they celebrate a Second Easter and keep a close watch to make sure the corpse doesn't rise from the dead. What do you say to that, eh?'

Che had considered the story. On the whole he believed it. Now seeing the congregation with every eye fixed on the crucifixion, he believed it more strongly. He had asked Pedrozo: 'What happened to the maid at the inn? Did she become pregnant?'

'I don't know. Is it important?'

'A second Christ as father – they would have had to worship the baby.'

Next day Pedrozo had been moved from his cell.

Che was no more than ten minutes in the church but when he came out it was a changed world. If you believed in a Second Easter you might as well believe in a Second Flood. Rain came down in drops so huge and relentless it was like a fog. The dirt streets were yellow mud. The paved plaza was a lake with stone islands rising above the floodwater. The drinkers had moved under the eaves of the *cantina* and were a line of ghosts behind the sheeting water running off the roof. Across the square was a rival *cantina* where the girls had gathered. Che halted, blinked, gaped. The girls were prepared for the *carnivalito* but not in frilled dresses with skirts flouncy with petticoats. Party frocks would be ridiculous in a place where it rained six times a day. T-shirts and jeans were the no-nonsense clothes. Even shorts, which were so quick and easy to slip off when wet.

But the masks! The masks!

The masks Che had seen the girls swapping in the boat were only a foundation. They were the underwear of masks in rainbow colours with slits to see and breathe. Larger openings allowed the girls' mouths freedom to kiss or to say no or later. The real masks were worn over those skintight face-coverings. These were glorious fancy-dress masks, even great headpieces. The girls shuffled their feet and preened and chattered. A Masai warrior talked to a Thai princess who was beside a forest deer who nudged a fairy castle with candles burning in the windows who whispered to an astronaut who embraced a *conquistador* who held the hand of a parrot who . . . Twenty, thirty, each mask different. The girls sheltered from the rain beneath the metal roof of the open-air *cantina*. Smoke came from a fire smouldering under a pot. At any moment a high priestess might appear and a sacrifice be made. In a village where people kept a vigil lest a drug inspector rose from the dead, anything was possible.

As Che began to move again music started. It came not from the local band but from a tape deck like some instrument from a space probe. Che assumed it was music, with a man singing to a frantic beat, but it might have been cries of pain from an alien civilization. In the middle of the plaza he was confronted by a black man holding an umbrella. Che thought he was being shunned by the drinkers under the eaves because of his colour. Then he decided the man was drunk when he said, 'Shall we dance?'

'I don't know how to dance to such music,' Che said.

'Like this,' the man said. Holding the umbrella above both of them, he gripped Che's elbow firmly with his free hand. Che was guided in something that had no relationship to the rhythm of the music. Perhaps it was the Puerto Vargas Waltz. The man asked, 'Where are you from?'

'Everywhere,' Che said. South America was his land and he hated narrow nationalism.

'Where are you going?'

'Nowhere,' Che said. He'd given no particular thought to a final destination.

'What brings you here?'

Then he realized that the man wasn't drunk or deranged or segregated. The drinkers under the eaves were watching. The Negro had been sent to check on the stranger.

'I have come to see Wolfgang Uhler.'

The rain had stopped as suddenly as it had begun. The black man put down his umbrella and inspected Che's face closely in the greater brightness.

'Why?'

'I have business with him. Is it usual to interrogate his business associates?'

'We interest ourselves in a stranger here. After all, you haven't come for the *carnivalito.*'

'When does it start?'

'Anytime. When the men have had another drink, when the girls begin to feel the music.'

'Does Señor Uhler come to the *carnivalito*?'

'He prefers to stay at his ranch.'

Che's eyes followed the nod of the other man's head. That way, somewhere outside the village, but not far. It was the end of a long, long fishing line that he had cast weeks ago in Potosi. Will the shark also come, smelling the bait? Che was certain. Rising excitement was all the proof he needed.

'Perhaps I could persuade him. He would need a mask.'

The black man tipped his head to one side. 'Men don't wear masks. A man doesn't have to pretend he's not doing what he is doing.'

'If we both wore masks,' Che suggested, 'he might not feel so shy doing it.'

The man considered this, then flashed a smile of stained and broken teeth.

Alsatians kept pace with Che on the other side of the wire, showing fangs like a crocodile's when they barked. Further off was an inner compound where Dobermanns hurled themselves against the netting. In the middle of the compound was a long low shed like a small factory. What was on guard inside that? Panthers? Trespassers will be eaten. That must be where the cocaine was cooked.

Beyond a line of trees was an airstrip. Lattice metal strips had been laid to provide stability on the sodden ground. A shed with open doors showed a small plane. The house rested on brick stilts to discourage floodwater, snakes and other animals. A verandah down one side was totally enclosed in mosquito netting. Cannas and zinnias made splashes of red and yellow. Blue was provided by the glimpse of a swimming pool set under palm trees.

He pressed the bell and waited. A head appeared behind the opaque glass of the front door and ducked down to look through the spyhole. It would not be Uhler himself, Che decided, but one of his staff who must now be disbelieving his eyes. An African witchdoctor had no business in Puerto Vargas. The door opened the width of a chain and a man servant squinted out.

'I've come to see Señor Uhler,' Che said. 'I'm an old, old acquaintance.' He leant forward, tapped his mask and said in a conspirator's whisper, 'It's to be a surprise.'

For some seconds the servant said nothing. A frown on his face deepened as he concentrated on the African mask in front of him. He peered closer as if he might recognize a long-lost brother. He pushed the door closed to unhitch the chain and beckoned Che inside. They went to a room at the side of the house where the servant knocked and opened the door.

'I think this is the man you were expecting.'

Uhler was at his desk. Possibly he'd been reading, possibly just toying with the pistol, an old Luger.

'Yes. Yes, I'm sure it is. Look at that scar on the side of his neck. You may leave now.'

When the door was shut, Uhler got up and came to stand in front of Che. He held the pistol loosely in one hand. With his other hand he patted Che all over. Not believing Che would have come unarmed, he turned him round and patted him again.

'Reckless of you but typical. I wondered how long it would be before you came. A former colleague informed me of the death of Doctor Quiroz, which the police were treating as suicide. Then I heard of the bizarre fate of Mendoza and your outburst. So I knew your mind would be on me next. Funny, I hadn't thought of you in a long time. In my mind you were the past, dead.'

He made a pause here but Che said nothing.

'Yesterday I heard an old man had been asking for me in Santa Cruz and I said to myself: Soon, soon. So I sent the men to the village to celebrate the *carnivalito* and had the dogs penned up. Do you imagine you'd have got in so easily otherwise?'

Still Che wouldn't speak.

There was the sound of a door shutting somewhere and a figure crossed in front of the window.

'Manuel is also going to the village, so we shall be alone. Better like that. Old times again?'

CHAPTER 19

It was dawn and as instructed by Gurdjiev the two guards took Tanner out to be killed. He was driven through streets washed grey by the early light. There were people about, preparing for the day with the solemn air of monks at morning devotions. A woman was piling a tray with oranges, building a careful pyramid. A man arranged newspapers on a table. Everything looks so normal, Tanner thought, even taking me out to be killed is a normal day's event here. Stopped at the intersection by a truck, Tanner caught a headline: 'SCANDAL OF THE FOOTBALL BRIBE.' Had the Bolivian national team actually been paid to lose? Was that necessary? On the opposite corner two policemen gazed at nothing in particular. The gun pressed into his side as a reminder. Daft, Tanner told himself, if they are going to kill me anyhow, what deterrent is a pistol now?

They passed a market where farmers unloaded fruit and vegetables from pick-ups. The bus terminal was crowded with passengers from a couple of overnight buses. They crossed the ring road and followed the sign to Cochabamba.

But they are *not* going to kill me, Tanner reminded himself, I am going to kill them. It would take luck and belief in himself and wit enough to seize his chance. Not in the car because of the noise and commotion it would cause. Also it was impossible with the pistol threatening him and the handcuffs restricting his movements. They had even tied his shoelaces together so that if he tumbled out of the car he could only hop. And be shot down like a rabbit.

The industrial belt gave way to slums and derelict fields. They entered a village where men sometimes lowered a pole to extract an illegal toll from cars. There was discussion between the other two whether to smash through the barrier or stop and pay up.

But the pole was raised and any chance that might have given Tanner was lost.

'What are your names?' Tanner asked. To his ears his voice sounded unnaturally loud. Perhaps to theirs as well for they both looked at him.

'Why do you ask?'

'I like to know who's going to kill me.'

The man next to him poked his ribs. 'Don't speak like that.'

'Is it a military secret?'

'Perhaps.'

The driver said, 'Tell him.'

'There are the names we were baptized with and there are our revolutionary names. Today we do an act of revolution so we use those names. The driver is Raul and I am Fidel.'

'Like the Castro brothers?'

'Yes,' he said, pleasure lighting up his face.

'And how are you going to kill me?'

The grin disappeared. There was something of an awkward pause. Raul's eyes lifted to the mirror and Tanner could see he was frowning. 'The comrade said to make it look an accident. So we cannot shoot you.'

The pistol prodded him again. 'Unless you try to escape.'

'Of course, people do have shooting accidents,' the driver went on. 'It is a possibility. Also I suppose the comrade would accept suicide as being as good as an accident.'

'I prefer the original plan,' Fidel said. 'If it is suicide by shooting I have to leave my gun with the body.'

'True.'

'I need my gun.'

'Yes.'

'Please understand,' he explained to Tanner, 'I am not a bank robber. But I need my gun to prepare for revolution.'

Tanner nodded. 'So if it's not shooting . . .?'

Raul said, 'I did hear of a way to kill someone with a pistol which is very clever because the police don't know the man has been shot.'

'How can that be possible? There is the bullet hole and the blood.'

'Ah,' Raul explained. 'You must insert the muzzle inside the anus and shoot up. The bullet causes a fatal amount of internal damage and comes to rest somewhere in the guts or chest. No bullet hole so no bleeding. Ingenious when you think about it. A Japanese method. Or is it Vietnamese?'

'That is absolutely disgusting. I'm not putting my pistol there.'

Tanner didn't probe further. He could do without creative suggestions like that. He felt his sphincter tighten in terror.

The sun was well up when they turned off the highway on to a dirt road that followed the river. Danger etched every detail more sharply: how Raul's knuckles were white on the steering wheel, how butterflies swarmed over a particular bush, how branches dripped with aerial roots, how the taller trees all seemed dead as if struck by disease. The river was brown shading to green at the edges and birds swooped low over the water. Death by crocodile? Death by snakebite? They'd have a struggle if they imagined they could drown him, even two to one, even handcuffed. The track was climbing now, lurching over stones and potholes, hammering the car's suspension so hard that Tanner thought: It's going to be death by shooting after all. That trigger-finger is going to slip.

He wondered where the track led. To some peasant's shack or a weekend hideaway or a hunting lodge. Perhaps the revolutionaries came out here for target practice. A parrot as gaudy as a paintbox flew into a tree. The leaves were such a brilliant green that the parrot's plumage looked subdued.

'Have you ever eaten parrot?' Fidel asked. Tanner shook his head. 'You can, you know, but it's not very nice. And don't ever eat the liver. Parrot liver is disgusting.'

'I'll remember that,' Tanner assured him.

They left the track to avoid a fallen tree. The sun was still shining but a sudden downpour rattled on the car's roof and was gone.

'Of course,' Tanner said, 'there's no need to kill me. You could simply turn me loose here and I'd be too late to stop Gurdjiev.'

'No,' Fidel said. 'He warned us about you. He said you were a tool of the imperialists and an *agent provocateur* and would offer us a bribe to let you go.'

'I'm not offering money,' Tanner said. 'I'm saving you from a terrible conscience for killing a defenceless man.'

'Don't listen to him,' Raul shouted. 'He warned us: The English speak with silver tongues. Close your ears.' They went on in silence. 'Anyway, we have arrived.' He turned the car into a clearing in the trees and switched off the engine. He turned in his seat to look at Tanner. 'Well, comrade.'

'He's not a comrade,' Fidel said.

'Of course. You are right.'

'Remember that. He's the class enemy. History has judged him and found him guilty.'

'Yes, that is true.'

'We are merely the executioners of history's judgement.'

'Yes,' Raul agreed, though his enthusiasm seemed dimmed for a moment by the thought of being executioners.

They're scared, Tanner realized, they've never done this before. They're holding the gun and they think that makes them invincible revolutionaries. But they're just kids who know nothing.

When they got out of the car, Tanner could hear the waterfall and birds everywhere. The birds chattered, chucked and screeched but never sang like they did in England. This could be a picnic spot, he thought, they've come here with their girls. Deserted, romantic, just the place for a foursome. Where can we take him? they must have asked each other. It can't be anywhere in the city, got to be somewhere isolated. How about where we chased Beatriz and Adela and they ran shrieking and let themselves be caught. Remember that day? Now they wouldn't want to come to this spot again. Get a grip. Tanner took a breath, angry with himself. They won't be going anywhere after this. It was time to take the initiative.

'Gurdjiev said it was to look like an accident,' Tanner said, 'so how have I got here?'

'Don't be silly,' Raul said, 'we drove you.'

'No,' Tanner said kindly. 'When the police find the body they'll say: Did someone drive him? Did a helicopter bring him?'

They looked at each other. 'You walked,' Fidel said.

'All the way from the main road?'

'Yes.'

'Then you'd better undo my shoelaces. I wouldn't walk with my shoes tied together.'

'Untie them,' Fidel said. Fearing some trickery, he retreated half a dozen steps. 'I'll cover you. And don't try to run, *Inglés*.'

The knot was undone and Tanner was instructed to walk across the clearing. He half expected a bullet in the back despite Gurdjiev's order. He stopped at the edge of a cliff where spray rose into the air. The waterfall plunged thirty or forty metres to rocks below.

'The idea is to push me?' Tanner asked.

There was no denial.

'I've come to admire the falls and tripped and fell? Wearing handcuffs? The police are going to find that hard to believe.' He held out his wrists.

'What do you think?' Raul asked.

'Better unlock them.'

'Now,' Raul said, pocketing the cuffs, 'face the edge please.'

'I'd like to smoke a cigarette,' Tanner said. 'A puff or two to give me courage.'

'You're wasting time.'

'It's the condemned man's last wish. Would you deny me that?'

'Give him a cigarette,' Fidel said. 'Hurry up.'

Tanner patted the side pocket of his jacket. 'I prefer English cigarettes. But I need a light. Better give me the box. The police will know something is wrong if they find I was smoking a cigarette but had no matches. So many details to remember . . .'

As Raul stepped close with the box of matches, Tanner put his hand in his pocket. *That's because you lied to me once*, Martina had said, slapping his cheek with her left hand. Then she'd loomed over him, slipping the pistol into his pocket before smacking him with her right hand. *That's because you tricked me once.* But only once. In the end she'd believed. It had taken his death sentence to persuade her.

He gripped the pistol and shot Raul through the jacket pocket. Raul stopped with the matchbox in his outstretched hand. His face showed puzzlement as if he couldn't account for the searing pain in his belly and the noise like a firecracker. His fingers faltered and the matchbox fell. Tanner stepped forward and grabbed a fistful of shirt. He brought the pistol out of his pocket and shot Raul in the chest. Aim for the heart, get it over with.

Raul coughed up blood and Tanner could feel a dreadful tremor in him and his mouth opened to shout.

'Gerardo,' he whispered, forgetting revolutionary principles.

His face changed. Tanner embraced Raul's dying body, using it as a shield. He looked over the shoulder to where Fidel at last grasped that the unimaginable was happening: that the prisoner who'd been thoroughly searched when he'd been first captured, had been manacled and watched through the night, was suddenly armed. This wasn't the class enemy to be executed: this was a dangerous and cunning *gringo*.

Fidel raised his gun and dodged to one side, hoping for a shot at Tanner that wouldn't strike his comrade instead. Tanner fired and missed even at that close range, fired again and hit Fidel in a shoulder. The pain surprised him and he gaped in wonder as the blood splattered on his shirt. With his next bullet Tanner killed him.

Tanner let the body of Raul slide to the ground. He stood swaying a moment at the edge of the cliff. Raul's blood was on his jacket but there was no time to go down to the river to wash it off.

Martina had watched Tanner being driven away and confronted the truth in herself. I was a coward, she thought and tried the word aloud: 'Coward.' She said it in English. Her face was reflected in the window and she told herself: Coward, where your guts? Why don't you save him? Since living in the United States English had become her first language. She would always sound a Cuban but her thoughts were in English. 'Cultural imperialism' was what that was called except it no longer seemed a full explanation. There was a slogan for every awkwardness. Someone somewhere must make up the phrases. Perhaps a whole committee of deep thinkers sat round a table with an agenda and a quota to fulfil. Today, comrades, our norm is six slogans, but to celebrate the anniversary of the revolution we should strive for seven. At the top of the list is *Murder*. That has negative associations and is liable to distortion by the capitalist media. Any suggestions? How about *People's Life Donation?*

Why am I thinking like this? she asked herself. Growing up?

Growing old? Growing apart? I'm no longer a believer. And it's terrible to lose your faith when it's the only thing that could have reconciled you to your lover being killed.

It wasn't a sudden revelation for she'd felt the change within herself for months. She would read a boast by some bunch of bloodthirsty crazies and she would think: Why? A bomb blew up a plane and six disparate groups shouted: Us! No, us! Or a contact would call and use the old comforting slogans but the comfort was missing. It had taken the shock of Tanner's death sentence to force her to recognize the change.

And not just Philip's death. Or was it Phil? Or Peeleep as the cop in the Sucre restaurant had called him? She'd never called him by name, though they'd been lovers. He'd given her news of Ben's death. He might have lied. It might be a trick. But the sickness inside told her it was the truth. Two lovers blown away. Love Martina and die. Put a government health warning over the bed.

'Coward.'

She'd slipped the gun in his pocket instead of using it herself to force his release. Would he be able to use it with the handcuffs on?

Suppose, suppose . . . A new and horrible thought opened in her mind. Suppose she had deliberately not saved him. Suppose she had put the gun in his pocket as a test. Save yourself, then come and rescue me to prove you are a man.

No, she told herself, don't search for a motive because there's always another motive behind the motive.

The greyness of dawn had grown to full daylight while she kept a vigil by the upstairs window. Sun was on the rooftops now. Well, it's decided one way or another, she told herself.

She went down to the kitchen to make coffee. When she opened the door, Gurdjiev's head snapped up. He was blinking from a doze. His face was pale and he seemed a size smaller than her memory of him at their meeting in Havana. Perhaps he hasn't been eating, perhaps worry is melting the flesh, perhaps he's just diminished in my sight.

'Do you want coffee?' she asked.

'After a long night, vodka is better,' he said. And after a bit: 'Yes, I'll have coffee.'

There was an electric kettle and she plugged that in and found ground coffee and filled two filters.

'Why did you have to kill him?'

'What? Because he's a British spy, that's why.' Gurdjiev said it with great certainty as if it was wartime.

'But why couldn't you just leave him under guard here?'

'Because he knows about Guevara.'

'Then how about the two who've taken him away? Don't they know about Che?'

'Not in the same way. They believe he's a madman we're going to expose. They're just boys who do jobs and don't think.'

How about me, Martina wanted to ask. Does everybody who knows the truth have to be killed? If Ben and Philip, why not kill Martina? But for what reason?

The kettle boiled and saved her from speaking.

'Those two will be back soon,' Gurdjiev said. 'They can drive us to the airport.'

He could kill me now, she thought, but he knows a body is swallowed up better by the jungle. Then she thought: But why get me all the way to a Bolivian jungle to kill me? Unless when he gets back to Havana or Moscow my death is to be explained as an accident. Why should that be? But no reason suggested itself. She wished she hadn't given away her gun.

Escape now? Or try to warn Che? Coward or martyr?

'You're worried about something,' Gurdjiev said. 'What is the problem?'

Warn Che? She realized how completely she had come to accept Tanner's way of thinking. She couldn't trace by what steps she'd reached this conclusion. Dialectic had played no part in it. It was an emotional change like falling in love. It terrified her.

'I'm tired,' she said.

Eight, nine, ten o'clock.

Gurdjiev said, 'Bolivian peasants. You cannot trust them to do the simplest thing. Let's not waste any more time.'

They walked out and stood on a street corner until a taxi stopped.

'El Trompillo,' Gurdjiev told the driver.

Tanner parked the car in a cul-de-dac near El Trompillo Airport. He left the keys in the ignition and was tempted to scrawl 'Please steal' on the dusty rear window. A stolen car would add another confusion. He had left his gun – Martina's gun – with the two bodies, close to Fidel's fist, and taken the .38 revolver in its place. The police might be puzzled, though not even Bolivian police could imagine a suicide pact where you began by shooting yourself in the shoulder. However it could be a week or more before the bodies were discovered and scavenging teeth and beaks would have destroyed much of the evidence. He moved his mind away from such thoughts. Even so he felt giddy for a moment.

It's the sun, he thought.

No, it's murder. Tanner wasn't a killer by trade though like all field agents he'd been sent to Bangs and Whimpers, as the gun-handling and unarmed combat courses were known. He'd only shot at a man once before, and missed because it was dark. Or missed because at the final instant he'd aimed aside. The man had run away and the gunfire was ignored as being part of the night music of El Salvador.

But today he'd shot to kill, and the images of surprise and pain and blood would be with him a long time.

He should find somewhere to eat except he didn't feel hungry. They hadn't offered him the condemned man's breakfast. He'd been kidnapped last night before he could eat dinner. There had been no restaurant at Tarija Airport. His last food had been over twenty-four hours ago at Sucre. No time now.

Soldiers guarded the perimeter fence. Police cars were parked by the terminal entrance. Doubtless a Cousin or two. A gate in the fence showed the way to a line of sheds and hangars. To the cop who guarded it Tanner spoke loud English with a drawl that would have made a Texan wince: 'Boy, you be good enough to open up the gate. I've come to see that Beechcraft *hombre* about my runabout. Lying bastard promised it for last week. Beechcraft, savvy?' He pointed to the office. Then he got out a wad of pesos. 'Perhaps you understand this better.'

The gate was locked after him. Knowing the cop would be watching, Tanner went to the Beechcraft office where he asked a stylishly dressed young man about a pilot called Baron who did air taxi work, and was directed to a distant parking area.

He was in time. Gurdjiev hadn't flown away. Baron was sitting on a little folding stool in the shade of the plane. His client was late but he seemed unconcerned, reading and smoking a fat little cigar in defiance of common sense and the *Prohibido Fumar* notice. No, he wasn't reading, Tanner realized, the book was in front of him but his eyes were raised. *Cien Años de Soledad*, the book's title announced. What trick are you trying to pull, the eyes asked.

'Señor Baron?' That sounded ridiculous to Tanner's ears.

Baron lowered the book and took a puff on his cigar. He had a face that must still cause a female flutter or two, the eyes tired now, grey threads in dark curls, a scar on a cheekbone such as a signet ring on a fist might cause. He waited.

'You have been hired by Señor Gurdjiev?'

'Don't recognize that name.'

'To fly to Puerto Vargas, the ranch belonging to Uhler?'

'Well?'

'I was afraid you might have left.'

Baron raised his hand and pointed the cigar at his plane. That was his answer to such foolishness.

'I want to go to Puerto Vargas myself.'

'Well,' Baron considered the burning tip of his cigar, 'at the last count there were about two hundred air taxis here. You should have no difficulty.'

'How much does it cost?'

'Depends. Depends on many things. But say five hundred US.'

'Is that what Gurdjiev paid you?'

Baron nodded.

Everything in Santa Cruz was expensive. It was cocaine inflation.

Tanner untied a moneybelt and removed a wad of notes, crumpled but inviting. He counted off ten one hundred dollar bills and replaced the moneybelt round his waist.

'My idea is this. What you do with the five hundred Gurdjiev gave you is not my worry. And frankly he's not going to be in any position to get it back. Keep it. Look on it as a bonus. Now do you see this thousand dollars? I like to think it will buy me a trip in your plane and not in one of the other air taxis. I would like a flight to Puerto Vargas, a short wait there, and a flight back. I would like to ride in the back of the plane and let Gurdjiev have one of the front seats. Don't give him the co-pilot's seat in case he should try anything reckless. You know, threatening you, grabbing the controls.'

All this Baron listened to with close attention. His face didn't show surprise or worry or shock. He'd been hired once but a new and more generous offer had come and this wasn't causing him any moral pain. Business was business. He was counting up fifteen hundred dollars for a morning's work and setting it against possible difficulties.

'Okay.'

As Baron reached out to take the money Tanner said, 'One thing. It could be that when Gurdjiev discovers I am now in the boss's seat he will become angry. He might decide that in a capitalist world he has been outbid so that all he has to do is make a higher bid. Say a couple of hundred dollars more than me. Or a thousand, or ten thousand. He should realize,' and Tanner made a brief pause so that it would be clear but not offensive that the warning was a general one, 'that in fact it is not a capitalist world we are operating in, it is the jungle. He knows what the law of the jungle is. He tried to have me killed this morning so he knows it very well.'

Baron's eyes dropped to the front of Tanner's jacket. The smear there was reddish-brown and fresh. He looked up again and nodded.

'He's coming,' Baron said from his position on the stool. 'He's got a woman with him, much younger than he is, good looker.'

Crouching at the back of the cabin Tanner checked the pistol for the third time and put it back in his pocket. Martina hadn't wanted him killed. She'd wanted to save him but wasn't saving herself. Did that mean she didn't believe Che was in danger? Or herself? Did she still imagine she was going to be offering him a life of ease and honour in Cuba?

'We're late,' he heard Gurdjiev say. 'Let's not waste any more time.'

'Not the co-pilot's seat,' Baron said. 'Take one of the passenger seats.'

'I've hired the plane and I'll sit where I like. I want to be where I can check the route.'

'It's a regulation. Only a qualified pilot can sit by the controls.'

'In Bolivia,' Gurdjiev said with a certain contempt, 'there are no regulations.'

'We're not flying in Bolivia,' Baron told him. 'We're flying in my aircraft.'

Gurdjiev climbed on board in a temper. Tanner could hear him muttering in Russian and paying no heed to Martina. She was forced to squeeze past Gurdjiev and as she was doing so she froze. Jammed behind a seat, Tanner's view was along the floor. He saw her feet stop as if something had caught her eye. Peering round, Tanner saw the heel of one of his shoes sticking out. It was too late to pull it in and Martina might shout there was an intruder.

Slowly he raised himself until his face appeared above the seatback.

'What's wrong?' Gurdjiev asked.

Tanner found himself staring into a pair of intense dark eyes. The eyes closed and she let out a breath.

'Nothing's wrong,' Martina said, and sat herself down.

CHAPTER 20

'Take off your mask. Why don't you? I know it's *carnivalito* but the tradition is for women to wear masks, not men. Do you know why?' Uhler went back to his chair, laying the Luger on the desk. 'Of course the vulgar opinion of outsiders is so they can enjoy sexual freedom without causing scandal. There is some truth in that because humans are not dogs that do it openly. But it is my belief the real reason is more subtle. At first it is just the young girls who appear masked and who flirt and dance. When darkness comes it is the wives who put on masks and come to the plaza. Ah, such masks. Have you seen them? The young girls' masks maybe, but as the years go by extras get added so that fantasies become more fantastic. The older women have added embellishments – a pair of cow's horns, a holy cross at a rakish angle, dried goat's testicles, a moustache, once a slither of skin reputed to be a foreskin. Grotesque additions, nothing to do with the style of the masks, but everything to do with the night to come. These are women showing their experience, you understand. Please, why don't you sit down? You must have had a tiring journey to get here.'

Through slits in the mask Che's eyes were visible. They were fixed on Uhler. When Uhler gestured at a chair with a carved wooden back, the mask scowled more fiercely. Or was that Uhler's imagination? He let his hand drop.

'So, imagine darkness has fallen. Picture the scene. There is a menace to night in the jungle, no denying it. But this has a whole separate layer of experience on top. During the night of *carnivalito* you don't notice the rustles and bird calls and shrill screams of dying animals. You hear music, taped music now, but later there will be pipes and drumbeats. The rum helps the dancing. For others cocaine liberates the spirit. The heat moves from the air to the bodies. I hope I'm not boring you. It's just I fear you will not have the opportunity of seeing it for yourself.'

He shook his head as if it was a matter of great personal regret to him. He looked again at the mask. There was something about the fixity of the expression and extraordinary silence that caused a slight shudder in Uhler. He talked and nothing was returned to him. It was like a dream where you pleaded with the figure of death and he waited until your words ran dry. Uhler swallowed and picked up his description.

'I have been an observer hidden in the shadows though I have never taken part myself. I have my position to consider and my authority. The people become intoxicated. It is not so much the liquor as the rhythmic beat and the heat and the body movements and the hypnotic lure of the masks. Then the married women have their pick of the men. Three, four, even five. Some use the forest, some the boats, some even the church. There are few lanterns and many black areas and much confusion. Now here is what makes the *carnivalito* more than just a louche romp. A wife will deliberately select her own husband and take him into the darkness and use every art she knows to arouse him, caressing, fondling, provoking. Some have full masks like yours, which makes kissing impossible but they use their fingers to make a mouth and make the man kiss that. And if he is an enthusiastic performer in the act of love, perhaps even taking an encore, then the wife unmasks herself and accuses the poor husband of only being so ardent because he believed it was another woman and that he never behaved so passionately with his own wife. Devious, wouldn't you say? But surely your experience has been that women are exactly that? My mother asked why I didn't marry but since she was a woman, how could I tell her?'

Uhler allowed himself a little smile. Why was he running on like this? He had planned something much more brisk and had cleaned the Luger and laid it out in readiness. It was that damn mask. We all make masks of our faces, he knew, but not like this.

'Here we are in a settlement on the banks of a muddy river separating Bolivia from Brazil, surrounded by rain forest, remote, isolated. And yet it could be Schindler writing a round of deceit and jealousy. Don't you find it amusing? Games in the jungle don't differ markedly from games in old Vienna. I said, Don't you find the intrigues interesting?'

Che moved his shoulders but it could have meant anything. Uhler started to reach for the butt of his pistol and relaxed with a sigh.

'You won't speak. And I can't see the expression on your face. Why do you wear the mask? Has something happened to your face? Some disfigurement you're ashamed of? Come, there should be no secrets between us. You have the shyness of a virgin and we're neither of us *virgo intacta.* We've shared too many intimate moments.'

He tried another smile. The full horror of that smile came back to Che. Uhler wasn't a Nazi thug. He didn't have the build of a bully boy. His body was slight and even now his face looked youthful in the way naturally trim people can. He had a yellowish tropical complexion and hair that was as much bleached by the sun as greyed with age; but really with his thick glasses he looked like the librarian in some Westphalian town. How old was he? Must be into his seventies. He had been an *Abwehr* major stationed in Algeciras during the world war, reporting on shipping movements. 'The English found out about BODDEN, which were the infra-red sensors. They never found out about GREGOROVIUS, the human sensor. I sent several hundred sailors for a final swim,' was how he had put it. He'd smiled as he said it.

Che felt the sweat on his body, a sudden flood of memories, fears, horror and hatred.

Uhler had the secret smile of a voyeur. But it wasn't the writhing of two bodies that excited him most, it was the writhing of one body. His ears had been eager for the screams, sobs and entreaties. His eyes had been round with an obscure thrill. He had been present at the worst times, not as a torturer, as a witness. He had been the one in the shadows. Quiroz or Mendoza had been in the foreground, Uhler had been the audience, Che had been the star. 'I am the aesthete of pain,' Uhler had said, 'and you are a virtuoso. You give a performance to savour.'

Yes, intimate moments, two lovers with their treasure trove of memories.

Che felt hot tears springing from his eyes, blessedly hidden by the mask. Why should he give Uhler the pleasure of seeing the suffering which the memories caused?

'In a sense the mask is appropriate,' Uhler said, breaking a silence he found uncomfortable. 'You started out as a doctor, you became a revolutionary, you end up as a witchdoctor. You are a symbol of the age we live in. You parallel the degeneration of Western culture.'

And you? Che thought. The screams were loud in his head, and the face in the shadows was lit by the hunger within.

'It's better we should be alone. We're two old men sharing a park bench, reliving old days. Do you remember when? And then there was that other time . . . Perhaps they have recriminations, but the heat has gone out of them. One stole the other's girl, one played a trick. It's thunder from a distant storm now.'

Che took a step forward.

'I owe you a lot,' Che said. His throat was painful and his voice seemed thick from concealing the weeping.

The smile played over Uhler's face again. The tortured and the voyeur have such a close link. 'I'm glad you see it that way. But while I'm happy to see you, I'm also curious why you came. Since you killed Emilio and Ruperto, I assumed you had come to kill me too, though I never personally did anything to you. Yet you have come unarmed.'

'I owe you a lot,' Che repeated because he'd been misunderstood the first time. 'Tell me, I was never in a position to ask you before, did you choose the name GREGOROVIUS yourself during the world war?'

'You came to ask me that?'

'Not primarily. But it will satisfy my curiosity.'

Uhler fingered the Luger, remembering his deeds as a young man in Franco's Spain. 'No, the *Abwehr* assigned covernames. When I escaped assassination in Tangiers, I was moved to Algeciras. It was the same work really but since BODDEN was compromised I was assigned a new covername by the *Abwehr*. So GREGOROVIUS was born.'

'He hadn't always been an interest of yours?'

'No.' Uhler was surprised at the turn of the conversation. 'But I set myself to find out something about him.' He got up, tucked the Luger into his waistband, and went to a bookcase. Here he searched a shelf of leather spines mildewed by the climate. His hand stopped on one volume and he drew it out. 'Here,' he said, blowing dust off the top. 'I confess it's years since I read it. You'd think in the jungle there was all the time in the world to read.'

'You know what I'm referring to?'

'Oh yes.' He gave Che a special smile. 'It was the first time Ruperto Quiroz performed one of his experiments – drowning you in milk, then reviving you. I remember it vividly. When you recovered you whispered to him, "What kind of doctor are you? Have you forgotten your professional oath?" Poor man, he was only interested in his research. Your life was never in real danger because you were too valuable for the experiments. That was the first time I spoke to you and I explained . . .' He'd found the place in the book, marking it with a finger. '*Die Welt . . .*'

'In Spanish.'

'You still refuse to understand German? It sounds much better. *Die Welt ist ein grösses Narrenhaus, nur sind die grössten Narren nicht eingesperrt.*' He looked up from the book at the mask covering Che's face. 'The world is a big madhouse, only the biggest madmen are free.' He closed the book. 'I think it was some comfort to you. Is that why you said you owed me a lot?'

But it wasn't and Che shook his head.

'You know, anticipating your visit and knowing the servants would be absent, I took the precaution of having a bottle brought in here. It is not real German schnapps but it is made by a German migrant to Argentina. I think you'll find it acceptable.'

Che shook his head again. 'I don't touch alcohol.'

'Really?' Uhler had uncorked the bottle and poured out two small glasses. 'Not even for a celebration? After all, this is the last occasion we shall be together. A toast to our reunion.'

He moved until he was only a couple of steps away from Che. A glass was in each hand and he held one forward.

'If certain persons in the old Germany, the ones who disappeared under the American bombers and the Russian tanks, if they could only picture this moment! I, a major in the *Abwehr*, exiled in the jungle, sharing a drink with a notorious revolutionary disguised behind a savage's mask. Is that a symbol of something? Must be, must be, but I can't quite see it.'

He smiled. Che stared at Uhler's eyes, distorted behind his

glasses. At the edge of his vision he saw lips twitching. When he focused on the mouth, the eyes seemed to glint with remembered delights. Eyes, mouth, eyes, mouth. Evil came and went and mocked.

'Perhaps this once I shall have a drink.'

'Wonderful. Though you realize you will have to lift off the mask. Otherwise it is like certain women who tonight will be unable to kiss.'

'You see, Uhler, what I owe you . . .'

'Please, we have known each other long enough: Wolfgang.'

'What I owe you is the knowledge of how I was betrayed twenty years ago.'

The smile came again.

Che reached up to remove the mask. From behind the mask where it pressed against his forehead, he fumbled as if with a fastening and brought out his pistol. Stepping forward while the surprise still lit Uhler's face, he rested the barrel on the spectacles frame between his eyebrows. Uhler's forehead wrinkled and his eyes squinted down the pistol and then changed focus to rest on Che's face. He pursed his lips. It was sadness more than anything.

'Oh. Oh no. Frankly you disappoint me. I thought the links we'd forged were too strong for such crudeness.'

CHAPTER 21

A man in his lifetime is faced by many surprises and most of them are unpleasant. That was Hershey's experience. At the same time that Uhler was being surprised by the pistol between his eyes Hershey was surprised by the phone call.

'Hello,' he said softly, not wanting to wake his wife.

'Bill, this is Harry,' was the response.

Hershey swung his legs out of bed and glanced at the digital alarm clock. Five bloody twenty-eight.

'Let me get to my desk. I'll ring you back.'

'I'm not at the head office. I'm at the Kensington branch. Got the number at home?'

'I know it. Two minutes.' Hershey put the phone down. He looked at his wife. Morning light coming through a gap in the curtains gave a serene glow to her dumpling cheeks and wavy hair. She had the closed eyes and absolute stillness of somebody who'd been listening but didn't want to be thought awake. Bloody time to ring. Bloody weekend too. Bloody head from bloody inky Burgundy. And bloody Abrams whose name wasn't Harry any more than Hershey's name was Bill. It was just the open line method of introduction meaning: The big one's come up. And since Abrams was Number 2 in the local CIA hierarchy, the big one could be anything from the Pope eloping to a declaration of war.

He put on his dressing-gown, a dark green silk affair. On the back was what the salesman had assured him was a Thai *naga*, though Hershey would settle for a black dragon with flames spewing from its mouth. He'd treated himself last birthday because it gave him a youthful image, still vigorous, breathing fire at all his enemies. He'd had a dream a short while ago where he'd worn it to the Bunker and Miss Bone, his vapid secretary, had come and breathed flames back at the dragon, and then burst into tears and had to be comforted. She'd sat on his lap for that. Dreams were another bloody thing. Subversive.

The telephone was answered on the first ring.

'Yes?'

'Dirk, this is Nicholas,' Hershey said, and this time they were their real names.

'Nick, I know it's early to call but us true defenders of freedom can't take time out to sleep.'

Already, in those first few words, something alerted Hershey. Not the words themselves but the tone of voice. Abrams sounded self-satisfied, even gloating, but he tended that way. Was there a smile on his lips as he spoke? If so, a grim smile warning of a settling of accounts to come.

'I wanted you to be among the first to know: we've tracked him down. Bolivia, some jungle village. CG himself, or his imitator.'

Too many emotions were suddenly struggling together in Hershey. Rage, jealousy, frustration jostled to come first.

'You still there, Nick? You haven't said anything, like congratulations old boy.'

'Congratulations old boy. The Yanks pull it off again.' But there was more. Hershey sensed there was more.

'That's right, we have. Thought you'd want to be told, knowing your continuing interest in him. Also there are some complications which may come as a surprise.'

The telephone on his desk was held to be a protected line, which was one degree less sure than a secure line. Hershey wasn't certain what the distinction meant but suspected a protected line was safe from a schoolboy with a screwdriver but would take a Telecom hacker five minutes to crack. Someone could be listening in, that was the caution they all lived with. The Russians, the East Germans, the Israelis of course. The Bulgarians would want to know who to stick their umbrellas in. And the French, oh yes. Not to mention the Cousins. And the Security mob. And 'C', just to check on backstairs plots. That was the theory even if it was paranoia. Still, Hershey knew, where would they be in a world without paranoia? Standing at the back of the dole queue.

'This surprise,' he said. 'In our line of work a surprise is always something unpleasant.'

'It's about your man you sent there. None of us knew about that. And now some questions are being asked about him. I think you should come over.'

We don't count for anything any more, Hershey knew. Now the Americans summon us as if they were the Emperor calling a tribal chief to Rome. If they do it to us, imagine how you've got to jump if you're a government official in some poor bloody Third World slum.

Abrams sweetened the summons a little. 'We have a satellite link-up, Nick. Keep us abreast of the action.'

My name is Nicholas, Hershey had once insisted. But by the next meeting he was Nick again.

'At this time of day, at the weekend, I should be there in an hour and a quarter.'

'Coffee will be waiting.'

'Is our man in trouble with the Bolivians?' Hershey asked, wanting just a hint.

'I'd say he was in the piss all round.'

'Oh.' Hershey was sorry he'd asked.

Abrams rang off without saying goodbye.

He went back to the bedroom and got clothes out of the closet. His wife watched from the bed.

'Surely you haven't got to work? This time of day?'

'Crisis,' he said.

'Must be important.'

'Small to middling.'

'Will you be back to lunch, dear?'

'Somehow I doubt it.'

He gave her rump a pat.

Bloody Tanner, what was he doing? Hershey tossed his dressing-gown on the bed and its pattern mocked him. What was a *naga* anyway? It didn't look fierce enough for a dragon. More your lizard with bad breath.

The Kensington branch, as Abrams had called it, was in a building in a backwater off Campden Hill. It was built of purple bricks so hideous that the council had winced and planted plane trees. It was a block of flats and on the top floor one had been leased for the London *pied-à-terre* of a firm of international marketing consultants. Because of the necessity of following commodity prices and stock market movements in Tokyo, Hong Kong and New York, permission had been granted to put a satellite dish on the roof. 'It's because of the Big Bang you had in your City,' one quiet market consultant explained to a neighbour, 'everything is so volatile at this time.' The old lady was disturbed by the advance of anarchy and kept her door locked as much as possible.

Pressing the bell, Hershey looked away at the cars parked nose to tail along both sides of the cul-de-sac. There were Mercedes and Porsches and Nissans and Volvos and Rovers and even a Sierra but there were no Buicks or Chryslers. There must be a CIA directive to avoid advertising. But he counted telephone aerials on half a dozen car roofs, an unusual concentration even for such a thrusting executive area. A movement at the edge of his vision brought him facing the door again and inspection by the security camera. He gave a one-sided smile to the staring eye and a voice crackled from the loudspeaker grille set into the wall.

'One hour twenty-three minutes. Okay, come on up.'

The door-release buzzed and Hershey pushed his way in. Out of sight of the lens, he made a face. Cheeky jumped-up New York lawyer. Should go back and sneer at the camera, he thought. He hesitated but the moment had passed. Now it would be a deliberate act of rudeness. Also Abrams wouldn't be wasting his time watching the screen. Hershey felt the unease again: the phone call at a gestapo hour, the summons, the insolence of timing his journey.

There was a very slow lift. 'I just *love* the sense of history everywhere,' Abrams had remarked of it when he was very fresh in London and still a little in awe of Hershey's breeding. 'I mean, Nick, this cage is simply too much.' Hershey peered through concertina doors at the stairs that spiralled up with him. And perhaps because he was trapped in a cage he began for the first time seriously to worry. Why had he been called? Why was a satellite connection established today? From Bolivia to Langley certainly, because they enjoyed that sort of immediate drama like seeing a space probe on its way. But why to London?

'This way, sir.'

Hershey had an escort from the lift to the front door of the flat. He was a respectful young man but ignorant of how well Hershey knew the way. They're all ignorant when they arrive, Hershey thought, and we do our best to put a bit of polish on them. But then – was his tone really respectful? Or was he to stop Hershey making a dash for freedom?

This flat was where Hershey and Abrams had met when they wanted to escape the formality of the Bunker or the annexe to the Grosvenor Square Embassy. Official meetings had rules and agendas and minutes. Secretaries and clerical officers might be loyal but more people meant less openness. So the Kensington branch had been set up and rising star Abrams put in charge. Those in the know referred to it as Host-Guest-Liaison. 'It's the Special relationship at its closest, Nick.' He'd made it sound a lovers' nest.

The American taxpayers' money had been put to liberal use. The sitting-room had been turned into a replica of the chairman's office in a smart advertising agency. There was an almost white carpet that needed shampooing every month and potted plants whose leaves needed spraying every week. At one end of the room was an Italian perspex table and chairs for anything so formal as a meeting with documents to pass round. At the other end it was leather and tubular-steel sofas, low tables for cups or glasses, a cabinet for the hospitality bottles. Abrams kept the key. Hershey stopped for this was where he was used to doing business with Abrams.

'No sir,' the young man said. 'This way.' He'd put his respectful tone away.

'What's the hurry? Why the panic?'

'It's not panic,' the American said. 'We don't waste time, is all.'

'What's gone wrong? The President been on the blower to you?'

Blower wasn't a word the American knew but he didn't like the sound of it. He jerked his head to get Hershey moving again. The place is on a war footing, Hershey realized, the atmosphere has quite changed. 'This here is the fun palace, Nick,' Abrams had said in easier times, smiling round at the plump sofas, the ice bucket, the bottles, 'only without the girls. No girls during office hours.' At the Bunker Hershey gazed past women as if they didn't exist but here at the Kensington branch he noticed their absence. He wished there was a girl here now, just a secretary, some softening of the hard line.

'What the fuck's keeping him?'

The voice came from the next room. It had been deliberately raised to carry and Hershey felt his ears reddening.

He followed his young escort to the next room which would have been the dining-room in more genteel days, for a hatch in the wall allowed access to the kitchen. This was where the busy international marketing consultants kept their electronic wizardry. There were a pair of TV monitors, telex, facsimile encryption unit, shortwave transceiver, tape and video recorders, metal boxes with esoteric functions, water fountain and coffee machine.

Abrams's eyes met his across the room and at first Hershey thought he wasn't going to be given the courtesy of a greeting. Then Abrams raised a hand to him but gave his attention to a microphone: 'What precise orders were you issued with, Lieutenant?'

There was a satellite pause before the answer came. 'Sir, Colonel Farr said that at all costs this must be seen as being part of Operation Purify. Sir, I don't know whether you are familiar with that but it is the anti-cocaine operation that Colonel Farr is running. He said that no Bolivian troops are accompanying us but that otherwise we play it as Purify right down the line. Sir, he said Colonel Dexter would have wanted that.'

'Right, Lieutenant.' Abrams covered the microphone and said to Hershey, 'Dexter was running the Guevara thing in Bolivia and was killed last night. That's in case you didn't know.'

This was the cue for everyone to stare. There was a force in the room and it was turned on Hershey. He was no longer in the top flat of an unlovely mansion block within sight of the treetops of Holland Park. He was deep in the heart of America and six American wills were massed against him and six hostile stares accused him. Hershey was stunned. He felt a physical shock as he took in that in their sight he was the one who'd given the order for Colonel Dexter's death. Even Glen Shortley, the FBI man whose puppyish features were unmarked by experience or understanding, even he was sending out waves of hostility.

By now the situation was well beyond Hershey. Questions crowded into his mind but had no obvious answers. Such as why he was thought to have caused Dexter's death. Why the FBI man was here. Why a CIA operation was being beamed to London at all. Now he felt the heat of their eyes go off him as they turned to look at the radio loudspeaker as if they could see Bolivia in it.

Abrams was telling the Lieutenant how much he appreciated being patched through and Special Operations was being good about it because of his continuing interest in the progress they were making. Now another voice came in. It was a three-way hook-up, and the other point of the triangle must be in Langley or Panama or wherever the CIA was directing the operation from. This third voice was the deepest Hershey had ever heard. It was like rich chocolate sauce. 'Well now, we're just glad to help you folks out,' it said and Hershey felt he'd listened to a whole speech. But there was more. 'We appreciate there are tough decisions to be taken by you over there in London.' That was another whole speech and 'over there in London' could have been out somewhere beyond Uranus. 'Especially,' he finished, 'since you could be finding yourself in a firefight with the Brits.'

Once again hostile eyes stared at Hershey. That's me, he registered, I'm the Brits. What have I done wrong apart from personally ordering the death of some gung-ho colonel?

'Nothing to report at this time, sir,' the Lieutenant said to whichever sir he felt himself serving. 'Just jungle down there, creeks, patches of grazing.' Then Hershey identified as an aircraft engine the background noise he'd thought was static. So there was a hook-up from a plane somewhere over South America to its base, then by satellite to Langley and rebeamed by satellite to London. In Technology We Trust. They should change their motto.

Abrams switched off the microphone and said to the others in general, 'Call me the moment when.' There was only one moment when, which didn't need filling in. He turned to go into the other room and passing Hershey he beckoned with a hand.

'Come.'

'Dirk, I think an explanation is due to me. Indeed I'm sure it is.'

In the sitting-room Abrams walked towards the conference table then changed his mind and came back to one of the steel and leather sofas. He bowed his head and pummelled his cheeks with the heels of his hands. It was the action of a weary person but when he looked up it was obviously anger he was controlling not exhaustion.

'Dirk.' Hershey felt uneasy saying it but Americans liked to hear their name. 'Dirk, I'm not accustomed to being treated in this manner. Do I have to remind you that this is the United Kingdom, not the United States. You operate by our grace and favour, as set out in the protocol. You do not operate as of right, or have you forgotten?'

Abrams might not even have heard this old-fashioned rebuke. 'You've got a man called Tanner, Phil Tanner, in your department. His hunting ground is Central America and certain parts of South America. Kind of a big territory but I appreciate your resources are stretched these days. That's one thing.' He stuck a finger like a dagger at Hershey. A second finger shot out. 'Two, when a certain Englishman is murdered in Florida, this Tanner is ordered to ask a few questions back here in London, right? Connections, background, that crap. Don't ask me why someone who knew the London scene better wasn't picked, but there it is. Your decision.'

'Because – ' But Hershey wasn't allowed to have the floor.

'All right, because he was Latin American-experienced and there were Latin American connections. So three,' another finger, 'amazingly he follows up with a quick flip to South Africa. Upset everyone he met, so I hear. Also our guy out there, Ed Mathews, Ed reported that your man was recalled by you to London. Except, Nick, you didn't bring him back to London. No sir. Four.' Now he gripped his four fingers as if they might break loose. 'You ordered him to Bolivia, without any liaising by your side with our side. That is what this apartment is for, what I am for. Host-Guest-Liaison, right?'

'Host-Guest-Liaison is to do with matters within the United

Kingdom, may I remind you. This is a different situation entirely.'

'Oh come *on*. One of your British demarcation disputes? Your unions going to call everyone out on strike? Everyone stop for tea? We're meant to be working together. At least that was the idea.'

He looked at his hand. There was only the thumb left and he abandoned the action. He went to the drinks cabinet where he poured himself a plain Schweppes tonic water, offering nothing to Hershey.

'In Bolivia there is a psychopath going round murdering people and claiming he's Che Guevara. Interesting since Guevara died way back. Well, at your Hyde Park Corner – your Speakers' Corner – you've got people standing up every Sunday and announcing they're Jesus Christ and the end of the world is on Tuesday and everybody cheers. Now I have never personally witnessed any acidhead claiming he's Guevara, but it's bound to have happened a few times. Weirdos imagine they're Martin Luther King and Einstein and Donald Duck. So are we to take every wild cry to be gospel? Still, on this occasion it did stir a little action back at head office. They went and got one of our guys out of retirement. There he was playing golf near Sun City, Arizona, and a helicopter swoops down and makes a mess of the fairway close by the third green. A certain Major Rixey who'd been in Bolivia in '67. He'd been pushing the Rangers who were closing in for the kill, but the actual final combat he didn't witness, nor did any of the other US advisers. Nor did they positively identify the corpse. Sure, a corpse was produced but after all those months living rough, sick, terrible diet, dirty, bearded, bloody, shot to pieces – hell, who knows what Guevara looked like at the end. Major Rixey says some Bolivian top brass swore the corpse was Guevara. Rixey further says, sure, it would have been possible to pass off some *other* dead guy for Che. Yep, sure would, our good Major opined, one dead G looks much like another. Pretty relaxed about the whole thing he was. After Bolivia, Rixey went and screwed up in Laos, so they raised him to Colonel. Just thought you'd like to know.'

He closed his eyes again, pummelling with his hands. Perhaps he thought Hershey was going to lodge another complaint at his shabby treatment for he suddenly jabbed out a finger.

'If that *is* Guevara, we want him, dead or alive. And the Soviets want him. And the Cubans. And the Nicaraguans would love him. And the Libyans and the Syrians and every little guerrilla group in the world will want him so they can salute this great hero and inspire themselves to fight harder. Analysts in Langley – and I don't propose to disagree with them – foresee a great upsurge of violence all over the globe. How could we respond to that? We send bombers to flatten a dozen capital cities? Send in the Marines? The Delta Force? Order TWA and Pan Am not to fly abroad because it's too dangerous? If that is Guevara, we *have* to have him.'

Abrams paused and listened for any sounds of action from the next room. He kept his eyes on Hershey's face.

'Let me tell you this operation was set up first of all on the personal order of the Director of the Agency. After Ollie North screwed up with Iran and the Contras, everybody was scary of taking an initiative in a situation like this. Morale was right down. People made jokes they were getting out to join the boy scouts because you saw more action that way, only they weren't kidding. But thank God this time we were on the road and actually running because the President himself came on the line: Get Guevara. Yes *sir*, you can have him for breakfast, sir. The President is not so dumb he'll let a simple propaganda victory go to the Russians, so now we have his authority. Not the say-so of the Director, or the Secretary of State, or the Chief of Staff. The President of the United States orders: Get him before the Soviets do. So we mount the kind of operation, Nick, that only we are big enough and well enough equipped and have the balls to do. We are going in and getting Guevara. At this moment in time.'

Abrams drained the last of the tonic water, eyeing Hershey over the glass. Go ahead, you've listened to my lecture, seemed to be the look on the CIA man's face. Now's your chance to raise an objection. Just try so I can shoot you down in flames.

'Last night, our Colonel Dexter who was commanding the task force was knifed by an intruder in his room. Throat slit. The police have no idea who did it. The Bolivian police couldn't find their ass with the paper except there was a sign pointing the way. Guevara had phoned a radio station and claimed he was in

Santa Cruz so maybe he did it. Maybe some other interested party did it. I don't know. But now we're getting down to the awkward bit. Apart from the death of one of our good men, this is the bit that really sticks here.'

Abrams put a hand to his own throat and squeezed so hard the colour rose to his cheeks.

'Our operation had transferred to Santa Cruz from some town in the hills. Except for one guy whose job was to do the round of the hotels and find out if any suspicious characters had checked out. In one hotel register he came across an entry for a US citizen so he thought he'd try the name on Langley: Mancilla, initial M. Pow! Lights flashed and we knew we were on to something. Two other foreigners had been staying there: a query West German called Gurdjiev who smelled like a Russian pig and a dear old Brit. Tanner, initial P. All of them checked out. Now guess what. Our guy spends a few dollars on the desk clerk and he says your man and our Cuban-American hot tamale had gone out to have dinner together and come back from dinner even more together. They'd collected their room keys but both disappeared in the direction of Tanner's room. According to the desk clerk, they were as close as two sheets on a bed.'

Hershey felt a growing sense of bewilderment. He'd lost his grip on his agent, on his operation, and on his American liaison. Forget any idea of a great coup as he bustled Guevara into hiding in one of the country houses. This was one of those monumental catastrophes where a head had to roll.

'What do you say to that?'

'The implications . . .' Hershey raised his hands in a hopeless gesture.

'Sure, Nick. The implications. Well, that's a modest reaction when you're told one of your men is collaborating with a Soviet agent. I guess over the years you've learnt to take such things calmly. Philby, Blunt, Burgess, good chaps at heart, what? Okay, we've got to the point. Our people out there have finally heard where this Guevara is going. Out to a remote ranch. So that's where they're headed now. When they get there – *if* they're in time – they're going to scoop up that crazy old man. But suppose they run into *your* fellow, what do you want done with him? Mmm? Do you read me? What's it to be? All I'm saying is, suppose he dies in the crossfire, who's going to be asking questions? Obviously Tanner isn't, and Langley isn't, how about you?'

Abrams watched and waited.

'Nick? What do you say?' He bent right down so he was on a level with Hershey's face. 'I need to know, Nick. You see, in a sense it's your life I'm saving, your professional life.'

Hershey stared at his face, not knowing the answer. All the certainties that had guided his life seemed to have lost their force. He saw his career was destroyed if he let Tanner get away, saw he was in thrall to Abrams for ever if he gave thumbs down.

'Damned if I do and damned if I don't.'

He pushed himself out of the sofa.

'What the hell does that mean? We're in the countdown now, Nick. I need an answer I can understand. Nick? Nicholas?'

Hershey started to walk out, saying nothing, gathering a tattered scrap of self-respect to him. It was Abrams who'd put him in this terrible dilemma and he realized now that he'd never liked Abrams.

One of the young men came to the door. 'Lieutenant Norwak's come on air again.'

CHAPTER 22

The plane heaved and sank in an air pocket. Tanner's stomach heaved with it. Suppose I throw up, he thought, nothing in my stomach except green bile but, oh God, suppose I throw up. Vomit had a pungency that would steal through the cabin. Gurdjiev had a nose made for twitching. He'd clamber over the seats to find the stowaway. If he was going to be airsick, Tanner decided he would have to swallow it again. Try to. His stomach revolted at the idea.

Think of something else. Consider this Wrigley's chewing-gum wrapper under the seat. How curious to find this piece of American culture tossed aside in an air taxi bumping over a South American rain forest. Chewing gum is a symbol. Think about it. Chewing gum is loved by kids all over the world but in the United States the habit clings on into adult life. Does that mean they haven't grown up? The plane gave a sickening jolt. Concentrate on the significance. Build a theory. Look for the political dimension. A radical like Boobs Becker would be quick with a political twist. Consumerism, waste, polluting the environment. Construct an entire philosophy on a discarded scrap of paper and condemn the mightiest nation in the world for its infantile retention syndrome. That's called sociology. Or something. Write a paper for a seminar. Propose research. Apply for a grant. Today Brent Council, tomorrow the world.

The queasiness passed.

Apart from a laconic 'Belt up,' from the pilot Baron before take-off, there was silence until Martina broke it.

'What plan have you made to get him out?'

Gurdjiev grunted, his mind on something else. 'Don't concern yourself with that.'

'You said to me right at the start: the escape plan was your responsibility. You made a secret out of it. Now the time has come and I want to know what it is. It is my concern because I'm coming too, right?'

To Tanner's ear that was a probing question. She'd had time to think and analyse since Gurdjiev had condemned him to death. The doubts gnawed inside her and Gurdjiev's answers were the worst he could give.

'We have this plane. Stop worrying.'

'But what route? Back to Santa Cruz? Brazil?'

In her insistence Tanner could hear the doubts growing stronger.

'Up north. Does it make so much difference? You have holiday plans, comrade? A boyfriend somewhere?' Gurdjiev made a poor attempt of humour to turn her enquiries.

'It matters to me if I'm included.'

'Of course you're included. This simply is not the time or the place to discuss it.'

Laying his head on the carpet and squinting between the struts of the seats, Tanner saw their feet two rows in front. The plane lurched again and Tanner's gorge rose. Oh God, look for the significance of their feet. One pair of men's shoes, smart but in need of a shine. One pair of women's flat-heeled lace-ups. You could tell his legs were crossed because one foot jiggled off the ground. Impatient. He faced straight forward. A bull wanting to charge. Her feet angled towards the window. Her body was turned away from him. She must be thinking hard about her future, as Tanner was.

Any operation in the field develops a momentum. There is a goal ahead and the agent gathers a force that thrusts him forward: the organization in London, local helpers, his professionalism, even the simple human need to achieve. Momentum had carried him until now. The target was almost in his grasp and the question now insisted he answer it: Why? Why take Guevara back to England? He wouldn't want to come and would have to be tricked or drugged. He wouldn't consent to stay. Essentially he would be a prisoner, under armed guard night and day. He would be a glittering prize for terrorists who would seize hostages and demand his release. Think of the expense and the hassle of keeping him.

A Royal tour is on the cards, Hershey had said, and we can't afford a rampant Guevara leading the peasants' revolt. A wilful Prime Minister wanted the Royal tour because it would show Britain's traditional values to the world. And Hershey wanted no hint of trouble that might cause the Queen to stay with the Royal corgis.

The more he gave his mind to it, the more Tanner felt a sense of alienation. His life was in supreme hazard because of the ambition of his boss. Another thing, Hershey had ordered Guevara killed rather than let anyone else get him. This put Hershey on the same moral plane as Gurdjiev. Morality was not to be considered during an operation, Tanner knew. But exhaustion plays tricks with what's allowed and what is forbidden.

The engine note changed as the plane began its descent. It tipped to one side and circled for ever, or so it seemed to Tanner. Nearly over, he thought, thank God. In his mind he'd pictured the worst scenario: Gurdjiev discovering him, mid-air shoot-out, pilot hit, plummeting crash. Tanner squeezed his eyes shut and breathed deeply. Be positive, he ordered, plan ahead, be a winner. Gurdjiev was sitting on the left side. Tanner's feet were in that direction so he manoeuvred himself until he was kneeling, a throbbing foetus, his head ducked down. Was a patch of shoulder visible between the seats? He could squirm no lower. The tyres thrummed while Tanner gripped his pistol in one hand and grasped the doorhandle with the other.

The plane was really a glorified limousine with no aisle but doors to each pair of seats. As the plane settled and stopped he heard Gurdjiev stand and open his door. Judging the moment when that thickset peasant body would be most hampered in the doorway, Tanner hurled himself out on to the lattice landing strip and was in position, legs apart, knees slightly bent, gripping the pistol two-handed with Gurdjiev's face blooming into surprise just a couple of paces from the end of the barrel.

'Don't move. Don't reach for your gun. Keep still.'

Tanner had witnessed people going through shock before: surprise changing to disbelief, belief, horror, panic like a slide show of emotions. Gurdjiev turned to go back.

'Stop. One more step and I'll shoot you in the back.'

Gurdjiev froze. Martina got down from the plane, ignoring

whatever Gurdjiev muttered to her. Gurdjiev looked sharply at her face, reading her expression, part defiant and part puzzled, like all recent defectors. He nodded his head to his own silent calculation. Tanner was against him and so was the woman. He should have shot them both himself in Santa Cruz. His head swivelled to the pilot's door.

Baron stepped out, rubbing the small of his back. He took in the little tableau and shrugged, showing more interest in the rainclouds that hovered above the tallest trees and had made the descent so tricky. His glance swept over the cocaine shed, the dog pen, the hangar and the fuel drums crowding it, the path that wound between banks of shrubs towards the house, the road that went towards the village hidden by jungle except for the cross on top of the church. Finally he rested his eyes on Tanner.

'Well, you wanted to come here. Now I wait?'

'Baron,' Gurdjiev said, 'I hired you and your plane. It is me you take orders from.'

Baron smoothed a cheek and scratched at some stubble under his chin. 'I guess you can't see but you have a pistol aimed right between your shoulderblades. I would say you are in no position to give any orders.'

'We shan't be long,' Tanner said. 'Gurdjiev won't be flying back with us though another man might.'

'Okay. Don't know whether it concerns you . . .' He put a cigar in his mouth and scraped a match. 'Just before we began the descent I did a search across the frequencies and my headset began to crackle.' He drew the flame into his cigar. 'Someone talking to Air Traffic Control at Santa Cruz.' He drew again. 'American talk.' He tossed the match aside. 'Just thought you might be interested.'

'What were they saying?'

'Wasn't normal aviation English. It was private. Big bird to nest, chipmunk, cinnamon toast. Things you could understand the words but they had no meaning.'

He gave Martina a smile. Hi little lady, what are you doing messed up in this? From the village floated the sound of drumbeats. For a few seconds their attention wandered there.

'Philip.'

Tanner moved fast at Martina's shout. He hit Gurdjiev on the side of his head with the butt of his pistol and stooped to gather up the gun he'd lifted from an underarm holster. Gurdjiev was on hands and knees, a trickle of blood coming down one cheek, shaking his head because of muzziness or because of the final evidence of Martina's change of allegiance. Why didn't I kill him, Tanner wondered, he would have killed me, he'd ordered my death once already.

A gunshot came from the house, muffled but distinctive. It couldn't be mistaken for a motorbike backfiring or a plank dropping or a single handclap. Someone had fired a gun, once.

'Come on,' Tanner said. 'Let's go.' He kicked the sole of one of Gurdjiev's shoes. 'You too.' And to Baron: 'Be ready for take-off when we get back.'

'I'm ready now.'

I am a far-flung soldier in Her Majesty's Secret Intelligence Service, Tanner reminded himself, but Her Majesty should be aware that it is no longer secret. Our plane has circled the ranch like a vulture above a dying animal. Three of us are marching bravely up the path to the house, one of us making a bold display of his pistol. But above all there are the dogs, descendants of the original hounds of the Baskerville, alerting the whole world.

The clamour of the dogs brought no one out of the house. No faces pressed against windows. No gardeners dropped their hoes. No servants demanded their business. Not even guards from the cocaine shed had them in their rifle sights. No Che, no Uhler. In Tanner's head was the echo of the single gunshot.

'No reason we shouldn't try the official way,' Tanner said. He rang the front door bell.

'What do you intend?' Gurdjiev asked.

'You say it's Guevara,' Tanner said. 'You're both convinced?'

Gurdjiev said nothing but Martina nodded.

'Why, Martina?'

'Because I took a plate to Havana with his fingerprints on. They matched his file in security headquarters.'

'What will you do?' Gurdjiev asked again.

'Simple,' Tanner said. 'I'll ask him what he wants. I'm not forcing him to do anything.'

'I doubt those were your orders.'

'South America is a long way from orders.'

'And me? What do you intend?'

'You told your two boys to kill me. You would have shot me yourself by the plane. What do you suggest I do?'

'Why didn't you shoot me just now when you had the excuse?'

Because Che and Gurdjiev, for differing reasons, were so desperate to have this encounter? Because of his own overpowering curiosity? Because he was British and the British had lost the will to be ruthless? Tanner had no answer. He listened for footsteps inside but all he heard were the drums in the village and the feral rumble of a distant crowd and the dogs. He rattled the doorhandle.

'Let's see if the back door's unlocked.'

Behind the house were sheds for garden tools and jeeps, a generator hut, a pigeon coop, hutches of rabbits, a line of washing, a kiddy's trike overturned in a mudslide, a doll. The kitchen door was open.

'Gurdjiev . . .' They all paused. 'Gurdjiev, the thing about a kitchen is you can be sure of finding a knife. When we pass through it might enter your head to grab a knife and make a lunge for me. He's grown soft, you say to yourself. Like the British grew too tender-hearted to hold on to their empire. Don't. We have these irrational moments when we fight like hell, such as the Falklands. I want you to know this: go for a knife and I'll kill you.'

Gurdjiev's head was half-turned to Tanner. The gun was firmly in the middle of his spine. His eyes moved to Martina. Any sign of support there? Her lips were parted and the sense of danger had brought a glow to her cheeks.

'You go first.' Tanner prodded the gun.

There could have been an air raid warning. The kitchen was littered with plates and cutlery and abandoned food, but maybe it was always like that. They went in procession through a silent house, Tanner opening doors to a larder, a dining-room, a small breakfast room, a toilet. Stairs led to an upper floor. A passage took them past the front door. The last door was to the living-room. They went in.

'There's no one here,' Gurdjiev said. 'They've got away.'

No, Tanner knew they hadn't left, nor were they hiding in an upstairs bedroom. He pointed to a door across the living-room, picturing to himself what lay beyond. 'They're waiting for us. They've watched us coming up the path, heard us ring the bell, followed our progress as we opened doors. They're listening to our voices now.'

'It's a trap. They're going to ambush us.'

Tanner looked at Martina.

'Or,' she said, 'only one person is waiting. Remember the shot.'

'Or nobody is waiting,' Tanner said. Che had achieved his objective and turned the gun on himself.

With the pistol jammed in Gurdjiev's back, Tanner reached past and grasped the handle. He twisted it and pushed the door open. From out of the room came not a smell of death but an overpowering stink of alcohol. A bottle lay in splinters on the carpet, a bullethole scarred the wall. Prodding Gurdjiev forward, Tanner and Martina followed through the doorway.

Tanner looked left and right, and his first feeling was one of puzzlement. He scarcely took in the room at all – a hazy vision of smuggled oil paintings in gilt frames, dark-wood furniture, the plumed helmets of Prussian cavalry officers, hunting trophies, books. Across the room was an old man, but surely not Che, not with blond-grey hair, a slight build, a face that was bleached by some emotion, a rigid posture. Prison, and everything that went with prison in South America, could change a man, but not turn him inside out. So where was Guevara?

Then Tanner realized what was wrong. The man was in the grip of terror and it had reduced him in size and confidence and willpower to someone who wouldn't even speak. Beyond him on the wall was the mask of an African witchdoctor, or a Haitian voodoo priest, Tanner didn't know. It was with a shock he understood the mask wasn't nailed to the wall, it was just behind the petrified man. A voice came from the black mask, and for a moment it touched the dread that hides in all of us: that there are dark arts which lie beyond our power to control.

'Who are you?'

The spasm of fright passed. Tanner became aware of the shoulders and chest of a solid man behind the mask.

'Fair question.' Tanner took his time, considering the look of terror on the seated man's face and what might have caused it. A witchdoctor's spell? More likely a solid and real threat pressed between his shoulderblades. 'My name is Tanner, and I've come from England. The woman's name is Martina Mancilla, originally from Cuba, now an American citizen. The man just in front of me is . . . well, you say, comrade.' There was no response to this prompting so Tanner went on, 'He says his name is Gurdjiev but he's probably worn out a dozen names in his life.'

'From Moscow?' the witchdoctor asked.

'From the Soviet Union, yes,' Gurdjiev said, like a dog's low growl.

'So you've come, you've come.' The voice was soft. He wasn't speaking for any ears but his own.

'Let me warn you about this man,' Gurdjiev said, jerking his head backwards. 'He hijacked my plane. He has a gun in my back. He is a spy from England.'

Full marks for courage, Tanner granted him, for speaking out like that. And yet . . . the sentences were so short and bald, and Gurdjiev had spoken them like a trader laying out his wares. These are the facts; admire their quality; you can't fail to buy them. To Tanner's ears there was a certain haste which showed desperation. And to other ears they didn't seem to be the right facts at all. Nobody responded.

'He intends to shoot me first, then you. He may not shoot the woman. He has already seduced her.'

Well, he's had his say, thought Tanner. He was too hasty. He did it too early when it sounds like the opening bid for greater disclosures. He should have kept it back to cast doubt on whatever I say.

'Someone has been going round causing mayhem and claiming to be Che Guevara. Is it you?' Tanner asked.

'Answer that.' The man seated at the desk jerked forward to a prod in his back. 'This is Uhler. He knows.'

Uhler nodded.

'Answer him.'

'Yes.'

'Say who I am.'

'You are Che Guevara.'

'Tell them. And tell them how you know.'

'We're talking of a long time ago.' He hesitated.

'Tell them.'

And Uhler did. Tanner had risked his life to reach this place. Others had already been killed. The secret armies of the world had mobilized. But Uhler repeated the facts as if they were dry sentences in a report destined for a dusty file.

'We're talking of twenty years ago, the time of the guerrilla movement in the province of Oriente. The leader was captured by the Bolivian army, wounded but alive. They didn't kill him straight off but thought to make use of him. Che Guevara must have secrets to tell. And when he had been squeezed dry, a show trial maybe, a full confession, a plea for mercy. That would be a great propaganda coup. But this is South America. It swallows up whole civilizations so one man can disappear very easily. Here he is, so important one day. Weeks pass and the feeling spreads among the bureaucrats that someone else is dealing with him. His existence is quite simply forgotten.' Uhler paused to catch his breath, or perhaps he hoped he'd said enough. There was a spasm in his body which Tanner put down to a sharp reminder in his back. Uhler went on in his flat unemotional style. 'For years he disappeared. Well, most thought he was dead already. Then Doctor Quiroz, who had treated his original wounds, chanced on him again. Doctor Quiroz arranged for his transfer to a special place of imprisonment. There he was kept for the purpose of questioning. I was present during certain sessions of questioning.'

'Questioning? You call it questioning?'

'He was interrogated. Also, certain experiments of a medical nature were carried out by Doctor Quiroz.'

'And why were you there?'

'I was . . . an observer.'

'An observer of what? Tell them what you observed.'

Uhler had answered his questions looking at Gurdjiev, or sometimes at Tanner. Now his eyes dropped.

There was a silence.

Tanner found the silence terrible. If Uhler had said: They did this, they did that to Guevara – it would have been words. The silence was filled by the screams of their imagination.

Che was the one to break the spell. 'I was only expecting the Russian. I don't know what to do with three of you. Why have you come?'

Do with us? Tanner had a pistol and Gurdjiev in front of him, much as he'd used Raul's body as a shield earlier. Nothing was going to be done to him.

'Knowledge of your resurrection – may I call it that? – has excited great interest in the world. Most opinions are sceptical, some are hostile. I represent an organization in Britain and was sent here to find out the truth, if possible. And to help your escape to England, if that is what you want. Arrangements can be made for you to live there in security with a new identity.'

'Come to England?' Che asked, taken aback. 'You mean to retire there like an English lord?'

Not exactly. In fact not at all, if Tanner was truthful. Hershey had something else entirely in mind. He wasn't forced to answer.

'He is a liar,' Gurdjiev burst out, 'an old-fashioned imperialist sent to kill you.'

'However,' Tanner went on, striking out boldly across the Rubicon, 'if you don't want to come to England, I respect that decision. I'm not going to kidnap you and force you to go at gunpoint. If I was going to murder you – as Gurdjiev suggested – I could have shot you through the mask already. Nor am I going to hand you over to the Americans or the Bolivians. Stay here or go – you choose. Also,' he finally reached the far bank of the Rubicon, 'mine is not the only offer open to you. Martina?'

She looked strangely at him. Well, it was a day for the political landscape to shift. Tanner had been very short in the offer he made and perhaps he was right. They weren't insurance salesmen holding out glowing prospects of a contented old age. Effusive greetings were out. She couldn't deliver them to a grotesque black mask. She chose a plain, businesslike tone.

'I live in the United States not because I have rejected the achievements of my country but for revolutionary reasons. I have maintained close links with many sections of the Party in Cuba which is how I was able to gain positive identification of you. I am empowered to offer you, on the highest authority, a sanctuary in Cuba, a safe retirement, all the honour that is due to you as a fighter for liberation in the past. Whatever is in the power of the Cuban people to give you will be yours as of right. There are greetings from Fidel and Raul but I will save those for a more appropriate time. The formal offer is: a haven of peace and honour.'

Well, two handsome offers there, Tanner thought. The grotesqueness of the situation wasn't lost on him: they were rivals pleading for his favour, courtiers anxious for his nod, lovers waiting for his smile. They had come to this jungle clearing in the most absurd country in the world and were confronting a man whose face they couldn't even see.

'Personal assurance of warmth and affection in Cuba,' Martina said after a pause. It seemed too bald otherwise. 'That is why I accompanied Gurdjiev.'

So attention moved back to the Russian. He shifted. Tanner felt the movement as a message sent back through the pistol. He wanted to wriggle out of his skin, shed his identity and escape to the safety of a distant land.

'I have waited for this,' Che began. 'I have worked for it.'

It seemed an explanation for why he wouldn't be rushed. He was savouring the passing moments. You don't want to hurry revenge. Love is a powerful emotion but it passes. Revenge consumes everything and lasts longer.

Che said to Gurdjiev, 'Why don't you take off your jacket?'

Tanner was not pleased at the idea. He would have to step back from Gurdjiev to let him remove the linen jacket, thus giving him the opportunity of hurling it or trying some diversion. A pistol nestling against the spine is proof against any trick.

But Gurdjiev said, 'I shall keep it on.'

'This is the jungle. Such formality is unnecessary.' Che had a playful tone, teasing. Gurdjiev didn't move. 'Then why not roll back your sleeves? Particularly your right sleeve, as far as the elbow.' Again Gurdjiev didn't respond. 'You don't want to do even that?' Che prodded Uhler and his tone hardened. 'Why should the man who now calls himself Gurdjiev not show us his forearm?'

'The tattoo,' Uhler said. 'The name is different but the tattoo is the same. He doesn't want to show it.'

'How do you know?'

'I told you this morning. You remembered but still you made me tell you.'

'Tell it again. Let them all know the story.'

Uhler lifted his head, twisting to see the man behind as if he could read his future in the witchdoctor's mask.

'They have to understand,' Che said. In his voice Tanner recognized the scruples of a civilized man who wants others of the human tribe to accept his motives for breaking the tribe's most powerful taboo: killing its own kind.

'In 1967,' Uhler said, 'Mendoza was a young policeman stationed in Santa Cruz. It was a wild town in those days, with a different rumour every day. Some rumours were of guerrillas – up in the *yungas*, in the hills near Cochabamba, hit-and-run tactics across Lake Titicaca. Another rumour said high-ranking Cuban military and police officers had come to foment rebellion, under the leadership of an international revolutionary from Argentina. You, of course. That was too ridiculous to be believed.'

'Speak to them, not me. Tell them how Mendoza was approached.'

'There was a bar Mendoza liked to go to, have a drink, then visit the brothel at the back. There was one whore in particular he liked – I have to tell you Mendoza was not a man of refined tastes – who was known as *El Cañon Grande* because of . . .'

Delicately, mindful of the pistol behind him, Uhler moved both hands up to indicate overflowing breasts.

'Her cleavage, you understand? One evening when Mendoza visited the brothel he was startled to find it was not the whore but a man sitting on the bed. He held a pistol, in case Mendoza took it into his head to become a hero. On his forearm was a tattoo, very striking, of an eagle. He apologized for postponing Mendoza's pleasure but he had information that would bring Mendoza much praise and promotion.'

'Did he identify himself?'

'He gave a name and said he came from Moscow because certain decisions had been made within the Party there and he was in Bolivia to implement them.'

'And Mendoza believed him?'

'Not at first but as they continued talking – '

Gurdjiev abruptly moved forward, catching Tanner off guard. Che, whose eyes had rested with hunger on Gurdjiev's face, was prepared. The pistol appeared over Uhler's shoulder.

'Stop.'

Gurdjiev stopped. But he turned his head to speak to Tanner. 'Do you believe any of this? A messenger from Moscow? Conspiratorial meetings in brothels? Do you think anyone would remember a fat whore all these years? It is a story they've made up and rehearsed together. They even tell it together.'

'Why should they do that?' Martina said.

'A runaway Nazi and a man in a savage's mask. They are both mad. We've wasted our time coming here.'

'But you have been to Santa Cruz before,' Tanner said. 'You admitted it yourself.'

Gurdjiev opened his mouth but they waited in vain for him to deny it. In the silence they heard a rumble: drumbeats from the village but louder now, a menacing sound. Tanner took a couple of paces forward to return his pistol to Gurdjiev's back.

'What was the information this Russian was passing to a junior police officer?' Tanner asked.

'Where Che Guevara and the guerrilla group were training.'

'Was he going to tell him? Show him?'

'A message would be sent to the Communist Party headquarters in La Paz. From there a jeep would be driven down to the base camp on an abandoned cattle ranch near Nancahuasu. The jeep would be left in a conspicuous position where an army patrol would be sure to find it.'

Tanner frowned, unable to see the point. When a revolution had triumphed, that was when it devoured its firebrands. It didn't betray its most famous son before it succeeded.

Che asked, 'Who was to drive this jeep?'

'She was called Tania at the time. She was called something else when you first met her in Berlin. That was when she acted as interpreter. I don't know her real name.'

'Tamara,' Che said, remembering her, 'perhaps.' She'd had a romantic beauty and Tamara had suited her long dark hair. For a time she'd dyed it blonde and been a different person. 'Also

Haidée.' But in Bolivia she'd been known by neither of those names but as Tania. 'What were her orders? What secret orders did this Russian pass on to her?'

'After she'd left the jeep she was to go to your camp. If you were away on a training march, she was to wait for you.'

'Impossible. To hang about the camp was forbidden. Those were my strict orders.'

'She was in love with you.'

Che nodded. She'd been in love with him. She'd said so. She'd also told other people. She had boasted of her love for this great guerrilla leader to her comrades, or confessed it to her masters in the KGB. Boast, confess – it didn't matter which. Here was a human frailty that could be exploited.

'What was the outcome?'

'Only partly successful. You sent her back to La Paz, and you left the camp before the army raided it. Mendoza had been finding extreme difficulty in getting his superiors to accept this story.'

'Hardly surprising,' Che said. 'I still marvel at it.' His eyes went from Martina to Tanner to Gurdjiev. 'A Russian arrives from the Soviet Communist Party and sets about betraying the revolution. If such treachery were known, even today, think of the impact it would have.'

'It would never be believed,' Tanner said. 'Why should the Soviet Union want to strangle the guerrilla movement in Bolivia?'

'That was the question Mendoza asked,' Uhler said. 'He had more than one meeting with the Russian. He said he'd gone to an army colonel who refused point blank to accept that the communists would betray their own. Why? the colonel demanded. It was a trap. There had to be a reason. The Russian finally said . . .'

'Go on. Mendoza told me often enough. You tell them.'

'Guevara is turning into a megalomaniac, a swollen-headed dictator. That was the view in Moscow. His ambition is not confined to Bolivia, he wants revolution in the whole of the continent. He sees himself as the Lenin of South America. It would be a situation beyond the control of Moscow. One country at a time was their goal. So Guevara must be halted.'

'Halted!' It was a poor word to describe his betrayal.

'Eventually the military authorities did send a patrol to look for the jeep. They found it, though the base camp was empty. But the jeep held vital papers.'

'Giving the names of miners' leaders in Potosi who backed the cause?'

'Yes.'

'The network in La Paz?'

'Yes.'

'The identity of the liaison officer from Cuba?'

'Yes. The entire organization to back up the guerrillas.'

'Thank you.' Che was the prosecutor who'd drawn out a witness: thank you for your damning testimony. He was the priest who'd listened to the condemned man: thank you for your confession.

In his mind Che was back in that special place where Mendoza had come in his uniform and practised his techniques of interrogation. After all, a torturer needs training as much as a doctor. The doctor, Quiroz in a well-cut suit and tie, didn't practise torture. As a professional man he donned a hygienic white coat and announced as if it was the subject of a lecture: 'Today we shall examine whether the body reacts more to a visual stimulus or to an aural stimulus.' Five kilowatts of light burnt Che's eyes out, 110 decibels of sound crushed his eardrums. He had one pair of hands. Did he choose to protect his eyes or his ears? Quiroz had been insane. Did that excuse such evil?

Against the wall, perched on the very edge of his chair, had been Uhler. This was how Che remembered him: his lips parted, his eyes shining, holding his breath, seeming to rise out of the chair at the very brink of exquisite pleasure. Sometimes he sipped a glass of wine.

Uhler's appetites had grown jaded by the repetition of physical acts. 'Tell him about the Russian,' Uhler had begged Mendoza. 'Tell him about Tania. Tell him how political love and a woman's love both betrayed him. Tell him the story again. Wait. It should be done by candlelight. Place the candle on the table so I can watch his face when he hears about the Russian sitting on the whore's bed.' He had an urgent whisper.

'Kill me,' Che had said the first time he'd heard. 'Why don't you finish off the army's work? I want to die.'

But dying was forbidden. Dying was a luxury he could not buy. Dying would be a loss to the others.

It had been the only time he pleaded to be killed. Then, alone at last, he'd said to himself: I will survive, one day at a time. His tears had not been for the pain but for the loss of faith.

There will come a day of judgement.

'Thank you,' Che had said. His voice was grave.

Remove the mask. Tanner wanted it so much. Some said the eyes were the windows of the soul but eyes were nothing without the face. Guevara's voice had been wiped clean of expression but what did his face show? Despair, agony, peace? Hunger? A calm madness?

After Che spoke there were some seconds of silence in the room. They became aware of the world outside. The thunderstorm was approaching. No, it was the unending growl of drums. Looking through the window they had a glimpse of people on the track from the village, a surging religious procession, a crucifix swaying, boys scampering, women in masks. The men seemed to be disputing something, to be quarrelling, or reinforcing their anger. Some waved bottles in the air, others had machetes, knives, hammers, axes. Some pointed to the airstrip, others pointed to the house.

Uhler saw the approaching crowd. The fear went from his eyes. His people would rescue him and once more Guevara would be his plaything. It had been *years* . . . His face relaxed in relief, the beginning of a smile.

That was the moment Uhler was shot, with that look of relief on his face. Che took a step back. The explosion of his pistol was deafening, like a barrage of artillery in the closed space of the room. Tanner swung round to see Uhler pressing with both hands on the desk, as if he wanted to rise to greet a visitor. He slumped back in his chair and a hand went to his neck to brush away a small red animal that clung there. The animal was a lump of his flesh and blood began flowing down, staining his shirt. Che fired again and Uhler was sent toppling to the floor, an arm dragging a pile of papers off his desk. Che stood over the body and fired a final time into the chest, though Uhler could have been dead already.

Che straightened up, satisfied, and came forward across the room. Tanner backed away, bumping into Martina. They stood together near the door. Gurdjiev looked round, seeing nowhere to hide, nothing to protect himself with, no escape through the barred window. Che walked with the pistol held up, pointing at Gurdjiev's chest. He stopped a couple of paces away, out of Gurdjiev's reach.

'Who sent you?' There was no answer. 'You must have some high official backing.' Gurdjiev wasn't saying. 'Or is it just a bit of private enterprise, knowing you'd be liquidated if any breath of the great betrayal got out?'

Outside were ugly cries as the crowd swarmed closer.

'I used to wonder in my cell if I ever caught the man they taunted me with, the Russian they said betrayed me, what would I do to him? How would I kill him? Slowly, painfully? A thousand deaths, as I had? Perhaps I should seek maximum world publicity, a great show trial? But what country would try him and on what charge and with what punishment? Or a quick death to show I could be merciful despite everything I suffered? The answer is: I am not going to kill you. Others will. Listen.'

They were coming up the path towards the front door, their voices a jumble of shouts and threats.

'They will find you alone with Uhler's corpse. He was their boss, their employer, their benefactor, bringing many dollars from his drug trafficking. You came by plane, as the anti-cocaine inspectors do, and have killed him. You will find they have a tradition here . . .'

'Enough,' Gurdjiev said. 'Don't you agree that's enough?' He swung round to try to rally support from Martina and Tanner, then came back to Che. 'You've had your revenge on the torturer. You and I are both fighters for social justice. Twenty years ago the Party made a terrible error of judgement but now it wants to atone. There is a new man in the Kremlin, a new spirit in the Soviet Union. Return with me and enjoy the hero's welcome that belongs to you. It will be a tremendous blow struck at the American imperialists, a rallying cry for freedom fighters everywhere. Come, show the greatness of your heart when it matters most.'

The African mask shook.

'When they come for you,' Che said, his voice firm, 'do not try to persuade them you are a Russian agent. They are used to such tricks. You are the killer of the man who gave them their living. Oh here, since you are the one who shot him, you'll need this.'

To Tanner's horror, Che thrust the pistol into Gurdjiev's hands. He is mad, an old man whose tortures have proved too much in the end.

Gurdjiev said, 'Stop! None of you move. Drop your gun, Tanner.'

Gurdjiev had the pistol pointed at Tanner's face. Tanner let his gun fall to the floor.

'Don't do that,' Guevara said to Tanner, stooping to pick it up for him. 'You may need it yet.' They heard a click as Gurdjiev squeezed the trigger, and another click, and again. There was desperation in it. 'Do you imagine I would hand over a loaded pistol? If there was even one bullet, you would use it on yourself when you discover what that lynch mob intends.'

Martina and Tanner went through the door. Che paused to say goodbye to Gurdjiev. 'Courage, comrade, you are about to discover the truth of what I have said: in revolution one lives or one dies.'

Che turned the key and followed Martina and Tanner along the corridor, past the front door, rocking under the thud of angry shoulders, towards the door in the kitchen.

CHAPTER 23

'What do you think?' Martina asked.

'It's the best we can do,' Tanner said.

They stared at each other. This is grotesque, Tanner thought, but the moment of doubt passed.

Che laughed. It was a wheezing laugh, rusty. The Englishman's head was enclosed in a beekeeper's mask found among the garden tools. A toy plastic duck was wired to the top like a mascot. A doll sat on the woman's head. It had a dirty gingham dress that smothered her face with a rip that let her dark eyes peep out.

'In *carnivalito* anything goes,' Che said.

Who would look anyway? It was the house they were storming. Once Uhler's body was discovered they'd have no time for a beekeeper and a Raggedy Ann. They would demand a sacrifice and the Russian was there to satisfy their blood-thirst.

Let them crucify Gurdjiev, Che prayed, nail him to the cross. It was the people's justice, his final revenge.

Across the yard, through poinsettia bushes, they could see the wooden cross being used as a battering ram. A roar greeted the smashing down of the front door. There came another roar from the landing strip as a little plane – their plane – heaved into view and climbed above the trees.

'Baron!' Tanner yelled, as if the bastard could hear. Through the trees he caught glimpses of the crowd that was swarming to the strip. Baron was not the man to enquire of a lynch mob what they thought they were up to. Baron had saved his own skin.

Abrams had returned to the communications room when the satellite link sprang to life again. Hershey had been walking for the front door and there wasn't even a plea for him to come back. Hershey didn't want to stay but he wanted to be asked. He was passing the hospitality cabinet and was suddenly furious at the lack of grace Abrams showed. Not even a sniff of whisky to soothe their troubles.

He poured himself a Haig Dimple that Abrams always referred to as Pinch. Chap simply couldn't adapt to local customs. Another of his faults. From time to time Abrams put on an extraordinary Colonel Blimp accent and used slang out of early Wodehouse. *Jolly good show, what. Absolutely ripping, old bean.* It would be offensive if it wasn't so juvenile.

Hershey could hear over the loudspeaker the lazy deep voice of the controller in Langley. It was like a record played at the wrong speed. What was he saying? Hershey couldn't catch the words. Odd, his glass was empty already. Well, since I'm here, he decided, it would be ridiculous not to find out what's happening.

No one paid any attention when he slipped into the communications room. They listened to the voice of Lieutenant Norwak bounced back from the helicopter over the jungle.

'It's making a circuit, sir. We're still about five/six miles off and can't see anything on the horizon. Too much haze. It just popped on to the screen so it has to have taken off from the strip at Puerto Vargas. Maybe it's looking at something on the ground. *Sir*, it's changing course. It's heading off now towards the top of the screen.'

'Lieutenant, refresh my memory,' came the deep voice, 'what is up in that direction?'

'Brazil, sir. I can see it now, sir. I have visual contact with the plane. The river is the boundary, then it's Brazil. The way that plane is heading, about fifteen hundred miles of Brazil.'

'Goddam.'

'As you say, sir.'

'Lieutenant,' Abrams broke in, 'if that is Guevara on that plane, we want it brought down.'

There were moments of silence.

'Lieutenant,' Abrams tried again. 'Do you read me?'

'Sir, I appreciate what you say but there are problems.'

'You have missiles clipped on?'

'Yes sir.'

'What problems then?'

'We are not in Bolivia on a military thing and shooting down an unarmed plane – '

'Lieutenant Norwak, do I have to get the President on the line? He is waiting to be told Guevara is no longer a threat, that he's been neutralized. He is your Commander-in-Chief and have you any idea what's going to drop on you if you disobey his order?'

'Sir, sir, another thing. We don't know for sure Guevara is on that plane. In fact we don't know at all.'

'Lieutenant, you shoot that plane down before it disappears just to make damn certain. Then you land to check it was Guevara you got. Is that understood?'

Abrams raised his eyes to heaven and then looked round at the rest of his crew with an expression: the schmucks I have to deal with. He saw Hershey holding an empty glass and wondered if Hershey's man was on that plane along with the Cuban woman and Che. Abrams turned back to the microphone and prepared to do battle again: Do you want me to get the Soviet leader on the line maybe, thank you for saving Guevara's life? Then he heard a distant voice, in a helicopter somewhere over the South American jungle, giving an order: 'Target that plane, Dan. Do it. *Don't give me that shit, just do it.*' The voice was off-mike but you could tell it was screaming.

They heard the explosion and didn't know what caused it. They heard a big bang but it was some moments until they heard the helicopter. Until then it had been the fading noise of Baron's plane and the growing anger of the crowd. They didn't see the explosion because they weren't watching the sky. What they saw, everyone's head snapping round, was the aftermath, the split second after the explosion.

The clouds were rolling away to the north and against a dirty blue was the starburst of Baron's plane. It was blown apart in a dozen different directions, leaving trails of grey smoke and brilliant tracers of flame and sparkles off bits of metal.

'What happened?' Martina swung round to stare at the masked face of Tanner. 'A bomb? Planes don't just explode, do they?'

Another thought struck her. 'My God, we should have been on that plane.'

Tanner thought: Hershey's just tried to have me killed. He shook his head to clear it. Exhaustion was eating him up. Paranoia had got a grip of him.

Then the helicopter came into sight, a brute of a transporter with US Army and a star emblazoned in white on the side.

'It's war,' Che said. 'America versus mankind.'

We can't stay, Tanner knew. To stay was to be crucified. Their plane had been blown up. The American helicopter was hovering over Uhler's ranch, swinging in an arc like a shark smelling out its victim. The river was the only way out. Instinct drew them to the water. Without a word spoken they began to walk down the path at the edge of the jungle.

Shouts suddenly erupted from the house. Uhler's corpse had been discovered and Gurdjiev was being dragged out for the pagan-Christian ritual. The screaming of a pig brought Che to a halt. He turned to watch. Could such a shrill sound come from that stocky peasant body? The dogs were in a frenzy, racing beside the wire, howling at the helicopter, the masked faces, the surging tide round Gurdjiev.

Revenge. It wasn't a thought, it was a feeling that swept through Che.

'Don't wait to watch,' Tanner said. 'Come on.'

Guevara shook his head.

'Hurry, man. Before the Americans spot us.' He spoke through his beekeeper's mask to a witchdoctor while a doll looked on. The Americans would recognize nobody.

The woman came and took Che's arm and he shook her off. 'Where would you have me go? England?'

'Cuba. You'll be safe among friends. There's a house waiting for you.'

Martina ripped off the stupid doll that masked her face. Che could see the pleading in her features. He looked back at the airstrip where the helicopter was making another circuit. At the crowd of villagers who were streaming in that direction. Back to Martina and Tanner. Take him to Cuba? He'd be the Holy Grail. He could picture it.

'I know what the house you have promised would be like.

Protected night and day against assassins. Armed guards patrolling the wall. On top of the wall barbed wire. A gate with a sentry. At night floodlights in the grounds. Dogs prowling. What does that remind you of?'

He set off once again along the path that led down to the river. He had a slight limp and his shoulders were stooped but he still had a briskness to his stride.

'Che,' Martina called out after him. 'Che.'

Tanner took her hand to hold her back from running after him. All the dangers, he thought, the days and nights of travel, the deaths of so many men, the destruction of the certainties of his life – and for what? The sight of an old man disappearing towards the jungle.

'Che,' Martina called again. 'You can't leave us like this. Take your mask off. I can never tell what you're thinking behind that mask.'

He stopped and turned. 'No,' he said. 'No. You've never seen me. You must tell the world I'm dead.'

He went on his way. Tanner, feeling the tension in Martina, put an arm round her shoulders and pulled her into him.

'And no survivors?' Abrams asked. 'No one baled out?'

'No sir.'

'Well done, Lieutenant. I am positive the President will be congratulating you in his own good time. And no sign of the Soviets?'

'No aircraft on the ground. It's impractical to come in any other way.'

'I don't get it. They sent one guy, one retired KGB oldie. Don't they care?'

'What they're doing,' Hershey said and stopped as the room turned to glare. But it was clear to him and he no longer gave a damn. 'They're leaving the bloody Yanks to make a bloody mess as usual and then they'll claim the propaganda victory.'

'Are you serious?' Spots of red blossomed on Abrams's cheeks. 'Here's a misquote. I've been reading your authors. Those who can, do. Those who can't, become analysts. Norwak?'

'Sir?'

'You're to go in to land now to check there's no Guevara, no Soviets, and nothing to connect us with this operation. That clear?'

How had this turned into Abrams's operation? It was clear to no one, least of all Norwak. He gave a dutiful, 'Yes sir.'

'Talk us through, okay? We're on the other side of the globe and we want to have some kind of a picture of what the hell's going on.'

'At this time we're taking one final swing over the village, sir. A few people in the plaza where the church is. They're staring up. Guess they don't see too many helicopters this way. A canoe pushing out on the river. Looks like a voodoo priest in it. No other action at the village, sir. Not many folk. Smudges of woodsmoke. Looks pretty primitive. No cars, no roads, no fancy houses, no offices, no factories. That the kind of stuff you want?'

'You're doing fine, son,' came a drawling voice from Langley. 'We like it so much we're taping it for you. Your grandchildren are going to hear what a great day you had.'

'Okay, we're turning now, circling the top end of the village. Some cattle in a field, then it's jungle again. Green hell, you can believe it. This place hasn't progressed since the stone age. Passing north of the ranch now. We're told it was built by some rich guy who beat it out when Nazi Germany fell. What a place to end up and he thought he was safe, nobody would ever look here for him and now here's a US army helicopter dropping in. This is where everybody's at. Not in the village, all out here, couple of hundred, three hundred, more, they're all over, and *weird*. Masked like Hallowe'en – trick or treat. Right, airstrip's coming up to meet us. Whoa there, Tom's just bounced us off the strip, or maybe he's just testing for firmness. Okay, we're back on mother earth.'

Abrams said, 'Lieutenant, you're doing fine. This is going to be a great day for you. How many men you got with you because you're going to have to go through that ranch now.'

'Twenty men. But sir, this is a time for leading from the front. I'll go first.'

'Attaboy.'

'I speak Spanish, sir.'

'Ah, the Puerto Rican Nowaks.'

'Sir? Sir, we do have a kind of problem. The Colonel showed us a twenty-year-old photo of a guy with a beard and hair to his shoulders and a beret with a star. So what does Guevara look like now? Hair fallen out? Beard gone white or shaved off? He had powerful eyes but maybe now he's short-sighted and wears glasses. Any guidance on that?'

'Well now,' said the Langley controller, 'none of us has seen him and there's no computer program we can run so I guess you'll have to use your initiative.'

'Sir, the sight outside now is incredible. I wish we had vision. Can you hear the drums? You should see the people, hundreds of them, like a football crowd along the strip. The women are wearing masks. Not itty-bitty masks but big things the size of trays that cover their whole face, their hair, everything. And crazy designs, crazy. Snow White and animals and princesses and spacemen and a cage with a live parrot. At the back of the crowd I can see a great cross, a crucifixion with a gaudy painted statue of Christ. It must weigh heavy. You know how they carry a cross upright, two maybe three guys do it? This is being carried by eight men and they're carrying it flat, like it was a stretcher. Or you see bearers carrying a coffin that way. Crowd is edging forward, the women in these fantastic masks, the men with work tools, hammers, axes, machetes. Few kids doing a dance to the drums, you know how kids get excited when there's a party. Well, I better go and speak with them. It is a little scary, sir, I got to admit that. We're in the jungle, all these masked figures, the drums, the tools and stuff the men are carrying. I'll just go and ask what they know about Guevara. I'm unclipping the mike so I'll be off-air for a spell.'

In London, at the Kensington branch, Hershey and Abrams and Shortley of the FBI and the others stared at the loudspeaker. The Lieutenant had sounded uneasy and they waited in silence.

THREE POSITIONS

by

Gary Marks

Deep Swing Publications

First published 2023
This edition published by Deep Swing Publications

ISBN 978-1-3999-6322-0

Cover Design by Gary Marks

Dedication

To those who have taken a beating from this game, which is all of us, and in the spirit of a never-ending search for answers, here are some thoughts on the golf swing that may be of interest.

TABLE OF CONTENTS

INTRODUCTION

The game of golf is incredibly difficult. Perhaps this is why there is so much instruction available for golfers to contemplate in their search for improvement. But with such a volume of material available to be filtered through, it is nigh-on impossible to figure out which bits and which ideas are worthy of pursuit, and which bits are likely to be a waste of time. Compounding this problem is that there is no generally accepted swing theory in existence for players to refer to. Something reliable, serving as a touchstone or place of refuge from uncertainty. Without a generally accepted theory, many speculative ideas are able to throw their hat into the ring and gain attention by staking a claim. Loose ideas on how to swing a golf club, make a better move, or – quickly gain ten or twenty yards. (Even thirty yards is being currently advertised!) Some of these ideas are non-starters. Others, little more than distraction and amusement (such as ground-force reaction), and some are interesting. All are harmless, so long as they are treated inquiringly and with caution rather than assumed worthy. In time, things get found out. However, the finding-out can sometimes cost years, as golfers – including tour pros – buy into hard-sell and run with an idea longer than they should (e.g. tying arms to body). It is easily done. We are all looking for improvement, and seemingly with nowhere to turn and feeling also like we are a step or two short of where we want to be as a player, we

become vulnerable to these hats when thrown in. Especially if the protagonist throwing the hat has their chest puffed out and is making grand claims, which is sometimes the case.

Many sports are advantaged over golf in that they have a considerable reflex/reaction aspect to their play. This reflex side of performance takes the mind out of things and is seen in all team field sports, all court sports and, perhaps we can include – all motor sports. Most of the world's *major* sports – soccer, NFL, basketball, tennis, baseball, rugby, ice-hockey, Formula 1, cricket. etc, have a significant reaction aspect as soon as play begins. But not golf. Golf has very little of reflex about it.

A normal routine: Taking advantage of being allowed to place the ball upon a tee peg, thereby sitting it up making it easy to hit, we begin preparation for the shot. Our playing partners stand back, stand still and stand quiet. They give us space, and watch as we go through our routine taking as much time as we wish within reason, to get ourselves comfortable and ready. The environment is close to perfect, and we even have time over the ball to choose a suitable swing-thought (from the many we know) to help our swing produce a good shot.

But when our swing gets moving what comes next is routinely *so* troubled that disaster is delivered upon the shot; it being mis-hit, mis-directed or… both. At this point it would be nice to be able to blame something, or some*one*, other than us. Many sports do offer-up possibility to shift a share of responsibility. A player can (in their mind at least) blame a few underperforming teammates, or – the opposition team for being so strong. The defeated tennis player can blame the

player on other side of the net for having the game of their life. With thoughts such as these we soften the sense of personal failure a little, and as a minimum (when playing the above-mentioned sports) we know that others are intrinsically involved in the allowing or disallowing of what we are able to do with our own performance.

But the golfer has only themselves to blame. And so, just as all roads lead to Rome, so too, all fingers point to one person regarding a failed golf shot. To the player. To them entirely and alone. If the failed shot repeats, and the golfer accepts they are the one causing it, then it will not be long before an inquisition is held and a golf swing is put on trial for treachery. It is, after all, our golf swing which lets us down when it cannot hit a small ball into such a large space.

Cause and effect are overtly pointed and personal in golf. In the perfect environment described above, the player is asked to hit a small ball measuring 4cm across into a target which is often one thousand times as wide. A target not only enormously wide, but also, without a goalkeeper in the middle forcing the player to play down one of the sides. Nevertheless, golfers in this perfect environment manage to miss the enormous target more often than they manage to hit it, including – on bright, sunny, and windless days.

Regarding some basics of cause and effect:

Our golf club has a flat face to strike with. The flat face has a simple (and obvious) relationship with the ball, in that – *the ball, when hit, will fly in the direction the face points.* Figuring things out from this starting point should not be too difficult.

But it *is* difficult, and this is where so many ideas spring from, from the desire to figure things out, or at least – find a better answer than the one we have.

When we talk of 'figuring things out', 'finding a better answer' or of any 'solution', we are usually talking about the golf swing. It is our golf swing which does the hitting and our golf swing which does the missing of the enormous target. Logically, therefore – we need a better golf swing. It is fair to say that many golfers are bewildered by their golf swing's lack of reliability, being that it routinely delivers levels of inconsistency and malfunction not appearing to fit fairly with their efforts.

This work will therefore explain much about how the full swing works, such that there will be less confusion going forwards (for all of us), and more certainty with any efforts we put into our own golf swing's development.

Before we start, though, let me take you back to the beginning. To where this all came from…

During one three-year spell in the early 1990's, I gave ten thousand lessons at Europe's busiest golf range (in London). They were half-hour lessons – short, and intense. It was a huge number of lessons to give and I learned most of what I know about amateur golf swings, and amateur play, from that three-year spell. Six months into those ten thousand lessons I adopted (without realising it at the time) what was to become a career-long teaching method, style, and theory. Thirty years have since passed and I still teach the same method. Nothing of significance has entered, been removed,

or been changed. In between then and now, I have kept close attention on developments in my profession, but nothing has arrived which offers the understanding that this theory of thirty years past offers. So, time has come for me to present it.

This book will deliver 'three positions theory' publicly, for the first time; and although it has remained quiet and out of sight for many years, I hope that readers will, by the end, recognise something original and of lasting value as having arrived in the field of golf swing theory. Little of what follows will have been heard before, although instructors will relate most easily to it as they use some of this theory in their day-to-day dealings. Including instructors, I believe it to be worthy of every golfer's consideration.

A final thought. The theory you are about to read captures all golfers. The routes forward (with technique) are the same whether applied to a 24 handicapper, a 12 handicapper, a 3 handicapper or, to a PGA Tour pro. Each would improve their technique in exactly the same way, using the same principles taken from this theory. That it applies to all golfers means also that it should be readable by all golfers, and when the final page of this work is turned there should have been reward for everyone. A learner, just starting out in golf, should be able to understand this work's core theory. Indeed, parts of this book have been written expressly for learners. Additionally, golf's more experienced players and studied readers will be able to understand the entire work and, just as parts of the theory have been written for learners, so too, some parts have been written for experts the world over – for

instructors (just mentioned), and for the highest performers at tournament level on the world stage.

Welcome to three positions theory.

A general theory of the golf swing, with application to all golfers.

FIRST CONTACT

If a non-golfer takes hold of a golf club and swishes it back and forth, they have a swing. And almost immediately the non-golfer can hit a ball with this swing. It is a scenario which plays out each day of the week at busy urban driving ranges. They are fun places, especially now, with automatic ball feeders and the latest screen technology in each bay ready to give the golfer information about their shot. If a player wishes to, they can even play virtual golf on a world-famous course.

New players often come along with friends to try golf. Two, three, four or sometimes a group of half a dozen will arrive to try their hand at something new. There are fast learners and slow learners, but all are able to hit the ball with their own version of a swing, in pretty quick time, even though it might be a first-ever attempt at the sport. Some of these first timers are a little timid with their hits, but although less powerful their efforts are just as technically able as the stronger hitters. Younger male learners often throw everything at the ball in an effort to out-do their friends and hit a huge distance. One of the features of modern screen technology is that it tracks the ball's flight as it leaves the bay, displaying precise distance feedback on the screen (along with numerous other data), and it *is* fun trying to beat a

personal distance record, or a friend's. Most new-to-golf first timers keep 'swinging away', taking delight when a good ball departs; and unlike experienced players (who have higher expectations and get irritated more quickly), only an unrelenting series of fails seems to frustrate or annoy them.

And so, one thing we see amid the goings on at urban driving ranges is that even complete rookie golfers own golf swings. Right from the off and without any instruction having been received. If these rookie first timers stay for an hour or so, and keep swinging, they will see some progress and gain a little confidence.

Here we are describing a fairly typical golf-range scene, and we will now focus it by imagining the scene is taking place in the evening, after work hours. A time of day when city ranges are at their busiest and most atmospheric.

To one group of friends who had come along to try golf, something happens. A player arrives and takes position in the bay beside them. There is nothing unusual about that, of course, but this player quickly catches their eye. His shots are different. His *swing* is different. It looks kind of wonderful to them and appears organised in some way... plus, there is a power about it despite it seeming simple and low on effort. So many things about this player catch their eye that they cannot stop themselves from watching *him* in the bay beside, instead of their friends when they are hitting in front. They watch, and his shots are all the same, all have the same flight and go to the same place. Something about this player is impressive. The friends can tell he is good, but what they do

not realise is that the golfer they are watching practise… is a leading tour pro.

Across the Spectrum

In the evening scene just described, and next to each other in adjacent bays, are opposite ends of a spectrum. The simplest, and least technical golf swing possible; alongside the most technical and most advanced. The first – achieved in rapid time (basically instantaneously). The second – crafted after many years of hard labour and study. Though they sit as polar opposites to each other in terms of swing development, these swings nevertheless (and perhaps surprisingly) have a few things in common. General things, yes; but significant things.

All Golfers

Both swings begin with the player standing to the ball ready to go. Both, at that point, are still; except for a few twitches or shuffles in the final moments before the swing begins. Both swings have two moves. One move away from the ball and the next move back at the ball in attempt to hit it someplace far away. Both swings have a necessary change in direction. A point where the backswing stops for a moment and the return swing begins. Both return moves have a follow-through. It is impossible not to have a follow-through. Momentum of fast-travelling arms and club carry the swings well beyond the ball. And both players have balance at the end of their swing. Even first-time rookie players

instinctively balance on their through-swing and hold an end position. There is nothing technical about it, but their follow-through is balanced and held for a few seconds as they watch a good shot fly. The tour pro also holds a balanced follow-through for a second or two, whilst he watches *his* ball fly.

If we include this ending, where both the novice and the expert hold still after the shot has departed, then both swings have an 'end' position to go with their 'start' position and 'change-of-direction' position. This is about all that these two extreme-opposite golfers have in common by way of anything that could be classed as technique. They both have a *start,* a *mid-point* and an *end* (with a strike taking place in between). These three 'places' give the novice and the expert space for movement. Movement which can rightly be called – a golf swing.

Look More Closely

In this imaginary evening scene, we are now going to ask the friends – the first timers – if they could stay a while. We would like them to take a seat and watch the tour pro practising. We ask them if they notice anything of interest about his swing.

(Remember, these friends know nothing about golf or its technique, and have no idea what to look for.)

Pretty soon one of them says, 'omg look at his head… it's not moving!' They look, and notice that the tour pro's head stays still whilst he swings. His legs, his hips, his arms and his

body, all seem to be moving but not his head. To them, the tour pros head appears to remain amazingly still.

Then another friend exclaims that the tour pro's left arm is 'dead-straight' on the swing back from the ball, staying straight all the way to the top of the swing. The friends also notice that on the way through the pro's body twists around on itself – corkscrewing. They notice at the end of the swing that he is balancing on one leg – on his left leg, and left foot: the other foot being on tiptoe. His hips and body appearing to have turned right around, such that they now face the target.

These above points would likely be all they would notice.*

It *is* possible they may also notice the tour pro's posture, it being more angular and clean looking than most amateurs and learners manage when standing to a ball. But we will not include posture. And so, with no prior knowledge or schooling, these rookies would have quickly identified three or four bits of technique, and in fact, three or four big bits.

- head steady
- left arm straight
- corkscrewed, balanced finish
- weight on forward leg

If they were to then go back to their bays to try and mimic what they had seen, they would without question make gains from the images now in their mind's eye, and would push their swings forward at a technical level as a result.

*(*The rookies would be unlikely to notice anything about the grip, unless perhaps it was held right in front of their faces. Detailing of a good golf grip is difficult to spot from a distance, and even up close, it is not easy to identify the level of precision possible from a perfectly formed grip.)*

Closer Still

When speaking about the level of care and detail with which a grip can be placed on a golf club, and the more angular and clean-looking posture that the friends might have noticed in the pro's starting position, signal was being given to something that will not surprise anyone, and which is of obvious importance – '*The finest swings, when looked at closely, show the finest levels of detail and precision.*'

This detail and precision in the finest swings can first be seen in the way the player stands to the ball, and then shows throughout the entirety of the swing. Detail and precision are maintained for the duration, which, after start, will include two more positions the player will enter. One of these two positions still to be entered is critical; the other, is important.

Reduced to Minimum

Perhaps the first thing about golfers in action that should be identified educationally, even if from a most simple of understandings, is that their golf swings (all golf swings) have two moves:

- Backswing
- Through-swing

(Potentially, golf could be played with only one move. We could hold the club in the air, get ready, and then swing at the ball. Baseball has only one move. As a method for playing golf this would be incredibly difficult.)

The second thing that should be identified when observing golfers in action (educationally only slightly deeper than the first), is that golf swings appear to have three positions.

When we look at golfers around us, whether they be learner, intermediate, advanced or expert; we see that they all have an arrangement from where they begin the swing. This arrangement is the ***first position.*** They then stop briefly (in most cases only a moment) after making the backswing move. This briefest of stops is the ***second position.*** We then see golfers playing through to a place where they are again, still, for a moment or a few seconds. This is the ***third position.***

So, there are two moves and three positions in a golf swing, and as this work develops, we shall see that the two moves and three positions are linked, so strongly, that any adjustment made to one, forces change upon the other. We shall see, also, that if we wish to make reliable progress with our swings, then this progress will depend on how well we understand the relationship which exists between *positions* and *moves,* because the implication for our golf swings that derives from this relationship, is – enormous. Saying such a thing alludes to (and is *meant* to allude to) dramatic consequence. With that in mind, plus awareness of a promise

I made to myself when commencing this work, we need to up the stakes a little.

Things are about to get serious.

THE THREE POSITIONS

There are three positions in a golf swing. ALL golf swings.

- start
- top
- finish

The first two are the more important, but the finish position is of high value also, and should receive its share of attention. These are the only positions that exist and which should even be considered such a thing. They contain the makeup and nature of - *all our golf swings;* and their significance is such that, with regards to technique, we can say the three positions are everything.

There exists no other position in a golf swing. Many people choose to include impact, but impact is not a position, and any swing theory – past, present, or future, which uses impact as a position, is making a mistake in doing so.

(Nb: The terms used to identify the three positions – start: top: finish – are the simplest of their kind and are the most user-friendly when being often repeated. There are other terms routinely used in reference to golf-swing positions, for example – set up, top of backswing and follow-through. But they occupy nine syllables instead of four. The fewer syllables the better.)

IMPACT

Impact is not a position, but it *is* a force; a transfer of energy that lasts a fleeting moment. This transfer of energy is from the golf club to the ball and it is, of course, the golfer who will with some level of exertion create the force delivered during impact. When impact is captured on camera in images of top professional players as they strike the ball, it looks important and meaningful. We see power and aesthetic, and a body arranged in such a way that everything makes sense. The incredible shot we have just seen, the player's proficiency, their status in the game and prowess as a ball-striker. Nevertheless, impact is not a position. No matter how hard we try to make it one.

When something is at rest, it has position. When something is moving it does not have position, and there are only three places in a golf swing where motion is at, or is close to being at, rest. Indeed, if the ball was removed as a player swung through (quickly pinched out of the way), there would be no impact of any kind, on anything. If this little trick took place on a tour pro and the ball was no-longer there to identify a location, would we still see a 'position' of some kind, somewhere; *anywhere,* between top and finish? … or specifically – around that area of the swing? No, we would not. Nothing even remotely resembling a position. Just a super-fast flow from one place to another.

Impact has its own definition unrelated to being a position. It has its own identity and its own contribution to make. We shall see this later. In the meantime, a general point:

'When a golfer artificially creates a body arrangement during strike (one that simulates their idea of what impact should look like) they are doing something with low-to-zero-to-negative value. Body arrangement at strike can only be enhanced (effectively) when being dealt with as a force delivered. A force delivered in dynamic moment. We must create a better 'force' if we wish to see better body arrangement.'

TWO MOVES

The three positions are linked by two moves.

From start position, as soon as a player's arms begin movement away from the ball the swing has begun. The swing will at that moment be on route to, and actively seeking out – top position. If left alone, the swing will make a smooth developing move all the way up to and into its arrival at top. This first move is the 'backswing'.

Then, from top, and at the moment when the player's arms* begin rapid acceleration toward the ball, the second move begins. This second move is typically longer than the first and delivers the telling blow upon the ball. It continues well beyond impact and professional players often have such long and free-flowing second moves that their torsos twist and corkscrew as they arrive into the resting place of their swing – finish. This second move is the 'through-swing'.

- 1st move – start to top = backswing
- 2nd move – top to finish = through-swing

Both moves completed in little over one second

*(*Not the movement of the hips, nor movement of the left knee, nor movement of any other body part should be considered the start of the downswing.)*

Moves in General

When we look at golfers playing, we see poor moves and dreadful moves; good moves and magnificent moves; competent moves and mediocre moves and, many other different move-types besides which could be judged or classified in a different way. But why is one move magnificent and another dreadful? What causes such a profound difference in appearance? The answer (despite the moves being our current point of focus and worthy, also, of such descriptions as 'magnificent', and 'dreadful'), lies outside the control of the moves themselves. Surprisingly, the moves are not responsible for their own level of magnificence or wretchedness, although they are often pointed at as if they were. The moves are usually trying and doing the best they can.

Backswing and Through-Swing

The backswing move is trapped between start and top. It cannot escape either position. The move has to depart from one position and then arrive into the other. Its very birth is delivered from start. The end of its life sees it disappearing as if it never even existed, into the second position – top.

Similarly, the through-swing is initially held in a grip by the technical arrangement at top, and from this gripping arrangement it must then depart and power forward (via impact) until it is caught and held by a new technical arrangement. This time, at finish. As in the case of the backswing, the through-swing cannot escape either position,

at either end. Each move is thus captured and held, and each move must try to deliver its best performance while operating under a kind of jurisdiction from the two positions which hold it; two positions which trap the move. And, critically, **it is the technical arrangement** of the two trapping positions which determines the success, or failure, of the move. The relationship between a move and the positions holding it is profound; not least because the relationship is largely one-way. The moves are surprisingly subordinate, such that we can go as far as to say – they are enslaved. Three positions RULE OVER THEM.

How Positions Rule

To get an idea of how positions rule the moves, we will use a couple of examples. In this first example we look at a player who is in their start position and is ready to play. The player has a poor set-up, with the following points worth noting:

- legs are overly bent (squatting almost).
- body too upright (partly a consequence of legs).
- arms reaching out excessively.
- wrists arched (consequence of arms).
- dreadful grip: right hand gripping 'fist-like', with thumb pressing on the right side of the club's grip.
- left hand equivalently misplaced.

This then, is the players start position, and despite it all the player is comfortable having repeated it so many times.

(Before continuing, we must remind ourselves that the backswing move is born from, and has no choice but to begin its life – attached to – this position.)

How can this player make a good move away from the ball? They cannot! Nor could anyone. It is impossible. This player may hold in their mind wonderful images of pros beginning their movement into their backswings. The player may be determined, focussed, and as far as they can tell – ready. But if they were immortal, still a million years would pass and they would not have made a single good move away from the ball. Here, they would be doomed to all eternity. Nothing could improve for them until they undid the technical mess limiting them so, in position 1 – at start.

Imagine another player. This player captured in their position at top:

- their head has lifted.
- left arm has collapsed.
- they have only 50 degrees of shoulder turn.
- their right knee has buckled sideways.
- they began with a poor grip (at start) and so their wrist-hinge is now, at top, conflicted.

As with the previous example, this player's downswing (their *move*) has no choice but to begin attached to what is a severely limiting 'arrangement', or – position. How can they make a good downswing when launching from such a situation? They also, cannot.

These are easy cases, but it gets subtler, the better we become and the closer we look. The point is that a player's best intention to swing well – to *move* well – is in trouble, perhaps deep trouble, if the positions do not sanction it. And so, if a player wishes to own a fine move, they will need to own fine positions. Fine 'technical arrangements' which will permit the move. The desired move will then develop easily.

The degree to which positions dominate movement in our golf swings is so substantial that we can make two statements with confidence:

IMPROVED POSITIONS = IMPROVED SWING

DEGRADED POSITIONS = DEGRADED SWING

Although up to this point we have been quite often referring to 'the moves' and 'the swing', it is important that we begin focussing less on these and more on the three positions – start, top, and finish. This need to switch focus, is necessary, if we are to begin making progress in the very things we are trying to get at – those moves we keep speaking of. So, let us focus our attention where it matters most. On the all-powerful three positions.

General principle:

When we upgrade a position, the move attached to it also upgrades, automatically and without effort from the player. This happens because the position's newly upgraded arrangement feeds directly *into* the move. If we upgrade two

adjoining positions – positions 1&2 together, or 2&3 together – then we upgrade *both ends of a move*.

This is more exciting, for an entire strip of swing is then caught between two upgraded positions and – **all of it** – lifts into higher order. The move cannot resist its own improvement. Trapped between two upgraded arrangements it has no choice but to upgrade with them. If a player has a fine start position *and* a fine top position, then the swing in between will struggle to avoid being anything other than fine, also. Short term, it may put up a fight. Long term, it has no choice.

So, in knowing this general principle, how can we use it and make it work for us? ... how do we improve a position?

What, specifically, do we improve?

IMPROVING & UPGRADING

To upgrade a position, we must improve the position's composition, i.e., its 'arrangement'. If we were to study a player after they had upgraded one of their three positions, we would notice a different appearance between old position and new. One piece (or more than one piece) of the upgraded position would look better than before. It is as simple as that. The piece selected by the player for improvement would have been selected after being identified as being 'faulty'. Then, after improvement, the faulty piece would look different – and importantly – *be* different. Superior. This visual difference might be subtle when viewed from distance amid the whole of a position, and it would be especially subtle (to the point of easily going unnoticed) amid the whole of a fast-moving swing. However, if image-frozen by camera and highlighted for closer study, the upgraded piece would show a pronounced change in appearance.

Here are a few examples where a piece of faulty technique could be seen to have been improved:

- A previously slouched posture (side view) would be seen to have measurably straightened, giving a straighter line-profile along much of the player's back.

(This would likely include an increase in hip-tilt. Hips set too close to horizontal (at start) are often part-cause of a slouched posture.)

- A fist-grip (right hand) would be seen, after improvement, to be gripping the club more in the fingers.

- 'Soft' arms at start would be seen to be straighter and firmer.

- A 60-degree shoulder turn at top would have become, perhaps – 70, 75, 82, 88 degrees, etc.

- An upright body posture – at finish – would show new, increased body-lean (side view).

These are just a few examples of the numerous ways in which a swing can be improved by focussing in on, and adjusting, a specific body part or piece of technique.

And on it goes… large pieces, small pieces, and subtle detail. The obvious and the not so obvious. Moving from one position to the next and back again as each position is assembled and then sculpted into finer composition. This work undertaken with knowledge that the three positions hold secret (if such a thing exists) to our ultimate golf swing. The process is not endless, and we can stop at any point, but the finer we wish our swings to become the more time we will have to devote to the sculpting of the three positions.

Pieces:

Whilst talking of pieces of technique, we can add that there are a precise number of such 'pieces' in the assembly of each position, and therefore, a precise number in the assembly of a complete golf swing. These pieces ought to be referred to

by their proper description – their noun form – and so from now on they will be known as **components**. Each of the three positions is formed, and valued, by the arrangement of its components. As stated, a precise number of them.

COMPONENTS

Components are the smallest relevant bits of 'swing matter'. We could say they are the atoms of a golf swing. All golf swings have them, and all golf swings have the same number of them; but most golfers' swings carry these components with varying degrees of malfunction, bringing corresponding degrees of malfunction to each of the *moves* of the swing. In all such cases the potential gains that could be realised (if these components were in good order), are missing. To get a first-level comprehension of how this works, we will look at perhaps the simplest of all components to relate to. The left arm.

Left arm, a study:

In this study we see that a given player's left arm is straight at start, and then bent at top. It is therefore *correct* at start and *faulty* at top. (A component in fine shape in one position will not necessarily be in fine shape when it arrives into another position.)

The degree of fault would equate to the degree of bend. A slight bend in the left arm would only marginally damage the position and subsequent move. A complete bend would damage the position at top substantially, causing loss of power and reliability into the downswing. From this example it also becomes evident that left arm is *twice* a component. That is, it is a component on two different occasions in two

different places. Once in each position. Although the left arm is only one body part, it nevertheless performs two component roles.

The left arm so far has two opportunities to succeed and two opportunities to fail.

1st opportunity – at start
2nd opportunity – at top

Additionally, the left arm has a third role to play, in that at top it should be on correct plane.

Value builds:

If a player has arrived into top position with their left arm straight *and* on-plane; a considerable amount of high-value technique has been achieved. It is for these reasons (reasons of uncertain form and implications thereof) that left arm is considered a component, and in its case, an important component.

Other components:

There are obvious and not-so-obvious body parts which qualify for definition as being a component, due to either their placement or their behaviour. *Body lean,* mentioned earlier (in finish position), is a component. *Grip,* also mentioned earlier is, naturally, a component. So too: *knee flex* at start, *right elbow* at top, *body coil* at top, *foot positioning* at finish. *Right arm* is twice a component at finish, etc. There are many others.

Non-components:

Our kneecaps are fixed in place (with regard to the golf swing) and cannot malfunction. For this reason, kneecaps are not components. Nor are forearms, or shins, or calves, or stomachs. There are others which can be added to this list.

But knees themselves *are* components. Knees can be bent too much, too little, or just enough. They can be bowed out, or pinched in, and these possibilities all occur in position 1 – start.

Knees also have a role to play in position 2 – at top, and it is because the knees are easily able to malfunction at this critical moment in the swing that they must receive whatever amount of training they require.

(We do not want to be thinking of our knees when we swing a golf club, but we may have to think of them during learning and training as we teach them correct behaviour. They can then make their valuable contribution to the performance of the swing. In this way knees are no different from any other swing-part, piece, or – component.)

Now, we skip forward... to a place we would all like to get to!

When the three positions possess ALL components in highest order, they permit and actively encourage the following from a golf swing:

optimal freedom
maximum harmony
optimal power
maximum precision

These four qualities brought together and acting in unison would deliver ultimate movement with regard to aesthetic and performance, and if we wish to take steps towards ownership of these highly desirable qualities, we must keep our attention held away from our swing's movement and instead hold it fixed, as it is right now, on the three positions.

We must study the three positions. First by choosing a model example: a player who is recognised as having a world-leading swing; or, perhaps... three players, each player offering a 'best example' of one of the positions: a player with the best start position; a player with the best top position, and a player with the best finish position. Then we must study our own positions. But importantly, we must become familiar with *individual components* held in each of the positions. We must not treat the position 'as a whole'. That will not help. Also, before we can become familiar with components by *feel*, we must become familiar with them by *eye*, and not just vaguely or approximately but with detail at the forefront of concern. We must check which components in our positions *look* correct, (or close to being correct); and those which look to not be correct when measured against model examples of that component. As each component is thus checked, assessed, and if necessary – improved; and then added to other improved components, the all-powerful three positions rise to higher order and release superior movement.

- Improving positions 1&2 releases an improved backswing.

- Improving positions 2&3 releases an improved through-swing.

(Components are not necessarily small, although some are. They may appear to be so, because they are not obvious and are easily overlooked or taken for granted. However, if they ***are*** *overlooked or taken for granted, the player is playing a risky game. Components will happily exact a cost when uncared for and there is no way for them to self-gather into glittering arrangement, by chance, for anyone.)*

TAKE A LOOK

Where are the components? How do we spot them?

An imagined scenario:

In this imagined scenario we visit a private golf club and ask a member if they would be kind enough to help us in a little experiment. The member we approach plays off a 15 handicap. We ask if he would be willing to try to assess a fellow member's start position. (The player whose start position is to be assessed, also plays off a mid-range handicap.)

Having initially been caught off-guard by the unusual request, the member nevertheless agrees to be the assessor and obliges by taking a look at the other member's start position, before saying that in his opinion it is 'Ok. Not bad'.

(From his answer it appears he is a little uncomfortable, steering for diplomacy and the wish to avoid possible cause of offence.)

But we are not happy with the answer (it is vague) and we ask him to be more specific by giving it a mark out of ten. He then gives the player's start position 6/10.

Good, we are getting somewhere, but… why does he say that? How does he make that call? Perhaps he gets an overall impression and, treating it therefore *as* a whole (which is

understandable) he thinks that it looks to be worth about a 6/10.

So, once again, although appreciative of his taking part, we are not satisfied and ask him to try to explain why he has decided on a 6/10.

He says 'well... it doesn't look like the pros look'.
We ask, 'What *exactly* about the player's position do you think looks so different from the pros that you deem this position to be worth only a 6?'
He says 'Some things don't look right... '

(He then apologises to the other member, who is not at all upset and is anyway quite interested to hear what will come next!)

Us: 'Which things?'

... 'he's bent over too much. You can see his back is curved... you know... a bit stooped. His grip looks... wrong somehow. I don't know why or what I really mean, exactly. And his hands and club are pushed too far forward, they are opposite his left knee; that can't be right, can it? He has his head tucked; I don't think his chin should be almost touching his chest.' etc.

So, the inexpert player is easily able to identify fault with a fellow player's technique, even though the inexpert player will not have studied golf swings like professional players and golf instructors have. The inexpert player *has* though, likely seen thousands of images of tournament professionals on television and so knows immediately when something is

right or wrong when looking at golfing friends and fellow club amateur players. The inexpert player may not appreciate nuance, or be able to apportion weighting and consequence, but they just *know* if a position is right or wrong when they see it.

Each of the bits which looked odd to the amateur judge in this invented scenario, each bit he drew attention to by himself, is, in fact, a component. So, components are not at all difficult to spot. They are very easy to spot if we just take a closer look at detail.

More Than a Few, & Value

The amateur adjudicator we were just with, drew attention to five components in the fellow member's start position. I have recently mentioned eight others and so we have thirteen quite quickly. Now, beyond the number thirteen we can say that there are, in fact, forty-eight components in a full swing. In terms of working on and achieving success with these components, most are easy, and some work on auto-pilot in the way they naturally fall into place.. There are only half a dozen or so from the forty-eight which can be considered difficult to own in top shape.

Just as relevant as the ease with which we can work on and improve the placement and condition of our swing's components, is their value. Components have unequal values in terms of what they bring to the golf swing. They each (every one of the forty-eight) impact the swing either directly, or indirectly; but there are a group of components which

deserve placement into a top bracket, a bracket of uppermost importance.

Of the forty-eight components there about fifteen which can lay claim to being key, and which are therefore worthy of being included in this uppermost bracket. Key components bring greater damage by way of their error, and greater gain by way of their success, and if a player wishes to own a good swing (good meaning good, and not meaning great) then they will need to have most of these fifteen components in decent order. A player may get away with having a few of them running poorly, but they will be pushing their luck and will likely need many of the others to be in top form. More than a few of these key components running weak, and the chances of a player swinging the club well will fall somewhere between difficult, and impossible.

On the other side of cause and effect we can say that certain components can exist with sizeable margins of error and still not subtract overly from the performance of a golf swing. As would be expected, a component which has potential to bring significant gain or loss to the swing, deserves a higher value-rating than a component whose potential to bring gain or loss, is lesser.

Whichever way we look at it though, there are forty-eight bits of technique and therefore forty-eight ways a flaw can take hold in a golf swing. As per the earlier analogy, components are like atoms. They are the nearest things to a DNA blueprint of golf's technique, and so we have in effect, a coding, where forty-eight individual components combine in a myriad of ways and bring a myriad of form to the golf swings we see

around us. Like species in nature. More to the point, with every component having a value we have a situation where every component has power to aid, or harm, in the making of one of these coded swings.

GRIP & WRISTS
A Component Study

Question: Why is the grip so important? The club will not fly out of a person's hands when they hold it to swing and hit with. So… why? What does it offer beyond a secure hold of the club?

Answer: First and foremost, the grip is important for power. It is also important (less so than people imagine) for the squaring of the clubface on its return to the ball.

During the swing, a golfer's wrists will hinge on the backswing and unhinge on the downswing. The hinge and unhinge has no purpose other than to add speed to the clubhead. The more hinge we have at top, the more lag, release, and whip we will get at the bottom, all else being equal.

At this point I will skip description of how the grip should be formed and use it instead as an example of a general principle. The principle of measuring value in technique.

We need to picture a golfer's left-hand grip as they take hold of the club and get ready to swing. The golfer may have placed their left-hand grip on the club *well*, or they may have placed it *poorly*. It might be described as being a 'good' left-hand grip, a 'bad' left-hand grip, or an 'average' left-hand grip.

This is true. It *could* be described like so, but such a modest level of evaluation is not helpful in 2023. Perhaps one-hundred years ago in 1923 it would have been enough to evaluate technique in such a way. But not today. We should have something more sensitive; and so instead of good, bad, and average, we will use the grade scale everyone is familiar with and which gives more information. The grade scale – zero to ten. When we do this, it then becomes possible for a golfer's left-hand grip to be valued more meaningfully. Using 0-10 we can identify a particularly poor left-hand grip and award it 2/10. We can identify an impeccable left-hand grip and award it 10/10; plus, we can identify many other levels of left-hand grip status with the grades at our disposal. We can then do the same for the right-hand grip.

Next, in this component study, we imagine we are looking closely at a club amateur's complete grip (inclusive of *both* hands). No one particular type of grip, just a commonly found case-type for us to consider as we develop this study.

Both of this golfer's hands are on the club, formed, and ready for action. But we ask the owner of the grip not to make a swing, and to instead, very carefully, remove one of their hands, leaving the other behind. The hand left behind still holding the club (exactly as it was before the partner-hand departed) can be graded *all on its own.* It has a value *all of its own* – out of 10. It is not dependent on the other hand, or, on the grip as a whole, for its grade. The hand left behind holding the club is a separate entity, and as such it is independent from all other technique in the golf swing. This understanding can also be applied to the hand that was removed and, if a swap was made (after re-forming the grip),

we could then grade the second hand in the same way we graded the first. Independently. Out of ten.

In practise, we do not need to remove either hand to be able to grade a player's grip. We can grade the whole grip all at once. The grip exercise was set up this way to show that although two hands come together to form a single bond, they are in fact separate entities with regard to the golf swing's technique, and as such, they may bring unequal values to the grip's bonded relationship.

The amateur player we were looking at may have had their left-hand grip grading 8/10. Their right hand, 3/10.

So, where earlier we were working with good, bad, and average, as value judgements being awarded to an overall grip, now we have a grade scale which allows us to measure the success or failure of a player's grip accurate to a margin of one twentieth. With this scale we can filter a mass of grips (millions of them) through the system and allocate, to each and every one, subtle but tangible values (and value differences). **These values will then be transferred into each player's swing.**

(The above sentence has the deepest of implications, for just as each of a golfer's hands (when gripping) will transfer their individual values into the golf swing, so too, will ***every*** *component from* ***each*** *position transfer its value – weak, strong, positive or negative (or, as we now know: 3/10; 7/10; 4/10; 6/10; 10/10; 2/10, etc.) – into the swing. In the writing of this work, and in all that is yet still to come, I doubt that a more serious message will be communicated.)*

Returning to the wrists and 'wrist action'.

The primary purpose of the grip is to enable utilisation of the wrists. Utilisation of the wrists means – for golfers – their contribution to power. Wrist action shows itself by way of the size of the blow that can be delivered upon the ball by their action.

Important – we must leave the face out of it. We must leave the 'squaring up' (of anything) out of it. We cannot conceptualise correct wrist action when our mind is cornered by the thought of a golf club and its square face. To better understand wrist action, we need to rid our minds of the straight-line edge and flat face that a golf club has, and instead, think of a baseball bat or a broomstick.

(In the following imagined experiment, we will use a broomstick. A broomstick has no face. It has no flat surface. It is just a round wooden rod without any prescribe to orientation. Easy to hold. Easy to swing. Easy to hit with.)

With this wooden rod we next imagine a heavy rug, outside, hanging over a line. We are to stand sideways to the rug and with the broomstick whack and smash the rug side-on as hard as we can, and as we do so, you, me – everyone – would hold the broomstick in a similar way. A way that would allow our wrists to hinge and unhinge, fully; powerfully.

I have not looked but I suspect that baseball batters, whose objective it is to slug the ball as hard as they can out of the park for a home run, and who do not have to worry about a flat surface or a straight hit, but only power and contact, will

all hinge their wrists in the way I am describing. This is the **main purpose** of correct grip placement with regard to golf and the golf swing. A correct grip allows the wrists to hinge properly. The hinge enables optimal or maximal (depending on which is desired) of deliverable force. The hinge and unhinge does *not* include (let alone necessitate) a flat or arched left wrist at the load point. A grip which necessitates a flat left wrist at the load point (at top) is lacking. A grip that allows for a full hinge is not lacking, although a player may choose to (or may have to) arrive at the load point flat-wristed or arched, for other reasons.

*'**All** grip arrangements offer ability to return a clubface to square **Not all** grip arrangements offer full use of the wrists for power. In fact, surprisingly few do.'*

I have spent thirty years or more looking at grips and their place in the golf swing. The degree of detail that is possible from a grip can certainly be divided into twenty parts. There are so many ordinary grips being used to play golf with, and which compromise the owner's wrist action, that when I see a really good grip I immediately appreciate what the player has achieved. The very best of grips – a grip that scores 20/20 – well, from Golf's perspective it is a small masterpiece. And yet, a grip of 15+ can be taught and learnt in a matter of minutes.

(Whilst here, discussing grips and our ability to measure and grade them, we ought to reiterate that just as a hand can be placed on the club in a variety of ways, and be assessed to have a variety of different grade values, so too, can assessment and grade value be given to all other parts of the golf swing. Once a scale is decided

upon (in this case out of ten) it is then just a question of deciding which bits of the swing are relevant for measurement, and how to measure them.)

PGA Tour

Collectively, PGA tour players demonstrate degrees of flaw in every one of the golf swing's forty-eight components. This may sound like a surprising statement, but it isn't really, if we think about it. It just means that where so and so, and so and so, and so and so – all have a flawless left-hand grip; there can be found a player on tour who does not have a flawless left-hand grip. And where so and so and so and so, etc. all have flawless hip placement at top; there can be found players on tour who do not have flawless hip placement at top.

Most players on the PGA Tour *do* have fine swings. Some have wonderful swings. The component flaws we are talking about are often relatively light (although not always) or are traded with a second flaw which acts as a neutraliser. A *fade bias* in one component will be neutralised by a *draw bias* in another; the two component errors cancelling each other out. But there will be a small loss. Two flawed components, means, two bits of swing-matter unable to deliver their potential into the swing. Equally, if a player has a fade bias (component assembly), without the neutralising draw bias, elsewhere; they will be left with a 'fade bias swing' and will almost certainly play the game that way.

If we look at a section of players on the PGA Tour who show example of this 'balancing' (there are many different groups

for different examples), we could choose a group who have varying degrees of a weak left-hand grip, at start; and who then have varying degrees of a flat or arched left wrist, at top. The weak left-hand grip should lead to an open club face. The flat/arched wrist should lead to a closed club face. These two flawed components will often cancel each other out, with regard to direction. The compromise results in a small loss of power, but no loss of accuracy. This power loss will not be noticeable for several reasons, including that these players will have enough power that they can comfortably afford the few yards it may cost them. No one would anyway notice. How would we know if they were 3 yds, 5 yds, or 7 yds down (on a 300yd drive) because of a grip compromise? Also, many tour players in this situation instinctively boost their arm or body actions, which *increases* power. There are also a few immensely strong individuals (Jon Rahm and Brooks Koepka come to mind) who can afford to sacrifice the power aspect that correct wrist-hinge brings, and instead concentrate more on their ability to hit straight.

Other PGA Tour players, rather than having only slight component error, have significant component error, but still they play PGA Tour. How does this work?

Again, the significant component error will usually be managed by way of there being a buddy component which has similar magnitude but opposite error-type, or… there may be several buddy components all putting in smaller amounts of flaw that together balance the single, larger flaw. It means the compromise will bear greater loss than in the earlier case where the player had modest error-trade. Oftentimes also, the significant error will be in a low-impact

component, one which catches the eye, but which has modest performance consequence.

When we watch these fine players on our tv screens it is easy to miss the detail. A well-timed full-powered swing which at the same time displays fine rhythm and tempo, hides the detail within, such that flaws are not easily noticed, especially when the said swing regularly hits the ball to 12 ft from 200yds. What our eyes see is the sum total. We see the 'wholeness' of the swing. Which is why we miss the detail.

SUMMARY

There is much still to come, but for now, a short recap:

- A golf swing has three positions which harness the swing's movement.
- A golf swing has two moves, each of which is trapped in between the positions.
- The quality of a move is determined by the quality of the positions trapping it.
- The quality of a position refers to the accomplishment of the position's technical arrangement.
- Technical arrangement refers to a set of body parts which need organising such that they support correct movement *into-and-out-of* a position.
- These specific body parts are classified as 'components'.
- There is a finite number of components in each position, and therefore, in a complete golf swing.
- Correct positions permit and encourage correct movement; movement that is free, powerful, and precise.

Additionally:

- Components can be individually graded.

- Positions can be individually graded as a collective of their component grades.

- An entire golf swing can be individually graded, with a number value given to its technical achievement.

Let us take a look at that last point…

With forty-eight components, we could, with a zero to ten grade for each component, grade a golf swing out of 480. All forty-eight components scoring tens would bring us to the magical number 480. Such a golf swing has never been seen before. A swing devoid of even a grain of sand's worth of imperfection.

The 480 scale would be interesting, but even more interesting would be a scale which accounted for component values. It would take a little time and thought to figure such a scale's numbers, but if we could, the scale would be more meaningful. It would likely come closer to a 600 scale. There would be several benefits to swing grading if it were available. (One day it will be.) Most notably that a computer, having scanned a player's swing, would then give a printout of the grades of all forty-eight components. The player would immediately know where to look for cause of any troubles. Being that some components affect accuracy, some affect power and some affect strike; a player would be able to identify the relevant component(s) highlighted by the

computer scan and grade report and know precisely where to get to work.

Another benefit would be our ability to map and monitor swing progress. In January, if a player had their swing scanned and graded at 218 (from the 480 scale), and then six months later they were again scanned, and graded this time at 245, they would know significant progress had been made, even if this progress wasn't yet revealing itself in play (which is sometimes the case). The player would be reassured that if they pushed on with their efforts, a breakthrough would soon be made. One likely to take them to the next level as a ball striker.

Also interesting would be the ability to compare our technique against each other's, just as we compare our handicaps against each other in a lightly competitive way (our handicap being like a badge worn with a sense of pride and progress (sometimes… decline!)). The same lightly competitive comparison would be made with our swing grade, and golfers would have a second virtual badge to wear, this one announcing the 'value' of their swing: its level of technical accomplishment.

In this way a swing grade would offer a sense of esteem to golfers who swing the club well but who have not yet become 'players' in the normal sense of the term. If a golfer plays only half a dozen times a year, it is understandable they cannot break 90, or 100; it is understandable that they have a handicap of 28, or higher. But they may have a good swing, they may be a good learner and, they may have better than average potential. Their swing grade would capture these

things and so, if the person was feeling a little uncomfortable at a social event (when the subject turned to golf) at having no handicap, or at never having broken 100, they might be able to say: 'but my swing grade is 285. Prospects are looking good if I can just find time to play!' They would feel less embarrassed in the company of 'players.' And rightly so. I have known many busy and hard-working people in this situation. They are good learners and have developed good swings but rarely get to play the game and so putting a score down, for them, is almost impossible. Their ability is as good as the next person's; but they have nothing on their side to suggest it and, because they are nevertheless classed as being a golfer, they feel unsuccessful. Even embarrassed.

So, there are several good reasons for a swing grade to be developed, the most important of them being its ability to pinpoint faulty technique. But for it to work there would need to be a standard model (three definitive positions) from which one grade scale could be produced ready to be developed into software. If two people, perhaps business associates, walk into different studios for a swing grading (one in London and the other, perhaps, in New York) there would then be no irregular or arbitrary results. Both players' grades would be relative to the standard model, and would therefore be - comparable.

FINISH
The Forgotten Position

Before we continue with any new branches of this theory, we ought to look at a neglected part of the golf swing. The follow-through, which means of course – finish.

Whilst start and top are the more important positions, in that their arrangements have greater bearing on the quality of the swing and shot that will follow, it should be recognised that finish also makes a contribution, even though its place in the order of things comes after the ball has departed.

Hogan said that if our downswing – into and through impact – is correct, then momentum would carry us naturally into a good follow-through. In other words, we do not have to think about follow-through because – *it is a consequence.* Perhaps so, and especially perhaps so if our downswing is as good as Hogan's was. But what if our downswing is not as good as Hogan's?

As we now know, the two moves of a golf swing live between three positions. We could even consider a move to be a high-speed revelation of the positional quality at either end. Well, one of those 'ends' is finish.

Thinking it through with some logic: if we depart from a good position at top, but track out way into a poor finish, the move will have to degrade as it travels. It is impossible for a

swing to be travelling in good form, at high speed, deep into follow-through and then suddenly leap, convulse, or transfigure itself into poor arrangement. The poor arrangement would start developing (and continue developing) *as* the swing travelled. Where the initial move into downswing would be good on departure, it would then be seen getting worse as it continued... and may be negatively affected (damaged) even *before* it has reached impact.

(As mentioned above, the linked flow of cause-and-effect can work back to such extent that an end position (with serious failure) reaches back and degrades/harms not only the approach into end position, but more importantly, the very downswing we are using to hit the ball with. A part of the golf swing imagined to be remote from and separate from – the flawed end.)

On the matter of possible neglect: if we neglect our finish position it can, in theory, do anything and go anywhere. It may behave perfectly well, or it may behave haphazardly. As time passes and hundreds and thousands of swings are put down, a through-swing will develop a habit *despite* neglect. This habit will become the swing's finish, and once its habitual finish begins repeating, it will ingrain itself becoming somewhat intractable. This (if it does happen) can be a concerning situation. Any significant component error/s will then become fixed as a feature and, being that most golfers do not appreciate the importance of finish, nor take care of it, these errors would stay put.

A finish position containing one or two destructive components relays negative impulses backwards – into – the

oncoming move. Spoiling a move that might otherwise have been progressing nicely. I once witnessed a tour pro spoil his impact (and therefore – his golf shots) by applying a misguided idea to finish.

This tour pro had the idea that his swing would be improved with a high-hands finish, similar to the high-hands finish of Seve. He clearly liked the idea, and probably the feel and look, too. But the high-hands finish did not match his position at top (which was neutral) and caused him to drop 'inside' on his route through impact. He lost his swing path as a result. A fair chunk of poor season came his way because he stayed with the idea for more than a few weeks, fiddling with various things in his swing in an effort to return to straight hitting. 'Various things' that is, except for the thing causing the problem – his high-hands finish. A previously true and straight swing was sent veering off-line by the powerful influence of this newly appointed (but faulty) finish, which sent its destructive impulses backwards into his move.

And so, from all I have seen and heard over the years, if I were to summarise a general theme that has been shown towards finish and its importance to the golf swing, it would be something along these lines –

'Finish, neglected time and again, and why? Simply, because it sits in the future. Because it comes after the main event. Because it is an apparent consequence. Because it is… borderline… irrelevant!'

Despite finish appearing to be irrelevant due to its place in the order of things, it offers an important area of gain (often

substantial) at club amateur level. Club amateurs can regularly achieve quick improvement with their swings, *and* their golf shots, by tweaking a few things in finish, or by working on one or two of finish's key components. When this is done successfully, finish acts like a force-for-good magnet, attracting the oncoming move, *helping* the oncoming move remain in good shape as it travels, and improving it if the player's finish position is superior to the move it feeds back into.

How important is finish? Well, finish is one of three positions on which an entire theory is built.

That tells you all you need to know about its importance.

KNOTS, GLITCHES & ROTTEN MOMENTS

It is tempting, when we see something in our swing which looks to be wrong, or which clearly *is* wrong – mid move – to stop precisely at that point and try to fix it. Try to teach it better behaviour. When we watch our swings played back in slow motion there are few of us who do not see something we hate, often to the point of making us want to turn away from the screen with an urge to curse out loud or kick the wastepaper basket to the other side of the studio! A knot, a glitch, a clench; or a moment that just looks plain - ugly. Call it more kindly 'a bad bit' if you like, but something we would very much like removed.

This bad bit could come anywhere and at any moment in the swing. It could be seen in the initial move away from the ball. It could be seen one third of the way back, or: halfway back, three quarters, seven eighths, four elevenths, etc. Or it could occur at transition, or just after, or anyplace you care to mention, including impact. On the follow-through perhaps. *Something* though, is seen to be wrong. A rotten moment – that bad bit we spoke of – and we hate it because it has been with us so long and, in a small way, it ruins our lives.

So, deciding that enough is enough, we go after it full of mean intent. *Anything* to get rid of it. We stop our swing where the bad bit occurs, go in, and bend-it-and-shape-it into better form. Hit it with a mallet if necessary. Then, when we are done, we move on with the rest of the swing believing we

have taught it a lesson, a lesson we are happy to teach it a good few times. Only, the lesson we think we are teaching it brings about no change. Our next video session shows the same bad bit – alive and well – in exactly the same place and of exactly the same magnitude!

The inclination to go in and tackle 'bad bits', is natural, and is probably why systems like Eight Step Golf Swing (8 positions) and P-System (10 positions) were created. I imagine the authors of those theories (Jim Maclean*, 8; and Mac O'Grady, 10.) believe that having numerous check points spaced around the swing, helps a player, in that the player can compare their bad bit against one of the eight or ten reference points. The player can then attempt to make their bad bit more closely resemble the relevant step, or reference point; before continuing. There is definitely some logic to the idea.

But questions arise...

What if our bad bit doesn't fall perfectly on top of one of the eight or ten check points? What if it occurs *between* two of the check points? Or a bit past, or a bit short of… what then? And if one theory suggests eight and another ten, is the number to some degree arbitrary? What are the authors' reasons for precisely eight and precisely ten? Can we have as many steps as we'd like? Why not twelve, fifteen or twenty? Things would then become more accurate. If we believe in the idea of checkpoints being of value during a golf swing, and we run with it, we will have a checkpoint every inch. Some three-hundred-plus of them. It would then be easy to capture overlay with our bad bit. But the madness of it all.

Leaving three hundred to one side, eight or ten is still too many. It complicates performance and additionally, creates an erroneous concept, for there are not eight, or ten positions in a golf swing. There are only three. Having only three positions is a good thing. It is simpler. And we can make things simpler still.

What comes next will surprise most, if not *all* readers!

*(*I have once or twice, before, been asked "who among the world's famous instructors do you have a high regard for?", and Jim Maclean always comes to mind and I mention him. The fact that I go against him here is no more than a coincidence, in that he (and Mac O'Grady for his) is famous for a theory based on there being a specific number of positions/steps that are relevant to a golf swing. That my theory disagrees with Jim's does not change the regard I have for him, it merely means I believe a stronger case can be made for there being three positions in a golf swing, than can be made for there being eight (or ten).*

Back to the surprise…

DO NOT TOUCH

We need to **cancel all contact** between positions. We should not touch any part of a move. A move is supposed to be free, and have purity about whatever it is trying to do.

In the case of the backswing, the move's purpose is to deliver all body parts to a new place and arrangement; a place from where we can make a successful strike of the ball. 'To a new place and arrangement' is the *only* purpose of the backswing. There is no importance to any particular part, or moment of the move; no importance to inch 5, inch 12, inch 23, or strip 30-36.

None of these points or segments have any value or bring any reward until they show they have delivered the body into a correct position at top. Adjustment mid-move *may* occasionally be needed to help components better align themselves *as* they move, but even this should be done in motion and without stopping the move dead; and it should be recognised that making adjustments mid-move has a degree of token gesture about it when compared to the value of dealing with the position directly.

Also, although a bad bit – mid-move – *can* be hands-on influenced into better form, this better form will only last if trapped between two improved or superior positions. Even greater profit comes if the two positions are high-grade. In such a case the bad bit will be disciplined to the nth degree as

two positions (one behind, one in front) send powerful impulses backwards and forwards, hitting the bad bit from both sides, gradually smoothing it out. In this way an ugly or poor piece of swing can largely be removed. In some cases, completely.

Strange Rehearsals

When watching PGA Tour and LPGA Tour golf, we sometimes see a player make what appears to be a strange rehearsal before playing a shot. Usually, on the backswing, but strange rehearsals are also seen on the down and through-swing. These rehearsals are always an exaggeration of a smaller move the tour player is trying to have included in their live swing – the swing they are about to make at the ball. Exaggeration is employed by the tour pro because they know that when they 'go live' there will be a wipe-out effect and only a trace of what they were rehearsing will make it into the live swing. The trace of desired move is the amount the player judges necessary to re-align a small error occurring at that particular point in the move. The tracking, or orientation of their *move,* is judged to be a trace out.

What is actually happening is that the trace of desired move they are rehearsing for, if achieved (during the live shot), enables **an improved top position** from which to play the shot. They are, in effect, improving top position. But they are dealing with a point on route which is not the best way.

When a player is practising a strange rehearsal on the downswing, it is a similar story. Something at top (possibly

at finish*) is out of place and is spoiling their downswing move, forcing it to be a smidge out. A 'smidge out' at full power with big clubs can lead to missed fairways and greens, and so the exaggerated rehearsal, like before, aims at capturing a trace of this rehearsed move. A trace being all they need. *But again*, if their position was correct at top, they would not need this trace of help on the downswing. They would be able to simply let go and make direct attack on the shot.

These players, when we see them make strange rehearsals, have correctly identified something wrong; and they deal with it where they spot it as a consequence, instead of where it was caused. Nevertheless, if the trace they require is achieved (which it often is), it will correct the position and deliver the move and the shot as intended. It is just an indirect way of doing things.

**It is unusual for a professional's finish position to be the cause of problems in their downswing. Professionals typically have neutral finish positions, in that their finish positions match (balance with) their top positions; and a pro's finish is also highly sensitive to shot call, in that it behaves like a kind of shape-shifter. A professional golfer's finish has learnt to instinctively adjust in support of any desired shot type. For example, call for a knock-down shot will prompt a very different arrangement of components, at finish, than the arrangement of components required for a high fade. Professional players need only think of a shot, or visualise one, for a whole sequence of subtle (or not so subtle) technical changes to immediately arrange themselves in support. Need for a punch… a high loft… a fade or a draw… will prompt these changes, without the pro even needing to think about it.*

TRAPPING

Trapping was mentioned early in this work, and has been mentioned again, recently. There is a side to trapping – its principle – relevant to all golfers, but perhaps most relevant to learners. By 'learners' I mean in particular: day-one learners.

Before we get to the principle, this introduction to 'trapping' offers opportunity for a brief aside, triggered by the thought in my mind and mention on paper, of teaching day-one learners:

With regard to teaching the golf swing and the detailing of its mechanics, when I am with a day-one student there is an extra element of pleasure for me. Within the first twenty to thirty minutes the student will have had a brief introduction to three positions theory before then experiencing all three positions in full, or close to full, form. This does not mean they will then be firing-off great shots already, but it does mean the frame of a fine swing is well under way. Most day-one learners are more capable of achieving this sprint-start to a good swing than they realise, even though it *is* quite demanding.

What I am about to say next, is of highest relevance...

I have little interest in the moves, and I have no interest in the mid-points, or checks, or steps, or stages along the way. Nor do I have interest in proceeding cautiously with the technique

– piece by piece – developing and attaching sections until the swing slowly fills out and reaches top; with a similar approach of careful build taken on the other side, developing the through-swing until it reaches a natural end. Nothing about this somewhat cautious approach is, to my mind, necessary (although I understand the logic behind it), and none of it happens. Instead, I arrange the day-one student's position at start and then sweep them up, and into, their top position, where I manipulate them whilst 'up there.' (Most instructors employ this method to some degree). The same then takes place at the other end of the swing – at finish. If the student has aptitude, and many do, they will have the frame of a fine swing with full or close-to-full positions and a good move, after only one hour. Indeed, delivery of three positions theory offers the fastest route to a fine golf swing. No other method of learning compares.

In such lessons the student needs to never have touched a club before. 'Day one' does not refer to an established player whom I see for the first time but who already has experience of play and practise.

Readers may be thinking, 'there is no way you could do that with me... my body wouldn't allow it'. Or 'you wouldn't be able to do that with an elderly person.'

Certainly, some people are more flexible than others, but I rarely teach a person whose self-assessment isn't shy of their capability. The more limiting factors are nearly always time, effort, and know-how.

Picking up from where we left off before looking at this one type of instruction, a type of instruction which utilises three positions theory to a maximum...

We said early in this work that the swing's two moves, the backswing and through-swing were 'trapped' at either end. That they were ruled over by the three positions. Now we put a different take on what appears to be unfortunate circumstance (of being trapped and ruled over), and announce that trapping can work *for* us, and... in a big way!

Two Fine Positions

Let us imagine a player who has a fine start position, and also, a fine top position to go with it. In the fine start position, among other things we would see:

- *correct body angle.*
- *left arm straight.*
- *wrists normal – (un-hinged).*

At top, also among other fine things, we would then see:

- *body angle retained (as at start).*
- *left arm straight.*
- *wrists hinged.*

Of the three components we are following in the two positions, any one of them could have begun to fail as the move into the backswing developed.

1. The body angle could have been lost (most likely lifted).
2. The left arm could have bent.
3. The wrists could have failed to fully hinge; or, hinged incorrectly.

One or more of these three errors could have occurred and been seen to occur during the move from start to top. But none of them *would* be seen to occur!

Let us look at the left arm:

If the left arm is straight at start *and* at top, why would it want to bend as it travels? This is a rhetorical question, for it would not want to bend. It would want to remain straight, throughout the backswing, and so be ready to meet its entry condition at top.

Now the Wrists:

The wrists are different, and this is why they have been chosen as one of the components for readers to follow. The wrists are a component that includes *change*, which is to say they are a body-part which shows a change in appearance from one position to the next. If the wrists are unhinged (as they should be) at start; but are then hinged correctly, at top; well, they will want to do their hinging as they travel so that they, too, can arrive with their 'entry condition' met. Which is to be – correctly hinged.

This phenomenon is as if a command is being sent back from the position ahead. In effect the command states: **'you must comply with this condition upon arrival'** and so, in the case

of the wrists (and many other components in a golf swing), the *movement* prepares the component ready for its arrival into the approaching position. In the case of the wrists, the movement prepares them (by progressively hinging) so they will satisfy their arrival condition at top, of being – hinged.

In this way components are trapped into proper form and proper behaviour – **as they travel** – by the two high-grade positions commanding events. Two positions which, as said – rule over the move. There is no possibility for bad bits to develop. They cannot even get started.

How Does It Know?

Going beyond the wrists, and looking at the swing in general…

In a correct golf swing our body is arranged in a specific way, at start. It is then arranged in a new and even more specific way, at top. During the move from one position to the other:

- *Some of the body will have stayed down, and some will have lifted.*
- *Some will have hinged, and some will be extended.*
- *Some will have turned, and some remained square.*
- *Some will have resisted, and some… gone freely.*

How will the body know how to coordinate these complex and contradictory developments? How will it know by how much? In which direction? At what rate...? ...the turn... the lift... the hinge?

Surely, we must help it. Surely, we must train the move progressively, and slowly. Take it by the hand and lead it along a careful route from one place to the next. Stop it from going wrong when it starts to go wrong. Re-connect it with the right route. Re-configure it when needed. Teach it to twist and hinge at certain points. This must be where steps and checkpoints become useful, as markers along the way, guiding the move to its destination.

Although many swings have been built this way, the learning of the swing doesn't need to be so deliberate. From the body's 'perspective', it could even be said to be interfering. Moves should be left alone to organise their own changes and sequencing as they travel from one place to the next.

This means that after a player has set themselves to the ball and is ready to go, they should just pull the trigger and set off to the next position with no conscious control of events along the way. All that is necessary is that the player *knows* the next position. (In this case, top.) Knows where it is, its configuration, its 'set-of-coordinates', if you like; and is familiar with them. The body will then (when left alone) find the simplest, most intelligent route of travel from the place it is in, to the place it is going. Included in this most intelligent route will be the making of any twists, turns, hinges and/or – *changes* – required.

When a player offers up this freedom to the move, the move is able to ignore interrupting checkpoints or steps; or prescribed routes, which, although trying to be helpful, generally are not.

The aim then, in the first instance, is to have free untouched passage between start and top. Then, similarly, when the swing departs from top it should once again be left free as it travels at high speed to its next destination – finish.

(If a player is altering a component in a position let's say – at top – then the desired change of this component will become the player's target instruction and their main thought. They should again though, simply depart from start with a determination to have the component in its new state, at top, and resist getting involved in how best to travel there.)

Are you sure?

Some readers may be thinking… can we be sure about this? It sounds risky. Even a little controversial to suggest we leave our swings unattended during their education. Why would we want to let go and take our hands off the controls? If we leave the move on its own, alone, how will it know what to do? Especially if, or when, we want it to learn, and do… something new?

With so much at stake, these are good questions; but…

It will not be alone.

SILENT GENIUS

Origin

Twelve years ago, I wrote a golf book, and Silent Genius was included in it. The concept came easily, was immediate, and Silent Genius (as a name well-suited) came more or less with arrival of the concept. As I began writing about Silent Genius, I tried to think of what was at its heart, and I considered this to best be described as Auto-Neuro-Response (shortened to ANR). Now, twelve years later, I try again to think about what is at the heart of Silent Genius, such that explanation of its method and function is relatable, and nothing better comes to mind. So, ANR it is, and remains, the driving force behind this incredible ability.

Behind The Scenes

ANR is the mechanism within us which coordinates complex movement according to any given set of parameters it has to work with. The parameters in our case, as golfers, are the three positions we must enter and exit during the swing. The grade or accomplishment of the three positions and the grade or accomplishment of the components within them does not stop ANR from functioning. Auto-Neuro-Response is ready to respond, if allowed, no matter who the golfer is and no matter how amazing or woeful their swing. If a player has

numerous component errors throughout, imbedded in their positions, then these numerous errors will become the parameters ANR will register and work with. This means that if there is a 'tangle' in a position, then ANR will recognise the tangle and proceed to the next tangle (if that is what lies ahead) as efficiently as is possible. In every instance ANR will deliver *best possible movement* as the swing proceeds from one place to the next; and this, as said, irrespective of the calibre of positions we are giving it to work with.

Despite what was advised earlier with regard to 'do not touch', you might still be reluctant to take your hands off that wheel, deciding after a bit of thought to ignore this unknown 'Silent Genius' and deal with the moves yourself. As we are at an early stage with this concept, I have sympathy with any reader preferring, still, to deal with the moves themselves. However, before you do, you need to know the following:

There is no amount of effort a player can consciously make in the manipulating of a move (including effort to hit steps or checkpoints), that can match the performance ability of their ANR mechanism. Silent Genius has such superiority over man-made attempts to coordinate movement, that if it could speak, it would say only one thing:

'Leave it to me.'

Silent Genius Steps In

In terms of coordinating a best-possible move, where 'best' means *most likely to succeed;* Silent Genius can also deal with direction. If a player is thinking 'Don't slice it' and senses they must do something to help the club-face square-up or turn-over during impact, then Silent Genius will figure a move which has the best chance of delivering on that directive, despite and inclusive of any component errors (at top) which have *slice* written large across them, and which at that critical moment before launch of the downswing seem to predict failure. Silent Genius, activated by the 'don't slice it' awareness, will try to find a solution, and in doing so will probably need to provide an ungainly body action to help with the squaring of the clubface. This ungainly body action will be natural to the player, unconscious and instinctive, and will likely deliver success. Success being a reduced slice, and possibly even – a straight shot.

Of course, while playing partners are shouting 'Nice shot Bill!' (We have chosen Bill for this one.) Bill has again felt the awful move in which his body refuses to stay down and back, and instead, hoiks itself together with the club, both rolling over the top as they, and he, play through impact. It is a move Bill hates feeling, hates even more to see, but it is a move he has had to live with for many years. What Bill does not realise is that the move was sent by Silent Genius to save his day, to give him a shot he could play golf with. Without the awful move he so hates (i.e., without Silent Genius' intervention) Bill, ironically, would have likely made a better and more attractive move but would have sliced his ball into the rough on the right.

Like many players, Bill sees the professionals make their 'slightly from the inside, slightly under, or, straight down the line' moves into impact, and comparing their moves with what he sees of his own move, sees *his* as being the blamed thing, the thing most relevant, not realising that his blamed move is predetermined by a poor position at top, which *destines* the move.

(There are a thousand ways in which Silent Genius helps us and gives us a chance of success. The most famous one of all, which many millions of golfers have been affected by over the years, is still, for the most part (although much progress has been made), misunderstood by the coaching and instruction profession. I shall not cover it here. It would be too big a distraction.)

In the meantime, Silent Genius is with us. The concept and the reality. It exists in all of us, waiting to help so long as we allow it. So long as we do not shut it out.

The Shut Out

When we try to force a move into existence – a move lacking positional integrity – Silent Genius gets shut out.

Positional integrity = component suitability for a given action; or move.

So, if Bill attempted to force good technique by trying to keep his head *back;* by trying to keep his head *down;* by trying to hit along the target-line, or, *from the inside;* these aspects of his move would have all looked better, would have *been* better;

but would have delivered the slice. ANR knows and senses this, and so, if Silent Genius is not shut out, is instead allowed to step in and deal with direction, it will coordinate the uglier move that helps Bill find the fairway.

Desired moves *can* be forced, but ironically, they will often deliver worse shots than those delivered from the inferior move. Moves are only willing partners when they are born naturally, when the positions at either end of the move, support the move.

TIME FOR CHANGE

The importance of the three positions should be clear by now. If they are in poor shape the moves will be in poor shape with them. If they are in good shape, so too will the moves be in good shape.

So… how can a poor position be improved? What is the process?

Improving a Position

There are several ways to do this, but basically it is as you would imagine it to be. A position is improved by improving the arrangement of the components within the position. Remember, components are simply: *hips, knees, feet, elbows, wrists, arms,* etc.

Method 1: Component Fix

The most obvious method is to go directly to the faulty area, which will have one, perhaps two components causing problems.

In the following example we imagine a player who has one particular component in a damagingly poor state, at top, and as a result their downswing pays a price:

When this player records their swing and reviews it on playback, they see (when pausing top) this poor component staring at them every time, and the downswing having the problem of trying to launch itself correctly – inclusive of – this dud component, which has become part of the position. There are, for the downswing, only two options…

Fail, or compromise.

To repair the damaged component this player will need to do a dry swing (no ball), from start, all the way up and into top position; and when up there *stay up there,* **correct the component,** *then hold it!* (keep the component captive in its new state, whilst at top, for several seconds) get the feeling for it, and repeat multiple times. Then – repeat again, then again, then again, and then… try it in motion but without a ball. If that test is passed the player can introduce the ball, although many shots will have to first be sent off at half power, maintaining strict focus on the component's new form. The player should look for an occasion when, after completion of the backswing, they are seen to have arrived into position with the faulty component no longer faulty. It must *arrive* fixed, or at least substantially improved such that there is no longer any need for the spot-fix (whilst) at top. This is key – **it must arrive fixed,** and the only chance a player has of succeeding at this is if the component's new state, at top, is tangible, distinct, and already somewhat familiar despite it being relatively early in the treatment process. This whole exercise repeated over and over until the change begins to show itself as reliable.

This method of component fix is used right from the get-go when we learn to stand to the ball. There is no feed-in move leading to a start position. Start is cold. It is statue-like, even though to onlookers there is a sense of something coming. When we learn the start position, we go straight in and give direct instruction to things. Things like hip angle, grip, body lean, arms extension, ball position, etc., each part being quickly put in place and honed until the player looks good and is 'ready to go'. When learning start position, component fix is often a hands-on physical adjustment of body parts, into their required form and location. This is certainly so with regard to instructors when teaching new-to-golf students.

The method of physically adjusting body parts can be employed with each of the three positions.

In theory, it is not necessary for a backswing to occur in order for a position at top to exist. A professional golfer is so familiar with the body arrangement at top, that they could be at a cocktail party with drink in one hand, sausage in the other, one moment; and the next moment be putting their drink down and the rest of the sausage in their mouth, before – in an instant – demonstrating top position (to the person they are chatting with) by going straight to it from cold. They would link two fingers and without a backswing just 'conjure' the position out of thin air. They would not need to go anywhere near their start position, nor need any kind of a backswing. They could do this with ease because they know, so well, the set-of-coordinates involved. Their bodies have memorised the arrangement upwards of two-hundred-thousand times.

And so, as with start, it is possible to hold top, or finish – with their faulty components exposed – go in, fix the components, hold for several seconds to gain awareness and memory, then continue the swing. Repeat, repeat, repeat. Over and over. If the work is done well, the newly upgraded component will form a relationship with neighbour components and thus secure its place in the position. An improved **move** will follow.

Method 2: Line Shift (easiest way)

This is where we leave components untouched and instead ask *the move itself* to bring about improvement in a position. We ask the move to change its trajectory, its path, its line of travel.

Example: A player has the following fault bothering them:

At top, and at the beginning of the downswing, they are outside of plane and so, come across the ball through impact.

Rather than using the first method of treatment – component fix – we can in this case suggest the player simply send their move away on a more inside path and continue this more inside path all the way up, and into, top. The inside line, or path, will effect a change in the player's position *at* top. Being that the move is now travelling in a different direction, it will arrive at a different destination (so long as it is continued all the way). The player will be more 'inside' than they were previously (hopefully enough inside), ready for that critical moment when they start down.

With the aid of a camera, a friend, or an instructor, the player could run a few experiments to decide how much path adjustment is needed.

This method is about 'direction of movement', and it is important that the newly chosen direction be continued all the way until coming to rest in the position ahead, that it does not travel in the new direction for only part of the swing. Line shift is easy, it works well, and it works for both the backswing move and the through-swing move.

Important:

The method of sending a move in a different direction – *steeper, flatter, in-out, or out-in;* will have little effect on component assembly. This means that if a player has, for example, a flying right-elbow and a buckled wrist-hinge when they are outside of correct plane; then, they will have the same flying right-elbow and buckled wrist-hinge even on the new improved plane, after having sent their backswing inside.

To clarify:

When we send a move on a different line of travel – *up, around, in or out, etc.* – it affects assembly LOCATION. Not assembly itself. If component assembly is poor, then the newly directed move will simply re-locate this poor assembly. An overall gain may be made, but it is unlikely to be in way of an improved arrangement of components. The one or two targeted components *will* improve, but line-shift

will not improve any components unrelated and in poor condition.

This can play out with dramatic consequence. Using the above example of a player who is outside of plane at top, and also at the beginning of the downswing (causing them to cut across the ball), if (unbeknownst to them) they have a saboteur component present, then the saboteur component will do exactly as suggested by name, despite their newly improved 'inside' position.

Let us quickly recap…

The player is trying to hit more from the inside by *being* more on the inside (at top). And they *are* more inside. So far, so good. But the saboteur component contradicts this path-and-plane desire, and so, although the player has an improved position after shifting their move inside on the backswing, when they begin their downswing they will be betrayed. Their swing will immediately shift outside of plane once again and deliver the across-the-ball swing. This is one of the reasons we see some golfers unable to fix their swing errors. They make rehearsals where all looks good and then fail with the ball. They try harder. Harder still. Their understanding of the desired move is correct. They see it being done by others, why not by themselves? Because a saboteur component makes it impossible, that is why. If they can identify and fix the saboteur component, then, all will be solved.

We cannot underestimate the power of components to support or ruin good movement. If a player desires a draw-ball (the player may have been dreaming of and fighting for

a draw-ball for months, or years), then they need *draw-bias components* to deliver the draw for them. Then it will be easy. Then they will barely even need to try. Without the draw-bias components the player will struggle. Yes, they can manipulate the clubface and have some success with that, but it won't be easy, and if they have a slice-bias assembly of components in any of their three positions – especially at top – then try as they might to hit that draw, they will not routinely be able to.

Some good news:

Although we have highlighted the case where an unnoticed saboteur component betrayed the player into their downswing, there are also many instances where a player's component assembly is perfectly good, in that it will support a desired move. In such cases, when the line shift re-locates the good assembly to the newly improved position, it sets up a green-light situation for the move to materialise and the player makes a big gain, in the easiest of ways.

Method 3: Working a component.

This is where we pick a faulty component (one which is spoiling a position) and work it into better arrangement.

For this example, we are going to look at the right hip:

A player's right hip is seen to be fine at start, but not at top. We see that during the backswing the hip has slipped sideways and is – all by itself – spoiling the player's top position at considerable cost. The hip-slide has resulted in the player (at top) having low-level body turn and a faulty left

arm plane with which to begin the downswing. (One component error (hip) has knocked two other components out of position. Now there are *three* component errors.!)

So, we work the right hip (by physical manoeuvre) into its correct placement at top. The hip will need to be active to get to its new place but: in a twisting/pivoting way. Currently it is active in a sliding way. Once the right hip has awareness (a strong awareness is needed) of its new destination, the pivot/twist will readily and happily repeat, being sensed as the best method for the hip to travel from the first place to the second. In this operation, once again, the critical part is the *destination* that the hip must find, and although we may initially need to help it on its way with a nudge or a twist, it is the precise coordinates of the hip's destination – at top – which carries full weighting in technical excellence. As soon as the hip becomes educated about its correct placement it will move there by itself, without need for any conscious effort from the player.

When the right hip locates to its new place in the position, it will at the same time bring about improvement in the two components which were failing as a consequence of it previously sliding. The two components ('body turn', and 'left arm plane') may be improved enough that they are lifted from poor status to fine status. This development, where the improvement of one component brings others along with it, is not unique to this example.

Additionally, to be considered: Shot call.

There is an additional way to affect components which needs mentioning, even though it does not, strictly, fit into this

chapter. It needs mentioning because it effects subtle changes to components and underpins much of the performance-based work we ask for from our swings. The subtle change to components... can be brought about by 'shot call.'

If a player's mind calls for and visualises a certain type of shot – a low ball, a high ball, a draw, a fade. A hook or a slice. The call may (depending on their skill level) prompt the shift in component arrangement necessary for delivery of the shot. Shot call will not transform or repair components, but it will affect their form and assembly at the hands of expert players whose swings are receptive to it, whose swings are not fixed one-dimensionally; but can bend, flex, or shift a little, one way or another, as required. Whose swings – through an abundance of play, practise and experimentation – have learnt to react quickly to impulses sent from the eye and the mind, regarding shot design.

Whichever way we go about it though: whether by method 1, 2, or 3. Whether by shot call, or, by any other method not mentioned. Whether directly or indirectly. Our swings *can* only ever, and *will* only ever – improve – via uplift in the quality of their three positions.

PROBLEMS OF MANY

A few of the swing's many components are related to direction; some, to power, and others to strike. Others still, have a general role and are not related to any one thing. There are forty-eight components in total, and we know that each bears an influence upon the swing which may be positive or negative. Each may assist, or impair, the attached move. Whilst reflecting on this and acknowledging the essential nature of components to the three positions, and thereby, to the overall golf swing; it must also be said that forty-eight components is an awful lot of detailed content to be managing. An awful lot for a golfer to have to worry about. Too much! it must be said!

That sentiment will resonate with many readers.

From a practical point of view it does sound daunting. Even off-putting. That aside, it is possible to put in place, tidy, and refine the majority of components fairly quickly, especially for learners under the care of a capable instructor. Just standing to the ball correctly takes up seventeen components, and there is no reason why we cannot all stand to the ball correctly.

The above concern about the number of components is fair, though. There *are* problems and complexities (both inevitable) as a result of there being so many components in a golf swing. But, even if we were to reduce the number to

the group of key components, we will still have fifteen or so, and if we tried to reduce further, to a group of *ten* key components (being that five are so simple to put in place at start); we will still have those ten; or – fifteen, twenty, thirty, forty or more components to tackle, and there is nothing we can do about it other than ignore the problem, or make a choice of where to start and which to prioritise.

Except...

In the background and hidden quietly from view, is a team of powerful allies, ready and waiting to be summoned. With 'problems of many' bearing down on us as we contemplate the realisation of having forty-eight components in our golf swings, forty-eight pieces of swing which may need care and attention; now is the perfect time to meet the four giants of technique.

THE FOUR GIANTS

Golf instruction and golf-swing analysis rightly speaks of mechanics. There are angles, planes, hinges, turns, levers and torques; all in a golf swing. We do, in many ways *build* a swing, and we also strive to make this swing machine-like in its reliability. The best swings in the world are so well put together, that on the range they demonstrate this machine-like quality by firing-off one ball after another with a repetitiveness that does appear to rival that of a machine. Most of all, though, the greatest golf swings – past, present, and future; excel (and always will excel) in four disciplines:

- STRUCTURE
- VOLUME
- ALIGNMENT
- CENTREDNESS

To own an impressive golf swing, these four are all and everything. Compromise one of these and the swing immediately begins falling short. Compromise more than one and it will struggle to reliably function at all. Try to add something else? Try to make it five disciplines – five giants? You will not be able to. Nothing else exists. These four giants of technique have everything covered when it comes to the mechanics of a golf swing. Collectively, they positively influence the behaviour and grade of more than 80% of the golf swing's forty-eight components. We need to get to know them. We need to work with them. We need to master them

and keep pushing to get the best from them. They are here to help us, but only if we drive them hard.

Their Powers

The Four Giants are to a large degree self-explanatory. At least, their names offer significant clue as to what each will bring. Despite their name-clues I shall nevertheless outline them, so that readers are able to grasp concept and create a usable understanding for each.

STRUCTURE

Structure gives strength and stability. The most important aspect of structure brought to the golf swing is, and are – the arms. Firstly, at start, where they should not simply hang limply from under the shoulders but instead should be held slightly out* from the body and held also quite firm. Left arm – straight; right arm – near-straight.

This though, is easy. It is what comes next that is difficult…

- The left arm should remain straight throughout the entirety of the backswing.

- The right arm should remain straight deep into follow-through.

Having our left arm straight half-way back, and our right arm straight half-way through, is not enough – *if they then bend as*

they continue. This again is where the three positions become so important, and is why a player must train the left arm to be straight, at top; and the right arm to be straight, at finish. If a player can maintain straight or near-straight arms at top, and at finish, then they will by that achievement alone be bringing considerable structure to their swing. Both tasks are demanding, but both can be learnt, trained, and maintained.

There are other aspects to structure (most notably posture, at start), but none is so important as the arms during the swing. More generally, 'arm-action' may be the defining feature of the world's best swings.

(*Precise arms extension at start depends on a few variables: how tall the player is, their limbs to body ratios and also the club being used. We needn't go to that level of detail here.)

Before we leave structure, we must all of us remember that with regard to ***components; positions and moves;*** *and now –* ***the four giants;*** *it is not a case of black or white, win or lose, succeed or fail. It is about progress. That each month we see a small but visible gain in the area of our efforts. This philosophy applies to ALL of our efforts, whether working (as now being discussed) the arms, for structure; or, on another giant; or on any given component in isolation. Small progress, repeating and accumulating over time, becomes – big progress.*

VOLUME

Volume is size of swing, which means – how far the club travels around us in its orbit during the swing. The volume

of the club's orbit is dependent on a three-fold contribution from:

- body turn
- arm lift
- wrist hinge

These three modes of club movement combine (with differing amounts in different swings), and the more we have of each, the greater will be the measurement of our swing volume. Backswing volume has greater value than through-swing volume, but through-swing volume is of relevance and should be added to the work schedule.

In simple terms

Volume = Room for acceleration = Speed = Distance

We all have our own largely fixed rate at which we can accelerate the golf club. (It is in fact *fixed*, but I say 'largely' because we can increase it by way of strength training.) That our rate of acceleration is fixed means that if we want to increase speed, we must increase *space and time* for the fixed rate of acceleration to deliver the increase in speed. The bigger our backswing, the more space and time we have, thus enabling greater club speed into the ball.

So far, we have defined the essence of volume with its relevance to the golf swing. Now, a few refinements…

Maximum volume comes from maximum use of each of the three modes of movement – body, arms, and wrists. Very few

of us are able to achieve all three modes to a maximum at the same time. It is an incredible effort, especially if we have to return for a precision strike. What is more generally relevant is that many golfers swing with at least one of the modes running low. Often considerably. In these cases, the low mode fails to contribute its fair share to the filling-out of the swing (particularly the backswing) which in turn leads to one of the other two modes exaggerating its role in an effort to make up for the 'lazy' mode. Whatever the reason or cause, it represents one area where a golfer can make quick power gains.

Correct volume:

Volume of the highest type includes not only the size of the backswing and through-swing combined (which is this giant's principal qualification), but also, the *stretch* created at top. When volume is increased it is important that the stretch (which builds) does not break in the process; or get dislodged. If the left arm collapses at top, then the stretch will be broken. Tension which had been building in that aspect of the swing will dissipate. If the right knee or right hip pop sideways, there will also be a break in the stretch (a part-collapse of structure) and again, in the tension that had been building.

'Dislodged' refers to the swing centre being pulled out of position.

These instances of a backswing breaking or being dislodged may each still include substantial and even vast swing volume, but with the stretch missing *the rate of initial*

acceleration into the downswing would reduce – and could never be recovered. Speed upon impact would be slower. This is important because volume's primary contribution to the swing is the enabling of club speed.

ALIGNMENT

This is, or should be, the easiest of the giants in which to achieve excellence. The alignment we are referring to is *swing line at ground level* (the line the club is travelling along as it meets and strikes the ball). We want the club to be travelling straight to target*.

There are lots of competing and conflicting forces in a golf swing – turns, lifts, twists, shifts, lags, releases. etc., and one of the main indicators that they are coming together in a meaningful way is when we see delivery of a target-line swing at ground level. The effort and act of delivering straight-line force into the ball at ground level, keeps the twists, turns, shifts, etc., in purposeful balance.

Ground level is where alignment matters most. It is easy to overemphasise the importance of alignment at top (where the club's shaft points to target when at horizontal), and whilst alignment at top *is* desirable, it matters not in comparison to alignment at ground level, upon strike. A player can be considerably off alignment at top, with their club pointing far to one side or other of target, and yet still deliver perfect ground-level alignment-force into the strike of the ball.

If you are wondering how to work on ground-level alignment, then take a tip from the tour pros. They routinely practise with alignment sticks placed on the ground. One for their feet, yes; but the alignment stick we most need for this giant is the one to be placed just outside the ball. An inch or two outside the ball and pointing at the target. We want our club to pass through impact in a line that runs parallel to this alignment stick. If this is new to you, then first practise without a ball. Get used to noticing (or looking for, if necessary) the flash-line of the club as it passes the point of would-be ball location at ground level. Additionally (and without a ball), practise shifting the flash-line to different angles – varying it at will – demonstrating mastery over the club's line of travel. Keep your feet parallel to target. We are looking to develop skill over swing-line *from* the swing; not by cheating with our aim.

The tricky part of this for some players will be the correction part, where their ground-level path is badly mis-aligned rather than marginally mis-aligned and a big correctional shift in the line is required. In such cases there are a few exercises and drills which can be used as straighteners. These drills will occasionally need to be severe, as path has shown itself time and again to be one of the most stubborn of features in club amateur golf swings. There may be, for some, quite a struggle. But there is not, nor has there ever been, a case of a player whose swing-line could not be straightened.

Once accomplished, maintenance of a straight path through impact is easy. A player need only keep an eye on things. The time for hard labour and tough drilling will be over, and a

major contributor to high performance striking will have been landed.

**straight-to-target is a reliable concept even if there is nuance to some of the facts.*

CENTREDNESS

Centredness relates to the head. Although the head is not actually the centre of the swing, it certainly feels like it is, and it should be treated as if it is. It is surprisingly easy for the head to be pulled away from its starting place during the backswing, even when a player is on-guard against such a thing. High-volumed, well-structured backswings place great strain upon centredness as it tries to hold its ground at top, and not be pulled away. Much of the good work *of* a high-volumed and well-structured backswing can be lost, if these precious forces and alignments, having been built, are then allowed to shift one way or another instead of remaining related to the ball and target. This happens, in particular, when the head no longer maintains 'square-to-target'.

Square-to-target is the most subtle and fragile aspect of centredness, being also the hardest error to spot, and yet it is responsible for significant complication and loss, despite this subtlety.

(Incidentally, alignment (the giant we have just discussed) appreciates any help it can get. In this way centredness plays a second role, for it supports another giant. It supports alignment.)

Centredness is not a tricky concept. Nor is it particularly difficult to tap into. However, it is very difficult to maintain centredness in combination with structure and volume. Huge stretch and strain from those other two giants pull upon the shoulder section and neck, and therefore the head. There is no easy route forward with this, but every minute spent striving and every inch gained in the bringing together of these three giants is a minute and an inch of profound type. You will be harvesting from the richest of fields. In the vast land that is golf's technique, no other field even comes close.

In theory, the four giants are able to operate independently, but in practise they are interconnected. They work with and complement each other, even though to fully employ one means to place strain upon another. They are not only interconnected by way of the conflicts they bring and share, but interestingly, each giant is dependent on at least one other giant to achieve its own highest state of existence.

- structure cannot achieve its highest state if centredness fails.

- volume cannot achieve maximum tension without structure (it would be slack volume).

- centredness and alignment prefer to work (and work best) with each other's support.

Tips On Using the Giants

When you get to know the four giants you can work all four of them simultaneously in one swing. This is the best way to use them, although, it takes considerable focus and experience. Despite the intensity involved in working all four together, you *do* need to try to get to this point after a month or two, because this is where they truly deliver. However, do not rush. Take your time. Take more than a month or two if needed. First, get to know and understand each giant on its own. Then, try two together; then three, and – *always* slowly (alignment is the exception and can be worked at speed, if worked in isolation). I do most of my training with a weighted club (no ball) so as to achieve full levels of mental and physical intensity, and I train outdoors, or in a room with enough space when the weather is poor.

Regarding working the giants with a golf ball:

When there is a ball to be hit there is a distraction, and a pronounced distraction if there is also a target. It is very difficult to lock-in fully on the giants when hitting a ball, but at some point you will be wanting to try a few shots whilst thinking of them. *This must not be done on the course.* At least, not in the beginning, and if you *do* use them during play, use only one (whichever is bringing biggest gains during practise). The giants are primarily to be employed away from the course. This means any balls being hit should be hit at the range, and again, you must avoid going to full speed with these shots (you will quickly get a feel for things, but I suggest half power as a maximum. If a normal seven iron shot flies 150yds, then... hit it 75yds). *For point of reference:* I usually

have **no interest** in the shots I am sending off (at half power or less). I am just 'removing' the ball in front of me, the ball I am looking down at in normal fashion. It can be hit poorly, and it can go anywhere. I do not care. The ball has no more significance to me than it simply being in the way of the club, as the club passes. I *do*, however (and you should, also), go to whatever feels like a personal maximum of technique. We are looking for excellence with each of the giants and so, go to maximum, or – beyond maximum.

(When pushing the giants to maximum or beyond, I repeat once more – swing in slow motion. You will be able to get more deeply into the technique when in slow motion, plus, you will avoid possible risk of a pulled muscle.)

The giants are for conditioning; for pushing beyond or maintaining the limit of our swing's technique. If your work with the giants is done well (away from the course), then your swing will without doubt carry profit from that work into action, when you play.

The four giants are assets of such value as to be indispensable. They offer us, as flailing golfers, aspects of machine-like performance.

Giants as Allies

Thus far, an outline understanding of the four giants has been presented, but I realise I have side-tracked slightly, because the giants were first introduced as being 'allies.' They were introduced as being allies in context of us having to

potentially take care of forty-eight components. We ought to know *how* they can be considered as allies.

Components beware!

The giants are allies in that their powers, which are immense, exert discipline across the entire swing. Where component error exists, the giants push back against it, reducing it to a minimum. They (components) have no option but to shape-up when the giants are in town, and many of our golf swing's wrinkles and creases are ironed smoother by their efforts.

It is not that the giants go looking for faulty components, as if they were trouble-shooters sent in to fix a problem or search out a culprit. They are unaware of the benefits they bring. They compel better form and better order only by trying to excel at their own tasks. That is all they care about. But they strengthen *all* golf swings, and this whether we are referring to the swing of a novice golfer or of the world's No 1 player. They enrich the swing's technique and deny component flaw where it might easily start developing, unnoticed.

Let us pause for a moment and reflect on this…

Okay. This all sounds like great news. So, with this great news in mind… where are we now? The implications… what are they? Does this mean we can leave the components alone? At least… we can leave them in the hands of the giants?

For answers to these questions we must move into the future. Perhaps quite a way into the future for some players, but not so far, for others.

Into the Future

We move forward to a place in time where a player is finished with the assembly and tidying of their components, or at least, is satisfied with them as they are, and has signed-off on them with regard to their condition and grades. By signing-off on components, the player will at the same time be signing-off on the three positions, and consequently – their swing.

(With regard to 'signing-off' – things do not have to be perfect. Far from it. Highly enjoyable (and competitive) golf can be played with imperfect technique, and a player may announce satisfaction or reconciliation with their swing, including its components and positions, whenever they feel like it.)

If the player has done this, and is accepting of the stage they have arrived at technically, feeling like they have done enough work and that for them the forward fight is over; that they are happy with what they have and where they are; then, from that point on and for the rest of their life the four giants will be all they ever need to care about with regard to their swing's technique. Literally all, literally ever.

You may be wondering *how* such a thing can be said...?

It can be said because the giants keep a hold on everything already established, already achieved; and in many cases they are able to improve upon it, too. They do have one or two modest limitations. There are a few bits of poor technique they cannot undo. The grip is an obvious example. The grip will not shift or improve by any type of influence,

no matter how strong the influence. Once placed, the grip is **fixed** (badly, or not) and may well remain a lifetime. There are also a few components within the three positions which escape the giants' influence.

In this way there will always be opportunity for some hands-on work, from us, in the targeting of detail; but we can forgive the giants this little short falling, for they bring us so much.

INTERMISSION

We have arrived at a place in between technique and performance. A hand-over place where technique sits out for a while and listens to what performance has to say. Of its teachings. Of its observations from watching those who play, play.

But before we enter the realm of performance, we will use this hand-over place to take a short time-out and with it, add one or two peripheral subjects to this work. Subjects not explicitly relevant to the main theory, but of some interest, nonetheless.

Children

Children are in many ways the best learners, as we know; but they are not the best listeners, and this often helps them. They are quickly bored by adults explaining in detail 'how to do it' and so they switch off. While the parent or instructor rambles on (which is how it appears to feel to the child!), the child is hearing a kind of white noise, and either waits patiently for the white noise to finish or ignores it and reaches for another ball. But, so long as children (fairly quickly) end up with a good start position, their swing will develop largely by itself, and nicely so. This is because from a good start position there are no errors in-built to spoil or deny access to a correspondingly good top position. And from this beginning the child's instincts will usually win out.

You might wonder why the same simple approach doesn't work so well for adults. Why, when adults are taught to stand to the ball well, their swing doesn't flourish like a child's swing does. In part, it is because adults are big enough to create power with an average length, or even a short, swing. Children love hitting the ball a long way (as we all do), but they do not have enough strength to rapidly accelerate the club like adults. On top of that they are not as tall, and so their swing arc is shorter. Children are not conscious of these things, but they are conscious of having to keep watching adults or bigger children boom it past them. They start out as short hitters but desire to be long hitters, and so they make up for their lack of strength and height with big backswings. Not all of them, but many of them. It is easy to make a big backswing at a young age, and natural to do so.

Another of their best qualities is their lack of distress over bad shots. They pull ball after ball and don't question what went wrong. They just go again. It is this which simplifies their style, and which allows the swing to develop largely by itself. This doesn't mean a few pointers won't be needed along the way, and good coaches know when to come in with a small correction or a nudge here or there, but also know when to keep out of the way, which they should for as much as possible, whilst keeping an eye on things and observing that the child's technique is developing nicely by instinct.

Adults have higher expectations and are more quickly frustrated. Plus, they have a lifetime of believing in cause-and-effect to overcome. (Cause-and-effect is relevant; but it can also be a bit of a blunt understanding.) They deconstruct and start interfering whenever something goes wrong. Often too soon, often too quickly.

On top of these differences there is the immersion level that a lot of good child players have. Many children play golf every day during holidays. It could easily amount to 40-50 games consecutively over a six or seven-week summer spell. I regularly used to play 36 holes in a day when I was a junior and I am sure many juniors still do the same today, whereas there are many adult golfers who play the same 40-50 games over a six or seven-YEAR spell. That's a compression multiple of x50 for the children!

Their freedom, their relentless play, their desire to be a long hitter when they have no strength, their lack of inquisition over a bad shot; these are the some of the things which,

together with a fine start position, lead to these wonderful swings we see in children.

Postscript: As mentioned above, much can potentially follow from a good start position, and many fine swings have developed (including some of the finest of all-time) without the owners being aware of having given any particular care to the three positions. The three positions can be crafted directly (with hands-on work, which is the fastest way) or, as result of long-term and intense desire to hit high-quality – ultimate, even – golf shots. Many fine players will have sculpted their three positions this way (somewhat unknowingly), through process of hundreds of thousands of intensely focussed golf shots being hit; each, with the player determined to deliver the result they are after, a result only achievable from superior positions. The positions then being slowly shaped, refined, and polished, as if by an unseen but master craftsman.

Pre-shot

A lot is made of the importance of pre-shot routines seen on the PGA Tour, and yet, although it is true that all PGA Tour players have a pre-shot routine, very few of these pre-shot routines will have been artificially made. They will have come naturally to each player when they were young, and that is how a pre-shot routine should come to all of us (even if we are not young) – naturally. In which case there should be no advice given, directly or implicitly, to go and work on one's pre-shot. A player doing this may force upon themselves implementation of a pre-shot routine not best suited to them, and they will never know because the better one, which would have come later (and been natural), will be blocked by the incumbent routine.

Also important to mention, and counter to the suggested importance of pre-shot routines, is observation that all club amateur golfers have a pre-shot routine anyway. The low, mid, and high handicappers who I and my peers regularly play alongside in the numerous pro ams and casual golf throughout the season, all – just like the tour pros – have pre shot routines. It does not help these amateurs play top-level golf. We need some perspective on this. And who can say two looks are better than one; or one look is better than three? ... How many waggles? – one, two, three, four, or five? And should the waggle be wrists only? Or should it include some arm? How to approach the ball? How to decide the order of foot placement? ... and how much shuffling is recommended? Which trigger move to employ: right knee press?... hands press? Or... cold start?

I can't see a way that these calls can be reliably made, and a message be given to a golfer to go away and work on their pre-shot, work on figuring the XY&Z of what needs to be done before they begin the swing. There is no sense to it. The only advice I would give on pre-shot would be to keep it simple. Cut out the fussing and let the pre-shot come in its own time, when it wants to come because it senses the time is right in that it fits with personality, and style of play.

Greats Falling

If a great player knows how they do it, and did it, and this knowledge is also held by the coach who is given credit for enabling the great player; then they both must know *how* it was done. If the player's form then falls off a cliff face and the player cannot find a way back, nor can the coach return the player to form, then it must follow that neither of them knew – in entirety – how they did it. An unknown element (obviously, key) has gone missing, and they can't figure what that bit is, or was, that they had when they had it. This may seem a little harsh, but there is some truth to it, and the game is so delicate when speaking of high performance that it is no particular surprise, either.

Removing, for a moment, speculation as to the degree of know-how in a great victory, part of a great victory (even *with* know-how) will still include the player's inspiration and their seizing of the moment. This alone is enough to be worthy of the highest admiration, and any player who wins – any time – deserves the fullest of respects for their win, and every bit of acclaim that comes their way as a result of it. We can add that many times, also (despite what was said in the opening of this piece), a player does know how they did it on a particular occasion, or on several particular occasions, in that they can tell you the swing-thought and mental process that led to peak form being delivered that week... can tell you what they had been working on in their swing. It might have been a specific 'feel' that they found on the range in the lead up to the tournament's opening round; a concept or move; something that felt tangible and that they felt good about.

Something which (as happens from time to time) delivered results immediately. Literally... within minutes. Of course, it must also be mentioned that the win/s may have come on the back of generally strong form, where a player is seen on the front page of leaderboards and it feels like only a matter of time before they do, indeed, start winning.

But the question still stands. Why can the same swing-thought and same mental process *not* work the following week? If we remove the inspiration that is needed to land a victory, and a player is left with their bread-and-butter game, including the ebb and flow above and below their standard middle-of-graph performance; then, if the player *truly* knows how they do things when they are winning, they would thereafter be seen regularly getting in the thick of things on Sundays, even when not winning. We would at least see them in contention numerous times throughout the season. But the great players we are speaking of when we refer to 'Greats Falling', went from world-leading, to no longer even making cuts.

Dramatic loss of form is a big mystery. Players like David Duval, who arrived on the golf scene and was for a few years a thrilling and bona fide superstar; and Seve, a golf hero of epic proportions, who could have been a central character in Homer's The Odyssey as much as a golfer of the twentieth century; loved and followed by millions in Europe and further millions around the world. These two come quickly to mind. There are others. We could name many fine players whose form was seen to plummet when they were at the top, or near top of their careers. Ian Baker-Finch, another. What was it they lost? Was it something unique and personal to

each of them, or was it something general that applied to all of them? This question (and one other) has occupied my mind more than any. The content of this book I have been teaching for thirty years, in-between tournament play, albeit for only half an hour or an hour to club players or learners who come along for their weekly or monthly lesson. By which I mean to say that I have not experienced any lasting mystery with regard to understanding the golf swing's technique, or the teaching of it. But the mystery of why great players – world no 1's and Major winners included – suffer sudden loss of form, never to return, has intrigued me since I was young. The wondering of whether these great players could be returned to their best, en masse, by way of a general explanation; a general understanding. I am convinced that collapse in form has a common aspect to it. Clearly, a critical aspect. Many of the players I am talking about were in the peak years of their career when they seemingly lost their swings (of course they *didn't* lose their swings. The answer lies elsewhere).

I believe there is an answer, and an answer which, when found, would return a mass group of struggling players back to form. If found it will be a general answer. It *must* be a general answer, or there will be little value in it. It will be an answer that enables 'falling greats' (and many lesser players, too, who have also lost their long game) to recapture a major part of what it was that made them great. I believe an answer is findable and I have one or two ideas that may be part of it, although I am not ready to elaborate on them here. I would need to be surer.

On Timing

Timing is important. I am not sure if anything is more important to a golfer, because timing is required for straight hitting, and if any reader considers themselves to be a 'master' of timing then I tip my hat in your direction. You are owner of the rarest skill in the game, a skill that, as a golfer with a set of golf clubs, puts you in an equivalent realm to that of a Samurai with his sword, and you can be imagined - 'swords' in hand - splitting fairways and staring down dangerous flags as you cut your way round the course. The greatest samurai was Miyamoto Musashi. Golf had no less with Ben Hogan.

So, what exactly is – timing?

Timing Pt 1:

Timing is the place or moment during the through-swing when the clubface returns to square. We want this 'square' moment to time its arrival such that it coincides with the golf ball. The golf ball will then fly towards the target, even if it has a curving flight due to path error. (A curving ball that flies to target, **still** – *flies to target!* Path error has not cost a bean. Clubface error will **not** fly a ball to target; and may cost the player everything.) Separate from the disparity in consequence between path error and face error, is that it is not necessary to get involved with path, to understand timing. So, we will not.

Every golfer's golf club opens on the backswing, and opens significantly. Our golf clubs are approximately 90 degrees open to target by arrival at top. They remain 90 degrees (or so) open as they are pulled hard into the downswing. It is during the second half of the downswing that the clubface will begin turning back to square. But will it make it in time? We can see from this question the use of time as the determining factor. It is, indeed, for many players, a race to get that clubface back to square.

For ease of understanding let us use the 90 degrees we spoke of as being the amount the clubface is open on the downswing when it begins squaring up. The ball sits and waits. The player's swing begins the squaring movement (it should be a release-roll movement, but many amateur golfers have the release without the necessary roll) and in a blink of an eye their club has met, and is in contact with – the ball. But did it return to square in time? No. They only managed to return 88 of the 90 degrees their club had been open. Their club is now in contact with the ball and the clubface is pointing 2 degrees to the right of target. This is where their ball will fly. At PGA Tour level a 2-degree open clubface with a driver will send the ball approximately 20yds to the right. A missed fairway. That's pretty tough on such a small error.

Another player may *over-roll* the clubface and, also in the blink of an eye, return the club 92 degrees instead of 90. Their clubface now points 2 degrees left as it meets the ball, which then flies 20yds to the left. Another missed fairway.

These examples are for a 2-degree error. A club returning a 5-degree error will send the ball 45-50 yds right, or a little less left (it hits the ground earlier), at tour level.

Think of it like this –

Imagine, as you look down ready to begin your swing, a thin line touching the back of the ball and perpendicular to the target. This line is analogous to a finishing line in a 100m race. The thin line touching the back of the ball is like the 100m tape, a place where judgement is made and awards are given out. Only, in our case as golfers, the photo-finish shows whether the squaring of the clubface is early, late, or on time; and the award given out is one given for a club that crosses the line with its face square-to-target.

If a player's clubface has *already* returned to square, and their club is still yet to reach the finishing line (ball), then, as it continues travelling and rolling for the remaining distance to contact, it will inevitably cross the line closed. It was square too soon, or – **early**. The ball goes left. If the clubface in another photo-finish is seen to have returned to square only sometime *after* it has crossed the line, then it was **late,** and will have crossed the line open.

So, this is timing, the moment on the through-swing *relative to the ball* when our clubface returns to square, and there are only three possibilities: late, early, or – on time.

Regarding rhythm: A player may take driver and make three swings, each with a lovely rhythm and… slice all three balls into the water on the right. Lovely rhythm. Late timing.

Regarding Tempo: Two friends playing together and teeing off; one has a quick tempo and the other, a leisurely tempo. But with their different tempos they both hook their balls into the rough on the left. Two different tempos, both *early* with the squaring of the clubface. From the next tee they both hit the fairway. One quick tempo – well timed. One leisurely tempo – well timed.

When we are at the range practising our swings, perhaps only generally, to stay sharp; or specifically, ie. – doing technical work for the purpose of improvement; then although we may be aware of good rhythm and tempo, we must nevertheless look to see that our shots are heading-off towards target, as confirmation that what we are doing fits with timing. If all *feels* good – the new technique and the rhythm of our swing – but the ball repeatedly cuts away to the right, then our timing is late, and we will need to somehow adjust it. Conversely, if the ball is hooking left, then we will need to do something to slow, or delay, the squaring-up rate. A push or a pull are still open or closed clubfaces, even if the path now gets involved to confuse matters. However, when we are at our best, there is definitely a coming together of rhythm and timing – they meld as one – and our swing feels easy because of it.

Do not trust feel. The pros do not. We trust the ball and deal with the ball's flight and with what that flight tells us. You may *feel* as if you squared the clubface as you came through, and you did (at some point), but if the ball flies into the trees on the right you did not square it soon enough, or – in time. You may tee off on hole number 7 and with anguished cry implore to your playing partners (as your ball sails over the

right-side out of bounds fence) 'I swear on my life I rolled my wrists and club on that swing!' Yes (you did) ... but way too late. The ball does not lie. Your feel does.

Timing Pt 2:

There is a second feature to timing. It has to do with whether or not a player delivers peak force at the moment of contact. If we have an involuntary flinch or twitch on our downswing, even if only tiny, it will cause a 'mis-time'. If we disconnect for a nano second in the same section of swing – the start down and downswing – there will be immediate loss of force as the player now gets out of sync with the club. Invariably, a mishit of some type follows. This aspect of timing is generally less relevant than the first aspect (return-to-square). We are all pretty good at timing our power such that we deliver it in the right place, ie, into the ball.

The most telling consequence of this aspect of timing (for us all, tour pros included), is when we are faced with a carry over water which is on the limit of our power output. If we need to go all-in with our 5 wood to carry the water in front of a green, and we have only 5 or 6 yards of spare with regards to failed carry, then a mistimed power output will almost certainly give our golf ball a watery grave.

It is the first understanding of timing that is the more important of the two, and is the one I recommend club players give most consideration to. This side of a golf shot (the timing of the return-to-square) is a life-long pursuit and trial (for most players, including me), as it rarely stays true for long before we have to capture it again. Even with a

heightened sensitivity to its importance, and due care given, its repeatability eludes most of us such that it becomes a seemingly every day, ever-present part of one's golfing life.

Once our timing is going well, however, things begin falling into place and our rhythm and sense of harmony more easily lock-in on the shot. A good day, or a good week or two on the fairways may well follow.

Incidentally, I do not consider timing to be an aspect of technique. Tiger, Rory, Ernie, Snead or Hogan, swinging at their best and missing a fairway, does not mean a bad swing being witnessed. Two degrees out at impact does not qualify a bad swing. Nor does four degrees. Their swings – and their swings' techniques – would still have been, as their shots missed the fairway, of an accomplishment to warrant inclusion into any list of 'best swings' you care to mention.

There is something abstract and to do with infinites about timing. And the finding of it and the delivering of it is a largely personal quest. Whereas principles of technique are neither abstract, nor personal.

End of intermission.

To continue…

TECHNIQUE & PERFORMANCE

This work has, until now, dealt largely with the technique of a golf swing. Explaining how we go from a beginner swing to the best swing in the world by shaping and refining the three positions. Now we leave the building of golf swings behind us, and instead, give thought to the other of golf's two branches – PERFORMANCE.

Technique and performance are the two material branches of input and output in golf. In most other sports, too. The mind sits unseen in the background, but we see the two branches clearly. Technique is seen by the swinging of the golf club, and performance is oftentimes stark and dramatic.

We *could* consider technique to also be a 'performance', in that we perform a swing. But that is not what we mean when we talk of performance and the term is better used when pointing to outcome.

So, let us get to the golf course! … where we can look at some of these swings, and outcomes.

TO THE TEE

As interesting as the golf swing is from the point of view of trying to figure its high technique, including means of possession, it is perhaps not as interesting (or as perplexing) as our attempts to divine satisfactory performance *from* the swing.

Performance might be best described as the act of going live, with what we have, under pressure. Attempting to deliver our best, or near best, when called upon to do so. The pressure we speak of needn't be of a specific type. It needn't be Ryder Cup or the back nine holes of a Major for a golfer to feel pressure. A Sunday morning four-ball with playing partners and a few others watching, by the first tee, will lift the heart rate a beat or two for most golfers, no matter how experienced, and test their ability to demonstrate competence in the presence of others. That slightly tense one-ball-one-chance moment, in front of an audience.

Or another typical pressure situation… where a player has a great score going through 14 holes of their medal round one weekend, and they know it. Let us see how calm, casual and nonchalant the player is as they play out the remainder of their round, trying to bring home a winning card. More likely than nonchalant they will be head down and fully gripped by events as on one hand they try to stay positive (perhaps even aggressive), while on the other they try to steer clear of

disaster and foolish mistake. A kind of high wire balancing act that leads, hopefully, to the safety of the clubhouse.

That there exist different levels of pressure throughout the different tiers of play can be appreciated easily enough. But pressure is also personal, and it can be argued that a club member, who after numerous failed years' worth of attempts, senses a chance to win their first-ever stroke play event (knowing they may never get another) would, at that moment, be more pressured and more nervous than any tour pro sensing a chance to win their umpteenth tour event.

And so, whilst society, together with the annals of golf's recorded history, fairly designates pressure-load by proclaiming significance of an event, it is the significance in our head which matters most and which has the greatest bearing on what comes next. In the life of the medal winner mentioned above, the handing in of that winner's card may equate to the conquering of a most dreamed of mountain, even though in the greater scheme of things it is just another weekend medal, among a thousand other weekend medals being played that day.

So, this much is one side of performance. 'High achievement', and the breaking of personal barriers; personal thresholds. But there is another side to performance. More basic. More modest. Humble. Yet also pressure packed. This side of performance applies to hundreds of thousands, perhaps a million or more golfers. It has less to do with prowess, and more to do with just – fitting in.

Fitting in – feeling ok about oneself as a golfer. Not being conspicuous by incompetence. Trusting that embarrassment will take a sidestep when, in front of people, we stand over a golf ball ready to swing. Knowing that we can at least get the shot away somewhere, *anywhere,* so long as it doesn't remain close by. Confident enough from the first tee, that we can, as near as is possible, predict we will at least get the club on the ball, even if where it goes is largely a matter of chance. Fitting in – being able to receive invitation from our boss or important client to join them for a game at their private members club, without having to decline the invitation. Or, having accepted, without fearing the day more and more as it approaches.

These modest asks, remote from any dreamy thought of placing a hand on a trophy, are born of a desire that we might consider ourselves, at least, vaguely – competent. There is no aspiration to strut a confident walk as we move about the club, passing by fellow golfers who all know and regard us well *as* a golfer. No aspiration to break a few of the club's smaller rules by straddling the plastic chains, wood railings and ropes dotted around the premises, rather than walking through the openings. A tiny breach but a big statement of fitting in (as all those who *do* fit in, seem to do it!). No urge for a wardrobe of fancy golf clothes and kit, so confident in ourselves that we are prepared to state as much with our walk and wear. All we wish for and need, if we are to be accepted quietly into golfing society and feel comfortable, is a degree of competence. Yet, it is so difficult!

If you are a reader who has still to achieve competence, then these next few chapters will help complete a picture of the puzzle. With that you will be able to see the piece missing from your own story, and so, have a good idea of what to do next.

Players and Learners

Because we are about to enter the field of play and performance, quite deeply, we should begin with insight into how 'the build of the swing' and 'the play of the game' cross paths and come together, for the overlap is not straight forward.

Let us therefore start simply, by dividing golfers into two groups:

Learners – golfers with no on-course experience, although they will be practising at the range and hopefully taking lessons.

Players – golfers who are experienced at playing the game of golf. Often, with a scorecard in hand.

(Learners, who in addition to taking lessons *also* play, qualify as players for the purpose of this piece.)

Learners, be Careful

When a learner golfer begins visiting the golf course for regular play *before* the swing is finished, they make the prospect of their swing-build ever *being* finished, remote. This is a serious point. Eagerness to get to the golf course is the main prohibitor against ownership of a fine swing, and prohibition is often life-long, for, whatever stage of development a player's golf swing is at when it starts being taken for regular play, will more or less be the stage it will remain at – ad infinitum.

It will be as if the evolution of the swing had been interrupted, and whatever (technique) is finished or unfinished, will remain - finished or unfinished; and that will be the way of the world for their golf swing going forwards. Taking our swing to the course for regular play is analogous to taking clay to the kiln for firing. When exposed to the extreme environment of on-course play, the swing bakes hard in whatever shape or form it arrives in. And it bakes quickly.

Although there are plenty of exceptions, this phenomena part explains the lack of high calibre swings we see from famous sports stars who take up golf. Champions in their own sport and proven as being possessed of the highest levels of physical ability and mental focus, they nevertheless struggle to distinguish themselves as being different from any ordinary golfer when it comes to swinging a golf club. They likely made the same innocent mistake many golfers make. Itching to experience the fun and excitement of play, they went to the course as soon as they thought their game was

good enough to get round, figuring they would improve as time passed and they played more. Certainly, they *will* have improved as they played more, but in context of their ball-striking capability they will likely have quickly plateaued.

Perhaps it is better we think of it like this:

If a learner has their swing 40% finished when they begin play, and the swing bakes at the 40% point, then even when they develop into an experienced golfer their ball-striking ability will have long ago been capped at around 40% of what was, and is, possible. Most tour pros have technical levels well above this, including many above 90%, and it is this swing value which gives them access to their elite striking; elite striking which is unavailable to the player who unknowingly caps their swing's technique at 40%. Chipping, pitching, bunker and putting are separate skills, and an experienced golfer with a middling long game may have an excellent feel for the short game to go with it. As for their long game, they may add a little here and there, but essentially they will have handicapped their ball-striking future by not finishing the swing build before becoming a player.

Although this is an important evidence-based point, I appreciate that use of the word 'finished' needs clarifying. No one ever finishes their swing to 100%. A learner has to factor how much time they have for the build of their swing, against their aspirations from the game. And then also, their opportunity for regular play. Most adults with full time jobs (and families) will not have enough time to chase down a technically accomplished golf swing before the desire to enjoy play overtakes them. Even for those learners with more time and opportunity, it will often be a good effort to get to

70% before they feel a calling from the golf course. It should also be mentioned that getting to a technical level during learning – of say… 70% – does not mean the learner will be able to immediately deliver this level into a ball-striking equivalence. It means only that components, positions, and moves, are in place; and are ***capable*** *of delivering equivalence in striking. A player still has to learn how to use, what they have.*

Staying with learning, and learners:

When we play, we are naturally concerned with our performance, which is completely appropriate, but it is a major problem for the learner golfer. As soon as they become concerned about the result of their shot, their swing (which is still learning how to operate as a single entity) will begin to pull apart as the 'one ball all consequence' anxiety takes over. For learner golfers especially, pressure to succeed is one thing, but pressure – **not to fail** – is on a whole other level.

When a learner fails it is often embarrassing for them: a thump of the ground (the ball barely moving), a whiff, or a shot that almost kills someone at the side. This 'whole other level' prompts rapid abandonment of the swing thoughts which were until that point needed to hold their swing together, but which are quickly proven to be suspect during play. With swing thoughts gone, instinct then drives the learner's performance based on some simple workings out –

'The ball is on the ground; must get it in the air!'
'The target is far away; must hit it hard!'
'Trouble everywhere … must hit it straight!'

Instinct, in this environment, will aim itself fully at survival and will not care a jot about the player's hard-earned but vulnerable technique. Any of the swing build which isn't yet secure will be compromised to a lower level, and this lower-level technique will then arrive for tomorrow's game, or next week's, and will begin to establish itself unless the learner – after each round – returns to the range for a re-boot before their next course visit. This 'one play one practise' routine is necessary for learners until they become familiar enough with the on-course environment that they are able to play *whilst using* the swing thoughts that got their swing to where it is; rather than defaulting to instinct. One play one practise will enable the player to hold on to their 40%, 50%, or 60% etc., swing value, until it secures. Without one play one practise, their swing's technical value will drop to the said lower level, where it will then, if they play regularly – set.

The established golfer is different. They will not see their swing pulled to pieces like the learner golfer because the mechanics of their swing will have long ago settled and become stable. They will, though, have similar difficulty implementing new mechanics during play in the early stages, unless they are able to disregard results, which is unlikely. Concern for results is the absolute *essence* of play. So much so, that trying to apply a new technique without having bedded it in properly, beforehand, is in fact *so* difficult, that a return to previous swing is almost a given. Even for a golfer of considerable experience. The player will stand on the first tee with their new swing and walk off the eighteenth with their old. They should not be defeated though. It can be done. They should return to the range and re-boot the new swing ready

for use again on their next course visit. It's 'one play one practise,' again!

The key for the established golfer is not to be only able to demonstrate the new swing (let's say... to friends, or to onlookers, or to your instructor) in other words – not to be able to demonstrate *only* the new swing, which would, however, represent a big success; but, and this is important: you must be able to demonstrate the new swing *with* performance-level golf shots resulting. If you can demonstrate the new swing, at the range, without loss to performance, there is no reason why you cannot take it to, and use it on – the course! None whatsoever.

The main take away from this is for learners. If you are scheduling your first few games in the not distant future and are likely to begin playing regularly thereafter, I recommend you cram, over the coming weeks and months, like a student approaching an important exam. Pack as much technical work and drilling in as possible, preferably under instruction, with realisation that the swing you start taking for regular play will become, for the most part, the one you use the rest of your life.

An Observation

Some years ago, as we were walking to the ball dispenser to get a hundred balls out for our lesson, a student asked me the following question: 'Why do I see so many people with poor and unconventional swings, and yet still they seem to play perfectly good golf?'

This student was wondering why he and I were working hard on technique at the range, when it appeared to him there might be an easier way to play this game well, including in it, allowance for some bad style. The student was happy to *look* unsightly, so long as he didn't *play* unsightly at the same time (showing an admirable lack of vanity) and it seemed to him that working on his swing's technique might be unnecessary, being as so many people he knew – played well – with what appeared to be poor, or at least poor-ish style. The question was quite amusing. He was looking for an easy way out and whilst he didn't for a moment dwell on it, it did highlight an intriguing observation.

'You do not have to own a good swing, to play – good golf.'

Let us take a look at that observation!

Local to Global

Look around us. What do we see?

A typical members golf club has enough members in it that if they were all playing at the same time they would put on display – and we would see – almost every type and style of swing imaginable. Included in-and-amongst this display would be many differently timed and styled yanks and tugs and shifts and lunges and snatches and jerks and re-routes; all taking place on the way from start to finish of the swings. Among the five hundred or so members would also be seen swings in the average, good, fine and outstanding categories.

But we are interested in the former category – the 'yanks and tugs' category.

The group of swings we are about to focus on, within the wider group of club golfer swings, is my favourite. I have deep affection for these golf swings which are found scattered around the fairways of the world; full of character, individuality and eagerness; closer to being unique than any other type of swing and whose owners show themselves disinterested in the fuss of form, being instead interested only in the hitting of the next shot, and the playing of the game.

Important to note is that on their own, no individual player will have more than a few of these complexities, but collectively, the club membership will contain pretty-well all of them. And if we widen this situation out to include *all* members clubs around the world, and therefore were able to see many millions of member golfers as they played, we would see hundreds of thousands of golfers playing golf with what could only be described as compromised golf swings. Some of them, considerably compromised. At the most interesting end of these compromised golf swings would be a percentage *so* compromised, as to fit deservedly into a category worthy of being titled – complicated. To try to copy these complicated swings at high speed would present a real challenge, even for an expert, and a near impossible challenge if the ball had to be struck sweetly at the same time.

And yet,

ALL of the owners of these swings are able to do it.

Every swing 'rule' that we can lay down as being important, or more than important – crucial; would be seen being broken by this club-member group of complicated swings. Put together as a collection, the technical complications on display would be bewildering in scope of variation and yet, as said, we would notice these same worrying swings delivering good golf shots, playing competitively from their handicaps and some of them, even, able to routinely post scores in the gross seventies.

We need to pause and reflect on this. These golfers do not look good, but they certainly play good (allowed, in modern English usage). They are successful golfers by any fair and proper definition of the term, and they have achieved this much *with* their complicated swings. More candidly we must say – in spite of – their complicated swings. Understanding the reason for their significant level of success, despite the unlikely looking prospects, is important for two reasons:

1) We are trying to piece together cause-and-effect with this game.

2) If we understand how *they* do it, we might be able to add a little of this know-how to our own game.

So – how do they do it?

This is a big question, and one that cannot be answered without an important piece (currently missing) of this work's general theory being called upon…

STRIKE & IMPACT

(A difference between amateurs and pros)

STRIKE

Strike relates to the centre spot on the club face – the sweet spot – and a player who impacts the ball with the club's sweet spot when swinging, achieves success with strike. This clean contact between sweet spot and ball transfers the club's forces *into* the ball. There is nothing more to strike than that.

Of the two subject matters – strike, and impact – strike is the easier to own and is the more important to own. With moderate strike success a golf shot is produced, and the player can play the game. Without this moderate success it is a different story, and a player will be lucky to achieve anything which could be sensibly called a golf shot, let alone one worth having.

Sweet Spot and Its Margin

Although we intend to strike the sweet spot every time, such a level of reliability cannot be achieved. That we cannot strike the sweet spot every time is fine, though (certainly at club level), because there is margin around the sweet spot which delivers enough of a strike so as to be usable.

Just as a bullseye on a target has an extra two or three rings around it (the rings *also* having value) so too, the sweet spot on a clubface has, in effect, a ring around it with value. The sweet-spot's extra ring is unmarked and so, is unseen; but it gives margin for mis-hit shots such that they work well enough for play. This unseen margin is actually the starting point for what we are considering as being moderate success with strike. Additionally, if a player is able to strike the ball from inside this unseen, but larger ring, it follows they will get a fair share of sweet spot hits as well. These will come randomly, like much else in this game, but nevertheless a good percentage of the player's shots will be struck sweetly.

How Big… the Margin?

The size of the circular sweet spot on an iron club is approximately half an inch (12.5mm) in diameter, perhaps a little more, depending on the make and type of club. The imaginary ring which delivers a usable strike is roughly twice this diameter. Mathematically, when we double the diameter of a circle we quadruple its area, and so the area on the clubface which allows satisfactory striking (at least, enough for competitive club-level play) is four times the size of the sweet spot.

The more we play and practise, the smaller our strike pattern on the clubface becomes. The best among us will gradually hone in on centre spot and may have skills such that we live there happily ever after, more or less never leaving it. Others among us will have issues pinning the strike down to this happy-ever-after level, but will demonstrate a generally fine

average of striking without ever quite managing to properly fix and secure it. Then there is a group which is a little unlucky, because for months at a time they play their golf striking sweetly, only to then see their ability with strike collapse on them. For no apparent reason they lose it completely, and there follows a desperate effort to re-find it. Players from this group are suddenly in a situation where they are out on the course, playing, without a usable golf game (the shank being the ultimate destroyer of games). On top of having lost strike, and with it their entire game, they typically have full diaries of pre-booked roll-ups, matches, medals and stablefords. This distressing situation can last weeks, sometimes months. Often, players in this group have no luck finding any explanation from which to navigate a way back to strike. But strike one day returns, out of the blue, just like it disappeared!

When we lose strike, which is to say – when we can no longer make contact inside the unseen margin for error on the clubface – we are left with no golf game. Even if only yesterday we were one of our Club's orbiting stars.

IMPACT

Impact is less dramatic than strike. It is, however (despite being less dramatic), more complex; because it involves the club's behaviour *during* strike. 'Behaviour', meaning – how the club is travelling, and its orientation *as* it travels. Which could be:

- in-to-out
- out-to-in
- straight (toward target)
- upward
- downward
- horizontally

Plus, clubface:

- open
- square
- closed

As a base understanding: At point of strike we want the club to be travelling in a straight line towards the target, with a slightly descending angle of attack, and with the face square-to-target. This, with irons.

Most club golfers do not deliver these characteristics when they swing a golf club, even given allowance for an agreeable tolerance of indiscretion. On the PGA Tour, with the same agreeable tolerance, these characteristics are found everywhere we look.

So, let's say that that, is fair enough. What, exactly, is being said? Does it matter if a golfer fails in achieving these characteristics? Do they lose much, or anything at all by not delivering this 'ideal' club behaviour? Short answer – yes, and by degree. The more relevant answer is yes, and often they lose significantly. The following example is common at club level:

With this example we will generalise a little, but only a little.

An average mid-handicap male amateur hitting with a six iron may have a club speed of around 70mph. In this study we need him to have a club speed of 90mph, and so we will give him an extra 20mph, free of charge. He now swings at the required speed of 90mph. His golf swing – including all of his club-behaviour characteristics – will remain the same. We are only adding speed. This amateur is going up against a tour pro to compare shots, and we want their club speeds to be equalised so that we can see the consequence of club behaviour – through impact – on the outcome of a golf shot.

One more thing. Not only do they have identical club speeds, they have identical strikes. They both deliver strike upon the ball from the centre of sweet spot. Elsewhere in their swings, however, and specifically during impact, there are differences…

The amateur:

Swing line 10 degrees across.
Club face 8 degrees open (to target).
Attack-angle up (+1 degree).

The pro:

Straight-line swing.
Clubface square.
Attack-angle down (–4 degrees).

Although the amateur and the tour pro have identical club speeds of 90mph, and identical success with strike, because of the differences in the way their clubs are travelling and are

oriented when meeting their respective balls, we see two distinctly different flights departing:

The amateur's ball flight is a lofted slice. High, and with a carry of around 155yards. The pro's ball flight is stronger; and penetrates as it flies toward the target. It also has greater backspin which gives a climb-and-hang aspect to the second half of its flight. Carry of around 190yards.

This huge loss of 35yards for the amateur, despite having matching club speed and an equally pure strike, is a result of those mis-aligned forces we see in the club-behaviour details and numbers, above. The amateur's club-behaviour details are (like the pro's) delivered through impact *by their swing* and determine that, in their own case, their ball receives a glancing blow.

As most golfers appreciate: if a golf club travels in one direction and its face points in another – a glancing blow results. The glancing blow might be marginal, or, something much more than marginal. It is quite often enormous. This type of club behaviour during impact and strike is very common, the most common type in golf, and the example demonstrates the potential for huge loss to a golf shot that poor impact qualities will deliver, even when delivering a perfect strike. With driver, the potential losses increase significantly.

(It should be noted that the amateur's true club speed was 70mph. He would therefore have already been 20mph down on the tour pro without the added losses which were to come from his swing's glancing blow.)

When we look at swing sequences of world leading players as they play through impact, we see in particular the evolution of excellence in the club's behaviour – *before, during, and after, strike;* and for every golfer somewhere in the world right now, standing over a golf shot and about to swing, it will be the behaviour of their club as it travels through impact that determines how true – in terms of trajectory and direction – the flight of their ball will be. Fortunately, as mentioned earlier, high-level impact ability is not an imperative, or even a requirement to be able to play this game; although it certainly *is* desirable.

To become a top amateur or a professional player, yes, we will need highest levels of club behaviour through impact.

For others, for golfers who are content with less, we can say the following:

- If you want to play from ten, twelve, fifteen or twenty handicap;

- If you want to be able to win club medals, stablefords, or matchplay knock-out competitions;

- If you want to have a lifetime of enjoyment walking home fairways, away fairways, and fairways of the world;

- If you want to feel like you fit in, like you are competent;

Then you only need to be good at strike. You MUST be good at strike.

With this in mind, we now return to the yanks and tugs:

These hundreds of thousands of golfers in the yanks and tugs category, achieve success with their complicated swings because they do the most critical bit well. This bit, as highlighted above, is – strike.

If we were to explore the phenomena we see when looking around us, we would notice that in many thousands of cases around the world there will be found club members who have unconventional and complicated swings, swings they and their friends *know* are unconventional and complicated, but – and this is important – swings that the owners of no longer worry about, and probably haven't worried about for a long time. Having accepted things as they are (despite the odd grumble and curse of dissatisfaction) they just get on with playing the game.

This long-time settled attitude towards their swing (acceptance of it) has meant that their hand-eye has had months, possibly years, even; to tune strike. A strike that each of these players and their swing has had to tune inclusive of a complex choreography of physical problem solving. This choreography, involving the very opposite of straight lines and straight-line forces, is over with in a flash, and captivates the eye, certainly my eye; especially when it whips a shot nicely into the fairway or toward the green.

This is not to say that these players have sweet and pure strike every time, but it *is* to say that their strike will generally be fine, and it being so means they will have a golf shot they can use to play golf with. Ironically, the key to their success

(their hand-eye skill) is the abandonment of swing development. Their success might be said to result from them no longer even caring about the swing.

For the most part: they leave their swings alone.

When a player leaves their swing alone by ceasing the pushing and prodding of its technique, then the swing, no-longer being disturbed, can begin to settle at whatever technical level it has arrived at and, as it settles – stabilise. **This is a key moment for all of us as golfers.** At this point the swing will begin to repeat better than at any time previously. It will repeat – despite-and-inclusive-of – each and every kink and glitch. In fact, each and every kink and glitch will occur in the same place and at the same time. It is *now*, when the swing is beginning to repeat for the first time, that it becomes possible for the player's hand-eye to anticipate events, tune in on them, choreograph the moves (including any yanks and tugs) and – deliver strike.

(Trying to improve our golf swing is a perfectly natural and logical thing to do, but when we do try to, we interfere with the sensitive collaboration that exists between technique and hand-eye. Each new push upon our technique requires a new tuning of the hand-eye to fit to it. It can take quite a while for our hand-eye to work out an answer, and there will usually be turbulence, including sometimes chaos, in the meantime. This disturbance to a player's shot is the main reason established golfers struggle to land significant swing upgrades. The disturbance de-rails them.)

Continuing forward, we are now at the juncture where a golfer has allowed their swing to settle, has given it time to

learn how to repeat, and then, given further time for hand-eye to establish strike. From here, Silent Genius will step in and take things to the next level.

Note: That club players around the world have a hand-eye skill that delivers strike, does not mean that the skill was, or will be, switched on like a lamp, simply by accepting the swing as it is and by no longer pushing or prodding it. Leaving our swing alone is only the first part. There is still lots to do. Most of all, the continuing effort to strike good quality, clean shots; and then also, the continuing effort to – direct – the clean shots we are dispatching. But there should be no thoughts as to how to do any of it. No thoughts to technique. Just a handing over of the tasks. First to hand-eye, and secondly, to Silent Genius.

To be able to fit in. To feel ok about ourselves as golfers. To not be worried about joining friends or business partners for a game. Competence. This much we can all achieve. This does not mean it will be easy, but it does mean we are all included. We can – all of us – enjoy this wonderful game.

What about me?

Despite the above message, it is possible that some readers may be doubting themselves, still. Doubting their ability to deliver strike, doubting their ability to find a source of direction, doubting even that they have within them their own Silent Genius. Enough to say that from many years spent instructing learner players, I have seen no evidence of these doubts being well founded. More likely any problems lie in a lack of play and practise. Which leads us on to…

GOLF'S RUNWAY

There is an element of runway and take-off with golf. Many learners never get to the point of take-off because their runway stage is too slow, and lasts what feels like an eternity. They never really get going with the game.

To explain...

Becoming a golfer has little to do with ability. Rather, it has to do with enough balls being hit and enough play being played. If you want to become a golfer you have to do a lot of both and, over a relatively short period of time. A good swing is not a requirement. Fine, if you have a good swing; but it is not essential. What you *do* need, though, is to hit a few thousand balls at the range and play in the region of fifty to one hundred games. Even then, the quantities mentioned are dependent on how densely they are packed together. If ten years pass before you play your seventy-five games. No take-off. If three weeks pass before every range session and, one month before every game – no take-off. If you play golf only when on holiday, it will not be enough. Assuming you take the average one or two holidays per year.

An airliner taxies into position on a runway and moments later it is brakes off, full speed ahead. All engines (two or four) pouring on the power. Many learners never make an effort equivalent to the plane on the runway in their attempts to achieve take-off as a golfer. Their output is spread thinly

over too long a time frame, often years, and as a result it is an empty version of thrust. If the game was easier, this slow route forward might work. With many other sports we *can* advance slowly, but not with golf.

One context:

This has not happened before, but if it did happen, and I was approached by someone for instruction who said to me – 'Gary, I am going to book twenty lessons with you and I'd like to schedule them such that I get as much from the lessons as possible... should I schedule the lessons every month, every fortnight, or every week...?'

I would tell them to schedule the lessons every day. For the next twenty days. The reason lies in the value of condensation and the way the body and mind respond to it, by retaining more, and compounding memory. While few students can offer such a strong start with the game, the principle is clear. You must load your efforts in the first six to twelve months.

The good news is that once you are up off the runway after a fairly-heavy engagement with the game, and are airborne (which is by far the hardest part), you will be a golfer! You will never have to put such effort in again. It is, as the saying goes, a one-off payment. Any additional bursts of effort and intensity (in play and practise) condensed like the first effort, will see your handicap tumbling.

THE PARABLE of CHARLIE NOOP

A short story of one man's adventures at the range.

Charlie Noop was a likeable fellow and a keen golfer who visited his local golf range for an hour and a hundred balls, every week, religiously.

He worked his hour in not untypical fashion, opening the session with full blooded drives and moving onto the smaller clubs when exhausted or fed up. Very little chipping or pitching, such that to some degree his sessions were spent heaving at the ball whilst trying to make it behave.

Of course, every week there were new ideas to try, which is one of the exciting things about the golf swing, SO many possible solutions. The latest thoughts on how to hit from the inside, stay on line longer, get a cleaner strike, or, five minutes worth (he gave up quickly) of trying to squat on the way down and press *up* on the way through; and, much more besides. He had launch angles to investigate and smash factors to reproach himself for, on top of keeping an eye on advances in equipment which seemed always to so-quickly render his current set obsolete. And he never went long before noticing things were amiss in one or more of the three 'delicacies' of the golf swing, each tantalising, but difficult to pin down: *timing*; *tempo*; and *rhythm*; they, being likely responsible for Charlie occasionally having 'his eye in' and reading more into it than was there; to then find he had *no*

eye in the following week. And he was sometimes led – captivatingly – by the 'sensing'… of something, (semi-mysterious); "a something of what, I am not quite sure, but I can feel it! and I have it!" that would lead to a great session, and a journey home excited about the weekend's game even more than usual.

But largely, as the months and years passed, the peaks and troughs of his play at the range remained the same. As did his handicap.

His 190yd fading-carry into the fairway remained a 190 yd fading-carry. And the more powerful drive he sometimes went after, and got, stayed the same also; in that it turned the fade into a slice that sent the ball out of play to the right. "At least, though," (he would tell himself) "My golf swing has another gear for added power!" He just couldn't find a way to square the face when using it.

Some time later (much later), ten years had passed, and although we could say that a lot of polishing – of what he had – had been done, and a lot of intimacy with his swing had been learnt, and some of its nuances put deep to internal memory; nothing about the way Charlie hit the ball had really changed. But despite a subconscious awareness of this and of a lack of obvious progress, he was unaffected by it, and remained 'captive held' by a love for his cherished game – golf. He could see, anyway, that most others were in the same boat as him, and thus – things appearing to be fair and equal – he continued living his happy golfing life; chasing balls, fairways, and greens; as well as looking forward to his weekly experiments at the golf range.

—

The reason for the parable is this: with those ten years Charlie had offered 500 hours of fairly intense practise, and 50,000 balls. If he had pursued for only half of those numbers, the polishing – not of his move, but of his three positions – he would after ten years have had a fine swing, perhaps one of the finest in the club, and his 190 yd carry would likely have become a 230yd carry (with a draw if he wanted a draw). It is true to say he would have needed help from an instructor with work done on the positions, but it would not have been difficult given the volume of training put in and balls being hit, and it would have been easier still, had the the four giants been called into action.

('of what he had' refers to Charlie's swing 'between' his three positions; (as limited by them); and the polishing of it and the getting to know it well is something that all golfers instinctively hunt down. Working on the 'between positions' part of a swing is, of course, working on – the moves. Developing what could be called 'move skills' to help the club through impact. When we work this way, we are usually looking for some instant sense of profit, or broader sense of security with our shots, this, achieved by tweaking, adjusting, or nudging an aspect of the swing that immediately touches the impact area.

It is this scenario of only ever polishing and refining 'what we have' that can lead to ten years of practise passing with no change being seen in our golf swing, like in the case of Charlie, who after ten years had the same swing he started with ten years earlier, because little or no work had been done on his three positions.)

Now, in a vein not dissimilar from the earlier piece where finish was seen to be uncared for; we tell the tale of Swing's unfair burden of responsibility.

DIMENSIONS

More Than the Swing Alone

A golf shot is resultant of three parts, in so far as it has three separate dimensions or aspects to it; and each dimension has a bearing on the shot's outcome. The three parts are –

- swing – proficiency of technique.
- strike – quality of contact.
- direction – accuracy of ball's flight.

Each of the three parts can fail, or soar, separately from the other two. They may blend together in appropriate balance (each showing a similar level of accomplishment) or, they may blend unevenly – one part excelling while one, or both of the other two, do not.

Who among us has not…

… felt a clean and sweet strike; only to then look up and see the ball sailing its way over the boundary fence!

... felt a perfectly good swing being delivered, only to then take a blast of mud and grit to the face as the club hits... ground-before-ball!

... seen – right in front of our eyes – a decidedly iffy-looking golf swing catch the ball cleanly and also, send it straight down the middle!

The golf shot that we hit, or witness being hit, *may* have its three parts balanced, i.e., the swing may be average, the strike may be average, and the direction may be average. But the parts are not tied to each other in the way one would expect them to be, and it is this confusing situation which causes problems when we are trying to learn, or improve, a golf swing. With three parts involved (and each part having potential for varying levels of accomplishment from its own contribution), there are numerous combinations possible that can make up a golf shot.

Some obvious combinations –

Poor. Poor. Poor.
As in – poor swing, poor strike, poor direction.
In need of another ball.

Good. Good. Good.
As in – good swing, good strike, good direction.
Ten feet from the hole.

Good. Good. Poor:
As in – good swing, good strike, poor direction.
Regularly seen from expert players. (How difficult this game is!)

It all makes sense, but is there any value in knowing this?

Yes, there is.

Here is the gist:

Throughout the years and still today, the accepted understanding has been that the swing is responsible for the success or failure of our golf shots. Solely responsible. Which means the swing has been held responsible for the success or failure of strike; and, that the swing has been held responsible for the success or failure of direction, also. *That the swing is in fact* ***everything.*** This understanding loads heavily upon the swing as being architect of all things successful and all things failure. The swing has consequently taken blame (decades worth) for everything that has gone wrong with our golf shots. The swing, in effect, is routinely and summarily held up and scolded. If it were not for the fact that swing has no feelings, this would be a sad thing to reflect upon, as it has often performed its part admirably.

Strike and direction are entities on their own and regularly ignore dictates from the swing. By not recognising strike's and direction's independence, this perennial blaming of the swing has been established as right and fair. Amongst other things it results in confusion, and a misdirection of many players' efforts. Efforts which often take them down dead-ends and blind alleys.

A bad shot begins to enter a player's game, and then, when it starts repeating (a hook or a shank, for example), it provokes a dive from the player into their *swing*, looking for the cause.

The player starts tossing all of their swing's bits up in the air like a madman looking frantically for an important *something* hidden at the bottom of a box and, after failing to find the 'something', they wrack their brains for other possible answers before rushing to a YouTube clip on 'how to re-wire a golf swing'. The panicking golfer is understandably concerned and is trying their hardest to fix the problem. But their efforts are nearly always mis-directed. Little or none of this drama is necessary. The two major catastrophes that might befall a golf shot – loss of strike, or, sideways direction – can each be worked on and repaired in isolation, with low-level engagement from the swing; and normal route of progress will need to include isolation work on strike, when strike disappears; and isolation work on direction, when direction disappears.

Important point of note: With this we are largely talking about established players whose form suddenly drops. We are not talking about learner players who will encounter strike and direction problems as a normal rite of passage into the game. (However, learner players should pay attention too!) The established golfer whose long game is suddenly stricken, will experience a good deal of dismay, as typically they will *not* have been meddling with their swing in the lead up. Things will have crept up on them slowly, and then – bang.

So, a few clues as to 'isolation work':

Strike

If a player has lost strike, they must seek solution by examining and adjusting – strike. *Not* the swing. Most strike errors are treated by adding an opposite amount of up, down, in, or out, to the strike error. This is at least a very good starting point and means, for example, that if a player is routinely shanking the ball (hitting it from the hosel, an inch or more to heel side of sweet spot) then the player must aim to strike the ball an inch or more to the toe side of sweet spot – **at strike**. Strike errors occur at strike, so deal with them at strike and not in the start position. A shank does not occur at start, and even if there is a shank influence hiding in the player's start position, there will be an element of 'guessing game' in trying to find it. More intriguingly, even if the player *does* find a hidden shank influence, it will often not solve the shank, whereas going to strike directly, most definitely *will* solve the shank.

If you are striking ground behind the ball, then try to strike ground *in front of the ball.* You can see the theme. We solve major strike errors by flipping them, by flipping the symptom, by… trying to do the opposite. More specifically (and more interestingly), this means we do not solve strike problems **by trying to do things correctly.** Nor do we solve them by doubling or tripling our resolve to 'do things correctly'. That may sound odd, but you are already trying to do things correctly *when* you mis-strike. If you want another mis-strike, try to do things correctly again!

Once the treatment (and you must commit to it) has jolted the strike away from its error, you can monitor the strike

evidence and reduce treatment dosage until things return to normal. At that point you will be able to do things correctly again.

Occasionally (not often, thankfully) I go to my local golf range to hit fifty or a hundred balls and, despite being a professional, I start the session hitting the ball with a heavy mat contact. A few of these heavy shots will not overly bother me but they will catch my attention. If, after another few minutes and half a dozen shots I am still hitting the mat heavily – *I trust the evidence* – and know from it that my hand-eye is slightly out (for whatever reason) and needs quick adjustment. In this instance I know I am swinging too low, such that if the mat was not there I would be swinging at a level *beneath* the mat. And so, I lift the low point of my swing so that it no longer even touches the surface on the way through. I may slightly thin one or two at this point, and happily so. It means I am in control. A few of these, then some clean hits where I take the ball only (still no contact with mat), and I can then gently lower my swing so that it again strikes the mat with the correct level of contact. At no point do I blame my swing. I simply flip the strike error.

Direction

If a player has a significant and repeating directional issue (not a moderate one – we all have moderate issues with direction), they must look to the clubface or to the club-path. These are the two major players with regard to direction. Again, be wary of being drawn into swing analysis. Swing analysis buys into a lot of uncertainty whereas grabbing by

the scruff of the neck – club-face control, and club-path control – does not. For example, the clubface's return-to-square moment (timing) would be the place to start. Taking it further, a player's best first attack on wild slicing or wild hooking would be to add or subtract club-roll on the down and through-swing, this, married with the aforementioned principle of 'flipping the symptom.'

The other directional loss, where a golf shot flies straight to the right or straight to the left, requires dealings with path, *and again…* flipping the symptom is the quickest way forward. If you are pushing, practise pulls. If you are pulling, practise pushes.

Not until these two hands-on and direct approaches have been properly tested and been seen not to help, should the player go in search of a guilty component.

Swing

Swing is different. Whereas with strike and direction a player can snap out of a problem just as quickly as they snapped into it (quicker, even), with swing it does not work that way. A player cannot just snap into ownership of a finer golf swing. However, when strike and direction are in normal health, it is then that the player is, in a sense, being encouraged by the game to get to work on their swing.

Any ball-striking improvements a player may be wanting to make, i.e., any desiring that their future good shots be more impressive than their current good shots, will mean the

player must improve – their swing. This will involve general work, work aimed at upgrading the three positions. As explained throughout this book, a player cannot own a finer move or a finer swing – one capable of hitting finer shots – if the required move, and swing, remain trapped between current-grade positions.

'Current-grade positions only enable current-grade striking.'

Bringing this branch of the theory to a close, perhaps a little suddenly, I appreciate that it could have been covered in more detail, even though it was signalled that time was short with 'here is the gist.' There are clues in what I have said. Actually, there are more than clues, there are strong pointers and with a little thought, readers will be able to experiment and by so doing, learn how to use Dimensions (with its three-parts concept) whenever needed. At club amateur level, many of golf's most traumatic spells of play can be quickly improved and sometimes completely remedied, by an understanding of and application of this branch of three positions theory.

Instruction and Demonstration:

Connected to the above, and whilst writing, I sometimes reflect on how much simpler it would be, if I were able to make a few demonstrations, was able to appear in front of readers on a mat with club and ball. One demonstration would save a thousand words, most likely more. Of course, I cannot appear in front of anyone, but nor is there time for another thousand words. I am running out of time generally. Tournament season will soon be upon us and I am behind

with preparation. That being said, and whilst now speaking of instruction, I do appreciate that instruction may be necessary for this theory to be brought fully to life. However, most important by far is that the theory be properly laid out and understood. That part is almost done. All going well, then after, I may be able to bring to golfers instructional content some of which will not have been seen before, including presentation of established ideas with a new slant, and there are likely a few things I can add to the 'visual book of knowledge' regarding the golf swing. This instruction must, for now, wait. (Including there being no guarantee of it ever materialising. I have to consider there being no interest in this work.)

Among other things, readers may also be wondering why I have not listed the 'key components' to help them. There are reasons for not publishing the list here, but they are ready and will be presented when the time is right. It should anyway be said that I would never merely write a 'list.' Such important content will need to be properly explained.

In short, with regards to what lies ahead, it can be said that *much* might lie ahead, including a headline, supported by this theory, that will catch the golfing world completely off-guard. A headline of near unimaginable significance.

Things will soon draw to a close, but before they do, I would like the reader to revisit grading, and the swing scale that comes with it. It is a revisit that captures much of this work's theory and consequence.

BEHOLD

Picture once more in your mind the theoretical golf swing described, where tens are delivered by forty-eight components and the definitive swing total of 480 is achieved as a grade. We take sight upon a shining vision of all that a golf swing can be, with three purest positions and two unequalled moves in both the backswing, and through-swing. But now, rather than climbing and aspiring towards 480, we are going to take hold of this incredible swing and travel in the opposite direction, degrading it as we go. We are going to injure its components at every opportunity, picking at each of them; one here, one there, another somewhere else, back here again; spoiling and disabling with every contact and immediately moving on to the next target, the next component. Both moves are quickly and inescapably caught by the attack, and regressing in parallel time, pulled ever more lowly as the targeted strikes come in. The swing soon collapses through 300, through 200... and into the low one hundred; its not-long-ago unequalled backswing and through-swing... now totally dependent on Silent Genius for help: for survival. But soon after, the once beautiful swing is seen unable to move. It exists no more. And its life-long friend, ever-present and always there when needed, is seen making its final struggle before falling, truly, silent.

(Have you noticed how simple the best swings look? Three positions in such good shape that movement is easy: it appears to be 'up down' or 'back through.' That's all! ... and Silent Genius has nothing to do).

END

I could have begun this work by explaining how to stand to the ball, how to grip, how to set posture, ball placement; where the golfer should feel balance, etc., but this is all common knowledge within relatively narrow margins of disagreement and is published and republished on a regular basis in golf magazines and golf books. I have written about something more meaningful. I have written about a universal theory.

I could have tackled questions arising from this work and answered them for the satisfaction of the reader. But all questions answered is not particularly interesting. Certainly not for those who are most deserving of the answers.

We have gone from the rookie first-timers, who had three positions and a swing on their first ever range visit, and who without any golf knowledge were nevertheless able to identify four key components in the golf swing; onward, to world leading PGA Tour players who work on trying to nudge trace improvements into their moves and positions; and then, beyond the tour pros, to the purest of all golf swings with a 480 grade out of 480. And in between, there is everyone else, including the out of shape businessman who struggles to identify with the swings he sees on television. But he should not doubt himself, for he and his swing fit right in alongside all others as equal players in this theory, and satellite professions which try to lay blame on his not being

an athlete as being reason for his swing problems should lower their heads a little. Surely, the average businessman cannot swing like Tiger or Rory, but that does not matter. It is what they *can* do that matters. And they can add five or ten degrees to their body turn; they can keep their left arm straighter on the backswing; they can sharpen their grip so it in turn sharpens their wrist and hand action; they can add speed and balance to their through swing… and on it goes. And with them, through any turbulence they may experience as they grapple with progress, will be the wisdom of Dimensions and the power of the Four Giants. They can do, and have, all of these things and more. And what does it mean? It means they can improve. 'When today I know more, tomorrow I will improve.'

Is there anything that brightens our tomorrows as much as the prospect we will be improved?

This theory is for everyone.

ABOUT THE AUTHOR

Gary Marks lives in London and is the attached touring professional at Roehampton Club. He is 59 years old and competes on the DP World Legends Tour.

In the U.K. Gary has won tournaments at Local, Regional, and National level. He has won five tournaments Internationally and is a two-time winner on the Legends Tour. His most recent success came in the 2022 Legends Open de France.

As well as competing on tour, Gary also gives lessons to a small number of private clients in London. He has given clinics for world-leading corporations and was in-house golf instructor at Goldman Sachs (London) for five years.

Gary is married with two children. Film, documentary, music, and reading, are his main interests away from golf.

Printed in Great Britain
by Amazon

39448387R00096